'Reacher **grab**  and
never lets go. [ ]ter'
KE[ ]

'The **coolest**
continuing series
character'
STEPHEN KING

'One of my
essential **guilty**
pleasures'
JOANNE HARRIS

'I am very much **in love** with Jack
Reacher – as a man and a role model.
If I can't **shag** him, I want to be him'
LUCY MANGAN

'I am such a
Lee Child **addict**'
MALCOLM GLADWELL

'**Indestructible** . . . lots of fisticuffs
and a **satisfying** denouement'
FREDERICK FORSYTH

Have you read them all?

The Jack Reacher thrillers by Lee Child
– in the order in which they first appeared.

KILLING FLOOR
Jack Reacher gets off a bus in a small town in Georgia.
And is thrown into the county jail, for a murder he didn't commit.

DIE TRYING
Reacher is locked in a van with a woman claiming to be FBI.
And ferried right across America into a brand new country.

TRIPWIRE
Reacher is digging swimming pools in Key West when a detective
comes round asking questions. Then the detective turns up dead.

THE VISITOR
Two naked women found dead in a bath filled with paint. Both
victims of a man just like Reacher.

ECHO BURNING
In the heat of Texas, Reacher meets a young woman whose
husband is in jail. When he is released, he will kill her.

WITHOUT FAIL
A Washington woman asks Reacher for help. Her job?
Protecting the Vice-President.

PERSUADER

A kidnapping in Boston. A cop dies.
Has Reacher lost his sense of right and wrong?

THE ENEMY

Back in Reacher's army days, a general is
found dead on his watch.

ONE SHOT

A lone sniper shoots five people dead in a heartland city.
But the accused guy says, 'Get Reacher'.

THE HARD WAY

A coffee on a busy New York street leads to a shoot-out
three thousand miles away in the Norfolk countryside.

BAD LUCK AND TROUBLE

One of Reacher's buddies has shown up dead in the California
desert, and Reacher must put his old army unit back together.

NOTHING TO LOSE

Reacher crosses the line between a town called
Hope and one named Despair.

GONE TOMORROW

On the New York subway, Reacher counts
down the twelve tell-tale signs of a suicide bomber.

61 HOURS

In freezing South Dakota, Reacher hitches
a lift on a bus heading for trouble.

WORTH DYING FOR

Reacher runs into a clan that's terrifying the Nebraska locals, but it's the unsolved case of a missing child that he can't let go.

THE AFFAIR

Six months before the events in *Killing Floor*, Major Jack Reacher of the US Military Police goes undercover in Mississippi, to investigate a murder.

A WANTED MAN

A freshly-busted nose makes it difficult for Reacher to hitch a ride. When at last he's picked up by two men and a woman, it soon becomes clear they have something to hide . . .

NEVER GO BACK

When Reacher returns to his old Virginia headquarters he is accused of a sixteen-year-old homicide and hears these words: 'You're back in the army, Major. And your ass is mine.'

PERSONAL

Someone has taken a shot at the French president. Only one man could have done it – and Reacher is the one man who can find him.

MAKE ME

At a remote railroad stop on the prairie called Mother's Rest, Jack Reacher finds a town full of silent, watchful people, and descends into the heart of darkness.

NIGHT SCHOOL

The twenty-first in the series takes Reacher back to his army days, but this time he's not in uniform. In Hamburg, trusted sergeant Frances Neagley at his side, he must confront a terrifying new enemy.

NIGHT SCHOOL

Lee Child

BANTAM BOOKS

LONDON • TORONTO • SYDNEY • AUCKLAND • JOHANNESBURG

TRANSWORLD PUBLISHERS
61–63 Uxbridge Road, London W5 5SA
www.penguin.co.uk

Transworld is part of the Penguin Random House group of companies
whose addresses can be found at global.penguinrandomhouse.com

First published in Great Britain in 2016 by Bantam Press
an imprint of Transworld Publishers
Bantam India edition published 2016
Bantam edition published 2017

Every effort has been made to obtain the necessary permissions with
reference to copyright material, both illustrative and quoted.
We apologize for any omissions in this respect and will be pleased
to make the appropriate acknowledgements in any future edition.

A CIP catalogue record for this book
is available from the British Library.

ISBN
9780857502704 (B format)
9780857502711 (A format)

Typeset in 11/14pt Times by Falcon Oast Graphic Art Ltd.
Printed and bound in Great Britain by Clays Ltd, Bungay, Suffolk.

Penguin Random House is committed to a sustainable
future for our business, our readers and our planet. This book
is made from Forest Stewardship Council® certified paper.

1 3 5 7 9 10 8 6 4 2

Dedicated with great appreciation to the men and women around the world who do this stuff for real.

NIGHT SCHOOL

ONE

In the morning they gave Reacher a medal, and in the afternoon they sent him back to school. The medal was another Legion of Merit. His second. It was a handsome item, enamelled in white, with a ribbon halfway between purple and red. Army Regulation 600-8-22 authorized its award for exceptionally meritorious conduct in the performance of outstanding services to the United States in a key position of responsibility. Which was a bar Reacher felt he had cleared, technically. But he figured the real reason he was getting it was the same reason he had gotten it before. It was a transaction. A contractual token. *Take the bauble and keep your mouth shut about what we asked you to do for it.* Which Reacher would have anyway. It was nothing to boast about. The Balkans, some police work, a search for two local men with wartime secrets to keep, both soon identified, and located, and visited, and shot in the head. All part of the peace process. Interests were served, and the region calmed down a little. Two weeks of his life. Four rounds expended. No big deal.

Army Regulation 600-8-22 was surprisingly vague

about exactly how medals should be handed out. It said only that decorations were to be presented with an appropriate air of formality and with fitting ceremony. Which usually meant a large room with gilt furniture and a bunch of flags. And an officer senior in rank to the recipient. Reacher was a major, with twelve years in, but other awards were being given out that morning, including three to a trio of colonels and two to a pair of one-star generals, so the big cheese on deck was a three-star from the Pentagon, who Reacher knew from many years before, when the guy had been a CID battalion commander working out of Fort Myer. A thinker. Certainly enough of a thinker to figure out why an MP major was getting a Legion of Merit. He had a look in his eye. Part wry, and part seal-the-deal serious. *Take the bauble and keep your mouth shut.* Maybe in the past the guy had done the same thing himself. Maybe more than once. He had a whole fruit salad of ribbons on the left chest of his Class-A coat. Including two Legions of Merit.

The appropriately formal room was deep inside Fort Belvoir in Virginia. Which was close to the Pentagon, which was convenient for the three-star. Convenient for Reacher too, because it was about equally close to Rock Creek, where he had been marking time since he got back. Not so convenient for the other officers, who had flown in from Germany.

There was some milling around, and some small talk, and some shaking of hands, and then everyone went quiet and lined up and stood to attention, and salutes were exchanged, and medals were variously pinned or draped on, and then there was more milling around and small talk and shaking of hands. Reacher edged towards the door, keen to get out, but the three-star caught him before he made it. The guy shook his hand and kept hold of his elbow, and said, 'I hear you're getting new orders.'

Reacher said, 'No one told me. Not yet. Where did you hear that?'

'My top sergeant. They all talk to each other. U.S. Army NCOs have the world's most efficient grapevine. It always amazes me.'

'Where do they say I'm going?'

'They don't know for sure. But not far. Within driving distance, anyway. Apparently the motor pool got a requisition.'

'When am I supposed to find out?'

'Sometime today.'

'Thank you,' Reacher said. 'Good to know.'

The three-star let go of his elbow, and Reacher edged onward, to the door, and through it, and out to a corridor, where a sergeant first class skidded to a halt and saluted. He was out of breath, like he had run a long way. From a distant part of the installation, maybe, where the real work was done.

The guy said, 'Sir, with General Garber's compliments, he requests that you stop by his office at your earliest convenience.'

Reacher said, 'Where am I going, soldier?'

'Driving distance,' the guy said. 'But around here, that could be a lot of different things.'

* * *

Garber's office was in the Pentagon, so Reacher caught a ride with two captains who lived at Belvoir but had afternoon shifts in the B ring. Garber had a walled-off room all his own, two rings in, two floors up, guarded by a sergeant at a desk outside the door. Who stood up and led Reacher inside, and announced his name, like an old-time butler in a movie. Then the guy sidestepped and began his retreat, but Garber stopped him and said, 'Sergeant, I'd like you to stay.'

So the guy did, standing easy, feet planted on the shiny linoleum.

A witness.

Garber said, 'Take a seat, Reacher.'

Reacher did, on a visitor chair with tubular legs, which sagged under his weight and tipped him backward, as if a strong wind was blowing.

Garber said, 'You have new orders.'

Reacher said, 'What and where?'

'You're going back to school.'

Reacher said nothing.

Garber said, 'Disappointed?'

Hence the witness, Reacher supposed. Not a private conversation. Best behaviour. He said, 'As always, general, I'm happy to go where the army sends me.'

'You don't sound happy. But you should. Career development is a wonderful thing.'

'Which school?'

'Details are being delivered to your office as we speak.'

'How long will I be gone?'

'That depends on how hard you work. As long as it takes, I guess.'

Reacher got a bus in the Pentagon parking lot and rode two stops to the base of the hill below the Rock Creek HQ. He walked up the slope and went straight to his office. There was a slim file centred on his desk. His name was on it, and some numbers, and a course title: *Impact of Recent Forensic Innovation on Inter-Agency Cooperation*. Inside were sheets of paper, still warm from the Xerox machine, including a formal notice of temporary detachment to a location that seemed to be a leased facility in a corporate park in McLean, Virginia. He was to report there before five o'clock that afternoon. Civilian dress was to be worn. Residential quarters would be on-site. A personal vehicle would be provided. No driver.

Reacher tucked the file under his arm and walked out of the building. No one watched him go. He was of no interest to anyone. Not any more. He was a disappointment. An anticlimax. The NCO grapevine had held its breath, and all it had gotten was a meaningless course with a bullshit title. Not exciting at all. So now he was a non-person. Out of circulation. Out of sight, out of mind. Like a ballplayer on the disabled list. A month from now someone might suddenly remember him for a second, and wonder when he was coming back, or if, and then forget him again just as quickly.

The desk sergeant inside the door glanced up, and glanced away, bored.

Reacher had very few civilian clothes, and some of them weren't really civilian. His off-duty pants were Marine

Corps khakis about thirty years old. He knew a guy who knew a guy who worked in a warehouse, where he claimed there was a bale of old stuff wrongly delivered back when LBJ was still president, and then never squared away again afterwards. And apparently the point of the story was that old Marine pants looked just like new Ralph Lauren pants. Not that Reacher cared what pants looked like. But five bucks was an attractive price. And the pants were fine. Unworn, never issued, stiffly folded, a little musty, but good for another thirty years at least.

His off-duty T-shirts were no more civilian, being old army items, gone pale and thin with washing. Only his jacket was definitely non-military. It was a tan denim Levi's item, totally authentic in every respect, including the label, but sewn by an old girlfriend's mother, in a basement in Seoul.

He changed and packed the rest of his stuff into a duffel and a suit carrier, which he heaved out to the kerb, where a black Chevy Caprice was parked. He guessed it was an old MP black-and-white, now retired, with the decals peeled off, and the holes for the light bar and the antennas all sealed up with rubber plugs. The key was in. The seat was worn. But the engine started, and the transmission worked, and the brakes were fine. Reacher swung the thing around like a battleship manoeuvring, and headed out towards McLean, Virginia, with the windows down and the radio playing.

The corporate park was one of many, all of them the same, brown and beige, discreet typefaces, neat lawns, some evergreen planting, low two- and three-building campuses spreading outward across empty land, servicing folks who hid behind bland and modest names and tinted glass in their office windows. Reacher found the right place by the street number, and pulled in past a knee-high sign that said *Educational Solutions Incorporated*, in a typeface so plain it looked childish.

Parked at the door were two more Chevy Caprices. One was black and one was navy blue. They were both newer than Reacher's. And they were both properly civilian, in that they didn't have rubber plugs and brush-painted doors. They were government sedans, no doubt about it, clean and shiny, each one with two more antennas than a person needed for listening to the ball game. But the extra two antennas were not the same in both cases. The black car had short needles and the blue car had longer whips, in a different configuration. On a different wavelength. Two separate organizations.

Inter-Agency Cooperation.

Reacher parked alongside, and left his bags in the car. He went in the door, to an empty lobby, which had durable grey carpet underfoot and green potted ferns here and there against the walls. There was a door marked *Office*. And a door marked *Classroom*. Which Reacher opened. There was a green chalkboard at the head of the room, and twenty college desks, in four rows of five, each one with a little ledge on the right, for paper and pencil.

Sitting on two of the desks were two guys, both in suits. One suit was black, and one suit was navy blue. Like the cars. Both guys were looking straight ahead, like they had been talking, but had run out of things to say. They were about Reacher's own age. The one in the black suit was pale with dark hair worn dangerously long for a guy with a government car. The one in the blue suit was pale with colourless hair buzzed short. Like an astronaut. Built like an astronaut, too, or a gymnast not long out of the game.

Reacher stepped in, and they both turned to look.

The dark-haired guy said, 'Who are you?'

Reacher said, 'That depends on who you are.'

'Your identity depends on mine?'

'Whether I tell you or not. Are those your cars outside?'

'Is that significant?'

'Suggestive.'

'How?'

'Because they're different.'

'Yes,' the guy said. 'Those are our cars. And yes, you're in a classroom with two different representatives of two different government agencies. At cooperation school. Where they're going to teach us all about how to get along with other organizations. Please don't tell me you're from one of them.'

'Military Police,' Reacher said. 'But don't worry. I'm sure by five o'clock we'll have plenty of civilized people here. You can give up on me and get along with them instead.'

The guy with the buzz cut looked up and said, 'No, I think we're it. I think we're the whole ball game. There are only three bedrooms made up. I took a look around.'

Reacher said, 'What kind of a government school

has only three students? I never heard of that before.'

'Maybe we're faculty. Maybe the students live elsewhere.'

The guy with the dark hair said, 'Yes, that would make more sense.'

Reacher thought back, to the conversation in Garber's office. He said, 'My guy called it career development. I got the strong impression I would be on the receiving end, not the giving end. Then he seemed to suggest I could get through fast if I worked hard. All in all, I don't think I'm faculty. Did your orders sound any different?'

The guy with the buzz cut said, 'Not really.'

The guy with the hair didn't answer, except for a big speculative shrug that seemed to concede a person with a strong imagination could interpret his orders as less than impressive.

The guy with the buzz cut said, 'I'm Casey Waterman, FBI.'

'Jack Reacher, United States Army.'

The guy with the hair said, 'John White, CIA.'

They all shook hands, and then they lapsed into the same kind of silence Reacher had heard when he stepped in. They had run out of things to say. He sat on a desk near the back of the room. Waterman was ahead of him on the left, and White was ahead of him on the right. Waterman was very still. But watchful. He was passing the time and conserving his energy. He had done so before. He was an experienced agent. No kind of a rookie. And neither was White, despite being different in every other way. White was never still. He was

19

twitching and writhing and wringing his hands, and squinting into space, variably, focusing long, focusing short, sometimes narrowing his eyes and grimacing, looking left, looking right, as if caught in a tortuous sequence of thoughts, with no way out. An analyst, Reacher guessed, after many years in a world of unreliable data and double, triple, and quadruple bluffs. The guy was entitled to look a little agitated.

No one spoke.

Five minutes later Reacher broke the silence and asked, 'Is there a history of us not getting along? The FBI, I mean, and the CIA and the MPs. I'm not aware of any kind of a big deal. Are you?'

Waterman said, 'I think you're jumping to the wrong conclusion. This is not about history. It's about the future. They know we're already cooperative. Which allows them to exploit us. Think about the first half of the course title. This is about forensic innovation just as much as cooperation. And innovation means they're going to save money. We're all going to cooperate even more in the future. By sharing lab space. They're going to build one new place and we're all going to use it. That's my bet. We're here to be told how to make it work.'

'That's nuts,' Reacher said. 'I don't know anything about labs or scheduling. I'm the last person for that.'

'Me too,' Waterman said. 'Not a strength, to be honest.'

'This is worse than nuts,' White said. 'This is a colossal waste of time. There are far too many far more important things going on.'

Twitching and writhing and wringing his hands.

Reacher asked, 'Did they pull you off a job to bring you here? You got unfinished business?'

'No, actually. I was due a rotation. I just closed out a thing. Successfully, I thought, but this was my reward.'

'Look on the sunny side of the street. You can relax. Take it easy. Go play golf. You don't need to learn how to make it work. CIA doesn't give a damn about labs. You hardly use them.'

'I'll be three months behind on the job I should be starting right now.'

'Which is what?'

'I can't tell you.'

'Who is doing it instead?'

'I can't tell you that, either.'

'A good analyst?'

'Not good enough. He'll miss things. They might be vital. This stuff is impossible to predict.'

'What stuff?'

'I can't tell you.'

'But important stuff, right?'

'Far more important than this.'

'What was the thing you just closed out?'

'I can't tell you.'

'Was it an outstanding service to the United States in a key position of responsibility?'

'What?'

'Or words to that effect.'

'Yes, I would say so.'

'But this was your reward.'

Waterman said, 'Mine too. I'm in the same boat. I

21

could say every word he just said. I expected a promotion. Not this.'

'A promotion for what? Or after what?'

'We closed a big case.'

'What kind of case?'

'A manhunt, basically. Years old and very cold. But we did it.'

'A service to our nation?'

'What's this about?'

'I'm comparing the two of you. And there's not much difference. You're very good agents, already fairly senior, seen as loyal and reliable and trustworthy, and hence you're given something useful to do. But then this is your reward for doing it. Which means one of two things.'

'Which are?' White said.

'Maybe the thing you did was embarrassing in certain circles. Maybe now it needs to be deniable. Maybe you need to be hidden away. Out of sight and out of mind.'

White shook his head. He said, 'No, it was well regarded. It will be for years. I got a secret decoration. And a personal letter from the Secretary of State. And it doesn't need to be deniable anyway, because it was completely secret. No one in those circles knew anything about it.'

Reacher looked at Waterman and said, 'Was there anything embarrassing about your manhunt?'

Waterman shook his head, and said, 'What's the second possibility?'

'This is not a school.'

'Then what is it?'

'It's a place where they send good agents fresh off a big win.'

Waterman paused a beat. A new thought. He said, 'Are you the same as us? I don't see why you wouldn't be. Why draft two the same and not three?'

Reacher nodded. 'I'm the same. I'm fresh off a big win. That's for damn sure. I got a medal this morning. On a ribbon around my neck. For a job well done. All clean and tidy. Nothing to get embarrassed about.'

'What kind of job was it?'

'I'm sure it's classified. But I'm reliably informed it might have involved someone breaking into a house and shooting the occupant in the head.'

'Where?'

'One in the forehead and one behind the ear. Never fails.'

'No, where was the house?'

'I'm sure that's classified too. But overseas, I expect. And I'm reliably informed there were a lot of consonants in the name. Not many vowels at all. And then the same someone did the same thing the next night. At a different house. All for good reasons. Which taken together means I would expect him to get better than this after-wards. I would expect him to get some input into his next deployment, at least. Maybe even a choice.'

'Exactly,' White said. 'And my choice wouldn't have been this. It would have been to do what I should be doing right now.'

'Which sounds challenging.'

'Very.'

'Which is typical. As a reward we want a challenge.

23

We don't want the easy commands. We want to step up.'

'Exactly.'

'Maybe we have,' Reacher said. 'Let me ask you a question. Think back to when you got these orders. Was it face to face, or written?'

'Face to face. It had to be, for a thing like this.'

'Was there a third person in the room?'

White said, 'As a matter of fact there was. It was humiliating. An administrative assistant, waiting to deliver a stack of papers. He told her to stay. She was just standing there.'

Reacher looked at Waterman, who said, 'Same for me. He kept his secretary in the room. Normally he wouldn't. How did you know?'

'Because the same thing happened to me. His sergeant. A witness. But also a gossip. That was the whole point. They all talk to each other. Within seconds everyone knew I wasn't going anywhere interesting. Just a meaningless course with a bullshit title. I was instantly yesterday's news. Immediately off the radar. I'm sure it's far and wide by now. I'm a non-person. I disappeared into the bureaucratic fog. And maybe you did too. Maybe administrative assistants and FBI secretaries have networks of their own. If they do, then the three of us are the three most invisible people on the planet right now. No one is asking questions about us. No one is curious about us. No one can even remember us. There's nothing more boring than where we are now.'

'You're saying they moved three unrelated but in-form operatives completely under the radar. Why?'

24

'Under the radar doesn't capture it. We're in class here. We're completely invisible.'

'Why? And why us three? What's the connection?'

'I don't know. But I'm sure it's a challenging project. Possibly the kind of thing three in-form operatives might regard as a satisfactory reward for services rendered.'

'What is this place?'

'I don't know,' Reacher said again. 'But it ain't a school. That's for damn sure.'

At five o'clock exactly two black vans pulled in off the road, and drove past the knee-high sign, and parked behind the three Caprices, like a barricade, trapping them in. Two men in suits got out of each of the vans. Secret Service, or U.S. Marshals. Both pairs of men looked around briefly, and gave themselves the all-clear, and ducked back to their vans to get their principals out.

From the second van came a woman. She had a brief-case in one hand and a stack of papers in the other. She was wearing a neat black dress. Knee length. It was the kind of thing that could do double duty, in the daytime with pearls in hushed high-floor offices, and in the evening with diamonds at cocktail parties and receptions. She was older than Reacher, maybe ten years or more. Middle forties, but doing well. Looking sharp. She had blonde hair, medium length, arranged in an unaffected style and no doubt combed with her fingers. She was taller than the average, but no wider.

Then out of the first van came a guy Reacher recognized instantly. His face was in the paper once a week, and on TV more than that, because as well as getting coverage for his own business, he was in a lot of stock photographs and B-roll footage, of Cabinet meetings, and tense shirt-sleeve discussions in the Oval Office. He was Alfred Ratcliffe, the National Security Adviser. The president's top boy, whenever it came to things that might not end well. The go-to guy. The right-hand man. Rumour had it he was nearly seventy years old, but he didn't look it. He was an old State Department survivor, historically in and out of favour as the winds changed and he didn't, but he had hung in there long enough until finally his backbone got him the best job of all.

The woman joined up with him and they walked together, with the four suits all around them, to the lobby doors, which Reacher heard open, and then he heard feet on the hard carpet, and then they all came into the classroom, two suits hanging back, two walking point towards the chalkboard, Ratcliffe and the woman following them, and turning when they could get no further, to face the room, exactly like teachers at the start of a lesson.

Ratcliffe looked at White, and then at Waterman, and then at Reacher, way in back.

He said, 'This is not a school.'

26

TWO

The woman bent decorously at the knee and laid her briefcase and her stack of papers on the floor. Ratcliffe took a step forward and said, 'You three were brought here under false pretences, obviously. But we didn't want a lot of fanfare. A little misdirection was better. We want to avoid attention, if we can. At least at the beginning.'

And then he paused, for the drama, as if inviting questions, but no one asked any. Not even: the beginning of what? Better to hear the pitch all the way through. Always safer, with orders from on high.

Ratcliffe asked, 'Who here can articulate this administration's national security policy in simple plain English?'

No one spoke.

Ratcliffe asked, 'Why aren't you answering?'

Waterman retreated behind a thousand-yard stare, and White shrugged as if to say the immense complexities obviously precluded ordinary language, and anyway weren't the notions of simplicity and plainness entirely subjective, and therefore clearly in need of a preliminary round of argument in order to agree definitions?

Reacher said, 'It's a trick question.'

Ratcliffe said, 'You think our policy can't be explained simply?'

'I think it doesn't exist.'

'You think we're incompetent?'

'No, I think the world is changing. Better to stay flexible.'

'Are you the MP?'

'Yes, sir.'

Ratcliffe paused again, and said, 'A little over three years ago a bomb went off in a garage under a very tall building in New York City. Personally tragic for those killed or injured, of course, but from a global perspective not a very big deal at all. Except at that moment the world went mad. The closer we looked, the less we saw, and the less we understood. We had enemies every-where, apparently, but we didn't know for sure who they were, or where they were, or why they were, or what was the connection between them, or what they wanted, and we certainly had no idea what they would do next. We were nowhere. But at least we admitted that to ourselves. Therefore we didn't waste time developing policies on things we hadn't even heard of yet. We felt that would generate a false sense of security. So as of now our standard operating procedure is to run around with our hair on fire, dealing with ten things at once, as and when they arise. We chase everything, because we have to. A little more than three years from now is the new millennium, with every capital city celebrating around the clock, which makes that one single day the greatest propaganda target in the history of planet Earth. We need to know who these guys are well ahead of time. All of them. So we ignore nothing.'

No one spoke.

Ratcliffe said, 'Not that I need to justify myself to you. But you need to understand the theory. We make no assumptions and we leave no stone unturned.'

No one asked anything. Not even: do you have a particular stone in mind for us? Always safer not to speak, unless spoken to. Better just to wait.

But then Ratcliffe turned towards the woman and said, 'This is Dr Marian Sinclair, my senior deputy. She will complete the briefing. Every single word she says is backed by me, and therefore by the president also. Every single word. This might be a complete waste of time and go nowhere, but until we know that for sure it gets exactly the same priority as everything else. No effort is to be spared. You'll get anything you need.'

And then the guy swept out, between two hustling suits. Reacher heard them leave the lobby, and he heard their van start up and drive away. Dr Marian Sinclair hauled a front-row desk around until it was facing the rest of the room, and she sat down, all toned arms and dark nylons and good shoes. She crossed her legs and said, 'Gather round.'

Reacher moved up to the third row and squeezed into a desk that put him in a neat and attentive semicircle with Waterman and White. Sinclair's face looked open and honest, but pinched by stress and worry. There was serious shit going on. That was clear. Maybe Garber had

29

dropped a hint. *You don't sound happy. But you should.*
Maybe all was not lost. Reacher figured White was
arriving at the same conclusion. He was leaning forward,
and his eyes were still. Waterman was motionless.
Conserving energy.

Sinclair said, 'There's an apartment in Hamburg,
Germany. A fashionable neighbourhood, reasonably
central, pretty expensive, but maybe a little transitory
and corporate. For the last year the apartment has been
rented to four men in their twenties. Not Germans.
Three are Saudis, and the fourth is an Iranian. All four
appear very secular. Clean-shaven, short hair, well
dressed. They favour polo shirts in pastel colours with
alligator badges. They wear gold Rolex watches and
Italian shoes. They drive BMWs and go out to nightclubs. But they don't go out to work.'

Reacher saw White nod to himself, as if he was
familiar with such situations. There was no reaction
from Waterman.

Sinclair said, 'Locally the four young men are taken
to be minor playboys. Possibly related to distant branches
of rich and prominent families. Sowing their wild oats
before coming home to the oil ministry. Standard-issue
Eurotrash, in other words. But we know they're not. We
know they were recruited in their home countries and
sent to Germany through Yemen and Afghanistan by a
new organization we don't know much about yet. Other
than it seems to be well funded, strongly jihadist, largely
paramilitary in its training methods, and indifferent to
national origins. Saudis and Iranians working together
is unusual. But working together they are. They were

well thought of in the training camps, and they were sent to Hamburg a year ago. Their mission was to embed themselves in the West, live quietly, and await further instructions. Of which they've had none so far. They're a sleeper cell, in other words.'

Waterman stirred and said, 'How do we know all this?'

'The Iranian is ours,' Sinclair said. 'He's a double agent. CIA runs him out of the Hamburg consulate.'

'Brave kid.'

Sinclair nodded. 'And brave kids are hard to find. That's one of the ways the world changed. Assets used to walk in the embassy door. They wrote begging letters. We used to turn some of them away. But those were old communists. Now we need young Arabs and we don't know any.'

'Why do you need us?' Waterman said. 'It's a stable situation. They're not going anywhere. You'll get the activation order about a minute after they do. Assuming the consulate mans the switchboard around the clock.'

Better to hear the pitch all the way through.

Sinclair said, 'It is a stable situation. Nothing ever happens. But then something did. A few days ago. Just a tiny random collision. They had a visitor.'

At Sinclair's suggestion they moved out of the classroom to the office. She said the classroom was uncomfortable, because of the desks, which was true, especially for Reacher. He was six feet five and two hundred fifty pounds. He was wearing his desk more than sitting in it. By contrast the office had a conference table with four

31

reclining chairs made of leather. Which enhanced level of comfort Sinclair seemed to fully anticipate. Which made sense. She had leased the space herself, after all, probably yesterday, or had an under-deputy do so on her behalf. Three bedrooms, and four chairs for the briefings.

The men in suits waited outside, and Sinclair said, 'Our asset was squeezed for every detail he had, and we think we can trust his conclusions. The visitor was another Saudi. The same age as them. Dressed the same as them. Product in his hair, gold necklace, alligator on his shirt. They weren't expecting him. It was a total surprise. But they have a thing like the Mafia, where they might be called upon to perform a service. The visitor alluded to it. It turned out he was what they call a courier. Nothing to do with them. Something else entirely. Just that he was in Germany on business and needed a safe house. Which is always a courier's pre-ferred option. Hotels leave trails, eventually. They're very paranoid, because these new networks are very spread out. Which means secure communication is theoretically very difficult. They think we can hear their cell phones, which we probably can, and they think we can read their e-mails, which I'm sure we soon will, and they know we steam open their regular mail. So they use couriers instead, who are really messengers. They don't carry briefcases chained to their wrists. They carry verbal questions and verbal answers in their heads. They go back and forth, from continent to continent, question, answer, question, answer. Very slow, but com-pletely secure. No electronic fingerprint anywhere, nothing written down, and nothing to see except a guy with a gold chain passing through an airport, alongside a million others just like him.'

White asked, 'Do we know if Hamburg was his final destination? Or was he breaking his journey to somewhere else in Germany?'

Sinclair said, 'His business was in Hamburg.'

'But not with the boys in the house.'

'No, with someone else.'

'Do we know who sent him? Do we assume the same guys from Yemen and Afghanistan?'

'We strongly believe it was the same guys. Because of another circumstance.'

Waterman said, 'Which was what?'

'By a statistically not very amazing coincidence, the messenger knew one of the Saudis in the house. They had spent three months in Yemen together, climbing ropes and firing AK47s. It's a small world. So the two of them had brief conversations, and the Iranian overheard some of them.'

'What did he hear?'

'The guy was waiting for a rendezvous coming up two days from then. Location was never stated, or at least never overheard, but the context suggested it was reasonably local to the safe house. He didn't have a message to give. He was there to be told something. An opening statement, the Iranian says. An initial position, of some sort. He says it was clear from the context. The messenger was to hear the statement and carry it back in his head.'

'It sounds like the start of a negotiation. Like an opening bid.'

Sinclair nodded. 'We expect the messenger to return. At least once, with a yes or no answer.'

'Do we have any idea what the issue is?'

Sinclair shook her head. 'But it's important business. The Iranian is sure of it, because the messenger was an elite warrior, just like himself. He must have been well thought of in the camps, or how could he have gotten the polo shirts and the Italian shoes and four passports? He wasn't the sort of guy used by small fish at either end of the chain. He was a principals-only type of messenger.'

'Did the rendezvous happen?'

'In the late afternoon of the second day. The guy went out for fifty minutes.'

'And then what?'

'He left, first thing the next morning.'

'No more conversations?'

'One more. And it was a good one. The guy spilled the beans. He came right out with it. He told his friend the information he was carrying home. Just like that. He couldn't help himself. Because he was impressed by it, we think. By the scale of it. The Iranian said he seemed very excited. These are young men in their twenties.'

'What was the information?'

'It was an opening statement. An initial position. Just like the Iranian thought it would be. Short and to the point.'

'What did it say?'

'The American wants a hundred million dollars.'

THREE

Sinclair sat up straight and hitched closer to the table, as if to emphasize her points, and said, 'The Iranian is by all accounts very smart and articulate and sensitive to the nuances of language, and the head of station went over and over it with him, and we firmly believe it was a simple declarative statement. During those fifty minutes the messenger met face to face with an American. Male, because there was no comment about it being a woman, and there would have been, the Iranian says. He's completely certain of that. During the meeting the American told the messenger he wanted a hundred million dollars. As a price for something. That was clearly the context. But that was the end of the transmission. What American, we don't know. A hundred million for what, we don't know. From whom, we don't know.'

White said, 'But a hundred million narrows the field. Even if it's an opening bid that gets knocked down to fifty, it's still a good chunk of change. Who has that kind of money? Plenty of people, you would say, but at least you can get them all in one Rolodex.'

'Wrong end of the telescope,' Reacher said. 'Better to

find the seller than the buyer, surely. What kind of a thing would guys who climb ropes in Yemen pay a hundred million dollars for? And what kind of American in Hamburg has such a thing for sale?'

Waterman said, 'A hundred million is a lot of money. That kind of price would worry me a little.'

Sinclair nodded and said, 'That kind of price worries us a lot. It sounds deadly serious. It's more than we ever heard of before. Therefore we're working every channel we can. All our assets worldwide have been alerted. Hundreds of people are working hard already. But we need more. Your job is to find that American. If he's still overseas, then CIA has jurisdiction, and Mr White will lead the effort. If he's back in the States now, the FBI has jurisdiction and Special Agent Waterman will step up instead. And because statistics tell us the overwhelming majority of Americans in Germany at any one time are serving U.S. military, we think we might need Major Reacher to be involved with either or both.'

Reacher looked at Waterman, then White, and saw issues in their eyes, and had no doubt they saw the same in his.

Sinclair said, 'Staff and supplies will arrive in the morning. You can have anything you want, at any time. But you will talk to no one except me, Mr Ratcliffe, or the president. This is a quarantined unit. Even if all you want is a box of pencils, you go through me, Mr Ratcliffe, or the president. Which in practice will be me. Subsequent paperwork will be generated inside the West Wing. You must not be identified personally. Because a hundred million dollars is a lot of money. Government involvement is not impossible. The American could be State Department, or Justice, or in the Pentagon. You might talk to the wrong person by mistake. So talk to no one. That's rule number two.'

Waterman said, 'What was rule number one?'

'Rule number one is the Iranian must not be burned. We must do nothing that could be traced back to him. We have a lot invested in him and we're going to need him, because we truly have no idea what's coming next.'

Then she pushed her chair back and stood up and headed for the door. As she left she said, 'Remember, hair on fire.'

Reacher lay back in his leather chair, and White looked at him and said, 'It has to be tanks and planes.'

Reacher said, 'Our nearest tanks are a thousand miles from Yemen or Afghanistan, and they take weeks and weeks and thousands of people to move. It would be easier to bring Yemen or Afghanistan to them. Also faster and less obtrusive.'

'Planes, then.'

'I guess a hundred million might get a couple of pilots to come on over to the dark side. Maybe three or four. I doubt if Afghanistan has runways long enough. But maybe Yemen does. So it's theoretically possible. Except planes are no good to them. They would need hundreds of tons of spare parts and hundreds of engineers and maintenance technicians. And hundreds of hours of training. And we'd find them five minutes later anyway, and destroy them on the ground with missiles. Or maybe we can do it remotely now.'

'Some other military hardware, then.'

'But what? A million rifles at a hundred bucks each? We don't have that many.'

Waterman said, 'It could be a secret, or a code word, or a password, or a formula, or a map or a plan or a diagram, or a list, or the blueprint of all of the world financial system's computer security, or a commercial recipe, or the sum total of all the bribes required to pass legislation in all fifty states.'

White said, 'You think data?'

'What else can be bought and sold unobtrusively and is worth that much? Diamonds, maybe, but they're in Antwerp, not Hamburg. Drugs, maybe, but no American has a hundred million dollars' worth ready to ship. That's South and Central America. And Afghanistan has poppies of its own.'

'What's the worst case scenario?'

'That's above my pay grade. Ask Ratcliffe. Or the president.'

'In your own personal opinion?'

'What's yours?'

'I'm a Middle East specialist. It's all worst case to me.'

'Smallpox germs,' Waterman said. 'That's my worst case. Or something like that. A plague. A biological weapon. Or Ebola. Or an antidote. Or a vaccine. Which would mean they already have the germs.'

Reacher stared at the ceiling.

Things that might not end well.

You don't sound happy. But you should.

As long as it takes.

Garber was like a crossword puzzle.

White looked at him and said, 'What are you thinking about?'

He said, 'The contradiction between rule one and the rest of it. We mustn't burn the Iranian. Which means we can't go anywhere near the messenger. We can't even stake out a location the messenger leads us to. Because we don't know the messenger exists. Not unless we got an inside whisper.'

'That's an impediment,' Waterman said. 'Not a contradiction. We'll find a way to work around it. They need that guy.'

'It's a question of efficiency. They need to know who these guys are ahead of time. They need to trace networks and build databases. Therefore they should focus on the messengers, surely. Verbal questions and verbal answers in their heads, back and forth, continent to continent, question, answer, question, answer. They know everything. They're like audiotape. They're worth a hundred inside men. Because they have the big picture. What has the Iranian got? Nothing but four walls in Hamburg and nothing to do.'

'He can't just be sacrificed.'

'They could pull him out the same moment they hit the messenger. They could give him a house in Florida.'

White said, 'The messenger wouldn't talk. This is a tribal thing, going back a thousand years. They wouldn't rat each other out. Not after the little we're allowed to do to them, anyway. So it's a smart play to keep the inside man where he is. They genuinely don't know what's coming. An early hint would be nice. Even part of a clue.'

Reacher said, 'Do you know what's coming?'

'Something unhinged. This is not the same as it used to be.'

'Have you worked with Ratcliffe before? Or Sinclair?'

'Never. Have you?'

Waterman said, 'They didn't choose us because they know us. They chose us because we weren't in Hamburg at the critical time. We were engaged elsewhere. Therefore we can't be the wrong people to talk to.'

A quarantine unit, Sinclair had said, and it felt like it. Three guys in a room, shut away from the outside world, because they were all infected, with an alibi.

At seven o'clock Reacher got his bags from the car and hauled them up to his bedroom, which was at the far end of three in a line, in a corridor that looked like an office corridor, and might have been the day before. The room was spacious and had a bathroom attached. An executive's suite. Designed for a desk, not a bed, but it worked.

Eating was a case of firing up the old Caprice and cruising McLean, turning by instinct into the kind of streets that might have the kind of eventual edge-of-town lots that might have the kind of restaurants he was looking for. Not everyone's choice. His metabolism helped. He saw neon up ahead, and shiny aluminium, next to a gas station, next to a highway ramp. A diner, old enough to be nearly authentic. Some dents and tarnish. Some miles on the clock.

He pulled in and parked, and heaved open the

40

chromium door, and stepped inside. The air was cold and bright with fluorescent light. The first person he saw was a woman he knew. All alone in a booth. From his last but one command. The best soldier he had ever worked with. His best friend, possibly, in a guarded way, if friendship was permission to leave things unsaid.

At first he thought it was another not very amazing coincidence. It was a small world, and close to the Pentagon it got smaller still. Then he reassessed. She had been his top sergeant during the 110th MP's glory years. She had played as big a part as anyone, and bigger than some. Bigger than most. Bigger than him, probably.

By being very smart.

Way too smart to be a coincidence.

He stepped up to her table. She didn't move. She was watching him in the back of an upturned spoon. He slid in opposite and said, 'Hello, Neagley.'

FOUR

Sergeant Frances Neagley looked up from her spoon and said, 'Of all the diners in all the towns. What were the odds?'

Reacher said, 'Carefully calculated, I'm sure.'

'I guessed you were likely to drive west, because subconsciously you would want to keep D.C. behind you. I figured the turns you would make, which meant this is about the only obvious place. And this is the obvious time. I figured two hours of briefing, and then break for dinner.'

'It's a school.'

'No it isn't. The course title doesn't even make sense.'

'They never make sense.'

'This one is worse than usual.'

'It's a school.'

'They wouldn't do that to you. Not while Garber lives and breathes.'

'I can't discuss it. It's too boring.'

'Let me hazard a wild-ass guess. It's cover for something. Given your current batting average, it's a high-level something. Which means you'll get whatever you ask for. Especially staff. So you'll be calling me in the morning anyway. Why not tell me twelve hours early?'

She was in woodland-pattern battledress uniform, the sleeves neatly rolled, her forearms on the table. She had dark hair, cut short, and dark eyes, and a tan. Her skin looked soft, but he was sure it wasn't. He had seen her in action. She was fast and exceptionally strong. She would feel hard and solid underneath. But he didn't know. He had never touched her. Never even shaken her hand.

He said, 'I don't know exactly what we're going to need. The percentage play would be to start making lists. From movement orders. Active-duty personnel physically present in Germany on a certain day. And civilians, too, from passport records.'

'Why?'

'We need to find a particular American who was in Hamburg during a particular fifty-minute window.'

'Why?'

'He's planning to sell something worth a hundred million dollars to a bunch of new-style bad guys from Yemen and Afghanistan.'

'Do we know what he's selling?'

'No idea.'

'Land borders might be a problem. I think you can drive right through. Because of the European Union. The passport records might be incomplete.'

'Exactly. It's only a percentage play. But we could help it a little. We could look at who was in and out of Switzerland, maybe the week before. When the guy was making his final decision. He was going to sell. He

43

was about to open the bidding. Which he knew couldn't last for ever. So he needed to be ready ahead of time. So he opened a secret Swiss bank account. Probably in Zurich. Standing by and waiting. Then he went back to Hamburg and named his price.'

'Which is also only a percentage play. Therefore it can't be an exclusionary factor. It could be an old account from years ago. This might not be a first-time bad guy. Or his secret account could be someplace else. Luxembourg, maybe.'

'Which is why I said I don't know exactly what we're going to need.'

'Do you think he's military?'

'He could be. The odds say so. Like Americans in Korea or on Okinawa. So that's another list we need, just in case. What could a military guy be selling? Is it intelligence? Or is it hardware? In which case, assume a shipping container, or a large van or a small truck, something unobtrusive, and make a list of what could fit inside and be worth a hundred million bucks.'

'It would have to be something reliable and simple to operate. There won't be support troops coming with it.'

'OK, bear that in mind. Make a master list of all the other lists. That's all we can do right now. Be ready to deploy about nine o'clock in the morning. I can't see them doing it any faster. After that everything goes through the NSC, via a woman named Marian Sinclair.'

'I've heard of her,' Neagley said. 'She's Alfred Ratcliffe's senior deputy.'

'Be ready with the things you need her to do for us. We shouldn't waste time.'

'Is this thing a big problem?'

'I guess it could be. If it's what we think it is. Which it might not be. It's one sentence plucked out of the air. It could be a joke. Or some kind of insider sarcasm. Could be obscure rope-climbing Yemeni slang for not very much at all. But if it's real, then yes, the price tag suggests a problem.'

The waitress came over, and they ordered. Neagley said, 'Congratulations on the medal.'

Reacher said, 'Thank you.'

'You OK?'

'Never better.'

'You sure?'

'What are you, my mother?'

'What did you think of Sinclair?'

'I liked her.'

'Who else have we got?'

'A guy named Waterman from the FBI. He's an old-school prowler. And a guy named White from CIA. He's a highly stressed individual. Probably with good cause. So far they've been adequate in several respects. They've had sensible things to say. Presumably they'll bring in their own staffers now. And presumably above all of us will be some kind of a National Security Council supervisor, babysitting us and relaying our messages to Sinclair.'

'Why did you like her?'

'She was honest. Ratcliffe too. They're running around with their hair on fire.'

'You should call your brother. At Treasury. He could watch for wire transfers. A hundred million dollars might be visible at government level.'

'I would have to go through Sinclair.'

'Are you going to stick to that?'

Reacher said, 'She thinks it could be anyone. She doesn't want us to betray ourselves to the wrong person. But she's missing a point. It isn't anyone. It's everyone. More or less. This is a broad sweep. No doubt our guy will prove to be one of many. We're going to catch all kinds of people in and out of secret meetings, and in and out of Switzerland with suitcases full of cash, all of them up to no good, buying and selling and trading all kinds of stuff. We're going to make a lot of enemies. Both military and civilian. But we can't afford too much background noise. Not yet, anyway. Secrecy will delay it. So right now I think we should stick with Sinclair. We'll reconsider as and when we need to.'

'Understood,' Neagley said.

The waitress brought their plates, and they started eating. Eight o'clock in the evening, in McLean, Virginia.

Eight o'clock in the evening in McLean, Virginia, was two o'clock the next morning in Hamburg, Germany. Late, but the American was still awake. He was on his back in bed staring at a ceiling he had never seen before. A naked hooker lay in the crook of his arm. It was her place. It was clean, and neat, and fragrant, and vaguely house-proud. Not cheap, but then neither was she. Which was OK. He was about to become a very rich man.

Therefore a small celebration had been in order. And he liked expensive women. They were a bigger thrill. His tastes were fairly simple. It was the degree of enthusiasm that counted. She had shown plenty. And then they had talked. Pillow-talk, literally. They snuggled. She had been interested in him. She had been a good listener.

He had said too much.

He figured hookers were better psychologists than real psychologists, and could tell the difference between bluster and boasting and bullshit and manic dreams. Which left a small category of truth. Not confessional truth. More like a happy thing. Like a bursting-to-tell-someone truth. It just came out, on a wave of excitement. He had been feeling great. She was worth the money. He was floating. He had mentioned his plan to buy a ranch in Argentina. About bigger than Rhode Island, he had said.

Which didn't mean much, but she would remember. And in Germany hookers weren't afraid of the cops. It was a welfare state. Everything was tolerated as long as it was regulated. So when the hunt began, she would be happy to drop by and tell them about the American she met, who was fixing to buy a ranch on the pampas bigger than Rhode Island. Some kind of compensation there, she would say. A take-me-seriously kind of thing. Because he was never real hard. And then the cops, being German, would write it all down, and then call someone who knew, and thereby discover a ranch on the pampas bigger than Rhode Island was a very expensive purchase.

A simple search of current real-estate transactions in one single country of the world would bring them straight to his brand-new door.

Stupid.

His own fault.

He moved around the room in his mind, retracing his steps, listing what he had touched. Which wasn't much, apart from her. Were his fingerprints on her skin? He doubted it. They would be smeared, anyway. His DNA was in her stomach, but it was being attacked there by powerful acids and digestive enzymes. And the science was still in its infancy. Still in its PR phase. It would refuse to take a case, rather than fail in public.

Safe enough.

Which was crazy.

But also logical. In for a penny, in for a pound. All or nothing. He was committed. He had wondered how it would feel. It turned out to feel like falling. Like sky-diving, maybe. The long, long free fall before the parachute opens. Falling, and falling. He couldn't fight it. All he could do was take a breath and relax and surrender.

He had left the hotel unseen, through the parking garage. No reason, except a shortcut to another bar he knew. She was driving in, ready to start work. Late evening, high end, high rollers. A different world. Except not any more. He could have anything he wanted. Asking was part of the fun. Right there in the garage. Suppose he was wrong? But he wasn't. He had seen her before. She smiled and named a very high figure. He would have paid ten times more, just because of the way she was standing. And she was fresh out the shower. Not a virgin, but as close as it got, on a day to day basis.

She drove, back to the place she had only just left.

Were there security cameras in the parking garage?

He thought not. He was the kind of guy who dealt in details. He was observant. He noticed everything. He had to. Part of his job. On the garage ceiling he had seen fireproof foam, and electrical conduits, and five-inch drains, and a sprinkler system.

No cameras.

Safe enough.

Which was crazy.

But also logical.

He rehearsed it in his mind, and then did it fast. At first she thought it was role play. Like he was acting out what he saw on VHS. He threw her on her front and straddled her, pinning her elbows under his knees, his butt on hers, crouched like a jockey on a horse, and she moaned like they all do, and he leaned down and strangled her from behind, fast and hard, shutting it all down double quick. She tried to buck and heave, but she could barely move. Only her feet, really, trying to get him in the back with her heels, but not quite making it, so they thrashed up and down uselessly, like swimming. And then they stopped, and he hung on tight until he was sure, and then he hung on some more, and then he let her go and got the hell out.

All or nothing.

FIVE

Reacher slept well in his executive bedroom, but woke early, and was already out and about when at seven o'clock a catering truck delivered industrial-size reservoirs of coffee, and a tray of breakfast pastries about the size of an on-deck circle. Much more than three people could eat. Which meant the staff was on its way.

It arrived at seven thirty in the shape of two mid-grade executive officers from the National Security Council. Personally known by Sinclair, she said on an introductory call, and trusted by her, presumably. They were both men, both in their thirties, both dour, as if worn down by the data they handled. By eight o'clock they were up and running, with secure phone lines established, and Reacher got in ahead of Waterman and White with his staffing request, and by nine Neagley was in the house, early enough to be already ordering up storms of information through the NSC before Waterman's help even got there, twenty minutes ahead of White's. Both new arrivals were men. They looked like younger versions of their bosses. Waterman's guy was called Landry, and White's was called Vanderbilt, no relation to the rich guy from history.

They hauled furniture from place to place, and set up a three-way joint control centre in the classroom, run by Neagley and Landry and Vanderbilt. The NSC baby-sitters were kept in the office, and Reacher and Waterman and White took conference calls at the table, in the leather chairs. By eleven o'clock the place was humming. By twelve o'clock it had some data. Sinclair called in on the speaker to hear all about it.

Reacher said, 'That day there were nearly two hundred thousand American citizens in Germany. About sixty thousand actively deployed military, plus nearly double that in families and recent retirees not gone home yet, plus about a thousand civilians on vacation, plus about five thousand more at trade conventions and board meetings.'

'That's a lot of Americans.'

Reacher said, 'We should go to Hamburg.'

'When?'

'Now.'

'Why now?'

'We'll have to go sometime. We can't solve this on paper.'

Sinclair said, 'Agent Waterman, what do you think?'

Waterman said, 'What I think depends on how fast these messengers get back and forth. Sounds like a slow process. When will our guy expect an answer? What would be a typical interval?'

'Elsewhere it seems to be about two weeks. Maybe a day or so less.'

'We want to be nearby when the deal is done. No question about that. But we seem to have time. I would go to Hamburg next week. I would want more background analysis first. It might save some effort in the long run.'

'Mr White?'

White said, 'I would assume I'm not going to Hamburg at all. Who would need me there, alongside the man-hunter and the assassin? Solving things on paper is what I'm all about. I leave the East Coast only when strictly necessary.'

Sinclair said, 'Major Reacher, on what grounds do you want to go to Hamburg now?'

Reacher said, 'On the grounds that Mr Ratcliffe said we'd get anything we want.'

Sinclair said, 'Would either Agent Waterman or Mr White object if Major Reacher went to Hamburg on his own?'

White said, 'No.'

Waterman said, 'As long as he goes on a do-no-harm basis.'

One advantage of communicating through the West Wing was instantaneous success with airlines and hotels. Within thirty minutes Reacher and Neagley were booked non-stop that night on Lufthansa, and rooms were reserved for them at a Hamburg business hotel not far from the apartment in question, in the fashionable neighbourhood Sinclair had described, reasonably central, pretty expensive.

They stayed in McLean the rest of the afternoon

and worked on eliminating personnel by matching manoeuvre reports to names. A guy couldn't be driving a tank on the eastern plains and walking around Hamburg all at the same time. The number of possibles dropped like a stone. Which felt like progress. Then the first reports from the airlines about Zurich started to come in. White's guy Vanderbilt seemed to get the point, and he volunteered to work late on the cross-check while they flew, and then to call them when they landed with anything of significance.

Cooperation school, Reacher thought. Who knew?

Neagley drove them to the airport in Reacher's Caprice and parked in the short-term garage on the government's dime. Her version of civilian dress was mirrored sunglasses and a battered leather jacket over a T-shirt, with pants Reacher took to be old Marine Corps leftovers like his own, but which turned out to be genuine Ralph Lauren items. She had a bag, and he didn't. Their seats were in coach, but were luxury items compared to the canvas slings on a military transport. They ate the food, reclined an inch, and went to sleep.

Twenty-four hours after the American left, the hooker's apartment was much less fragrant than it had been before. Or more fragrant, to be accurate, but with the wrong scent. It was becoming noticeable, out in the corridor, and through the kitchen vents. Her neighbours, already resentful, called the cops in the middle of the night. The dispatcher sent a squad car for a look. Or a sniff, as it turned out. Which resulted in the super being roused, with a pass key. Which led to four hours of detectives, and questions, and caution tape, and crime scene technicians, and then finally an ambulance and a rubber body bag.

Good news and bad news, from the police point of view. Hamburg was a rowdy port city, with a world-famous red light district, and drugs and graffiti at the train station, but even so homicide was relatively rare. Less than one a week. A dead body was still an event. Careers could be built. And the police department claimed a success rate close to 90 per cent. That was the good news. The bad news was the remaining unsolved 10 per cent was all either stabbed junkies or strangled prostitutes. Occupational hazards. Not likely to be one for the textbooks. The perpetrator was probably at sea already, in a bunk on a ship, a hundred miles away, heading for the open ocean.

Reacher and Neagley had West Wing cash in their pockets, for operational purposes, so they took a Mercedes taxi into town from the airport, through watery sunshine and morning traffic. The street with their hotel was quiet and leafy, full of buildings made of glass and pale foreign brick, and lined both sides with small but expensive cars. Their rooms were on the fourth floor, modestly elevated, with rooftop views. Hamburg was an ancient Hanseatic city, with more than a thousand years of history behind it, but none of the roofs Reacher could see was more than fifty years old. Germany had bombed Britain, and Britain had bombed back, and had gotten pretty good at it. In 1943 they had started a firestorm that all but wiped Hamburg out. Flames a thousand feet high, temperatures of a thousand degrees, the air on fire, the roads on fire, rivers and canals boiling. Forty thousand dead in one raid. Britain had lost sixty thousand in the whole war. *They have sown the wind, and they shall reap the whirlwind*. Hosea, one of the twelve minor prophets, but dead on the money in that case.

The room phone rang. Neagley, arranging to meet for breakfast. Then it rang again. Vanderbilt, up late in McLean, Virginia, with the names of thirty-six Americans who had travelled from Hamburg to Zurich during the week in question. *We're going to catch all kinds of people*, Reacher had said.

He went downstairs to the breakfast buffet, which was very European, with cured meats and smoked cheeses and exotic pastries. He sat with Neagley, at a table in a window. Nine o'clock in the morning, in Hamburg, Germany.

Nine o'clock in the morning in Hamburg, Germany, was half past twelve in the afternoon in Jalalabad, Afghanistan. Lunch was being prepared in the kitchen of a white mud house. Outside was a hot desert climate, like Arizona. The messenger was waiting. He had arrived during the night, after four commercial airplanes and three hundred rough miles in a Toyota pick-up truck. He was given breakfast and shown to an antechamber. He had waited there before, many times. Back and forth, back and forth. Such was his life. He was the only man in the house without a beard or an AK47.

Eventually he was led to a small hot room. The air was full of flies, moving slowly. Two men sat on pillows, both bearded, one short and fat, the other tall and lean. Both were in plain white robes and plain white turbans.

The messenger said, 'The American wants a hundred million dollars.'

The men in robes nodded. The tall one said, 'We will discuss it tonight over dinner. Come back first thing in the morning, for our answer.'

Neagley had taken a Hamburg street plan from the concierge station. She opened it and tilted it to catch the light from the window. She said, 'A fifty-minute absence suggests about a one-mile radius, don't you think? Twenty minutes there, ten minutes talking, twenty minutes back. What kind of place would they use?'

Reacher said, 'A bar or a coffee shop or a park bench.'

They found the rented apartment on the street plan. Neagley spanned her finger and thumb and traced a one-mile radius. The resulting circle covered a nest of streets that Reacher figured would be mostly residential but a little bit commercial too. He had been in a lot of cities, and he knew how they worked. In that part of the world, in that part of town, there would be low-rise apartments from the second floor up, with discreet stores and offices at street level. Delis, obviously, in a small way, and maybe jewellers and dry cleaners and insurance bureaus. And bakeries and pastry shops and coffee shops, and restaurants, and bars. A neighbourhood. Plus there were four pocket-handkerchief parks, which meant maybe eight benches available, and probably pigeons to feed, which was what spies did in the movies he saw.

Neagley said, 'It's a nice day for a walk.'

A one-mile radius meant a three-mile area, which was more than two thousand acres. They found the apartment building at its centre, and walked past without looking, and then stood on random corners with their map, like tourists. Of which there were others. They didn't stand out.

From the get-go they racked up one possibility after another, including in the first five streets alone a boutique bakery with two gold tables, and three regular coffee shops, and two bars. Reacher said, 'But the meeting was in the late afternoon. Which means the bakeries aren't right. Bakeries are morning places. I think they met in a bar.'

'Or a park.'

'Where would the American feel dominant? This is a negotiation, we assume. He'd want a psychological advantage. He would want to be comfortable, and he would want the other guy to be uncomfortable.'

'Are we assuming he's white?'

'The odds say he is.'

'Then a skinhead bar.'

'Is there one in a neighbourhood like this?'

'They don't put a sign out front. It's an attitude.'

Reacher looked at the map, for the right kind of

shapes, for wide streets meeting, where traffic would be worse, and rents would be lower, and there would be side streets for parking. He found a possible location. They could take in two parks along the way.

He said, 'It's a nice day for a walk.'

The parks were a disappointment in a horticultural sense. They were mostly paved over, with planters, and flowers as bright as lipstick. But they had benches, two each, and a certain kind of seclusion. One guy could have sat on one bench, and the other guy on the other, and the first guy could have spoken, and then gotten up to leave, and no one would have been wiser. Just a guy on a bench. Then another. One arrives, and one leaves.

The parks were possibilities.

The high-traffic area was not night and day different, but there was a little more hustle and noise. The commercial spaces spilled off the main drag into the side streets, a couple of units back. One of them was a bar with four guys outside, drinking beer. Ten o'clock in the morning. All four guys had shaved heads. All hacked and scabby, like they did it themselves with knives, and were proud of it. They were young, maybe eighteen or twenty, but large. Like four sides of beef. Not from the neighbourhood, Reacher thought. Which raised issues of turf. Were they claiming something?

Neagley said, 'Let's get a cup of coffee.'

'Here?'

'Those boys have something to say to us.'

'How do you know?'

'Just a feeling. They're looking at us.'

Reacher turned, and they looked at him. Tribal, with a hint of challenge, and a hint of fear. And animal, as if they were suddenly quivering with fight-or-flight secretions. As if the rubber was about to meet the road.

He said, 'What's their problem?'

Neagley said, 'Let's find out.'

So he stepped ahead, on a direct line to the door.

The four boys closed ranks.

The boy at the front said, 'Are you American?'

Reacher said, 'How could you tell?'

The boy said, 'We don't allow Americans in this bar.'

SIX

Afterwards Reacher conceded that if a guy his own age had said it, he would have hit him right away, *bang*, before the last word had even died away to silence, because why let a guy who wants to start a fight do so on his own schedule? But this was a kid, and compassion demanded at least one do-over. So instead Reacher asked, very slowly, 'Do you speak English?'

The boy said, 'I *am* speaking English.'

'Because you got your words wrong back there. It came out all mixed up. It sounded like you think there are bars in Germany where Americans can't walk right in and feel at home. That can't be what you meant to say. I could teach you the right words, if you like.'

'Germany is for Germans.'

'Works for me,' Reacher said. 'But here I am, nonetheless. Just passing through. Looking for a cup of coffee. Trying to give you an opportunity to back off and save face and not get your ass kicked.'

'There are four of us.'

'How long did it take you to count that high? No, seriously, I'm curious.'

There was a face at the window of the bar. Staring out, then ducking away.

Neagley said, 'We can go now. This ain't the one. Our guy couldn't get in.'

Reacher said, 'What about our cup of coffee?'

'Probably lousy.'

The boy said, 'It's not lousy. It's good coffee here.'

Reacher said, 'You just made my mind up for me. Now step aside.'

The boy didn't.

Instead he said, 'Here we say what happens. Not you. The American occupation is over. Germany is for Germans.'

'You sound like you're fixing to fight me over it.'

The kid took a step forward.

He said, 'We're not afraid.'

He sounded like the bad guy in an old black-and-white movie.

Reacher asked, 'You think tomorrow belongs to you?'

'I think it does.'

'Doing the same thing over and over and hoping for a different outcome is insane, you know. You ever hear about that? That's what doctors are saying now. I think it comes from Einstein. And he was German, right? Go figure.'

'You should leave.'

'On a count of three, kid. Step aside.'

No answer.

'One.'

No response.

Reacher hit him on the two. Cheating, technically, but why the hell not? The do-over was long gone. Welcome to the real world, kid. A straight right, to the solar plexus. A humanitarian gesture. Like stunning a cow. The second guy wasn't so lucky. Momentum was against him. He stumbled into Reacher's elbow, smack between the eyes, and on his way down he impeded the fourth guy, just long enough that Reacher had time to get to the third guy, with the same elbow coming back, arcing, stabbing down like a knife, which left the fourth guy pretty much wide open to a variety of options. Reacher chose a kick in the nuts, for the minimum effort, and the maximum reward.

He stepped over the tangle of legs, and walked into the bar. There was an old guy behind the counter. No customers. The old guy was maybe seventy. Like Ratcliffe. But in much worse shape. He was seamed and lined and grey and stooped.

Reacher said, 'You speak English?'

The old guy said, 'Yes.'

'I saw you looking out the window.'

'Did you?'

'You knew about those boys out there.'

'What about them?'

'Wanting only German customers in here. You OK with that?'

'I have the right to choose who I serve.'

'Want to serve me?'

'No, but I will, if I must.'

'Your coffee any good?'

'Very good.'

'I don't want any. All I want is an answer to a question. Something I've always been curious about.'

'What is it?'

'How does it feel to lose a war?'

They moved on, and gave up five streets later. There were too many plausible locations. Guessing at personal tastes and preferences narrowed the field, but still left multiple options for every scenario. There was no way to predict where the two men would meet.

Reacher said, 'We'll have to do it the other way around. We'll have to hole up and wait for the messenger to come back, and then follow him out to the rendezvous. And see who he meets with. Which will be very difficult, all things considered. It will take a lot of craft, on these streets. And a lot of people. We'll need a specialist surveillance team.'

Neagley said, 'We can't anyway. We can't burn the Iranian.'

'We would stay hands off. And we would wait. As long as it took. All we need now is a look at the guy he's meeting with. If we know who he is, we can come at him later, and from a different angle. We can fake a line of inquiry that gets to him some other way. Or reverse-engineer a real line of inquiry. In either case there would appear to be no involvement on the part of the messenger. The Iranian's status wouldn't change.'

'Does anyone even have specialist surveillance teams any more?'

'I'm sure the CIA does.'

'In every consulate? Still? I doubt it. Plan on you and

me only. Which will be very difficult. Like you said. Especially because the apartment building almost certainly has a service entrance. We'll be split from the start.'

Reacher said, 'Maybe Waterman has people.'

'This should be a bigger operation.'

'We can have anything we want. That's what the man said.'

'But I'm not sure he meant it. He'll say even watching the apartment is a risk to the Iranian. Which it is. It could be two whole weeks. One slip, or if they see the same guy twice, then the safe house is blown, and they'll figure out why. Our hands are tied.'

Reacher said nothing.

They walked back towards their hotel, and on a street two blocks from it saw four police cruisers parked in a line at the kerb, and eight cops in uniform out on their feet, going from building to building, pressing buzzers, talking to people in lobbies, and then leapfrogging ahead to the next address. Door-to-door inquiries. Something bad.

They would have walked on by, but a cop stopped them and asked, in German, 'Do you live on this street?'

Reacher said, 'Do you speak English?'

The guy said, in English, 'Do you live on this street?'

Reacher pointed ahead. 'We're staying at the hotel.'

'How long have you been there?'

'We arrived this morning.'

'Overnight flight?'

'Yes.'

'From America?'

'How could you tell?'

'By your dress, and your manner. What is the purpose of your visit?'

'Tourism.'

The guy said, 'Your papers, please.'

Reacher said, 'Really?'

'The law in Germany requires you to identify yourselves to the police on request.'

Reacher shrugged and dug in his pocket for his military ID. Easy enough to find. Not much else in there. He handed it over. Neagley did the same. The cop wrote their names in his notebook and passed the cards back, politely.

He said, 'Thank you.'

Reacher asked, 'What happened?'

'A prostitute was strangled. Before you got here. Have a pleasant day.'

The guy walked on, leaving them alone on the sidewalk.

At that moment the American was less than five hundred yards away, renting a car from a small franchise shoe-horned into two ground-floor units in a parallel street of low-rise apartments. He wanted to get out of town. Just for a few days. A few hours, even. An immature response, he knew. Like a child. *I can't see you, so you can't see me.* Not that he was worried. Not at all. No fingerprints, no DNA, no cameras. She was only a hooker. They would give up soon. He was sure of that. But in the meantime there was no point in lingering. He would drive to Amsterdam, maybe. And then come back. It was like falling. No way of stopping now.

Reacher and Neagley got back to the hotel and the clerk behind the desk told them a gentleman from America called Mr Waterman had called twice on the phone. Twelve noon in Hamburg. Six o'clock in the morning on the East Coast. Some kind of urgent business. They went up to Neagley's room, which was closer, and called back from there. Waterman's guy Landry answered. They were all at work already. Then Waterman himself came on the line and said, 'You need to get back here. They just picked up more chatter. They think everything's changing.'

SEVEN

They took Lufthansa in the early evening, sitting together among mostly young people travelling mostly alone, some of them scruffy, some of them weird, some of them like a postgraduate field trip. The flight got them back to the States two hours after they left Germany, in the middle of the evening, eight hours in the air minus six time zones, and they collected the old Caprice from the short-term garage, and drove it through the dark to McLean, and parked it next to the newer Caprices, which looked like they hadn't been moved. Next to them were two black vans. They went inside and found everyone including Ratcliffe and Sinclair crammed in the office. Waiting for them. But they hadn't been waiting long. Rank had its advantages. Ratcliffe said, 'You're right on time. The FAA kept us informed about Lufthansa, and the police kept us informed about the traffic.'

Reacher said, 'What have we missed?'

Ratcliffe said, 'A piece of the puzzle. What do you know about computers?'

'I saw one once.'

'They all have a thing inside that sets the date and the time. A little circuit. Very basic, very cheap, and developed a very long time ago, back when punch cards were the gold standard and data had to be squeezed into eighty columns only. To save bits they wrote the year as two digits, not four. As in, 1960 was written as 60. 1961 was 61. And so on. They had to save space. All well and good. Except that was then and this is now, and before we know it 1999 is going to change to 2000, and no one knows if the two-digit systems will roll over properly. They might think it's 1900 again. Or 19,100. Or zero. Or they might freeze solid. There could be catastrophic failures all around the world. We could lose utilities and infrastructure. Cities could go dark. Banks could crash. You could lose all your money in a puff of smoke. Not even smoke.'

Reacher said, 'I don't have any money.'

'But you get the point.'

'Who designed the circuit? What do they say?'

'They're all either long retired or long dead. And they didn't expect the programs to last more than a few years anyway. So there's no documentation. It was just a bunch of geeks standing around a lab bench, trying to figure things out. No one remembers the exact details. No one is smart enough to work it out again backwards. And there's a feeling they might have misunderstood the Gregorian calendar. They might have forgotten 2000 is a leap year. Normally anything divisible by a hundred isn't. But something divisible by four hundred is. So it's a real mess.'

'How does this relate?'

'The world is increasingly dependent on computers. The Internet could be a big thing by the year 2000. Which would multiply the problem, because everything would be connected to everything else. So the stakes are getting higher. People are starting to worry. They're waking up to the dangers. In response smart entrepreneurs are trying to write software patches.'

'Which are what?'

'Like magic bullets. You install their new code and you fix your problem. There's a lot of money to be made. The market is huge. Millions of people all around the world need to get this done ahead of time. It's urgent. So urgent we anticipate people will install first and think second. Which leaves them vulnerable.'

'To what?'

'Another fragment of conversation. We picked up a whisper there's a finished patch for sale. Supposedly it looks good, but it isn't. It's a Trojan horse. Like a virus or a worm, but not exactly. It's a four-digit calendar, but it can be paused remotely, on command. Through the Internet. Which gets bigger every day. Computers all over the world will crash. Government, utilities, corporations and individuals. Think of the power that gives a person. Think of the chaos. Think of the blackmail potential. Someone would pay a hundred million for that kind of capability.'

'That's a stretch,' Reacher said. 'Isn't it? People would pay a hundred million for a lot of things. Why assume this thing in particular?'

Better to hear the pitch all the way through.

Ratcliffe said, 'It takes a certain type of talent to write

a thing like that. A certain type of mind, too. A kind of outlaw sensibility. Not that they see it that way, of course. It's more of a hipster thing with them. Not an uncommon type, they tell me, among software programmers. And about four hundred of them just got together at an overseas trade convention. Four hundred of the hippest geeks in the world. About half of them were Americans.'

'Where?'

'The convention was in Hamburg, Germany. They were there while you were there. The convention broke up this morning. They all left town today.'

Reacher nodded. 'I think we saw some of them on the plane. Young and scruffy.'

'But the convention was still in full swing on the day of the messenger's rendezvous. There were two hundred American programmers right there in town. Maybe one of them slipped away for an hour.'

Reacher said nothing.

Ratcliffe said, 'Our people tell me such conventions in Western Europe have a different flavour. They tend to attract the oddballs and the radicals.'

Ratcliffe left after that, with his bodyguards, in his black van. Sinclair continued the briefing. She said the focus would switch to computer programmers. She said the FBI had a new unit dedicated to such matters. Waterman would liaise with it, but only through her or Ratcliffe or the president, or with anyone else who might be useful, but again, not directly. White would identify all two hundred Americans, and start background checks.

Reacher would have no immediate role, but should remain on the premises. Just in case. The Department of Defense had computers, and programmers, and in fact the first real concerns about the date issue had come from there. Maybe the bad guy had been drumming up demand ahead of arranging supply.

Waterman and White went to work, but Reacher stayed in the office. Him and Sinclair, all alone. She looked at him, top to bottom, and said, 'Is there a question you would like to ask me?'

He thought: *Did you eat dinner yet?* She was in another black dress, knee length, shaped to fit pretty tight, with more dark nylons and more good shoes. And the face and the hair, the unaffected style, combed with her fingers. And no wedding band.

But he said, 'You really think this is something that guys who climb ropes in Yemen would like to buy?'

'We don't see why not. They're not unsophisticated. In a way the price tag proves it. That's either a rogue corporation's support, or a rogue government's backing, or access to a very rich family's capital. Any of which would suggest familiarity with modernity, certainly including computer systems.'

'That's a self-fulfilling prophecy. You're talking yourself into it.'

'What's your point?'

'Improvisation is a good thing. But panic is a bad thing. You're clutching at straws. You might be wrong. What happened to leave no stone unturned?'

'Do you have another viable line of inquiry?'

'Not as yet.'

Sinclair asked, 'What happened in Hamburg?'

'Not much,' Reacher said. 'We saw the apartment. How's the Iranian?'

'He's fine. He checked in this morning. Nothing doing. Some local excitement four streets away. A prostitute was murdered.'

'We saw it,' Reacher said. 'We saw a lot of things. Including way too many destinations. We can't start at the far end. We're going to have to follow the messenger from the apartment to the meeting.'

'Too risky.'

'No other way.'

'You could find the American before the meeting even rolls around. That would be another way. And probably a better way for all concerned.'

'You're getting pressure from above.'

'The administration would be very pleased to wrap it up soon, yes.'

'Hence it feels good to narrow it down. It feels like progress. Two hundred feels better than two hundred thousand. I understand that. But what feels good isn't always the smart play.'

Sinclair was quiet for a long moment. Then she said, 'OK, when the others don't need you, you're free to work on your own.'

Which was a restriction of a different sort. The gravity squeezed out the freedom. It felt like one strike and you're out. One attempt at a theory.

Neagley said, 'Every avenue comes back to the exact same question. What is the guy selling?'

Reacher said, 'I agree.'

'So what is it?'

'You wrote the list.'

'I didn't. The list is blank. What kind of intelligence would they want from us? What's worth a hundred million dollars to them? They already know what they need to know. They can read it in the newspaper. Our army is bigger than their army. End of story. If it comes to it, we'll kick their ass. Why would they spend a hundred million dollars to find out precisely how and how bad? What good would that do them?'

'Hardware, then.'

'But what? Things are either too cheap and plentiful or else they need a whole regiment of engineers to make them work. There's no middle ground. A hundred million is a weird price point.'

Reacher nodded. 'I said the same thing to White. He thought tanks and planes.'

'What hardware would they want from us? Give me one good example. Something designed for use in the field, obviously, in the heat of battle, by an average infantry soldier. Because that's the standard they must be aiming for. Something simple, rugged, and reliable. Something with a big red switch. And a big yellow arrow pointing forward. Because they don't have specialist training or a regiment of engineers.'

'There are lots of things.'

'I agree. Man-portable shoulder-launch ground-to-air missiles would be useful. They could bring down civilian airliners. Over cities. Except they already have thousands. We gave thousands to the rebels and the Soviets left thousands behind. And now the new Russia is busy selling the thousands they brought back. And if that's not enough they can get cheap knock-offs from China. Or North Korea. It would be physically impossible to spend a hundred million dollars on shoulder-launch missiles. They're too common. Too cheap. It's Economics 101. It would be like spending a hundred million dollars on dirt.'

'What then?'

'There's nothing. We have no theory.'

Ten o'clock in the evening, in McLean, Virginia.

Which was half past seven the next morning in Jalalabad, Afghanistan. The messenger was once again waiting in the antechamber. Early sun was coming in a high window, catching motes of dust, and stirring newborn flies. Tea was brewing in the kitchen.

Eventually the messenger was led to the same small hot room. It too had a high window, with a shaft of morning sun, and dancing dust, and waking flies. The same two men sat below the sunbeam, on the same two pillows. Both bearded, one short and fat, one tall and lean, both in the same plain white robes and the same plain white turbans.

The tall man said, 'You are to leave today with our answer.'

The messenger inclined his head, respectfully.

The tall man said, 'The way of the world is to bargain. But we're not buying camels. So our answer is simple.'

The messenger inclined his head again, and turned it a little, as if presenting his ear.

The tall man said, 'Tell the American we will pay his price.'

EIGHT

Four hours later it was eight o'clock in the morning in Hamburg, Germany, and the city's chief medical examiner was starting work at the central morgue. He had completed his autopsy late the previous evening. Unpaid overtime, but homicide was rare, and careers could be built. Now he wanted to review his notes before presenting his conclusions.

The victim was a tall pale-skinned Caucasian female. According to her papers she had been thirty-six years and eight months old at the time of her death. Which was consistent with the physical evidence. The woman had been in good shape. A dieter, judging by her low body fat. A gym member, judging by her muscle tone. She had eaten a couscous salad about six hours prior to death, and had swallowed semen about an hour before. Then she had been strangled from behind, savagely, by a right-handed assailant. The tissue damage was marginally greater on the right side, indicating stronger fingers.

The victim's pale skin had permitted perimortem bruising in other locations. Not dramatic, but well defined. In particular there were incipient contusions on the backs of her elbows, from her assailant's knees. He had pinned her down, straddling her, riding her like a pony. And her buttocks were faintly bruised, from the pressure of his. He was bony, in the medical examiner's opinion. Strong, but wiry. Sharp-edged, in the hands, and at the knees. A skinny-ass dude, they would say on the television. Possibly charged with energy, possibly nervous in his manner, and capable of violent outbursts.

A picture was emerging.

And best of all, the linear measurement between the bruises on the victim's buttocks and on her elbows was self-evidently the precise distance between the sharp base of the assailant's pelvic girdle and his kneecaps. Which after standard deductions for the joints in question gave the precise length of his femur. And the length of the femur was considered an infallible guide to a person's height.

The assailant was one metre seventy-three tall. In American, five feet eight inches. And American had to be quoted, because the victim was a prostitute. GIs still had money to spend. But either way, not a dwarf and not a giant.

The medical examiner clipped a personal note to the back of the file. Not standard practice, but he was a little caught up in the excitement. The note said in his opinion the guilty party was a right-handed man of average height, probably less than average weight, with pronounced bone structure, and a strong physique, but wiry rather than muscular. Like a long-distance runner, perhaps.

Then the medical examiner sealed the file in an envelope, and asked for it to be biked immediately to the chief of detectives, in the city's police department.

The chief of detectives was not thrilled to get it. Not at first. He got more excited later. His name was Griezman. He was considered successful. His department's 90 per cent record was impressive. But on this occasion Griezman didn't want impressive. He wanted a short investigation, and then he wanted the case far away in the distance, on the other side of the divide, firmly in the 10 per cent of cold and forgotten failures.

He had read the notes from his detectives. One said normally the victim drove from her home to the hotel, late in the evening, and parked in the garage, and worked the bar. But that night no one had seen her arrive. Normally the client would use his own hotel room. Normally she would leave in the middle of the night, or sometimes early the next morning. The bartenders and the housekeeping staff might be able to generate a list of men she had been seen with.

Another note said it was unusual for her to entertain clients at her own apartment. Unusual for hotel hookers generally. Perhaps the client had been a repeat customer. Known and trusted. In which case close investigation of regular clients might pay dividends. Over the past year or two, perhaps. It was assumed the relationship had begun in the bar. Perhaps the hotel workers would remember the original meeting. Most of them had been there a very long time.

A third note said she was extremely expensive.

Griezman closed his eyes.

He already knew that. And he knew she worked the bar. The notes were wrong in some respects. It wasn't unusual for her to use her own apartment. Not at all. Sometimes quite naturally she would meet people in the bar who weren't staying in the hotel. Local gentlemen, perhaps unwinding after a hard day at the office. With homes of their own nearby, but of course those could not be used. Because of wives, and families, and so on.

Local gentlemen, like himself.

He had been her client. Almost a year earlier. Three times. OK, four. All at her place. The first time from the hotel, indeed. *What's your room number? I'm not actually staying here. I'm just here for a drink.* They had gone in separate cars. He had an insurance policy, recently matured and paid out, with a bonus, all of it supposed to go in the savings account. For the children. And now she was dead. Murdered. He would be on the list of men she had been seen with. Close investigation would be disastrous. Someone would remember. He would be fired, obviously. And divorced, of course. And shamed.

He opened the medical examiner's envelope. He read the cold, hard facts. He knew that neck. It was long and slender and exquisitely pale. He knew she liked couscous. He knew she swallowed.

He turned the last page and saw the personal note. Right-handed, average height, underweight, pronounced bone structure, wiry rather than muscular.

Like a long-distance runner.

Griezman smiled.

79

He was two metres tall, and weighed 136 kilograms. Six feet six inches and three hundred pounds, in American. Most of it fat. He ate sausage and mashed potato for breakfast. The last time he had seen a bone had been on an X-ray.

Nothing like a long-distance runner.

He told his secretary to call a meeting. His team came in. His detectives. He said, 'It's time to set some new parameters. Let's say the victim drove to the hotel, but got picked up before she got in the door. A chance meeting in the garage itself, maybe. Possibly a regular client. Possibly a long-time-no-see thing. Which tells us he's rich enough for her, but doesn't stay in the hotel, or she'd have suggested his room as first preference. So he was either local or bunking elsewhere. The question is, did he have a car? Probably, because he was in the garage. But possibly not, because the garage is also a shortcut to the other side of the block. In which case the victim might have driven him to her home herself. In which case we should fingerprint the inside of her car. The door handles and the seat belt latch at least.'

His detectives made notes.

Then Griezman said, 'And best of all we now have really solid intelligence from the pathologist. The perpetrator is average height and skinny. That's scientific information. And that's what we're looking for. Nothing else. Forget the past clients, unless they happen to be average height and skinny. We're not interested in anyone else. No doubt a waste of time, because no doubt he's a sailor with back pay, long gone over the ocean, but we have to be seen to do something. But focus. Don't waste time. Average height, skinny, his prints in her car. Check those boxes. Nothing else. No wild goose chases. Save your energy for the next thing.'

The detectives filed out, and Griezman breathed out, and leaned back in his chair.

At that moment the American was in Amsterdam, showering. He had gotten up late. He was in a hotel one street away from prime time. It was small and clean and some of the guests were airline pilots. It was that kind of place. He had been down for coffee and had seen the German papers in the breakfast room. No headlines. They were nowhere. He was safe.

At that moment the messenger was in a Toyota pick-up truck, just five miles into three hundred by road. To be followed by four separate airports, and three safe houses. All arduous, but the worst came first. The road was rough. Hard on the truck, and hard on the passenger. It was fatiguing. In places it was barely a road at all. In places it was more like an extinct riverbed. But such was the price of seclusion.

The sun rolled west, first lighting up the Delaware coast, and then the eastern shore of Maryland, and then D.C. itself, the city temporarily magnificent in the early light, as if designed specifically for that single moment of the day. Then dawn reached McLean, and the catering truck arrived in the corporate park, with coffee and breakfast. Everyone was awake and waiting. Landry and Vanderbilt and Neagley were quartered in the second of the three buildings on the Educational Solutions campus. Same deal, beds where desks had been. The NSC guys played team tag out of the third building, always one on duty, always one asleep.

White said, 'All but ten of the programmers are either back in the States already or ticketed en route. The missing ten are ex-pats. They live in Europe and Asia. One of them lives right there in Hamburg.'

'Congratulations,' Reacher said. 'You cracked the case.'

'It's a question of priority order. Is an ex-pat more likely to be a bad guy or not? Should we look at them first or second?'

'Who is the guy in Hamburg?'

'We have a photograph. He's a counterculture guy. Into computers early. He says sooner or later they'll make the world more democratic. Which means he steals and breaks things and calls it politics, not crime. Or performance art.'

Vanderbilt dug out the picture. It was a head and shoulders shot at the top left of a page torn out of a magazine. An opinion piece, in what felt like an under-ground journal. The photograph was of a skinny white guy with a huge shock of hair. Like he had his finger in an outlet. Part mad professor, part merry prankster. He was forty years old.

White said, 'The Hamburg head of station did a little walking surveillance. The guy isn't home right now.'

Reacher said, 'If he lives there, why did he schedule the first rendezvous while the convention was in town? That's a busy week. And there are folks who know him. They might notice. Better to do it before or after.'

'Therefore in your opinion the timing proves it was a visitor to the convention.'

'In my opinion this whole thing is Alice in Wonderland.'

'As of now it's all we've got.'

Reacher said, 'How far do these messengers travel?'

'Not as far as here. Not yet. Not as far as we know. But they go all through Western Europe, and Scandinavia, and North Africa. And the Middle East, of course.'

'So the best you can do is keep track of the programmers who made it home, and wait for one of them to go back again for the second rendezvous. For the yes or no answer. But not necessarily to Hamburg. Your theory says Hamburg was convenient the first time around because of the convention. Therefore somewhere else might be more convenient the second time around. Paris, or London. Or Marrakesh. Your theory makes no prediction as to location.'

'We'll know what ticket the guy buys. We'll know where he's headed.'

'He'll buy at the last minute.'

'We'll still know what plane he gets on.'

'But too late. What are you going to do then? Get the next flight out and arrive four hours after the deal is done?'

'You're a real ray of sunshine, you know that?'

'Your theory says at the same time the messenger will also be moving. Towards the same destination.'

'We don't know what name he'll be using or where he'll

83

be coming from. Or what passport he'll be using. Pakistani, possibly. Or British. Or French. Too many variables. We looked back two days before the first rendezvous, and there were five hundred plausible contenders through the Hamburg airport alone. We can't tell one from the other on paper. We wouldn't know who to watch.'

'Drink more coffee,' Reacher said. 'That usually fixes things up.'

In Hamburg it was lunch time, and Chief of Detectives Griezman was minutes away from a fine spread in a cellar restaurant not far from his office. But first he had work to finish. Part of his role as chief was to pass on intelligence to those who needed it. Like an editor, or a curator. Someone had to be responsible. Someone's fat ass had to get fired if the dots didn't join up afterwards. That's why he got the big bucks, as they said on the television.

Naturally he tended towards caution. Better safe than sorry. Practically everything got sent somewhere. Before lunch every day. He scanned carbons and Xeroxes and made separate labelled piles, for this agency and that. His secretary had them biked out, while he was eating.

Near the top of the pile was another report from the prostitute investigation. Among the names gathered during the door-to-door inquiries in her street were a U.S. Army major and a non-commissioned officer who claimed to be there for the purposes of tourism. The reporting officer had followed up by checking with border control records at the airport. He had discovered both Americans had indeed arrived that morning, as claimed. Therefore both could be eliminated as suspects, but the reporting officer wished to point out they didn't look like tourists.

Better safe than sorry. Griezman tossed the report into the space labelled *U.S. Army Command HQ Stuttgart*, where it was so far the only entry of the day.

Then he read a routine one-paragraph cover-your-ass statement from the uniformed branch. It said several days ago an individual member of the public had contacted them by telephone to report that in the late afternoon he had seen an American in conversation with a dark-skinned man probably from the Middle East, in a bar just out from downtown. The member of the public further claimed the dark-skinned man was acting in an agitated manner, no doubt due to life or death secrets related to regional unrest due to historic inequities. But local officers were quick to advise that the informant in question was a known paranoid and fanatic, known for making frequent phone calls of similar doomsday content, and anyway the Middle Easterner was entitled to act in an agitated manner, because it was a hardcore bar, and his presence would not have been welcomed or long tolerated. All that said, the matter was still considered worthy of recording.

Therefore worthy of passing on up the chain, Griezman decided. Two could play the cover-your-ass game. But passing on to where? The American consulate, of course. Partly as a tweak about the bullying behaviour. Why would an American invite an Arab to a bar like that? The invitation certainly couldn't have been the other way around. It couldn't have been the Middle

Easterner's first choice of venue. What had been the purpose?

But mostly he passed it on because an American was talking to an Arab. All of a sudden they were very interested in things like that. There were brownie points to be earned. There were careers to be built.

He tossed the paragraph into the space labelled *U.S. Consulate Hamburg*, where it was also the only entry of the day.

NINE

Reacher and Neagley set up in the control centre in the classroom. They worked on the manoeuvre reports. They took out a hundred, two hundred, five hundred names at a time. The military was pretty good at keeping track of people. Except people on leave. Family time, in the German suburbs. Or cheap fares home. Or vacations, or adventures. Folks all over the world. Thousands at a time, minimum.

No information.

Neagley said, 'We also have three AWOLs in the mix. Plus an O-5 who refuses to say where he was that day.'

A lieutenant colonel.

Reacher said, 'Who are the AWOLs?'

'All PFCs. One infantry, one armoured, and one medic.'

Privates first class.

Reacher said, 'Medics are running away now? When did that start? How long have they been gone?'

'The medic a week, the infantryman a week and a half, and the armoured guy four months.'

'Four months is a long time.'

'They can't find him. He hasn't attempted to use his passport. So he's probably still in Germany. But it's a big country now.'

'Who's the O-5 who won't say where he was?'

'Infantry commander.'

'Did you ask around?'

The world's most efficient grapevine.

'He's solid,' Neagley said. 'But he didn't see much in the Gulf and now he's staring east through the mist at the Soviets, except they're long gone. So he's frustrated. And he's occasionally vocal about it.'

'A malcontent.'

'But not the worst ever.'

'Why don't they know where he was?'

'He wrote himself a roving brief. Research into new weapons and tactics. All that kind of bullshit. The future is flexible and lightweight and so on. He travels extensively. Normally he doesn't have to say where. But this time they asked him and got nothing out of him.'

'Where is he now?'

'They sent him home. Because the question came out of the West Wing. It's the commander in chief asking. No one knows what to do next. No one knows if it's something or nothing.'

'We should put those words on our unit patch. Like a motto on a scroll below two crossed question marks.'

'I'm sure the guy is billeted close to the Pentagon. He's got high-level discussions in his future, I'm certain of that. We can find him if you want to talk to him.'

Then she said, 'Wait.'

She dug through her pile of lists.

She said, 'Wait a damn minute.'

She found the right list. She checked it once, and she checked it again.

She said, 'I know where he was a week before.'

Reacher read the list upside down. Names and flight numbers. Thirty-six Americans. Vanderbilt's work.

'Zurich,' he said.

Neagley nodded. 'Exactly seven days ahead of the rendezvous, arriving in time for afternoon coffee, and getting back again late, after dinner. But he can't be our guy. Our guy would have a cover story for the day in question. Wouldn't he? He would lie. He wouldn't just clam up. What does he think we're going to do? Take his word as a gentleman?'

Reacher said, 'Find out where he is. Make sure they know it's the commander in chief asking. Tell them we're coming over to pick the guy up. Tell them we're going to take him for a ride around the block in the back of our car.'

The guy was at Myer, in a billet in their visiting officers' quarters. Reacher figured the new get-in-the-car orders would have hit about twenty minutes previously, probably via the Joint Chiefs' office. Which would have added to their gravity. He figured the guy would have either run away right then or gotten ready. Turned out he had gotten ready. He stepped out his door as soon as the black Caprice pulled to a stop at his kerb.

Neagley was driving, and Reacher was in the back, on the right side. The guy climbed aboard and sat behind Neagley, upright, back straight, hands on his knees, like he was in a pew and everyone was watching. His name was Bartley. He was the wrong side of forty, but not by much. He was average height and lean. A stamina guy. Endurance, not strength. Just starting to lose it. A leader of men, but not as down-in-the-mud credible as he once had been. He was in battledress uniform, nicely creased. He smelled of soap.

Reacher said, 'Repeat your orders for me, if you would, colonel.'

Bartley said, 'I am to get into a vehicle containing two military police officers, and for avoidance of doubt I am to consider myself legitimately under their jurisdiction at all times, and I am to answer their questions truthfully to the best of my ability, because for further avoidance of doubt I am to consider these orders personal to the commander in chief.'

'He has a way with words, doesn't he?'

'He was a lawyer.'

'They were all lawyers.'

'What questions do you have?'

Reacher said, 'You picked the wrong day to go missing, colonel.'

'I have nothing to say about that.'

'Not even if the commander in chief is asking?'

'It's a matter of privacy. That day has nothing to do with my professional performance. Nothing to do with my duties.'

'That's good to know. But I think that's the point. They want to know what you do in your spare time. You're a senior officer. There are implications. These things can be either good or bad. You should tell

90

us about it. You risk our imaginations running riot.'

'I have nothing to say.'

'That's a tactical error. You're drawing attention. Where there's smoke there's fire. This is an event horizon, colonel. This is where it all goes wrong. Possibly for nothing. Possibly for some little thing other guys have gotten away with. But you're going to crash and burn. Best case, you're going to stall. Best case, you're going to get an asterisk against your name for ever. As in, we can't be sure about that guy.'

Bartley rubbed his palms against his pant legs and said nothing.

Reacher said, 'I don't care what you did. Except if it was one particular thing. But I don't think it was. I mean, what are the odds?'

'I'm sure it wasn't that thing.'

'There you go.'

'There's no reason for you to be interested in me.'

'I'm sure you're right. But I have to look people in the eye and give them an honest opinion. If it wasn't that thing, then I'm happy to say so, and nothing more. I'm happy to say don't ask, it was something else altogether. Your secret stays here. But first I need to know what kind of something else it was. Because I need to be convincing. I need to speak with the kind of confidence and authority that comes from a solid foundation of facts.'

'It was nothing of importance.'

'This is make or break, colonel. When you're in a hole, you should stop digging. I truly don't care what it is. I won't even report it. Sex, drugs or rock and roll, I don't give a damn. As long as it's not that one particular thing. Which we agree is unlikely. All I really want is to ask you a completely different question. Something else entirely.'

'What question?'

'This is not it, OK? This is just a little supplementary first. A minor inquiry. Like batting practice. Do you go to Zurich every week?'

The guy said nothing.

Reacher said, 'It's a simple answer, colonel. The truth can set you free. One little word, and you can move on up without a stain on your character. Or not.'

Bartley said, 'I go most weeks.'

'Including the day they're asking about?'

'Yes.'

'Still got the plane ticket?'

'Yes.'

'Arrive after lunch, leave after dinner?'

'Yes.'

'You go to a bank?'

'Yes.'

'With what?'

'Money, of course. But all of it mine. All of it legal.'

'Care to explain?'

'What happens if I do?'

'Depends what it is. Depends if it disrespects the uniform.'

'What if it does?'

'You take your chances.'

Bartley said nothing.

Reacher said, 'You figure it out, colonel. You're a smart guy. I'm sure you have a postgraduate degree.

This is not splitting the atom. The order to get in this car came from the White House through the Joint Chiefs. Therefore who are we working for?'

'The National Security Council.'

'How bad can they hurt you?'

'Very bad.'

'Worse than you can imagine. A million times worse than a scandal about carrying money to Switzerland. If it is a scandal. Which it might not be. Not if it's all yours, and it's all legal. Which you said it was.'

'I'm hiding it from my wife. I'm going to divorce her.'

'She done you wrong?'

'No.'

'But you're taking the money anyway.'

'I earned it.'

'Earned what? You're an O-5. I know what you get. With all due respect, I doubt if your life savings keep Swiss bankers awake at night. And don't tell me every little helps. There's no point carrying two dollars a week to Zurich. The airfare would become a factor.'

'The airfare is a factor. As are the fees. But I did the math.'

'What money?'

'Our house. Here at home. Mortgages, mostly. I want to get the equity out. I transfer it as fast as they allow. I take it out of Germany in cash. By that point it no longer exists on paper. I keep it in a safety deposit box.'

'You're a prince among men, colonel. That's for damn sure. But what I really need to know is who else you saw. In Zurich. Back and forth, maybe, like you. Or new guys, just once. Did you get to know anyone?'

'Like who?'

'Other Americans.'

'It's a private situation. You don't necessarily see anyone.'

'What about at the airport? Or on the street?'

Bartley didn't answer.

Reacher said, 'I need a list, colonel. Dates and descriptions. Military and civilian. The very best you can give me.'

'What are you going to do? Who are you going to tell? What are you going to say?'

'The president will tell the Joint Chiefs you're of no interest to the NSC. Not in this matter. After that it's unpredictable. Depends who you have to talk to, I guess. And how much fuss your wife chooses to make.'

They let him out on the kerb, outside his billet, and then they drove away, back to McLean.

All kinds of enemies.

They wrote up the Bartley conversation and lodged it in the central file. Then Neagley took a call, and told Reacher the four-month AWOL was a guy named Wiley. From Texas. He was one of a five-man crew working a Chaparral air defence battery. Twelve missiles on a tracked vehicle. Four on the rails, ready to launch, and eight more waiting. To protect armoured vehicles and personnel on the forward edge of the battle area. The idea was to sit in behind the front line of tanks and use radar and binoculars to scan the low horizon ahead. For incoming fighter-bombers or attack helicopters. And then, fire and forget. Heat-seeking, like an old

Sidewinder, but better. Designed for low altitude only. As the enemy swooped down for the kill.

Reacher said, 'Perfect for bringing down civilian airliners over cities. During take off or landing. When they're low in the sky.'

Neagley said, 'Too big. The missiles alone are ten feet long. The truck is gigantic. Plus it has tank tracks and camouflage paint. People would notice, in the airport parking lot. Plus they use forward area alerting radar. And the infrared sensors are complicated. There was an upgrade. Same problem. It's a specialist expertise. All due respect, a training camp in Yemen is not the same thing as Ford Aerospace. Same problem with the price, too. Twelve missiles per vehicle. Top speed less than forty miles an hour. It would take an all-day convoy to reach a hundred million dollars' worth. Like a parade in Red Square. Plus the guy has been gone four months. He can't go back to organize it now. He would be arrested on sight.'

'Keep an eye on him anyway,' Reacher said. 'I don't like four months. That's shameful. Someone needs his ass kicked. What the hell is going on over there?'

In Hamburg night was falling. The Iranian was taking a walk. An evening stroll, with a newspaper tucked up under his arm. Lights were coming on in the stores and the offices and the delis, and the jewellers and the dry cleaners and the insurance bureaus. Bright, clean, crisp white light. But not harsh. A softer type of neon. More European. The bakeries and the pastry shops were dark. Their day was done. The restaurants and the bars were lit up amber, low and welcoming, as if they were all friendly dim spaces, panelled with oak. On the streets, traffic was steady. Cars passed by, every detail of the glowing scene duly reflected in their waxed panels, their new headlights probing ahead, restlessly, unnaturally blue.

The Iranian reached a pocket park and sat down on a bench. He leaned back and rested his arms along the rail. Cars passed by. He stared straight ahead. There were no pedestrians.

He waited.

Then he got up again, no rush, and like a conscientious citizen he put his newspaper in the trash can, and he left the park, and strolled back the way he had come.

Thirty seconds later the CIA head of station stepped out of a shadow and crossed the street. He went straight to the trash can, and he took out the newspaper, and he tucked it up under his own arm, and he walked away.

Thirty minutes later he was on the phone to McLean, Virginia, direct from the consulate.

TEN

Vanderbilt took the call, and brought White to the phone. White listened, and his eyes went through their entire repertoire of squinting long, and focusing short, and narrowing, and looking left and right. He made notes on a piece of paper. Two separate subjects, Reacher thought. Two separate headings. Two blocks of hand-writing, neat and cursive.

Eventually White hung up the phone and said, 'Two pieces of news. The Iranian requested a dead drop. Half an hour ago. He left a report hidden in a newspaper. Some of it could be called speculative. It's partly a cultural analysis. Almost an essay. He says the Saudi who knew the messenger is very excited. As if something big is going to happen. Bigger than they dared to dream. Tied in with the hundred million dollars, obviously. As if they got somewhere they never expected to get. The Iranian stresses he has no specific details, and neither does the Saudi kid. It's a faith-based thing. It feels to everyone like a whole new ballgame. He says the Saudi kid is smiling like he's looking at the promised land.'

Reacher said, 'What was the second piece of news?'

'The consulate got a cover-your-ass report from some low-level Hamburg cops about an American talking to an Arab in a bar. Some weird thing. Except it was exactly the right day, and exactly the right time. It's possible the first rendezvous was witnessed.'

White called the consulate back and got the local numbers he would need, including two for the main man, who was apparently a big fat guy named Griezman. The chief of detectives. The consulate knew him well. It was after the end of the regular day in Hamburg, but the guy was still in his office. Still at his desk. He picked up right away. White put the phone on speaker and asked him about the police report. Reacher heard the guy going back through a stack of paperwork. He couldn't remember it. Then he got it. The weird thing with the Arab in the bar.

Which went to the U.S. Consulate.

Which meant there were brownie points to be earned.

The guy said, in English, very politely, 'How may I help you?'

Like a concierge in a hotel.

White said, 'We need a name and address for the witness. The same for the bar. Background information on both. Possibly surveillance on both.'

'I don't know.'

'I could have your chancellor call you. Your head of state. Then you would know.'

'No, I mean I don't know. I don't know the details. I'm

the chief of detectives. Those reports pass through my office, that's all. And anyway it says here the witness is a lunatic.'

'Can he tell the time?'

'OK, I'll get the details for you. Certainly. End of the day tomorrow.'

'Are you kidding me? You've got an hour. And tell no one what you're doing or why. Consider this matter top secret. And keep this line open for when I call you back.'

In Hamburg Griezman took a breath, and looked out at the evening gloom. Then he set to work. It was not taxing. It was merely a sequence of telephone calls. One number led to another. Like a neural pathway. An organization in action. Something to be proud of. The validation of a theory. As granular as he wanted. He could take it all the way back to the hapless trooper who took the original call. If he wished. Which he did. With fortunately simple questions. Names and addresses, of a person and a place.

In Virginia Waterman's guy Landry said, 'Bigger than they dared to dream doesn't sound good to me. Neither does it sound like stopping someone's clock. It sounds much worse than that.'

Reacher said, 'We're hearing it third-hand. We can't judge the tone.'

'But?'

'I heard the words whole new ballgame. As if it was a big step up. As if it was unexpected to the extent of feeling accidental. Like they dropped a nickel and found a quarter. Such that guys in their twenties who wear Italian shoes and go out to nightclubs are getting all excited. It sounds erotic to me. Are computers that big of a deal?'

Landry said, 'We think they are. And they're certainly going to be in the future. Even now the damage would be catastrophic. Lots of people would die. But I agree, it's not erotic.'

Vanderbilt said, 'It's not a grand gesture either. Which they tend to value. It's not like blowing up a building. It has no single moment of climax. It's a little too technical.'

Reacher said, 'So we all agree we're wasting our time with computers.'

'Where else would we start?'

'What is the guy selling?'

'We've been over that.'

'An hour is up,' Waterman said.

White dialled the Hamburg number again. The guy named Griezman answered. He had names and addresses, for the witness and the bar. The witness was a municipal worker. He started his duties early in the morning and finished them after lunch. Hence the bar in the afternoon. He was a man of strong convictions. Some of them were offensive and all of them were erroneous. The bar was five streets from the safe house. It was said to be a hardcore place. But not visibly. It looked civilized. Stern, but discreet. Men in suits, mostly, with normal haircuts. And not yet anti-American, as long as the American was white.

After the call ended Neagley found the bar on the street plan she had. She said, 'Not the place we liked so much. Better part of the neighbourhood. And a very easy walk from the apartment. Less than twenty minutes. The timing works. Do you think it was the rendezvous?'

Reacher said, 'It was the right place at the right time. And the right feel.'

'We need a description from the witness. Maybe a police sketch.'

'Can we trust the Hamburg cops? Or should we go do it ourselves?'

'We don't have a sketch artist. And maybe the witness doesn't speak English. We're going to have to trust them. The State Department would insist, anyway. Otherwise it would turn into a diplomatic incident.'

Reacher nodded. He had dealt with German cops before. Both military and civilian. Not always easy. Mostly due to different perceptions. Germans thought they had been given a country, and Americans thought they had bought a large military base with servants.

There was the noise of a vehicle on the driveway. Swooping in, past the knee-high sign. Then another. Two vehicles. Two vans, no doubt. Black in colour. A minute later two men in suits came in through the door, followed by Ratcliffe and Sinclair, with two more men in suits bringing up the rear. Ratcliffe was out of breath. Sinclair was a little flushed. Her throat, and high on her cheeks. She was in another black dress, looking as good as ever. Maybe better. Maybe the flush helped.

Ratcliffe said, 'I hear we have an eyewitness.'

Reacher said, 'That's our current operational assumption.'

'We're going to roll the dice. You and Sergeant Neagley will go back to Germany tonight. The State Department will give you passport photographs for all two hundred programmers. Including the ex-pats. First thing in the morning you will interview the eyewitness. The Hamburg police department is being leaned on as we speak. Then immediately the eyewitness picks out a photograph, you will call here with the name, and we'll have the guy picked up at home. Which will be a neat and timely conclusion.'

Reacher said nothing.

They got the same Lufthansa flight. Early evening departure, six time zones, scheduled arrival at the start of the business day. Neagley brought her bag. This time Reacher had one too. It was a red canvas tote from the Air and Space Museum. Presumably some State Department staffer's lunch bucket, requisitioned in an emergency and repacked with two hundred passport photographs. Which was a large quantity. Each photograph was glued to an index card, with a name and a passport number. Reacher and Neagley looked at some of them. They dealt them back and forth like playing cards. They found the ex-pat Hamburg resident. The counter-culture guy, with the shock of hair. His government picture was better quality than the underground journal. Glossier, and much crisper. Regulation size, white background. The guy was showing a head-on stare, and a challenge in his eyes. A large head, and a thin neck.

'It's not him,' Reacher said.

'Why not?' Neagley said.

'Because of his hair. He has to do something to make it look like that. Even if it's doing nothing at all. It's a choice. It's a statement. He's saying, look at me, I have interesting hair. Like guys who wear hats. They're saying, look at me, I have an interesting hat. All a little desperate, don't you think? Insecurity, I suppose. As if what's inside ain't quite enough. And such people don't write software patches that could blow up the known universe. If you're smart enough to write a thing like that, and you're smart enough to sell it for a hundred million bucks, all in secret, then you're not insecure. Not even a little bit. You're the best there ever was. You're the king of the world.'

They put the pictures back in the bag, and ate the meal. Neagley had the window, and she went to sleep leaning away, her head against the fuselage wall. Less danger of accidental contact that way. Reacher stayed awake. He was thinking about the eyewitness. The municipal worker with the offensive views. Possibly a waste of time. Possibly the man who saves the known universe. Reacher wanted to get a look at him. He felt like the plane, racing east to meet the dawn.

The American was brushing his hair, in the bathroom mirror in his Amsterdam hotel. He was up early. No reason. He had slept. He was calm. But it was time to get back. He would shower and pack and hit the road before the morning rush got going. After that it was plain sailing.

But first he wanted coffee, so he dressed in yesterday's clothes and brushed his hair. It was sticking up at the top, from the pillow. He used water and slicked it down. He checked the mirror. Acceptable. It was just a quick down-and-up trip in the elevator. In the lobby he took coffee in a go-cup from a silver urn on a table outside the breakfast room. On a matching table the other side of the door were newspapers. Dutch, obviously, plus British, and French, and Belgian, and German, and the *Herald Tribune* from home. All neatly laid out, all perfectly squared away.

There was nothing in the Berlin paper. No headline, no story. Nothing on the front of the Hamburg paper, either. Or on page two. Or three.

There was a headline on page four.

Low down, and not very big. Plus two inches of story. Mostly boilerplate. Police said the case was receiving maximum attention, and progress was being made.

Specifically, they were about to fingerprint the inside of the victim's car.

The American put the paper back in the stack. He closed his eyes. She had agreed right there in the garage. She had turned around, enthusiastically, theatrically, and she had beckoned him to her car, urgently, with a complicit smile, like she couldn't wait. Then she had driven him home. In a neat three-door coupé, tiny but built like a bank vault.

He got in again in his mind. The outer door handle. Black finish, slightly textured. Sporty. Maybe not a problem. The door pull on the inside was leather. Part of the moulding. A void for the fingers. Vinyl in there, probably, to save money. But pebbled like the visible areas. Grained, like it should be. Maybe not an ideal surface for prints. Maybe safe enough.

The seat belt tongue was shaped like a T. The cross-piece was made of black plastic, stippled like fine sandpaper. For grip, he supposed. Some regulation or other. Safe enough. Then later the release latch. His left thumb. He remembered clicking it down. Elbow back, thumb fumbling. A red plastic bar, firm and ridged.

A partial at best. Maybe smeared when the tail of his jacket swung across it. He remembered pressure on his nail, mostly. Vertically downward. Unrushed. Unhurried. Slow, even. A precise little click, in keeping with the jewel-like car. And to let the anticipation build. Before he unwrapped his gift. His favourite moments, in many ways.

The seat belt latch was safe enough.

But the door release wasn't. The door release was a small chrome bar, cool to the touch, with space scooped out behind for fingers. In his case, the middle finger of his right hand. Slipped in there alone, and elegantly, he thought, even suggestively, and then held there for a polite shall-we-go second, the whole pad of the fingertip pressed hard against the back of the chrome, and then harder, to trip the lock, another precise and respectful click, and then his finger had extricated itself, just as elegantly, he thought.

No smearing.

Smooth, cool chrome.

Stupid.

His own fault.

ELEVEN

Evidently German immigration had been pre-warned, because as soon as Neagley handed over her passport the guard in the booth made a sign, and a big fat guy got up off a hard chair in the next lobby and stood ready to greet them. He said his name was Griezman. He said he recognized Reacher's and Neagley's names. They had been recorded by a street cop and described as tourists. But clearly they weren't. Now he understood. He said he was happy to help in any way he could. He said the witness was already waiting at the police station. Very willingly and very eagerly. He had been told his opinion was being sought on a matter of national security. And it was a day off from work. With pay, because he was performing a civic duty. Griezman said the guy spoke no English. There would be a translator present. And yes, it was normal in Germany for a witness to be shown photographs of possible suspects.

Griezman had a department Mercedes on a no-parking kerb. They got in and he drove. His seat crushed back under his weight. He was a huge guy. An inch taller than Reacher, and sixty pounds heavier. More than twice what Neagley weighed. But most of it fat. No danger to anyone, except himself.

Reacher said, 'On the phone yesterday you called the witness a lunatic.'

Griezman said, 'Not literally, of course. He's obsessed about certain things, that's all. No doubt rooted in racist and xenophobic pathologies, and worsened by irrational fears. But otherwise he's quite normal.'

'Would you trust his word in a court of law?'

'Certainly.'

'Would a judge and jury?'

'Certainly,' Griezman said again. 'In everyday life the man functions very well. He works for the city, after all. Like me.'

The police station turned out to be Hamburg's finest. It was big and new and state-of-the-art. And integrated. Its labs were built in. On the paths outside there were forests of signs at every corner, pointing to this department and that. Inside was the same. It was a complex facility. More like a city hospital. Or a university. Griezman parked his Mercedes in a reserved slot and they all got out. Neagley carried her bag, and Reacher carried his. They followed Griezman into the building, and turned left and right in his wake, along wide clean corridors, to an interview room with a wired-glass window in its door. Inside was a man at a table, with coffee and pastries in front of him, and crumbs scattered all around. The man was maybe forty. He was wearing a grey suit that might have been made of polyester. He had grey hair, thinly flattened across his scalp with oil. He wore steel eyeglasses. Behind the lenses his eyes were pale. His skin was pale. The only colour on him was his necktie. It was a swirl of yellow and orange. It was wide and short, like a fish hanging down from his collar.

Griezman said, 'His name is Helmut Klopp. He's an easterner. He came west after reunification. Many of them did. For jobs, you see.'

Reacher was still looking in at the guy. Possibly a waste of time, possibly the saviour of the known universe. Griezman made no move to enter the room. Instead he lifted his cuff and checked his watch. As he did so a woman turned the corner and walked towards them. Griezman saw her and shot his cuff back into place, satisfied. Right on time. German precision.

'Our translator,' he said.

She was a short stocky woman of indeterminate age, with hair lacquered into a wide globe around her head, like a golden motorcycle helmet. She was wearing a grey dress, some kind of thick gaberdine, as stout as a uniform tunic, and thick wool stockings, and shoes that might have weighed two pounds each.

She said, 'Good morning,' in a voice that sounded like a movie star.

Griezman said, 'Shall we go in?'

Reacher asked, 'What does Mr Klopp do for the city?'

'His job? He's a clerical supervisor. At the moment for the Department of Sewers.'

'Is he happy in his work?'

'He's in an office. It's not what you would call a hands-on position. He seems happy enough. His performance reviews are good. He's considered meticulous.'

'Why the weird hours?'

'Are they weird?'

'You told us he starts early and finishes after lunch. That sounds manual to me, not clerical.'

Griezman said a long word in German, the name of something, and the translator said, 'There was a proposal to reduce pollution by reducing congestion at rush hour. Workers were encouraged to stagger their office hours. Naturally local government was expected to set an example. Clearly the Department of Sewers voted for the early start and the early finish. Or they got stuck with it. But either way the city has announced that beneficial results are already visible. The latest tests show particulate emissions have lessened more than seventeen per cent.'

She made it sound like the greatest thing ever. Like a 1940s movie, black and white, a giant silver screen, the strait-laced guy agreeing to do the very bad thing, all because of the breathy way she asked him.

'Ready?' Griezman said.

They went in, and Helmut Klopp looked up. Like Griezman had said, he seemed happy enough. He was centre stage for once. And ready to enjoy it. A frustrated man, probably. German, but an easterner in the west, with all an immigrant's resentments. Griezman made an opening statement in German, and Klopp replied, and the translator said, 'You have been introduced as top-level operatives who have come from America at a moment's notice.'

Reacher said, 'And how did Mr Klopp answer?'

'He said he's ready to help in any way he can.'

'I don't think he did.'

'Do you speak German?'

'Maybe I picked some up. I've been here before. I understand you're only being polite, but my sergeant and I have both heard worse than anything this guy can say. And accuracy is more important than our feelings. This could be a very serious situation.'

The translator glanced at Griezman, who nodded.

She said, 'The witness told us he's glad they sent white people.'

'OK,' Reacher said. 'Tell Mr Klopp he's an important figure in a current operation. Tell him we intend to debrief him thoroughly across all policy areas. Tell him we want to hear his opinions and his advice. But we have to start somewhere, and the beginning is always best, so our initial focus will be a detailed physical and behavioural description of the two men. Starting, randomly, with the American. First we want to hear it in his own words, and then we're going to show him some photographs.'

The translator said it all in German, facing Klopp, with animation and careful enunciation. Klopp followed along, nodding gravely, as if contemplating a long task of great difficulty, but willing to give it his best.

Reacher said, 'Does Mr Klopp go to that bar often?'

The translator translated, and Klopp answered, quite long, and the translator said, 'He goes either two or three times a week. He has two favourite bars, which he rotates to match his five-day work pattern.'

'How long has he been going to that bar?'

'Nearly two years.'

'Has he seen the American in that bar before?'

There was a pause. Thinking time. Then, some German, and, 'Yes, he thinks he saw him there two or possibly three months ago.'

'Thinks?'

'He's as sure as he can be. The gentleman he's thinking of two or three months ago was wearing a hat at the time. Which makes it hard to be certain. He would be prepared to admit he might be wrong.'

'What kind of hat?'

'A baseball cap.'

'Anything on it?'

'He thinks a red star. But it was hard to see.'

'Long time ago, too.'

'He's remembering it by the weather.'

'But either way the American is not a regular customer.'

'No, he's not.'

'How does he know the guy is American?'

There was a long consultation. A long list. The translator said, 'He was speaking English. His accent. The loudness of his voice. The way he dressed. The way he moved.'

'OK,' Reacher said. 'Now we need a description. Did he see the American standing up or sitting down?'

'Both. Walking in, sitting alone, sitting with the Arab, sitting alone again, and walking out.'

'How tall is the American?'

'A metre seventy, a metre seventy-five.'

'Five feet eight inches,' Griezman said. 'Completely average.'

Reacher asked, 'Is he fat or thin?'

The translator said, 'Neither.'

'Solid?'

'Not exactly.'

'Strong or weak?'

'Quite strong.'

'If he played a sport, what sport would he play?'

Klopp didn't answer.

Reacher said, 'Think about what's on the TV. Think about the Olympic Games. What sport would he play?'

Klopp thought hard and long, as if going through the whole sporting calendar, in great detail. Eventually he spoke in German, a long speculation, arguments for and against, a little of this and a little of that. The translator said, 'He thinks probably a middle-distance runner. Perhaps the fifteen hundred metres upward. Maybe even a long-distance runner, up to the ten thousand metres. But he wasn't an unnatural stick insect like a marathon runner.'

'A stick insect from Africa, right?'

'He added that, yes.'

'Tell me everything, OK?'

'I apologize.'

'So the American is average height, on the wiry side of average weight, possibly full of bounce and energy? That kind of guy?'

'Yes, always moving.'

'How long was he there before the Saudi guy showed up?'

'Perhaps five minutes. He was just a man in a bar. No one was interested in him.'

'What did he drink?'

'A half litre of lager, quite slowly. He still had most of it left after the meeting had finished.'

'How long did he stay, after the Saudi guy left?'

'Perhaps thirty minutes.'

'What did the Saudi guy drink?'

'Nothing. He would not have been served.'

'What kind of hair has the American got?'

Klopp shrugged at the translator, and she chided him, telling him to think. He said something, awkwardly, clearly not his field of expertise, but then he carried on, determined to muster all the details he could. It turned into a long speech. Eventually the translator said, 'The American had fair hair, the colour of hay or straw in the summer. His hair was quite normal at the sides but much longer at the top. Like a style. As if he could flop it around. Like Elvis Presley.'

'Was it neat?'

'Yes, it was neatly brushed.'

'Product?'

'What is that?'

'Oil, like he uses. Or wax, or something.'

'No, just natural.'

'Eyes?'

The face as described went with the hair and the build. Deep-set blue eyes, tight skin on the forehead, prominent cheekbones, a thin nose, white teeth, an unsmiling mouth, a firm chin. No visible damage. No major scars, no tattoos. An old tan, and some lines around the eyes. More likely squint lines than laugh lines or frown lines. A groove down one cheek. From the clamp of the jaw, and maybe a missing tooth. But all of a piece. Narrow, but all horizontal. The brows, the eyes, the high cheekbones, the thin slash of the mouth, the clamped and working grimace. His age was more likely thirty-something than twenty-something.

Reacher said, 'Tell Mr Klopp we'll want him to repeat all of that for the sketch artist.'

The translator passed on the message, and Klopp nodded.

Reacher asked, 'What was the American wearing?'

Klopp answered, and the translator said, 'Actually a Levi's jacket the same as yours.'

'Exactly the same?'

'Identical.'

'Small world,' Reacher said. 'Now ask him why he feels the Saudi guy was agitated. Only first-hand evidence. Only what he saw or heard. Tell him to leave the political analysis for later.'

There was a long discussion in German, with Griezman chipping in, with a lot of back and forth to get it all straight, and then the translator said, 'On reflection Herr Klopp feels excited might be a better word than agitated. Excited and nervous. The American told the Arab something, and the Arab reacted in that manner.'

'Did Mr Klopp hear what was said?'

'No.'

'How long was that part of the discussion?'

'Possibly a minute.'

'How long did the Saudi guy stay?'

'He left immediately.'

'And the American stayed another thirty minutes?'

'Almost exactly.'

'OK,' Reacher said. 'Tell Mr Klopp it's time to look at the photographs.'

Reacher put his tote bag on the table. He said, 'Tell Mr Klopp there are a lot of photographs. He should feel free to take a break whenever he needs to. Tell him to bear in mind everything he told us about the man's face, all those details, and to use them as a mental checklist for when he's deciding. Tell him hair can change, but eyes and ears never do. Tell him it's OK not to be sure. He can make a pile of possibles and check them again later. But tell him not to make mistakes.'

Neagley unpacked the bag. Two hundred cards. She separated them into five equal stacks of forty each. Less daunting that way. She slid the first stack over to Klopp. He got to work, without visible enthusiasm, but with a degree of efficiency. Like a clerical supervisor. Reacher watched his eyes. He seemed to be following the checklist suggestion. One item after another. Eyes, nose, cheekbones, mouth, chin. Every step of the way was a separate yes or no decision. Most candidates failed early. The discard pile grew large. Fat faces, round faces, dark eyes, full lips. No one in the first stack of forty made the cut. Not even as possibles.

Neagley slid the second stack into position. She caught Reacher's eye and winked. He nodded. The Hamburg ex-pat was top of the pile. The counterculture guy, with the shock of hair. Klopp rejected him immediately. Reacher saw why. No cheekbones, and pouty rosebud lips, not a thin unsmiling slash.

The discard pile grew tall.

There was no possibles pile.

Neagley slid the third stack into position. Klopp got to work. The translator sat quiet. Griezman went out and came back and a minute later a man came in with a pot of coffee and five cups. Klopp didn't pause. He took cards off Neagley's stack, one at a time, left thumb and index finger, and brought them closer to him, and looked at them, and slapped them down, one after the other.

The discard pile grew taller.

There was still no possibles pile.

Klopp said something in German, and the translator said, 'He apologizes for not being more helpful.'

Reacher said, 'Ask him how sure he is about his discards.'

She did, and said, 'A hundred per cent.'

'That's impressive.'

'He says he has that kind of mind.' Then she paused. She glanced at Reacher, who had told her to tell him everything, and then at Griezman, as if for permission to do so. She said, 'Mr Klopp trained as an auditor, in East Germany, and was second in command at a very large factory near the Polish border. He wishes us to understand he is overqualified for his current position. But all the better jobs here in the west are prohibited to ethnic Germans and given instead to people from Turkey.'

'Does he want to take a break? He's got about eighty more to look at.'

She asked, and he answered, and she said, 'He is happy to continue. He has the American's face fixed firmly in his mind. Either it is here or it is not. He invites you to check his work against the sketch he will produce with our artist. He thinks you will find his conclusions to be accurate.'

'OK, tell him to get it done.'

There was nothing in the fourth stack. Not even a possible. A hundred and sixty gone by. Neagley slid the final forty into place. Reacher watched Klopp. One card at a time, left thumb and index finger, held easy, not near and not far. Decent vision, with his glasses on. Genuine concentration. Not a bored blank stare or an impatient sneer. A calm focus. He was interrogating the photographs, one by one, point by point. Eyes, cheekbones, mouth. Yes or no.

No, time after time. Always no. The cards slapped down. By that point Reacher had seen more than a hundred and seventy versions of what the guy wasn't. Which started to define what he was. Which was what Klopp had said. Deep-set blue eyes, prominent cheekbones, a thin nose, an unsmiling mouth, a firm chin. There were no other variants left. All under hair currently the colour of straw, currently normal on the sides and long on the top. Like a style.

Reacher watched.

The discard pile grew taller.

There was still no possibles pile.

Then Klopp scrabbled up the last card, and looked at it, the same focus as every other card, and he put it on the discard pile.

Reacher called from Griezman's office. He got Landry,

who got Vanderbilt, who got White, who sounded sleepy. It was five o'clock in the morning in Virginia. Reacher said, 'The guy saw the rendezvous. No doubt about it. The choreography was exactly right. The odds against the same type of thing happening in the same neighbourhood at the same time are astronomical.'

'Did he ID the American?'

'No,' Reacher said. 'Ratcliffe is wrong. This is not about computers. He put two whispers together, for no reason at all. There's no connection. They're separate. Just random.'

'OK, we better tell him. You better get back here.'

'No,' Reacher said. 'We're staying.'

TWELVE

The sketch artist wanted to work alone, so Griezman took Reacher and Neagley on a walking tour of the station. They saw more interview rooms, and offices for officers, and squad rooms, and the booking area, and the holding cells, and the evidence room, and a cafeteria. Serious people were working hard everywhere. Griezman seemed proud of it all. Reacher figured he should. It was impressive.

They pushed through a door and took a second-storey pedestrian skybridge to a new part of the complex. The science centre. Forensics. The labs. First up was a large white room with ranks of computers on long white benches. Griezman said, 'We think this is how people will steal from each other in the future. Already three per cent of Germans use the Internet. More than fifteen per cent in your own country. And we're sure it will grow.'

They walked on, past clean rooms with airlock doors. Like operating rooms in a hospital. Chemical analysis, firearms, blood, tissue, DNA. Laboratory benches, hundreds of glass tubes, all kinds of weird machines.

The budget must have been immense. Griezman said, 'The university co-funds some of it. Their scientists work here. Which is good for both of us. And we get a lot of federal money too. It's a shared facility. For the German army also, under certain circumstances.'

Reacher nodded. Like Waterman had said, back in cooperation school.

They took stairs down to the ground floor. The air was fresher, like there was open access to the outside. They went through a door to a vehicle bay. Like a service station or a tyre shop, but immaculately clean. Almost antiseptic. Slick white paint on the floor, white tile on the walls, bright white light. No oil stains, no dirt, no clutter. There were two vehicles in there. One was a big sedan, with a damaged front corner. Worse than a fender bender, but not a wreck. Not a write-off. Griezman said, 'There was a hit-and-run accident. A child was badly injured. The driver didn't stop. We think this was the car. The owner denies it. We hope to find blood and fibres. But it will be a challenge.'

The other car in the shop was a pretty little coupé, with its doors standing open. A guy in a white coat was leaning in. Griezman said, 'We're fingerprinting the inside. There was a homicide. We think the perpetrator might have been the victim's last passenger. She was a prostitute. It can be a dangerous profession.'

Reacher wandered over and took a look. It was a cute car, especially compared to his recycled Caprice. And immaculate. It shone under the lights. It fit right in with the antiseptic atmosphere. He said, 'This is a very clean automobile.'

Griezman said, 'So was her apartment.'

'Did she have a housekeeper?'

'A service, I think.'

'Then she probably had her car washed too. Maybe on a regular basis. Waxed and detailed. Inside and out. Which is good. Not many old prints.'

Griezman spoke German to the guy in the lab coat. A request for a progress report, possibly. The guy answered and pointed here and there. Griezman stuck his head in for a better view. Then he backed out again, ponderously, and said, 'We think there's a partial left thumb on the seat belt release. But it's narrow, because the button is ridged. And smudged somehow. Possibly the same thing on the seat belt tongue, but the surface is hopeless. Hard plastic, with tiny pimples for grip. A regulation, no doubt. We should have a word with the department concerned. They're not helping us.'

Reacher said, 'What kind of a car is this?'

Griezman said, 'It's an Audi.'

'Then Audi has already helped you. I had a friend with the same problem. About a year ago. Fort Hood, which is about the same size as Hamburg. Off-post married quarters. A Jaguar, not an Audi, but they're both premium brands. They put chrome on their door-release levers. Looks expensive, feels great, and it gleams in the dark so you can find it. All of which enhances what they call the user experience. The passenger puts his middle finger in and pulls. Not his little finger, because he thinks it's too weak, and not his ring finger, because he thinks it's too clumsy, and not his index finger, because his wrist would need to rotate an extra twenty-five per cent, which borders on the uncomfortable. Always his middle finger. So you need to take the door apart, and print the back of the lever. That's what my friend would say.'

The guy in the lab coat said something in German. Unknown words, but an indignant tone. Clearly he could follow along in English. Griezman said, 'That was going to be our next step anyway. Did your friend secure a conviction?'

'No,' Reacher said. 'The chain of evidence broke down. He could prove the guy's print was on the lever, but he couldn't prove the lever came from the ex-wife's car. Defence counsel said it could have come from anywhere.'

'What should he have done?'

'Before he started he should have engraved his initials on the front of the lever. While it was still right there on the door. With a dentist's drill. He should have had himself photographed doing it. Wide shots, to establish the car, and then close-ups.'

Griezman spoke in German, a long list of instructions. Reacher caught the word *Zahnarzt*, which he knew from having a toothache in Frankfurt meant *dentist*. The guy in the lab coat listened and nodded.

They got back to the interview room just as Klopp was getting set to leave. The sketch artist gave them a copy of a drawing made with coloured pencils. Griezman told them he would fax a further copy to McLean, Virginia, and then keep the original on file.

Reacher and Neagley carried their copy to the door,

where the wired-glass window let in some natural light. The American looked exactly like Klopp had described. The artist had done a fine job capturing his words. The wave of blond hair. The skin stretched tight over the skull beneath. The brow and the cheekbones, horizontal and parallel and close together, like two bars on an old-style football helmet, with the eyes flashing out from way behind. The mouth, like a gash. Plus two vertical lines, the nose like a blade, and a crease down the right cheek, as if the most the mouth ever moved was in a lopsided and sardonic smile. The guy was shown in a jacket like Reacher's. Pale denim, authentic in every respect. Under it was a white T-shirt. His collarbones stood out, like his cheekbones. His neck was shown corded with sinew. A hardscrabble guy, no longer young.

Neagley said, 'Military?'

Reacher said, 'Can't tell by looking.'

'Then why are we staying?'

'I don't know. Ratcliffe said we could have what we want. I guess what I want is not to be trapped in some-one else's mistake.'

'The second rendezvous might not even be in Hamburg.'

'I agree. It's probably ten to one against. Which means if we stick around we have a one-in-ten chance of being in the right place at the right time. Whereas if we go back to Virginia we have a zero chance. They're not going to meet at the Washington Monument. That's for damn sure.'

The translator came over and said, 'Mr Klopp is

asking when you want to schedule the rest of the debriefing session.'

Reacher said, 'Tell Mr Klopp we're done with him. Tell him if I ever see him again I'll pop his eyeballs out one at a time with my thumbnail.'

Then Griezman came over and said, 'Will you be my guests for lunch?'

Twelve noon, in Hamburg, Germany.

Which was one o'clock in the afternoon in Kiev, Ukraine. The messenger was getting off a plane. He had been driven through the mountains to Peshawar in Pakistan, and had flown to Karachi, and then to Kiev. He had used a different passport for each of the flights, and he had changed his shirt once, from pink to black, and added shades and a Donetsk soccer supporter's hat. He was untraceable and anonymous. Ukraine border control gave him no problems. He walked through baggage claim and out of the terminal. He joined the taxi line and smoked a cigarette while he waited.

The taxi was an old Czech Škoda, and he told the driver the address he wanted, which was a flower market five streets from his real destination, which was a small apartment occupied by four of the faithful from Turkmenistan and Somalia. A safe house. Always better to make the final approach on foot. Taxi drivers remembered things, the same as anyone else. Some even made notes. Mileage logs, gasoline consumption, addresses. He didn't know the four guys. But they were expecting him. Kiev was not the same as Hamburg. He couldn't just walk in. A messenger had been sent ahead. Of

124

the messenger. Such were the necessary precautions.

He got out of the Škoda at the flower market. He walked between stalls crowded with bright blooms, into a humid hall full of rarer specimens, and when he came out the other end he was back in his pink shirt and the hat and the sunglasses were gone.

He walked the final five blocks and found the right building. It was a squat concrete tower, set off-centre in a row of older and more elegant buildings. Like a false tooth. As if long ago a bomb had fallen, randomly, and made a space. Perhaps it had. The lobby smelled of ammonia. The elevator worked, but with unpleasant noises. The upstairs hallways were narrow.

He knocked on the door and waited. He counted the seconds in his head. He had knocked on a lot of doors. He knew how it worked. One, they hear the knock, two, they get up off the couch, three, they thread around the clutter, four, they step to the door, five, they open it.

The door opened. A guy stood there. On his own, with silence behind him.

The messenger said, 'You're expecting me.'

The guy said, 'We have to go out.'

'When?'

'Now.'

The guy was Somali, the messenger thought. In his twenties, but already worn down to nothing but dusty skin and sinew. Primitive, like an ancestor species. The messenger said, 'I don't want to go out. I'm tired. I have to be on my way first thing in the morning. I have an onward flight.'

'No choice. We have to go out.'

'The point of a safe house is that I don't have to go out.'

'The Kiev soccer team is playing an evening game in Moscow. It's on the television in the bars. It starts soon, because of the time zones. It would be weird for us not to go. We would stand out.'

'You can go.'

'We can't have anyone in the apartment. Not this afternoon. Someone would notice. It's a big rivalry. Like a patriotic thing. We're supposed to fit in here.'

The messenger shrugged. Such were the necessary precautions. And soccer wasn't so bad. He had once seen it played with a human head. He said, 'OK.'

They took the stairs down, an unspoken agreement not to risk the elevator. They walked away from the flower market, in a new direction, past grand but faded apartment houses, with rusted ironwork and peeling stucco façades, and then between two of them into an alley the Somali said was a shortcut. It was a narrow brick passage, echoing and almost uncomfortable, but a building's depth later it opened out into a small court-yard, not much bigger than a room, which was walled in by the blank four-storey backs of other buildings. There was a small patch of sky, way up high. The walls were pierced here and there by blind or whitewashed windows, and they carried fat rainwater pipes and aimless loops of antenna cable.

There were three guys in the courtyard.

The messenger thought one of them could be the Somali's cousin. The other two were also a pair. From Turkmenistan, no doubt. The guys from the safe house.

For a happy second the messenger thought they were meeting there and all going to the bar together. Then he saw there was no other exit from the courtyard.

Not a shortcut.

It was a trap.

And then he understood. Clear as day. Perfectly logical. He was a security risk. Because he knew the price. A hundred million dollars. Which was the single most dangerous component of the whole enterprise. Such a huge amount would set alarm bells ringing everywhere. Anyone who knew about it was automatically a potential leak. Classic theory. They had studied it in the camps, with hypothetical examples. They had gamed it out. A pity, they had said. But necessary. A great struggle required great sacrifices. A great struggle required clear minds and cold hearts. The guy sent on ahead had not asked for the guest quarters to be aired out and made ready. He had carried a different instruction.

The messenger stood still. He would never talk. Not him. They must know that. After all that he had done. He was different. He was safe. Wasn't he?

No, these were men who played soccer with human heads. They had no room for sentiment.

The Somali guy said, 'I'm sorry, brother.'

The messenger closed his eyes. Not guns, he thought. Not in the centre of Kiev. It would be knives.

He was wrong. It was a hammer.

In Jalalabad it was half past four in the afternoon. Tea was being served in the white mud house. The new messenger had been brought to the small hot room. She was a woman. Twenty-four years old, long black hair, skin the colour of tea. She was wearing a white explorer shirt, full of loops and pockets, and khaki pants, and desert boots. She was standing at attention in front of the two men, who were sitting on their cushions.

The tall man said, 'It's a matter of very little importance, but there's a need for speed. So you'll fly direct from Karachi. No need for caution. No one has ever seen you before. You'll meet with an American and you'll tell him we accept his price. Repeat, we accept his price. Do you understand?'

The woman said, 'Yes, sir.'

The fat man said, 'The American won't mention the price, and you won't ask. It has to stay a secret. Because he's embarrassed we beat him down so low, and on our part we don't want the others to think we're broke and that's all we can afford.'

The woman inclined her head.

She said, 'When shall I leave?'

'Now,' the tall man said. 'Drive all night. Get the morning plane.'

THIRTEEN

After lunch Griezman drove Reacher and Neagley to the hotel they had used before. They thanked him and waved him away but didn't check in. Reacher didn't like to stay in the same place twice. A habit. Unnecessary, some said. He said he was thirty-five years old and still alive. Had to mean something.

They checked Neagley's map. She put her fingernail on the safe house. She said, 'Of course, they might have more than one.'

'Possible,' Reacher said. 'This whole thing is a percentage game.'

They set out walking, and found the street they had seen before, where the four cop cars had been parked. Where the hooker had been killed. They made a left, towards the safe house, close but not too close, and they checked the side streets on the way. Not easy to do. Not like some parts of the world. There were no big signs. No flashing neon, no shingles swinging in the wind. Prohibited, presumably. On grounds of good taste. Every commercial unit had to be eyeballed individually. They saw a car rental franchise occupying two side-by-side addresses. Other operations were also self-explanatory. But some weren't. Reacher stepped into a lobby with armchairs and a reception desk, thinking it was a hotel, but it turned out to be a tanning salon, with the booths in back. The woman at the desk laughed, and then tried to suppress it, and then further atoned by mentioning a boutique establishment a block away. Which turned out to be a good-looking place. There was a guy in a top hat, standing ready to open the door.

'You got money?' Neagley asked.

'Ratcliffe will pay,' Reacher said.

'He doesn't know we're here.'

'We'll call him. We should anyway.'

'From where?'

'A room. Yours or mine.'

'We won't have rooms. They won't let us check in without money.'

Reacher pulled out his wad of walking-around money. Logged out, but never logged back in. A modest sum. Neagley had the same.

Reacher said, 'We'll get one room. For the time being. Until the NSC calls them.'

Neagley paused a beat, and said, 'OK.'

They went in.

At that moment the American was three streets away, slowing to a stop outside the car rental franchise they had just seen. He had stopped for an early lunch in Groningen. With a glass of wine. Therefore he lingered, to let it wear off. Just in case. The laws were tough. So he took a walk. It was a pretty town. Then he drove on, across the nominal border, and he hit the fast road through Bremen. He enjoyed every mile. Like a premature nostalgic feeling. It would be a long time before he saw Europe again. Maybe never.

He gave back the key and walked away, out of the neighbourhood, towards the water. Towards his place. Rented, with less than a month left on the lease. Waste not, want not. Good timing.

The room they got had dark green wallpaper and pewter accents all over the place. But the phone worked. Reacher got the duty NSC guy, who undertook to finance their stay through the consulate. Then White came on the line and said, 'Vanderbilt went back four years with the Switzerland thing. Then he cross-checked. There were exactly one hundred Americans in Germany that day who had visited Zurich on a prior occasion.'

'Good data,' Reacher said. 'But not definitive. He might have used the Cayman Islands. Or Luxembourg. Or Monaco. Or maybe he went to Zurich for a vacation. I did, once, and I sure as hell didn't go to a bank while I was there.'

White said, 'Understood.'

'But tell Vanderbilt thanks.'

Then Waterman got on, and said, 'They're nervous about you.'

Reacher said, 'Who are?'

'Ratcliffe and Sinclair.'

'He said we should roll the dice. No point all doing it in the same place.'

'Getting anywhere?'

131

'Are you?'

'We're nowhere.'

'So are we. And there's no point being nowhere all in the same place either.'

'Sinclair will want to speak to you.'

'Tell her I'll check in later. After the consulate comes through. That might give them an incentive.'

'And there's mail from the Department of the Army for Sergeant Neagley.'

'Urgent?'

'I don't think so.'

'Put it on hold until I've spoken with Sinclair.'

'Can we agree a time?'

'Tell her two hours from now,' Reacher said.

They went to find the bar where Helmut Klopp had seen the rendezvous. It was twenty minutes away, the same as it was from the safe house, but on a different vector. Like two spokes of the same wheel. They walked past it, not slowing down, not speeding up, looking straight ahead, inspecting the place obliquely. It was on the ground floor of an older building made of stone, which once might have been a tenement or a factory, probably burned out in the wartime firestorm but deemed repairable. The bar had a centre door in a planked wood façade. But it wasn't a rustic look. Not like the side of a barn way out in the country. The planks were tight and true and planed smooth. They were dark gold in colour, heavily varnished and shiny, like a rowboat on a lake in a park. There were small windows, with cream lace café curtains hung behind the bottom halves, and loops of small paper flags hung on strings behind the top halves. All the paper flags were German. The light inside looked dim and amber.

Neagley said, 'We have two people following us.'

Reacher said, 'Where?'

'On the corner fifty yards behind us.'

He didn't look.

He said, 'Who?'

'Two males between thirty and forty. Bigger than me and smaller than you. Probably not Germans. They walk like Americans.'

'How do Americans walk?'

'Like us.'

'How long have they been there?'

'I'm not sure.'

'Cheekbones?'

'No. Also too tall.'

'OK,' Reacher said. 'Let's get a cup of coffee.'

They strolled on, at the same lazy pace, and came to a pastry shop with a display case full of confections, and an espresso machine, and four small tables with two chairs each. The tables and chairs were metal painted silver. They were right up against the windows, with a good view of the street. Neagley sat down and Reacher went to the counter. He ordered two double espressos and called, 'You want a cake?'

'Sure,' Neagley said. 'Apple strudel.'

'Two,' Reacher said to the woman at the register. The old army rule. Eat when you can. The next chance could be days away. The woman pantomimed that Reacher should go sit down and she would bring a tray.

Reacher pantomimed that he wanted to pay right away. His own rule. He might need to leave without warning, and he didn't like to stiff ordinary working folk. He got his change and stepped over to the table and sat down, and Neagley craned her neck, very discreetly, and said, 'They saw us come in here. They sped up. We'll see them in a minute.'

Reacher checked the view left and right. There was another coffee shop across the street, twenty yards farther on. Tables in the window. A good view. Anyone with any sense would stop in there. They could wait as long as they needed to, raising no suspicion at all, and then they could resume the tail whenever their quarry moved.

'There they are,' Neagley said.

Reacher saw two guys, as advertised, in their thirties, bigger than her and smaller than him. Maybe six feet and two hundred pounds. Short hair. Walking like Americans. Dressed like Americans. Specifically, to his practised eye, dressed like off-duty American military. Put a civilian in uniform for an hour, for a movie role or a fancy-dress party, and he looks wrong, somehow, as if uncomfortable, or unaccustomed. Equally, put a guy who has worn a uniform for the last ten years in jeans and a jacket, and he looks wrong, too. Equally unaccustomed. Wrong posture, too neat, creases too sharp, no slouch or shuffle.

They came on, the same way Reacher and Neagley had passed the bar, not slowing down, not speeding up, looking straight ahead, checking the scene in the corner of their eyes. Big hard faces, worn hands. NCOs, probably. Lifers, by the look of them. They ambled on, and one whispered something to the other, and the other nodded, and they ducked in at the coffee shop twenty yards farther on, across the street. Cars drove by, both ways, and shoppers and office workers hustled past on the sidewalks. The guys got a table in the window and sat there, pretending not to look at Reacher and Neagley, just as Reacher and Neagley were pretending not to look at them.

'Who are they?' Reacher said.

'Can't tell by looking,' Neagley said.

'Ballpark guess?'

'Army, obviously. Terminal at sergeant. Probably not combat troops. Old sergeants in the battle area look different than that. Those guys are some other thing.'

'But they're not company clerks.'

'No. They're muscle workers.'

'Agreed. They're support troops of some kind. Transportation, maybe. Maybe they load trucks. And unload them.'

'What are you thinking?'

'I'm wondering why they're here,' Reacher said. 'How did they know?'

'Griezman? Maybe he made a call. As soon as he left us at the hotel.'

'But we didn't stay at that hotel. They didn't follow us from there. Because we didn't start from there.'

'Which means the NSC leaked it. They're the only ones who knew what hotel we were in. Which is ridiculous.'

'Agreed. Therefore they didn't follow us from either

hotel. We came to them. They were waiting here.'

'Why?'

'Maybe that bar is more than just a place for like-minded folk. Maybe it's a rendezvous for all kinds of people. Maybe money is earned there. So what happens when two unexplained military cops show up in town? They post sentries, just in case. And here we are. We just tripped their wire.'

'They don't know we're military cops. They don't know our names. No one even knows we're in the country.'

'How did we find out about Helmut Klopp?'

'Griezman passed on some dumb police report. To the consulate.'

'Because he's a noble citizen?'

'No, because he was covering his very considerable ass.'

'Such a guy would also pass on a dumb police report about two military personnel recorded in a homicide investigation. Walking past the scene and claiming to be tourists. Our names are right there in black and white. So he had to pass it on. Probably straight to HQ in Stuttgart. Where someone looked us up, and saw the 110th in our recent pasts, and hit some kind of a secret alarm button. Like in a bank. No one heard anything, but people started scrambling all over town. Who are we here for? This is a broad sweep. We're going to upset all kinds of people.'

'Suppose these are the right people?'

'You take the one on the left, and you can have the Legion of Merit.'

'They would never give a Legion of Merit to a sergeant.'

'They're not the right people. I'm a lucky man, but not that lucky.'

'So who are they?'

'Can't tell by looking,' Reacher said.

They chased the last strudel crumbs around their plates, and drained their coffee cups down to the muddy paste at the bottom, and then they stood up fast and hustled out the door.

FOURTEEN

Reacher and Neagley dodged pedestrians on the sidewalk and cars on the street, and headed diagonally towards the second coffee shop on the other side. Through the window they saw the two guys startle and sit up straight. Too late. They were sitting together on the far side of a corner table for four, where their angle was good. Which left two empty chairs between them and the rest of the room. Neagley went in first and took one of the chairs. Reacher followed and took the other. Which meant the two guys were trapped. All quiet and genteel and civilized, but they had no way out. Not unless Reacher and Neagley stood up again to let them by. Which was not on the immediate agenda.

Reacher said, 'Listen carefully, guys, because I'm going to say this once and once only. We have a one-time special offer. We'll help you if we can. Minimum sentences in exchange for full disclosure. Unless it's the one thing we're interested in. But I don't think it is. I think you're the wrong kind of guys for that.'

The guy on the left said, 'Get lost.'

He was closer to forty than thirty, with greying black hair buzzed short, and a doughy slab of a face, like an uncooked loaf. He had dark eyes and calluses on his hands. His accent was from Arkansas, or Tennessee, or maybe Mississippi.

Reacher said, 'You know our names, because someone checked us out and raised the alarm. Therefore you know we're MPs. You're under arrest as of this moment.'

'You can't do that.'

'I'm pretty sure we can. The Uniform Code says so. We could arrest the Chief of Staff if we wanted to. We would need a pretty good case, but in theory we could do it. You present much less of a problem.'

'You have no jurisdiction.'

'That's a big word.'

'We're not military personnel.'

'I think you are.'

'We're not American either.'

'I think you are.'

'You're wrong.'

'Prove it. Show me ID.'

'Get lost,' the guy said again.

'The law in Germany requires you to identify yourselves to the police on request.'

'German police. Not you.'

'You're doing this wrong. Now you're heading for maximum sentences.'

The guy said nothing. The other guy was watching the conversation, his eyes going back and forth, like tennis.

Reacher said, 'Show me ID.'

The guy on the left said, 'We'd like to leave now. Please step aside.'

'Not going to happen.'

'We could make it happen.'

'You could try,' Reacher said. 'But you'd get hurt. You're out of your league. You're up against something you never saw before.'

'You have a mighty high opinion of yourself.'

Reacher nodded at Neagley. 'I'm talking about her. I'm just here to clean up the mess.'

They looked at Neagley. Dark hair, dark eyes, a tan. A good-looking woman. She smiled at them. Her forearms were on the table. Reacher noticed her nails. They were shiny with clear polish, and neatly filed. Even on the right, which she must have done left-handed. She wouldn't use a nail salon. She couldn't bear her hands to be touched. She looked at one guy, and then the other.

The guy on the left shrugged and raised up an inch off his chair and dug in his back pants pocket. The other guy did the same. Reacher watched. Safe enough. No one kept a weapon in his back pants pocket. Uncomfortable. Not readily accessible.

The guys came out with two IDs each. Plastic, the size of credit cards. But not. They were national identity cards, and driver's licences. Both had *Bundesrepublik Deutschland* at the top. Germany. The Federal Republic. The photographs were right. The guy on the left was named Bernd Durnberger, and the guy on the right was named Klaus Augenthaler.

Reacher said, 'You're German citizens?'

The guy on the left took his cards back and nodded.

'Naturalized?'

The guy nodded again.

'Did you have to take a test?'

'Sure.'

'Was it hard?'

'Not very.'

'What state are we in?'

'Germany.'

'That's the country. It's a federal system. There's a clue where it says Bundesrepublik. It means it has states, like America. Only sixteen of them, not fifty, but the principle is the same.'

'I guess I forget.'

'Hamburg,' Reacher said.

'That's the town.'

'Also the state. Like New York. Next to Schleswig-Holstein and Bremen. Then comes Lower Saxony. Did you change your name?'

'Why not?'

'Why Durnberger?'

'I like the way it sounds.'

'Did you retain your American citizenship?'

'No, we renounced. We're not dual. So there's nothing you can do.'

'We can be impolite.'

'What?'

'Americans often are, overseas. You Europeans are always complaining about it. We could just sit here in the way.'

'No, we're going to leave now.'

'Why?'

'Because we want to.'

'You need the bathroom?'

'No.'

'You got a pressing engagement?'

'We got freedom of movement.'

'Sure you do. Like a person in Times Square, trying to get to work on time. No way to do that, unless he runs right over the tourist in front of him.'

The guy said nothing.

Reacher looked at the other guy, and said, 'How did you choose your name?'

'The same,' the guy said. 'I liked the sound of it.'

'Really? Say it for me.'

The guy didn't answer.

'Say it for me,' Reacher said again. 'Let me hear how nice it sounds.'

No response.

'Say it for me.'

Nothing.

Reacher hooked his thumbs under the edge of the table top and clamped down hard with his fingers. He leaned forward. He said, 'Say your name for me.'

The guy couldn't.

Reacher said, 'So we got one guy who can't remember Germany has states, and another guy who can't remember his own name. You're not doing a real great job of convincing me.'

He was clamping the table and leaning forward not for the drama, but to be ready for what came next. And it came right then. The guy on the right shoved the table hard, aiming to jab Reacher in the midsection with it, like a punch, or even to knock him over backward in his chair, but Reacher was ready, and he shoved back ten times as hard and drove the wooden edge into the guy's gut. A satisfactory blow, but the movement of the furniture gave the guy on the left a widening gap to stand up in, which he did, and then he slid around behind Reacher's seated back and hustled for the street door. Except by then Neagley was also on her feet, stepping left, leading with her shoulder, drifting towards the guy, and then rotating savagely and slamming a roundhouse right into his chest, dead on the solar plexus, which stood him up panicked and breathless, like he had swallowed an electric cattle prod. Which gave her plenty of time to call her next shot. Which was her left knee to his groin, followed by her right knee to his face, as he crumpled to the floor in front of her.

Reacher kept the other guy hemmed in behind the table. He said, 'See what I mean? Now I have to clean that up.'

He turned his head, and saw an old lady behind the counter getting ready to scream or faint or grab the phone. He called out *'Sexueller Angriff'*, which he knew from taking a prisoner to a civilian courthouse in Frankfurt meant *sexual assault*. He pointed to himself and added *'Militärpolizei'*, which he knew meant *military police*. The old woman calmed down a little. The forces of order were in control. And actually nothing was broken. The guy had gone down and missed everything. Neagley was a precision worker. There was blood on the floor, but not much. Nothing a minute with a mop wouldn't take care of. No harm, no foul, overall.

Reacher said to Neagley, 'Ask to use her phone. Call Stuttgart and find out who we know who could get here today.'

'For these guys?'

'The background noise is starting. We're going to need garbage disposal.'

'Not through Sinclair?'

'This is army business. We shouldn't bore her with the details.'

Neagley spoke no more German than Reacher, so she mimed with raised eyebrows and her right-hand thumb and pinky, the universal dumb-show for a telephone, and the old lady bustled off to the far end of the counter and came back with an old black instrument tethered by a wire. Neagley dialled and waited and started talking.

Reacher turned back to the guy at the table. He was pale. He had a buzz cut growing low on his forehead, and old acne pits on his cheeks. His gaze was alternating between Reacher and his pal on the floor. Back and forth, like a metronome. Panic in his eyes.

Reacher said, 'I'm going to take a wild-ass guess and say you're not the brains of the operation. Which leaves you in a vulnerable position. But luck is on your side. I'm a reasonable man. The one-time special offer is still open. For you only. Minimum sentence in exchange for full disclosure. I'm going to count to three. Then it's gone.'

More panic in the guy's eyes. He opened his mouth, but he couldn't speak. Not very bright. Not very verbal.

Reacher said, 'Who told you to be here today?'

The guy pointed at his pal on the floor.

He said, 'He did.'

Reacher said, 'Why?'

'We sell things.'

'Where?'

'In the bar.'

'What kind of things?'

No answer.

Reacher said, 'Big or small?'

'Small.'

'Handguns?'

The guy nodded.

'Beretta M9s?'

The guy nodded.

Reacher said, 'Anything else?'

'No.'

'OK, you sell sidearms to skinheads. Congratulations. New or used?'

'Only old ones.'

'From where?'

'We take them from the scrap trucks.'

Reacher nodded. Retired U.S. Army inventory, listed as worn out or defective or destroyed, but never quite making it to the smelter. Not uncommon. He said, 'Ammunition too?'

The guy said, 'Yes.'

'In that same bar?'

The guy said, 'Yes.'

'Where did you get the phoney ID?'

'Same place. In that bar. There's a German guy.'

'What else happens there?'

'All kinds of deals.'

'Do you go there a lot?'

The guy looked at his pal on the floor. He nodded. He said, 'It's where we sell things.'

Reacher took the police sketch from his pocket. The American. The brow, the cheekbones, the deep-set eyes. The floppy hair. He unfolded the drawing and flattened it out and reversed it on the table. He said, 'Did you ever see this man in there?'

The guy took a look.

He said, 'Yes, I've seen him.'

FIFTEEN

Neagley put the phone down and mimed a thank-you to
the old lady and came back to the table. Reacher said,
'This guy has seen our guy in the bar.'

Neagley said, 'How many times?'

The guy said, 'About three.'

'Over how long of a period?'

'About the last few months. Sometimes he wears a
hat.'

'What kind of a hat?'

'A sports team, I think. The NFL, maybe. Something
with a red star.'

'Do you know his name?'

'No.'

'What does he do in the bar?'

'Nothing much.'

'Is he army?'

'Last time I saw him he had no hat and his hair was
too long.'

'When was that?'

'About two weeks ago.'

'What was he doing two weeks ago?'

'He was at a table near a window drinking beer by himself.'

At that moment the American was waiting to get on a city bus, to head into town. He had things to do. Last-minute errands to run, and a shopping list. Hamburg was a passenger port, with ferries and cruise ships in and out, so travel supplies were not hard to find. And suitable clothes, for a long journey. All cash purchases, all from different places. A strict timetable, but necessary. The clock was ticking.

The bus arrived, and the American got on.

Reacher hauled the guy up off the coffee shop floor and pushed him out to the sidewalk. Neagley took his partner. They checked Neagley's map and headed down to a pocket park. The guy Neagley had hit limped and shuffled. His nose was broken, from her second knee. It didn't make him any prettier. Or uglier.

They made it to the park and took two benches. Neagley and the dumb guy sat on one, and Reacher and the casualty sat on the other. They waited. The dumb guy kept very still. He seemed scared of Neagley. Maybe not so dumb. The damaged guy got slowly better. Reacher sensed him getting restless. Sensed him glancing around, calculating the angles, weighing up his chances. At one point a city bus roared slowly past, close and huge and loud, full of passengers heading into town, and Reacher sensed the guy stir, as if the noise and commotion presented an opportunity, so he put his hand on the back of the guy's neck, like a friendly gesture, and he squeezed, and the guy yelped silently, and then the bus was gone.

They waited. The afternoon grew late. Then a blue car drew up at the kerb. A big Opel sedan. A General Motors product. At the wheel was a guy in army battle-dress uniform. Beside him was another. Behind both of them was a floor-to-ceiling plastic screen. A cop car.

The passenger got out. Short, wide, and dark. Manuel Orozco. Late of the 110th. *You do not mess with the special investigators.* His phrase. A good friend. He said, 'I thought you were buried in a school somewhere.'

Reacher said, 'Is that what you heard?'

'Everyone was talking about it, man. Like you died.'

'The NSC got us for a secret thing. We're shaking a tree. A whole lot of extra crap is falling out. You're going to have to clean it up for us. Without mentioning our involvement. You can claim them as your own, if you like. Get another medal. Start with these two. They're selling scrap M9s to skinheads in a bar.'

'I won't get a medal for that.'

'It's really about the bar. Could be the tip of an iceberg.'

'What happened to his nose?'

'Neagley.'

'Outstanding.'

'We need background on the bar. Apparently all kinds of deals go down there. Write it up as a separate report, OK? And then feel free to go fishing. But not until we say. There's one particular guy we're looking at, and we don't want to scare him away. Assuming he plans to come back anyway. Which he probably won't.'

Orozco said, 'You got it, boss.'

'I'm not your boss any more.'

'I'm sure you're still the boss of something.'

Orozco put the two guys in the back of the car, behind the plastic screen, and he climbed in next to his driver, and Reacher and Neagley waved them away. Then they walked back to their boutique hotel, where the clerk confirmed the consulate had indeed come through, and as a result they now had two upgraded rooms side by side on the top floor. They went to Neagley's first, where they dialled McLean, Virginia, to check in with Sinclair.

At that moment the fingerprint technician in the police garage was on the phone with Chief of Detectives Griezman. He said he had taken an excellent print off the back of the chrome lever. Clear as a bell. By shape, to his practised eye, it was a right-hand middle finger, and it was average size for a man, or large for a woman. It showed no hits in any of the federal databases. Therefore the perpetrator was almost certainly not German.

The upgraded rooms had fancy console telephones, and Neagley put hers on speaker and sat on the bed. Reacher sat in a chair. In McLean the phone was also on speaker. Reacher heard the spacey echo, and then he heard Sinclair say hello, and then Waterman, and then White. He guessed they were all in the office, at the conference table, in the leather chairs.

Sinclair said, 'Are you getting anywhere?'

She sounded tired.

Reacher said, 'The German witness was a man named Klopp, and we got a good description and a good sketch. Which was faxed to you. Klopp says he's seen the guy twice. Since then we have another witness who has seen the guy three times. All in the same bar. Which seems to be partly a right-wing political hangout and partly an underground marketplace. All kinds of deals, apparently.'

'Will that be the location of the second rendezvous?'

'The odds say no. They could choose anywhere from Scandinavia to North Africa.'

White spoke up and said, 'We're cross-checking lists in several different lateral ways. State has put some big computers on it. We're watching about four hundred American names. Which is way too many to be useful. Their recent travel destinations include about forty countries. Which is also too many to be useful.'

Reacher said, 'It all comes down to the same old question. What is the guy selling?'

No answer.

'We got a weird piece of news,' Sinclair said. 'From our people in Ukraine. Just routine police blotter stuff. The Kiev police department reported a dead Arab in an alley downtown. Killed by blows to the head, probably with a carpenter's hammer. In his twenties, and wearing a pink polo shirt with an alligator on the front. Which is what caught our eye. Probably nothing. Kiev police say there was a soccer match on the TV. The locals lost to Moscow. Lots of unhappy young men in the bars. An Arab on his own in a pink shirt might have been irresistible.'

151

'Or?'

'It's stupid to base it on the shirt. But maybe he was one of them. Maybe there's a civil war going on.'

'Does it change our plan?'

'No, we should assume the messenger is still on his way. We should act as if the second rendezvous is still imminent. What we need to figure out is whether you and Sergeant Neagley should stay in Hamburg or come back here.'

'They won't meet in McLean, Virginia. That's a certainty. Whereas they might meet in Hamburg again. That's at least a possibility. A small chance, maybe, but slim is better than none, surely.'

Sinclair was quiet for a long moment. Nothing on the line except echo and static. Then she said, 'OK, but stay away from the safe house.'

'Even if that means missing the rendezvous?'

'We'll cross that bridge when we come to it. You need to be clear on this. It's not your decision.'

In Jalalabad dinner had been eaten and the plates had been cleared away. The men in the white robes were back in their small hot room. Half of their conversation was made up of cautious ritual reminders that nothing had yet been achieved. Not definitively. Not for sure. They were close, but not certain. Ancient proverbs were quoted, old tribal incantations along the lines of not counting chickens until eggs were hatched. But the other half of their conversation was all about counting those chickens. They counted them over and over again. Glorious, dreamy speculation. They made lists, and revised them endlessly, smiling and rocking on their cushions. It was as close to erotic as those guys got.

They had to choose ten cities. They agreed Washington D.C., New York and London had to be included. They were non-negotiable. Which left seven more. Paris could be the fourth. Then Brussels, because of NATO headquarters and the European parliament. And Berlin, because why not? Which left four. Moscow might be important to their brothers in the eastern part of Europe. And Tel Aviv, obviously, although really that was a separate argument. Which left two. Amsterdam? Chicago? Los Angeles? Madrid?

Then they reminded themselves once again not to count their chickens. That resolution lasted less than a minute. They rocked in silence, and then they started over with the fourth spot. Should San Francisco go ahead of Paris? The Golden Gate Bridge?

The American got out in the heart of the downtown shopping district. He had a small smile on his face. The bus had slowed to take a corner near a pocket park, and out the window across the aisle he had glimpsed two guys he had done business with in the bar. They were sitting on benches. Small world. They were with two friends, a man and a woman. The man had been wearing the exact same jean jacket as him. An even smaller world. What were the odds?

He crossed a cobblestone plaza and stopped at a foreign exchange booth. He swapped a fistful of Deutschmarks and dollars for Argentinian pesos. Then he did the same thing at another booth a street away, and then another. Always used and crumpled bills of mixed denominations. Always cash for cash. No huge amounts. Nothing memorable. No records.

He changed his final wad up at the train station. Which was a sad place now. There were homeless people and disturbed people hanging around. There were furtive men with swivel eyes, their hands thrust deep in capacious pockets. There was spray-can graffiti on the walls. Nothing compared to the South Bronx or inner-city Detroit or south-central LA. But unusual for Germany. Reunification had been a strain. Economically, and socially. And mentally. He had watched it. Like living a comfortable life in a nice little house with your family. And then a whole bunch of relatives moves in. From someplace where they don't really know how to use a knife and fork. Ignorant and stunted people. But German like you. As if a brother had been taken away at birth and locked in a closet. Then in his mid-forties he comes stumbling out again, pale and hunched and blinking. A tough situation to manage.

He measured his pesos between finger and thumb and was satisfied. They were for incidental expenditures only, nothing more. The banker would do the heavy lifting, as arranged, by wire or telex, or whatever other secret way they did it. The cash was for tips and taxis and porters at the airport. That was all.

Next, clothes. And then a pharmacy. And then a hardware store, and a camping store, and a toy store.

* * *

Reacher and Neagley went out for an early dinner. They had seen plenty of spots in the neighbourhood. They chose a meat-and-potatoes place down three steps in a semi-basement. It had brown wood panelling and accordion music on ceiling loudspeakers.

Neagley said, 'Marian Sinclair is going to fly over here.'

Reacher said, 'Why would she?'

'I think she bought your argument about slim being better than none.'

'It shouldn't need selling.'

'And she wants to keep an eye on you.'

'She knew what she was getting. I'm sure Garber told her.'

'Ten bucks she'll be here tomorrow.'

'You good for it?'

'I won't need to be. And don't give me government money. Make sure it's your own.'

'She won't come,' Reacher said. 'It would be like backing a horse. Those people don't do that.'

Then the lights seemed to dim as Chief of Detectives Griezman walked up to their table. Six-six and three hundred pounds. Billowing grey suit the size of a pup tent. The floor creaked. Griezman said, 'I am very sorry to interrupt.'

Reacher said, 'You hungry?'

Griezman paused a beat, and said, 'Yes, a little, actually.'

Lucky guess, Reacher thought.

He said, 'Then please join us. Be the Pentagon's guest.'

'No, I couldn't allow that. Not in my own city. You must be my guests.'

'OK,' Reacher said. 'Thank you very much. The United States Treasury is grateful.'

Griezman sat down. A waiter hustled over with a third cover. Water was poured and bread was brought.

Griezman said, 'I want to ask for a favour.'

Reacher said, 'First tell us how you found us here.'

'Your hotel told us where you're staying. They're required to. Any booking by an embassy or a consulate or a diplomatic mission has potential security implications. So there's a system now. Then I put men in parked cars with radios. They passed you from one to the other until you came in here. I didn't want them to try following you on foot. I thought you'd spot them.'

'Have we done something wrong?'

'I need to ask for an important favour. Personally, face to face.'

'What kind of an important favour?'

'We found a fingerprint, in the dead prostitute's car. Remember? Exactly where you said we would. On the back of the chrome lever. A middle finger from a right hand.'

'Congratulations.'

'It has no matches anywhere in our databases.'

'Is that usual?'

'It is if the print is foreign.'

Reacher said nothing.

Griezman said, 'Will you run it through your systems for me?'

'That's huge,' Neagley said.

Reacher nodded. 'That's political. That's a can of worms. Probably involves all kinds of NATO crap, as well as the Fourth Amendment. We're knee-deep in PR people and lawyers. It would take them a year to even think about it.'

Griezman sighed, and said, 'That's always my problem. I'm not political. I'm just a simple detective, hoping for a favour from one to another.'

'Bullshit,' Reacher said. 'You're paying for dinner tonight because I said the word Pentagon. Maybe you'll run for mayor one day. This is a liberal city in Western Europe. The voters wouldn't like to hear the uncouth warmongers bought you a meal. So you'll have an expenses fight tomorrow, instead of an embarrassment ten years from now. I would call that fairly political, on a scale of one to ten.'

'I'm just trying to catch a bad guy.'

'Why would he be an American?'

'Statistics. Crime figures.'

'And you think we'd admit that out loud? As in, you've got a dead hooker, so sure, it makes total sense to round up the Americans. We can't just meekly accept a presumption of guilt. Wouldn't play well at home. This stuff is way above my pay grade.'

'Personally I agree with you. I think it was a sailor. One of a hundred nationalities. But you're a large foreign group in Germany. I could eliminate a large number of possibilities.'

'So now you think it wasn't an American?'

'I would like to prove that, yes. An attempt will be

expected of me, before the case goes cold. Which is what I want, frankly, as soon as possible.'

'Why?'

'Well, for one thing, we're wasting too much time on it.'

'Because she was a prostitute?'

'Ultimately, I suppose. But only through bitter experience and data. Most prostitute murders are committed by itinerants. That's a fact. This guy is already halfway across the Atlantic, I'm sure. Happy that he got away with it.'

Political. Reacher felt played. He said, 'I'll think about it. Have a copy of the print sent to the hotel, just in case.'

'Don't need to,' Griezman said. He took a small envelope from his inside pocket. 'There's a copy on film in here. And a card with my number.'

Reacher took the envelope and put it in his own pocket.

After dinner they elected to walk back to their hotel, so Griezman drove away in his department Mercedes without them. They detoured via the safe house. Just an evening stroll. Just a corner-of-the-eye glance, as they passed. Not that they knew which apartment. There were fifteen windows plausibly related to the lobby in question. Some of them were dark. Some showed the blue glow of television. Some had low, warm light. No people were visible. There were cars on the street, and occasional pedestrians. Early evening, in the city. They walked on.

There was a blue car parked at the kerb outside their hotel. An Opel sedan. Manuel Orozco's cop car. He was waiting for them in the lobby. He said, 'There's something you need to know.'

SIXTEEN

They went back outside and leaned on Orozco's car. The evening was cool and damp. They could sense the water nearby. Reacher said, 'You could have called.'

'No,' Orozco said. 'This is better done face to face than on the telephone.'

'Why?'

'You gave me the small story. You missed the big story.'

'Are they selling something worse?'

'No, about forty scrap M9s over six months or so is all it was. Plus a thousand rounds of ammunition. Not the end of the world. We've all seen worse.'

'So what's the big story?'

'Their ID was genuine.'

'They're real German citizens?'

'No, they're American as apple pie. Arkansas and Kentucky. They barely speak English, let alone German. Their names are Billy Bob and Jimmy Lee. Or something like that.'

'So their ID was phoney.'

'In that sense, yes. But it was also genuine. In the

160

sense that it was way too good to be faked. So good we think it must have been manufactured for them by the German government itself. In their regular plant. Alongside all their regular Kraut stuff.'

'They said they got it from a guy in the bar.'

'They said that to me too.'

'And?'

'And I believe them.'

'So?'

'Where did the guy in the bar get it from?'

'How sure are you about this?'

'I asked around. We had a debate. Some say it's complicated because when the Wall came down a whole bunch of communist forgers lost their jobs. And they were really good. All kinds of mischievous documents came out of the old East Germany. So now those guys are working for someone else. Best case, that would be organized crime. Worst case, it's the new German intelligence service. Either way, best to keep this off the phone lines. We don't know who's listening.'

'German intelligence can afford its own sidearms. They wouldn't need to print up phoney IDs for a couple of small-time crooks.'

'Agreed. But let's assume their intelligence service has a document creation division. Like they all do. Staffed by the usual array of eccentrics. Like they all are. Suppose one of them is bent? Suppose he does his business in that bar? Billy Bob and Jimmy Lee make that place sound like the stock exchange. Buy, sell, trade, anything you want.'

Reacher said, 'The first witness who saw our guy is a

government worker. I guess there could be others in there.'

Orozco nodded. 'You need to take care. You keep on shaking that tree, all kinds of crap could fall out. Some of it could be heavy duty.'

Orozco left and Reacher stopped by Neagley's room to call White in Virginia. He said, 'We're getting solid intelligence that genuine German ID is for sale in that bar. So far we've seen identity cards and driver's licences. Nothing to say you can't get passports too. Nothing to say our guy didn't buy one. So watching four hundred American names is a waste of time. A buck gets ten he'll travel under a German alias.'

White was quiet for a long moment. Then he said, 'You're right there in town. You could find out who sold what to him, and you could find out what name he put on it. Date of birth and passport number would be good too. These types of vendors keep records, usually. For security, and blackmail.'

'That's all or nothing,' Reacher said. 'They'll panic if we hit that bar. Word will get around fast. Our guy will go to ground immediately. And maybe he has more than one passport. There's more than one bar. Our witness splits his time between two of them.'

'It's still our best chance.'

'Talk to Ratcliffe. I would want to know how on my own I am.'

Then Reacher went next door to his room and went to bed. He was tired. He had been awake more than thirty hours. He put his shoes side by side under the window, with his socks draped over them. He folded his pants seam-to-seam and laid them flat under his mattress to press. He took off his jacket and hitched it straight on the back of a chair. A pocket crackled. Griezman's envelope. The fingerprint. He had thought about giving it to Orozco, but he had forgotten.

Next time, maybe.

He took a shower, and cleared a dozen green brocade pillows from his bed, and then he climbed in and went to sleep.

The American's bedtime routine had not changed in several days. He started with ten minutes of pleasure, and then he did twenty minutes of work. The pleasure came from a map of Argentina. Large scale, fine lines, a lot of detail. The ranch he was going to buy was right in the middle. It was a huge square parcel, fully thirty miles on a side. An hour's drive, at city speed limits, from corner to corner. A total of nine hundred square miles. Nearly six hundred thousand acres. Practically visible from outer space. But not, truthfully, bigger than Rhode Island, which was about twelve hundred square miles. But it was bigger than the largest single contiguous property in Texas, which was only eight hundred square miles. Both were dwarfed by the Anna Creek sheep station in Australia, which was more than nine *thousand* square miles. Nearly six million acres. About the size of Massachusetts. He had read a story about its owner. The guy had put a hundred thousand miles on his truck without ever once leaving his own property. But still, the new place in Argentina would be in the top ten in the world. It was a big-ass spread. No doubt about that. His house would be fifteen miles behind his own fences. Which was the kind of isolation he would need, in the new world he was helping to create.

He folded his map and started his twenty minutes of work, which was all about improving his Spanish, by listening to language tapes. He was going to need workers, and he couldn't expect them to learn English. So he lay in bed with foam headphones clamped to his ears, listening, repeating, learning, until his brain got tired and he fell asleep.

Neagley knocked on Reacher's door at eight o'clock the next morning. He was awake. He had showered and dressed. He was ready for coffee. The elevator was like a gilded birdcage on a chain, inside a shaft made of filigreed wrought iron. They heard it coming up to meet them. They stepped in. There was a credit card on the floor. Or a driver's licence. Or something. Face down. Dropped by accident, presumably. Not a Bundesrepublik Deutschland identity card. Wrong colour.

Neagley bent down and picked it up.

She looked at it.

She said, 'You owe me ten dollars.'

It was American ID. A Virginia driver's licence. The photo was sharp. A woman. An open, honest face. Blonde hair, medium length, an unaffected style, no doubt combed with her fingers. Marian Sinclair. She was forty-four years old, and her home address was Alexandria. A suburban house, judging by the street number.

Reacher pulled cash from his pocket. He separated two American fives, and handed them over. He said, 'She must have just checked in. After the night flight. I'm losing my touch. I didn't think she would come. And I especially didn't think she was the type of person who would lose her driver's licence in an elevator. She's number two at the NSC, for God's sake. The future of the world depends on her.'

The elevator arrived at the ground floor. They stepped out. Breakfast was in the basement. They followed a winding stair and came out in a pretty room with double glass doors standing open, with a sunken courtyard beyond. Sinclair was right there, at an outdoor table in the morning sun. Drinking coffee. Eating a pastry. Wearing a black dress. They walked over, and said, 'Good morning.'

Sinclair looked up.

She said, 'To you too. Please join me.'

They sat down, and Reacher asked her, 'Why are you here?'

She looked straight at him and said, 'Slim is better than none.'

'You dropped your driver's licence in the elevator.'

'Did I?'

He handed it over. She put it on the table next to her cup. She said, 'Thank you. Very careless of me. Very lucky you found it. I'm not using my real name here. They wouldn't have known who to return it to. You just saved me a bunch of DMV paperwork.'

'Why aren't you using your real name?'

'Hotels report to the police. My name would trigger a diplomatic alert. And I'm not here officially.'

'You have an alternate identity?'

'Several. We have a document creation division. Just like the Germans. I spoke to Major Orozco this morning and got the whole story. Naturally we were watching your friends. You disobeyed me. I told you only me, Mr Ratcliffe, or the president.'

'It was private business.'

'No business is private. Not in this matter. But please don't blame your friend for ratting you out. He had no choice. And don't feel too bad, either, because both Mr White and Special Agent Waterman have already done the same kind of thing. With their friends. Not unexpected. We were briefed about your backgrounds.'

'It wasn't relevant.'

'It was, because of the ID. That changes everything. ID for sale good enough to get through multiple foreign borders is very rare. We didn't include it as a factor. Now we must, which reduces our chances to less than zero. Our American will be one of ten million anonymous people going to one of ten thousand different places.'

'Our chances are better than zero,' Reacher said. 'He'll want a place where he feels at home and the messenger doesn't. Which means a big Western city. With direct connections by air. He won't want to travel more than he has to. And he's already familiar with Hamburg. He might come back. Our chances are one in ten, maybe.'

'You're pushing to watch the safe house.'

'I think we need to.'

'They might have more than one.'

Reacher nodded. 'They might have ten in every town

on earth. It's a percentage game. We have to start somewhere.'

Sinclair nodded in turn. 'We're taking it under consideration. In either case we'll be alerted as soon as the messenger arrives. If he ever does. Then we'll take it from there. Last time the wait before the rendezvous was forty-eight hours. We'll have time for a decision.'

'How does the Iranian communicate?'

'On the phone if he can. If it's safe. Or by dead drop. And the Hamburg head of station just arranged a very basic early warning. Under the circumstances we felt it was necessary. If the Iranian can't get to the phone or arrange a drop, he'll move a lamp on his bedroom windowsill. From the edge to the centre. As soon as the messenger shows up. His bedroom is in the back of the building, and the window is visible from the next street over. The head of station is doing four drive-bys a day.'

A waitress with yellow pigtails came by for the newcomers' orders. Sinclair dug in her bag and came out with a large brown envelope. She gave it to Neagley and said, 'This is your mail from the Department of the Army.'

Neagley said, 'Thank you, ma'am,' and opened the envelope. She checked the contents, put them back, and smiled an only-the-army kind of a smile.

Reacher said, 'What?'

'Nothing.'

Sinclair said, 'You can speak freely in front of me, sergeant. I have a security clearance.'

'No, ma'am, it's really nothing. Not relevant at all.

167

Except I guess it proves once again the most efficient unit in uniform is the press room. I asked for information about a four-month-old AWOL case we found. A purely tangential inquiry. Nothing to do with anything. But Major Reacher asked me to keep him up to date with it.'

'Why?'

Reacher said, 'That's a command I want to avoid.'

'And the press room responded?'

Neagley said, 'They sent two generic newspaper articles about the guy's unit. The best they could do. Trying to be helpful. In fact one of them isn't even an article at all. It's an advertisement. Because obviously they don't know anything about the guy himself. Because they're only the press room. But they're very willing and very fast.'

'And nothing from the units that do know something about the guy?'

'Not yet.'

'Is four months unusual?'

'It would be in a unit I worked for.'

Reacher said, 'They're putting people in advertisements now?'

Neagley took out the envelope's contents for the second time. An old *Army Times*, and a trade show handbill. The *Times* had a bland piece about the ongoing drawdown out of the Fulda Gap, near Frankfurt, where once upon a time great swirling tank battles had been envisaged. Now the enemy was gone, and the border had moved hundreds of miles farther east, like an ebb tide, and front-line units had been stranded like fish on a beach. Some had pushed onward, just in case, and others had streamed back to immense storage lagers, where they were mothballed. Just five Chaparral units were still on active duty, including the AWOL's crew, who were featured in a photograph at the top of the story.

The photograph was a posed picture, with the camera set low behind the men and their vehicle, all of which were facing away towards an imagined incoming threat. The missiles on the truck were in their launchers, aimed at a low horizon ahead, and the guys were staring at the same spot in the sky, some with binoculars, some with hands shading their eyes, as if the sun was coming up. As if the viewer of the photograph was cowering twenty yards behind their manly and vigilant protection. From the rear the men looked like a useful bunch, lean and purposeful and energetic. Reacher knew people from similar units. In his experience they acted halfway between regular artillerymen and the flight deck crews on a navy carrier, all hustle and bustle, with a little maverick *Top Gun* aviator mixed in. They thought of their trucks as parked airplanes. Morale and unit cohesion tended to be high. These particular guys all had Mohawk hairstyles, with two-inch-wide tufts running front to back across otherwise shaved skulls, all spiked up with soap or wax. Not strictly legal, according to Army Regulation 670-3-2, which said that haircuts should be neat and conservative, and that extreme, eccentric, or faddish styles were not authorized. But clearly a wise commander had turned a blind eye. Some battles were not worth fighting, especially when more important battles were on the horizon, literally.

The trade show handbill had been printed up to look like a newspaper article, by a uniform manufacturer touting a new urban camouflage pattern. Aimed at the Department of Defense, possibly, or at police SWAT teams. The main picture looked like it had been shot in a giant indoor studio, and it featured the same Chaparral crew as the *Army Times* piece, and their vehicle, all of them decked out the same way, men and machine alike, in a design that looked like digital noise, made up of tiny printed rectangles, all different shades of grey. The men's faces and hands and part-bald heads were painted the same way, as was the truck, and as were the missiles themselves. They were all posed in front of an artificial painted backdrop, like a theatre set, that showed a ruined cityscape. This time the camera was set high and in front of them, like an incoming pilot's eye view. Like an attack helicopter coming in low and close, for a pre-emptive strike. In which case the new camouflage was doing an excellent job. The men and their machine were barely visible. They merged into the background more or less perfectly. They were a ghostly presence, both there and not there all at the same time. No details were clear. Even the missiles themselves were hard to make out. Only the Mohawk hairstyles were obvious, five in a line, because they were the only things not painted. Very impressive. Except the manufacturer had the luxury of designing the studio floor and the theatre backdrop itself, any old way it wanted. Which in this case had been to match the camouflage exactly. Which helped. The real world might be different.

Sinclair put a fingernail on the ghostly half-hidden missiles and asked, 'Could things like these be stolen and sold?'

'Not for a hundred million bucks,' Neagley said. 'That's the problem. We've been over and over it. It's a catch-22. There's no middle ground. Everything is devalued now. There's too much cheap old stuff coming out of Russia and China, and too much cheap new stuff for sale anyway. Arms manufacturers have been hustling ever since the Wall came down. They're worried. They're feeling the pinch. Every month there's an arms fair somewhere. If you've got the right kind of chequebook you can get anything you want. Except nuclear. Which kind of proves my point. There's no middle ground. To get to a hundred million, you would have to go nuclear.'

'Don't say that word out loud.'

'We have to, ma'am. If only to dismiss it instantly. We have bombs on air bases back home, and missiles in silos in the badlands, and missiles on submarines under the sea. All of them are under heavy guard, and we'd notice if one went missing. The smallest and most accessible portable piece in our current inventory is probably a Minuteman ICBM, and selling and delivering the Brooklyn Bridge would be a thousand times easier. Plus no individual ever knows the complete arming codes. Regulations mandate that arming codes must always be split between two personnel. That's a basic nuclear safeguard.'

'So in your opinion this is not military?'

'Unless it's intelligence.'

'What kind of intelligence is worth a hundred million dollars?'

'We don't know that either.'

'Should we audit our physical inventory?'

'That would take for ever. And I can tell you exactly what it would find. We have a million small things missing, but no big things.'

'How do you know?'

'I would have heard.'

'The world's most efficient grapevine,' Reacher said. 'Someone just told me that.'

The table went quiet.

Reacher said, 'We should watch the safe house.'

'We'd need a clandestine team,' Sinclair said. 'We don't have one in Hamburg. And it would be hard to justify bringing one in. Taking one-in-ten chances is not a policy stance.'

'Neither is running around with your hair on fire.'

'Griezman could do it for us,' Neagley said. 'His guys were pretty good. They tracked us to the restaurant last night. And he owes us. He told Stuttgart about us.'

Reacher took the sketch out of his pocket. The American. The brow, the cheekbones, the deep-set eyes. The floppy hair. Recognizable. Griezman's guys could watch for him, from strategically parked cars. With radios. Day after day. They might be successful. He said, 'It would be a very big commitment. A lot of hours. We'd have to trade favours.'

Sinclair said, 'What could we offer him?'

'A prostitute got strangled. He has a fingerprint. He wants us to run it through our systems.'

'We can't do that.'

'What I told him.'

'Anything else?'

'Not that I can think of. Food, possibly. There's a lot of him.'

The table went quiet again. Sinclair bent down and dug around in her pocketbook, and came out with her purse. It was a fat leather thing, blue in colour, fastened with a tab and a popper. She scooped up her driver's licence, from the table next to her cup, and she unsnapped her purse, and made ready to slide the licence into its customary slot.

Then she stopped.

She said, 'I have my licence. It's right here.'

She pincered her fingertips and pulled it out from behind a plastic window.

Two licences, side by side. Everything the same. The Commonwealth of Virginia, the number, the name, the address, the date of birth, the signature.

Even the photograph was the same.

Two licences.

Identical.

SEVENTEEN

The back part of Reacher's brain checked doors and windows, and the front part checked facts and logic. Facts and logic won. But certainty was a dangerous illusion, so he said, 'Maybe we should go inside.'

Neagley went first. Sinclair grabbed her pocketbook in one hand and her purse and her two licences in the other and hustled after her. Reacher brought up the rear. They stepped through the double doors and walked through the breakfast room and up the stairs to the lobby. No one there. Sinclair said, 'We should check my room.'

Reacher asked, 'Where is it?'

'Top floor.'

The elevator shaft was empty. The birdcage was on an upper storey.

Reacher said, 'Wait one.'

He stepped over to the desk. The clerk who had checked them in was on duty. She was a stout old matron, and no doubt very competent. He asked her, 'Ma'am, did a woman who resembles my friend here ask for a key? Did she show you ID?'

The clerk said, 'Resembles?'

174

'Looks like.'

'No,' the woman said. 'No one asked. No one came in. There was no woman. Just a man. He waited by the elevator. Possibly meeting a guest. But then I had to go in the office. I didn't see him again.'

She pointed behind her, at an office door.

Reacher said, 'What did the man look like?'

'He was small. He was wearing a raincoat.'

'Thank you,' Reacher said.

He stepped back to the others.

He said, 'Let's take the stairs.'

Neagley led the way, staying close to the wall, craning her neck, looking upward. The stairs wrapped around the elevator shaft. They could see into it through the filigreed wrought iron. Nothing was moving. Just chains and cables and an iron slab of a counterweight, all immobile. They made it to the second floor. Then the third. They looked up and saw the underside of the elevator car. The birdcage. It was waiting on the floor above. The top floor.

Reacher said, 'If it moves, we'll race it back to the bottom. We'll get there first. It's pretty slow.'

But it didn't move. It just sat there. They walked up to where they could see into it. It was empty. Gate closed, waiting. They came around behind it, then alongside it, climbing all the way, and then finally they stepped out into the top-floor hallway.

Empty.

Sinclair pointed. Third room along. Next to Reacher's own. Upgraded. Only the best for the United States government. The door was closed.

Neagley said, 'I'll go.'

She moved silently over the thick corridor carpet. The hinge side of the door was closest, and the knob side farthest. She ducked under the peephole's field of view and flattened against the wall beyond the door. She reached out and tried the knob backhand. Long training. Always safer. Guns can shoot through doors.

She mouthed 'Locked', and mimed that she needed the key. Sinclair tucked her purse and her licences up under her arm and scrabbled in her bag. She came out with a brass key on a pewter fob. Reacher took it from her and tossed it to Neagley, who caught it one-handed and put it in the lock, from the same position, backhand again, at a distance, out of the line of fire.

She turned the key.

The door sagged open an inch.

Silence.

No reaction.

Reacher stepped up and flattened against the wall on the hinge side, symmetrical with Neagley, equally safe, and he spread his fingers and pushed the door wide.

No reaction.

Neagley pivoted around the jamb and ducked inside. Reacher followed. Long training. Smallest first, biggest last. That way both parties got an unobstructed view. And the bigger party didn't get accidentally shot in the back.

There was no one in the room.

Just a wide bed with a dozen green brocade pillows, and a lone wheeled suitcase with a lock, in the middle of the floor.

No one in the bathroom.

No one in the closet.

Sinclair came in and dumped her stuff on the bed. Her pocketbook, her purse, the two driver's licences. They spilled and fluttered. Reacher closed and locked the door. He checked the window.

Nothing to see.

Safe enough.

Sinclair said she knew her real licence by a long-forgotten smudge of ballpoint ink in one corner. From cashing a cheque in a D.C. bank, she said, where she needed ID, and where the writing ledge was cramped and narrow due to the thickness of the teller's bulletproof window. The exuberant underline beneath her signature had swerved off the cheque and touched her licence. She had rubbed the mark with her thumb, removing some of it and spreading the rest.

She put her real licence back in her purse, and she put her purse back in her pocketbook. She left the fake licence on the bed, and sat down next to it. She trapped it under her fingernail, as if it might float away. She said, 'I guess this raises a large number of questions.'

'One, at least,' Reacher said.

'Only one?'

'Have you ever mislaid your licence before?'

'Is this the question?'

'Yes.'

'No, never.'

'Then I would say Mr Ratcliffe has work to do.'

'Why him?'

'Because they won't want to give it to the FBI. Too high a risk of a scandal.'

'Who won't?'

'The White House.'

'Forget the White House. Someone is running around Hamburg pretending to be me.'

'Or vice versa.'

'What does that mean?'

'You might be a foreign spy,' Reacher said. 'Maybe it's the real Marian Sinclair who's running around Hamburg.'

'Are you kidding?'

'No stone unturned.'

'That's ridiculous.'

'Do you follow baseball?'

'What?'

'Baseball,' Reacher said. 'Do you follow it?'

'Socially, I suppose.'

'Where do you go?'

'The Orioles.'

'What do you see beyond the right-field wall?'

Sinclair said, 'A warehouse.'

'OK, you pass the test.'

'Were you serious?'

'No, I was pulling your leg. Obviously you're real, because you brought Neagley's mail.'

'There's a time and a place, major.'

'These are as good as any. We could get depressed otherwise.'

'The White House didn't forge a copy of my driver's licence.'

'I agree.'

'We're a stone's throw from a bar where this stuff is for sale.'

'Coincidence,' Reacher said.

'I don't believe in coincidence. Neither should you.'

'Sometimes we have to. If that licence had been made here in Germany, however good these people are, they would have been forced to use a press photograph. From a newspaper or a magazine. Re-shot on regular film, to make it look like the real thing, and definitely you, but it couldn't be the exact same photograph as on your real licence, because they don't have that photograph. Only the Virginia DMV has that photograph. You never mislaid your licence, so it can't have been copied direct.'

'So who made it?'

'The Virginia DMV.'

'Which is many things, but not a criminal organization.'

'Far from it. They did it as a statutory duty. As a service to the public. When you mislaid your first licence and requested a replacement.'

'But I never did. I told you that.'

'They didn't know it wasn't you. Someone filled out the form, with your name and address, and mailed it in, and then monitored your mailbox until the replacement arrived.'

'Who?'

'Someone who works in the White House travel office. An older person, who has been in government service a long time. Hence the potential embarrassment. Hence Ratcliffe won't give it to the FBI.'

179

'Why the travel office?'

'Partly because DMV paperwork needs more than just your name and address. There are all kinds of numbers. The people who book your flights and your cars and your hotels would know them all.'

'My lawyer knows them all. My accountant knows them all. Probably my housekeeper knows them all.'

'You were eating breakfast under an assumed name four thousand miles from home. Your replica DL was dropped twenty feet away. You don't believe in coincidence. Who knew you were here?'

Sinclair paused a beat and said, 'The White House travel office.'

'Who else?'

'No one else.'

'Not even the hotel desk,' Reacher said. 'You're using a different name. Only one possible explanation. Someone in the travel office made a phone call.'

'To who? Some local woman trained to impersonate me?'

'There is no local woman. No one went to the desk. No one entered the lobby except a small man in a raincoat.'

'So what happened?'

'The small man in the raincoat knew your ETA. The night flight, on Lufthansa. Someone in the travel office told him all about it. He followed you from the airport to the hotel, he hung around across the street, he saw you check in, he saw you get in the elevator, he snuck in the lobby, he called the elevator back down, he dropped the licence on the floor, and he turned around and walked away.'

'Why did he do all that?'

'It was a message. I think you were supposed to find the licence yourself. You went up to dump your bag, and he expected you to come back down again for breakfast.'

'I took the stairs.'

'Evidently.'

'Why an older person who has been in the travel office a long time?'

'You can figure that out. In fact I think you already have. You're not wondering who the man in the raincoat was. Because you know.'

'I don't.'

'You're pretty sure.'

'There are things I can't tell you.'

Neagley said, 'Let me hazard a wild-ass guess. You guys ran a black operation somewhere and gave our side German papers. For false-flag cover. Or just for the fun of it. Or the Israelis did, with your permission. The German government found out and got upset. You wouldn't admit it or discuss it, so now their intelligence service is applying some very civilized German-style pressure. They're saying, see, we can do it too. They're asking, how do you like it now? There's an element of showing off in there, I guess, but why not? It's all very discreet, and ultimately harmless. But unsettling, I imagine.'

'Why an older person who has been there a long time?'

'They have embassy people who could have done it, but deniability is always a good thing, so they called on a local asset. There are no new relationships of that type. Not for the new Germany. They're all historic survivors from the old East Germany. Some young U.S. government worker, way back when, hoping for a revolution, copying documents and leaving them under a rock in a park. Then he buys a house and needs some cash, and it rolls on, until eventually the new Germany and its new intelligence service inherit him. Now finally he's useful. He knows your home address, because he's in the travel office now. So he runs the licence scam, and he delivers the replacement to the embassy. Ratcliffe's too, maybe, plus whoever else they're tweaking. Where they all wait patiently in a drawer, until the first of you comes to Germany. Which would be you, this morning. Lufthansa cooperated, because it's a state airline. You didn't fly alone. A German embassy worker got a last-minute seat, with your licence in an envelope. Which is why the man in the raincoat had to follow you from the airport. He could have waited here, because he knew where you were headed, because the travel office booked your room, but he had to meet the flight first, because the embassy worker had to hand off the envelope. The licence was about two minutes behind you, all the way into town.'

Sinclair was quiet for a long time. Then she said, 'I won't comment on any of that. But obviously we couldn't admit it. If such a thing had happened. Which I'm not saying either way.'

Reacher asked, 'Are you going to respond?'

'That would be a complicated double bluff, wouldn't it?'

'You could go to Griezman. Make him bluff. He'll make nice to you, but then he'll bury it behind your back, in order to be seen as a reliable guy by his own government. Which would do him good. He might regard that as a favour. He might watch the safe house in return.'

'Simpler for him to insist on us running the fingerprint.'

'Which we should anyway. A woman was killed. It would be the right thing to do.'

'That's the view from the cheap seats?'

'Should be the view from every seat.'

Sinclair said nothing.

Reacher said, 'We could run it privately. If it's a null result, we could tell him. If it isn't, we could figure something out as we went along.'

'What are the odds?'

'Soldiers use hookers but don't usually kill them. And she was expensive, judging by the neighbourhood. Which makes it even less likely.'

'No,' Sinclair said. 'It's a can of worms. Too much political risk.'

At that moment the new messenger was in the immigration line, at the Hamburg airport. There were four booths operational, two labelled for European Union passports only, and two for other passports. Hers was Pakistani. She was fifth in line. Not nervous. No reason to be. She was a clean skin. Brand new. She was in no databases. She had never been anywhere. Never seen, never fingerprinted, never photographed except literally once in her life, for the passport she was carrying. Which was completely real, except for the name, and the nationality.

Now she was fourth in line. She could see her reflection in the glass of the booth. Her hair was mussed, and her eyes were sleepy. Vulnerable. Her explorer shirt was still white and crisp. All treated and antimicrobial. Unbuttoned two down. *Never three*, she had been told. *Unless it looks accidental. Pick a line with a male official.*

Now she was third in line.

Reacher and Neagley left Sinclair in her room. They leapfrogged Reacher's billet and went to Neagley's, so they couldn't be heard through the wall. Reacher said, 'I don't know why she came. She won't watch the safe house.'

'She's here because slim is better than none.'

'Except she's deliberately opting for none.'

'Is she?'

'What are you talking about?'

'Never mind,' Neagley said. 'Take a break. The East Coast won't be up and running for another hour. We'll get together then. I'm sure a conference call will cheer us up.'

Reacher went out for a walk. He found himself in a street full of menswear shops. And belts and gloves and watches and wallets. Clothing and accessories. Like an unofficial outdoor mall. He stopped in at a basic place and bought fresh underwear and a new T-shirt. The T-shirt was black, and spun from a fine grade of cotton. It cost about four times what he was accustomed to paying. But it fit. Germans were tall, on average. Not as tall as the Dutch, who were world champions, but taller than Americans, as a whole.

He changed in the store's cubicle and dumped his old stuff in the trash. Like Neagley had said. A million small things missing. An olive drab undershirt, right there, once issued, never returned or reported missing or destroyed, and therefore now suddenly subtracted from an inventory that as a consequence would be out of balance for ever.

He walked on. Halfway down the street there was a barbershop, like the centrepiece of the unofficial mall. It was tricked out to look like an old-time American place. Two vinyl chairs, with more chrome than a Cadillac. A big old radio on a shelf. Not a marketing plan, but a tribute. There was no large number of U.S. military nearby. And the PX barber was always cheaper. To Reacher's practised eye the place looked more like a diner than a barbershop, but it was a brave attempt. Some of the accessories were good. There was a visual chart taped to a mirror. An American publication. Reacher had seen hundreds of them in the States. Black and white line drawings, twenty-four heads, all with different styles, so the customer could point, instead of explaining. Top left was a standard crew cut, then came the whitewall, and the flat top, and the fade, and so on, the styles getting a little longer and a little weirder as they approached the bottom right. The Mohawk was in there, plus a couple of others that made the Mohawk look a model of probity.

A guy inside beckoned Reacher in.

Reacher mouthed, 'How much?'

The guy held up his hand, fingers and thumb all extended.

Reacher mouthed, 'Five what?'

The guy came to the door and opened it and said, 'American dollars.'

'My regular barber is cheaper.'

'But I'm better. You get your uniforms tailored, right?'

'Do I look like I wear a uniform?'

'Oh, please.'

Reacher said, 'Five bucks? I remember when five bucks got you two hamburgers and the back row of the movies. Plus car fare for her, if you fell out along the way. A shave and a haircut was two bits.'

'Was that a homage?'

'What?'

'Did you say that deliberately?'

'Sometimes I let things out by accident, but generally only one syllable at a time.'

'Therefore you said it deliberately. It was a homage. You were building the energy.'

'What was I doing?'

'You like this place.'

'I suppose.'

'Then support it by paying the full five bucks.'

'I don't need a haircut.'

The guy said, 'You know the difference between you and me?'

Reacher said, 'What?'

'I can see your hair from the outside.'

'And?'

'You need a haircut.'

'For five bucks?'

'I'll add a shave for free.'

Which turned out to be a luxurious experience. The water was warm, and the lather was creamy. The steel was perfect. It hissed through, on a molecular level. The mirror was tinted, so the finished job looked tan where it was probably pink. But even so, it looked pretty good. *Call it a buck*, Reacher thought. *Which leaves the haircut costing four. Which is still outrageous.*

The guy swapped the razor for scissors and started in on Reacher's hair. Reacher ignored him and looked at the visual chart instead. The twenty-four styles. He went through them in order, only his eyes moving, carefully, as if studying them, from the plain number one at the beginning, all the way to a fantastically elaborate DA at the other end of the scale.

He looked back at the Mohawk.

The guy said, 'What do you think?'

Reacher said, 'About what?'

'Your new haircut.'

Reacher looked in the mirror. He said, 'Have you done it yet?'

'Are you in doubt?'

'It doesn't look like it's just been cut.'

'Exactly,' the guy said. 'The best haircut looks like it was done a week ago.'

'So I pay five bucks for a haircut that already looks grown out?'

'This is a salon. I am an artist.'

Reacher said nothing.

He looked back at the Mohawk.

Then he dug in his pocket and gave the guy five American dollars, and asked, 'Do you have a phone?'

The guy pointed at the wall. An old Ma Bell pay-phone. All metal. For outside a gas station rather than inside a barbershop, but points for effort.

Reacher said, 'Does it work?'

'Of course it works,' the guy said. 'This is Germany. It was rewired as a normal telephone.'

Reacher dialled the number on Griezman's business card. From the envelope with the fingerprint. He got ring tone. The phone worked. Germany. Rewired.

Griezman answered.

Reacher said, 'We're just simple detectives, you and I, hoping for favours, one to the other.'

Griezman said, 'You're going to run the print.'

'If you do something for me.'

'What something?'

'Two somethings, actually. Put some guys in cars around that bar. Where Klopp goes. With radios. Watch for the guy in the sketch. But don't be obvious about it.'

'And?'

'There's an apartment five streets away. Same thing, cars and radios. Not obvious. Sooner or later a Saudi kid is going to show up. He's going to stay home for a spell, and then he's going to come out again and head for a rendezvous. I need to know where he goes, in real time.'

'That's a lot of people and a lot of cars.'

'This is Europe. What else do you need them for?'

'When?'

'Immediately.'

'That won't be possible. It will take time to arrange.'

'Do you want me to run the print or not?'

Griezman was quiet for a second, and then he said yes, he did, and he said it with a little more enthusiasm than Reacher expected. The guy had a lot of departmental pride. He wanted to close his case.

Reacher said, 'You do your best for me, and I'll do my best for you.'

Griezman said, 'OK.'

Then Reacher called the hotel and asked the desk for Neagley. She was in her room. He said, 'I need Orozco. Right now. And then five minutes after that you and I need to meet with Sinclair.'

'She's looking for you anyway. She has something for you.'

'What?'

'I don't know. Something Vanderbilt did. She's all excited.'

'Tell Orozco I'm in a barbershop three blocks from the hotel. Tell him to be quick.'

'What have you got?'

'I know who the American is.'

EIGHTEEN

The hairdresser guy made coffee, and Reacher sat in the barber chair, and the guy asked him questions about his childhood memories of old-time America. Hoping to build the energy, Reacher figured. Truth was Reacher had spent virtually his whole childhood outside the continental United States. He was the son of a Marine officer who had served all over the world. Reacher had gone with him, with his brother and his mother, as family. The Far East, the Pacific, Europe. Dozens of bases. Which helped, in a way. Old-time America had always been a myth to Reacher. So he repeated the same made-up crap he had lived on then, about bubblegum machines and Cadillacs with fins, and endless sunshine, and drive-in movies and waitresses on roller skates, and cheeseburgers and cold Coca Cola in green glass bottles, and baseball on AM radio, out of Kansas City, static and all. The hairdresser guy's smile got wider and wider, as if the energy in the room was indeed building to a satisfactory level.

Then Orozco's sedan squelched to a stop on the street outside, and Reacher hustled out to join him. He got in the passenger seat. Orozco said, 'Nice do, man.'

Reacher ran his fingers through his hair. He said, 'You can tell?'

'Picks up your cheekbones big time. The ladies will love it.'

Reacher took out Griezman's envelope.

He said, 'I want you to run this print.'

'Through what?'

'Army, navy, air force, and Marines. But very quietly.'

'What happened?'

'A hooker was killed. Local cops figure this is the guy who did it.'

'Any reason to believe he's American military?'

'None at all, but I need a favour.'

'We can't do it.'

'Which is why I said quietly. Your eyes only. Then mine. Then it's on me.'

'The words court and martial spring to mind.'

'Hasn't happened yet.'

Orozco sat still for a long moment. Then he took the envelope. But he said nothing. He made no promises. Deniability, from the start. Always a good idea. Reacher got out and Orozco drove away. Reacher hustled for the hotel.

They met in Sinclair's room again. Her big news was that Vanderbilt had been struck by a bolt of proactive initiative and had taken the faxed sketch of the American to Bartley, over at the Fort Myer visiting officers' quarters. The lieutenant colonel, who had refused to say where he was on the day in question. The guy bleeding equity out of the family home, ahead of divorcing his unsuspecting wife. He recognized the face in the sketch. He said he had seen the guy at Zurich airport. On his last but one trip. They had been on the same flight back to Hamburg. Exactly two weeks before the first rendez-vous. The guy had been carrying a glossy multi-pocketed folder with a bank logo on it. The kind of thing you got when you opened an account. The lieutenant colonel had one of his own, from a year before, when he had rented his safety deposit box.

'It's not definitive,' Sinclair said.

'But it's suggestive,' Reacher said. 'Klopp has seen the guy, and Bartley has seen the same guy. I think the sketch is a good one.' He took out his own copy. Unfolded it. The brow, the cheekbones, the deep-set eyes. The hair. The colour of hay or straw in the summer. Quite normal at the sides, Klopp had said, but much longer at the top. Like a style. As if he could flop it around. Like Elvis Presley.

Reacher said, 'How do you get hair like that?'

Sinclair said, 'I guess first you grow it long all over, and then you tell the stylist how you want him to shape it.'

'Or you start with a Mohawk, and you let it grow out. Four months later it's normal on the sides and long on the top, because the top got a running start. Early on you wear a hat, until it stops looking weird.'

Neagley said, 'You wear a ball cap with a red star on the front.'

'Probably the Houston Astros, because Texas is where

you're from. Your name is Wiley, and four months ago you walked away from an air defence unit hundreds of miles east of here.'

Sinclair said nothing.

Neagley said, 'And you bought a new passport, so you never have to use your own. Which means the MPs will never find you.'

Sinclair said, 'That's a big bet on a hairstyle.'

Reacher said, 'Order up his personnel jacket. Show his photo to Klopp.'

At that moment the new messenger was knocking on the apartment door. It was the first apartment door she had ever knocked on. It was the first apartment door she had ever seen. But she knew how it would feel. She had been coached. It would feel like a long time, but really it was nothing more than counting from one to five. She had been coached about everything. She had taken the bus into town. First time ever. She saw paved roads for the first time ever. But due to long hours of stream-of-consciousness briefing from the others she knew how to do it. She was prepared. She didn't stand out. She stumbled once or twice, but so does every weary long-distance traveller. Perfection would have stood out worse.

One, two, three, four, five.

The door opened.

A young Saudi guy said, 'Who are you?'

The new messenger said, 'I seek sanctuary and haven. Our faith requires you to provide it. As do our elders and betters in this venture.'

The Saudi boy said, 'Come in.'

He closed the door after her, and then stopped and said, 'Wait a minute. Really?'

The new messenger had been coached. She said, 'Yes, really. The tall one sets the strategy, and the fat one works the angles. In this case including a messenger no one could possibly suspect is a messenger, because she's female.'

'The fat one?'

'On the left. More flies around him.'

She had been coached.

'OK,' the kid said. 'But wow. Although I guess we always knew this was important.'

'How?' she said. She was in her first apartment ever, but not her first danger ever, of bungled alliances, or outright betrayal. She was from the tribal areas. She said, 'How do you know this is important?'

The kid didn't answer.

She said, 'Did the first messenger tell you?'

'He told us the price.'

'He's dead now. They killed him. They sent me instead. They told me not to ask the price. They don't like it if someone knows the price. So you should forget it as soon as you can.'

The kid said, 'How long are you staying?'

'Not long.'

'These are cramped accommodations.'

'A great struggle requires a great sacrifice. But don't get ambitious. I heard they killed my predecessor with a hammer. The same will happen to you. If I say so. Or if I don't get back.'

She had been coached.

Sinclair did as Reacher had asked. She unlocked her suitcase and took out what looked worse than the first wireless telephone ever invented. Like a brick.

'Satellite phone,' she said. 'Encrypted. To the office.'

She pressed buttons and waited for answering beeps, and then she said, 'I want the personnel jacket for U.S. Army Private First Class Wiley, first name unknown, currently four months absent without leave from an air defence unit in Germany. To me in Hamburg, seriously fast.'

Then she clicked off.

The National Security Council.

The keys to the kingdom.

There was a knock at the door.

For an illogical split second Reacher thought, *seriously fast, you bet your ass.*

But no.

The door opened. A guy came in. Busy, bustling, sixty-something, medium size, a grey suit, a tight waistband, a warm and friendly face. Pink and round. Lots of energy, and the start of a smile. A guy who got things done, with a lot of charm. Like a salesman. Something complicated. Like a financial instrument, or a Rolls-Royce automobile.

'I'm sorry,' the guy said. To Sinclair only. 'I didn't know you had company.'

American. An old-time Yankee accent.

No one spoke.

Then Sinclair said, 'Excuse me. Sergeant Frances Neagley and Major Jack Reacher, U.S. Army, meet Mr

Rob Bishop, CIA head of station at the Hamburg consulate.'

'I just did a drive-by,' Bishop said. 'On the parallel street. The kid's bedroom. The lamp has moved in the window.'

NINETEEN

Bishop wouldn't let them see for themselves. He said he had driven by, and then driven by again, immediately, which was one time too many on any given visit. But he had to, because something wasn't right. But even so, he couldn't allow a third go-round. He knew which window to look for, and they didn't. He would have to crawl past and point it out. A third consecutive pass, driving slow, four people hunched down in the car, craning their necks. Too obvious. Not going to happen. Couldn't risk it.

Reacher asked, 'What wasn't right?'

'The kid was supposed to move the lamp from the edge of the sill to the middle of the window. But it's only halfway there. It's way off centre. It's not exactly the prearranged signal.'

'Which means what?'

'One of three things. First, maybe he only had half a second. In and out, real quick. Or second, maybe he felt moving the lamp all the way was too obvious. Maybe the others are in and out of his room all the time. They might notice. Who takes a moment to move a lamp the

197

same day their old pal shows up again? These guys are not interior decorators. They have other things on their minds. Maybe it was a bad idea.'

'He hasn't called?'

'Presumably that's difficult right now. Presumably they're all in a huddle. They're excited about this, remember.'

'What's the third thing?'

'He's trying to tell us something.'

'What kind of something?'

'Something has changed. Some new factor. As if he's trying to say, it is but it isn't. As if for instance the messenger is here in Hamburg, but the rendezvous is somewhere else. Maybe the guy told them he has to take the train to Bremen. Or Berlin. They could meet on the train. That could be a smart way to do it. They could meet accidentally and talk for a minute. Or it could be something else completely.'

Sinclair said, 'We have forty-eight hours to figure it out.'

'If they stick to the same schedule,' Neagley said. 'Which they might not. It's a lottery. Travel could be delayed. I imagine they're making connections all over the place. Including third-world countries. So I assume they build in extra time. If the planes go on schedule, then they get to hang out for two days. But if the planes are late, then they have their meetings more or less immediately. Or somewhere in between. That would be my assessment.'

Bishop said, 'We need eyes on the apartment building.'

'Can't do it,' Sinclair said. 'Can't risk the safe house.'

'We're blind if we don't. We're passing up a solid-gold chance of getting the guy.'

Reacher looked at Bishop. An unexpected ally.

Sinclair said, 'There are future considerations.'

'That's then and this is now.'

'Can't do it,' Sinclair said again.

'We're already doing it,' Reacher said.

'What?'

'Chief of Detectives Griezman agreed to watch the apartment building. Plain-clothes officers in cars. They're pretty good. We saw them at work. Or rather, we didn't.'

Sinclair went pale. Anger mostly, Reacher figured.

She said, 'Starting when?'

'Maybe this afternoon,' he said. 'Depends on his scheduling issues.'

'Why is he doing it?'

'I asked him to.'

'In exchange for what?'

'I'm running the fingerprint.'

Sinclair said, 'Major, I need to talk to you.'

Reacher said, 'You are talking to me.'

'In private.'

Neagley said, 'Use my room. We won't hear you from there.'

She tossed her room key, a soft underhand arc, and Sinclair caught it, one-handed, no trouble at all.

She said, 'Follow me.'

Which Reacher did, down the corridor, to Neagley's

room. Sinclair went all the way in, to the window, and she turned around with the light behind her.

Taller than the average, but no wider.

The black dress, the pearls, the nylons, the shoes.

The face and the hair, combed with her fingers.

Looking good.

She said, 'You disobeyed an order.'

Reacher said, 'I don't remember an order. I don't remember much of anything after the National Security Adviser told us we get anything we need. And we need this. It could save us a year. Without it all we get is a regular manhunt. For a guy already four months AWOL, with a brand new foreign passport. Instead of that we could have a Saudi kid in a pink shirt and pointed shoes lead us directly to him. Right here and now. Who wouldn't take that deal? The future means nothing if we don't live to see it.'

'So you broke the law, but only because you thought you had a good reason. You and everyone else. There are lots of good reasons. Too many good reasons. Which is why we have a special structure, to decide between them, when they compete one against the other. That structure is called the National Security Council. We weigh things up and we judge priorities. You just blew a year's hard work, major. You should resign. Before the after-action report comes out. You'll get a better deal that way.'

'OK,' Reacher said. 'I will, if it turns out bad.'

'You also just blew up forty years of legal precedent about which databases are secret and which are not. That's a court martial offence all by itself. It's a federal crime.'

'OK,' Reacher said. 'If it turns out bad, I'll plead guilty.'

'You're guilty however it turns out.'

'Doesn't work that way. If it turns out good I get the Legion of Merit.'

'What is this, a joke?'

Reacher said, 'No, it's a gamble. And so far I'm beating the house. The messenger is back in Hamburg. That was ten to one at best. But it just paid out. We should ride the wave and keep on winning. Griezman's OK. He won't blow the safe house. The boys inside are very complacent. They pay no attention. They have a roommate who's making secret phone calls, and composing secret messages for dead drops, and heading out to the park for no reason at all, and they haven't noticed any of that. Why would they notice a car parked a hundred yards away?'

Sinclair waved it off, like he was missing the point. Then she said, 'The fingerprint issue is serious. Legal and political. No one can make that go away.'

'I could say I worded the promise very carefully. I said I would run the print. That was all. I didn't say I would share the result. A deception for sure, but hey, welcome to the major leagues. I could say for people like me it's always the same gamble. Eggs get broken, the omelette gets made, and if it turns out tasty, then all is forgiven.'

'And if it doesn't?'

'I'm always open to new experiences.'

No reply from Sinclair.

Reacher said, 'If this turns out bad, you're going to turn me in. You're going to give evidence at the court martial. I understand that. And you'll give it willingly. I understand that too. You command us, but you don't approve of us. I've played this game before. No hard feelings.'

'What if it turns out good?'

'Then you won't turn me in and there won't be a trial. You'll get a glowing letter in your file, and I'll get another medal.'

'Which will it be?'

'Honest answer?'

'Always.'

'It's in the bag. It's a done deal. This is an AWOL soldier. He and I are in the same city. It's money in the bank.'

'Are you always this confident?'

'I used to be.'

'What are you now?'

'Even more.'

'Are you sleeping with your sergeant?'

'No, I am not. That would be inappropriate. And generally frowned upon too. Not least by her.'

'She's crazy about you.'

'We get along, as friends and colleagues.'

Sinclair said nothing in reply.

There was a knock at the door. Neagley herself, Reacher figured, right on cue, checking if Sinclair had killed him yet. Or Bishop, checking if he had killed Sinclair. He opened up, standing to one side, out of the line of fire.

Long training.

Neither Neagley nor Bishop.

It was a young American man in a department-store suit and a Brooks Brothers tie. He was carrying a rubber pouch with a zip. It looked to have half an inch of paper in it. That kind of size. That kind of stiffness.

The guy said, 'For Dr Sinclair. From the consulate. The document she requested.'

Seriously fast.

You bet your ass.

Reacher took the pouch and handed it to Sinclair. The guy in the suit went back down the stairs. Reacher and Sinclair went back to her room, where the others were waiting.

Sinclair unzipped the pouch and Reacher smelled copier paper still hot from the printer. There had been a flurry of phone calls, he guessed, and then a high-speed digital transmission incoming from somewhere, either Personnel Command back home, or Stuttgart maybe, directly into the Hamburg consulate, where a high-speed machine had done fast work, and where the young attaché in the Brooks Brothers tie had caught the tumbling pages and butted them together and zipped them up and grabbed a cab. The National Security Council. Even faster than the army press room.

The pages were crisp clear monochrome copies of a standard-issue army personnel file, for Private First Class Horace-none-Wiley, who was thirty-five years old, and from Sugar Land, Texas. He was coming to the end of his first three-year hitch. He had been a thirty-two-year-old recruit. He was five feet eight inches tall, and lightly built. Like a long-distance runner.

The second page had his photograph. It was clipped to the top right corner. Not a passport thumbnail like the old days, but a bigger print. Maybe three inches by two. The Xerox process had bleached out the highlights, like liquid neon, and made the shadows sooty. The image of the paperclip itself looked photographic, but also radioactive.

It was the same guy.

The Xerox imperfections gave the picture a hand-made quality, like a sketch done in charcoal. Like the sketch done in pencil. The same sketch. The same guy. No question. Zero doubt. The brow, the cheekbones, the deep-set eyes. The nose, like a blade. The crease in the cheek, exactly parallel. The set jaw, like he was clamping his teeth. The mouth, like a thin wound, completely expressionless.

Only the hair was different. The photograph was three years old. Horace-none-Wiley had signed on with a regular country-boy buzz cut. A slam dunk, where Army Regulation 670-3-2 was concerned. The extreme, the eccentric, and the faddish had all come later.

'We'll show the photograph to Mr Klopp,' Sinclair said. 'But there's really no doubt about it. Congratulations, major. And sergeant. Outstanding work. You started with two hundred thousand.'

Reacher said, 'Only because someone made a dumb note about a dumb phone call, which survived about seven different levels of bureaucracy before winding up with the United States government itself. We're always trying to cut down on paperwork. Maybe we should rethink that.'

'What now?'

'Now we wait. For a Saudi kid in a pink shirt and pointed shoes to come on out and take a walk.'

TWENTY

Sugar Land was what Wiley intended to call his new ranch. Or Sugarland, all one word. Not that he would grow sugar. It was cattle country. He was going to have the largest herd in the world. And the best. But first he would need a name across the top of his gate. Fancy wrought iron. Maybe leave it in red primer. Sugar Land would look good. All in capital letters. Or all one word, Sugarland. And it would be a kind of personal tribute. To an old ambition. Once upon a time he had tried to make it in Sugar Land. But it was a tough old town. Now he was buying a place forty times bigger than the entire incorporated municipality.

All good.

It was like falling. At first he had fought it, and then he had gone with it. And then he had fallen even faster. Everything had speeded up around him. Which was why he was ready way too early. Ready for the meeting. He felt he had to be prepared. Especially now. The endgame would happen quickly. It always did.

In Sinclair's presence Reacher called Griezman from

the room phone, on the speaker, and he gave him Wiley's name, to go with the face, and he told him as far as they knew the messenger had already arrived, and then he reconfirmed all the various protocols, about how to call it in if something happened, and above all about being cautious around the apartment. But not so cautious he would miss something. A tough job. But Griezman sounded on top of it. He agreed to all the points. His language was convincing. Reacher saw Sinclair relax a little. Then she looked at him, right in the eye, a level gaze. He wasn't sure why. Either half approving, because the crazy plan might be working after all, or half disapproving, because now he had made her complicit.

Then Bishop went back to the consulate, and Reacher and Neagley left Sinclair in her room and stopped in at his, to read Wiley's file front to back. Their first question was why the guy had waited until the age of thirty-two to join the army. Abnormal behaviour, right there. But there was no note from the recruiter. Nothing to explain it. Neagley called Waterman's guy Landry, back in McLean, and suggested he get the background check started right away. Thirty-two years of it, from the day the guy was born to the day he put on the green suit. There had to be a reason.

An old man or not, Wiley's early progress looked conventional. He completed basic training without complications, which indicated he had a certain amount of aptitude and fitness. He was promoted Private First Class, which indicated he had a pulse and was still in the army. He was sent to Fort Sill, to the artillery school, for assessment. He was then trained and deployed in Germany with an air defence company.

'I can picture it,' Neagley said.

Reacher nodded, because he could, too. The bland notations in the file were more than just marks on paper. They were like a box score in baseball. A person could make a whole big story out of it. This happened, and then that. The artillery school was the pivot. Not for dummies. Wiley was clearly an acceptable soldier. Probably up there near the top of his class after basic. Not elite school material. But maybe his CO had seen an aptitude. Or invented one. Some COs counselled people based on old wives' tales. As in, left-handed people couldn't be snipers. People who were small and wiry should be artillerymen. And so on. But either way it had worked. Wiley had fit right in. Not easy. The Chaparral was a weird machine. It had to stop driving and be more or less rebuilt before it could fire. Then packed up and driven on and stopped and rebuilt all over again. The crews were like the pit stop crews from a Nascar automobile race. As complicated as a ballet, timed to a tenth of a second. An incoming airplane could get real close in a tenth of a second. It was team work at its finest. Almost gymnastic. And Wiley had earned his place. Maybe small and wiry helped for real. The guy was a competent soldier. No question. But dead-ended. Three years later he was still a private. The armoured divisions were no longer hiring. The front line was a thing of the past.

Had that been a surprise to him?

Reacher said, 'Did the MPs on the original AWOL

out there talk to his buddies from four months ago?'

Neagley nodded and said, 'I already requested the transcripts.'

'What is he selling?'

Neagley didn't answer.

Instead she said, 'How mad was Sinclair?'

'Less mad than she could have been,' Reacher said. 'I blew the safe house.'

'How? Griezman won't let you down.'

'That's what I told her. But she wasn't convinced. Then I understood. The safe house was blown as soon as Griezman heard about it. Simple as that. It was no longer our secret. That's what she meant. And I can see her point. Sooner or later Griezman will pass it on to his intelligence service. That's his MO, and he's obliged to anyway. So then the Germans will want a finger in the pie. It's their turf. Which is too many cooks. Pretty soon the surveillance vehicles will be double-parked on the kerb outside. My fault.'

'Unless we get the guy.'

'I told her that too. But it doesn't solve her problem. Win or lose, the Krauts will always know about that safe house.'

'We would have told them anyway. Sooner or later. Next year, or the year after. This shit will go international. Believe me. We're all going to be cooperating our asses off. You got in early, that's all.'

'She said the fingerprint thing is worse. It's a federal crime.'

'Same thing. If we get the guy.'

'Or if I double-cross Griezman. If I steal his labour and give him nothing in return.'

'Did she ask you to do that?'

'I suggested it myself. I told him I would run the print. That was all. Why did I choose those particular words?'

'Subconscious wiggle room.'

'Doesn't feel good.'

'Would going to prison feel better?'

'He's a homicide cop with a fingerprint. What am I supposed to do?'

'What did you think you were doing?'

'I guess I was figuring I would tell him if it's negative, and if it's positive, maybe I would stall. I figured I could deal with it direct. That way everyone's a winner, and I don't break the law. Which I'm happy about, because I like that law. I like to control whether or not our people go on trial in foreign legal systems. So I made two separate errors of judgement.'

'Why?'

'The price,' Reacher said. 'A hundred million dollars. I keep seeing it in my mind. It's a lot of money. It's front-burner money for sure. But I'm letting it get out of proportion. It's all I can think about.'

'Evidently.'

'What does that mean?'

'Why do you think Sinclair was less mad at you than she could have been?'

'Maybe she secretly agrees with me.'

'No,' Neagley said. 'She likes you.'

'What is this, high school?'

'More or less.'

'OK,' Reacher said.

'Trust me,' Neagley said. 'She was there, and you were here. Now she's here too. Not rocket science. Slim is better than none, whatever the target. She's lonely. She lives in a big empty house on a suburban street.'

'You know that?'

'I'm guessing.'

'I don't think she likes me at all,' Reacher said.

'Do you like her?'

'What are you, my mom?'

'You should have listened to her more.'

'Who?'

'Your mom. She was French. Those ladies have got it going on.'

'What exactly are we talking about here?'

But Neagley didn't answer that, because the room phone rang. Griezman. Reacher put him on speaker. Griezman said his people were in position, and that surveillance could be considered officially active as of that moment. The apartment house lobby fed six separate units, one to the left and one to the right of the walk-up stairwell, on each of the second, third and fourth floors. Records showed a Turkish family and an Italian family also in residence, both diplomatic households, plus three German families, all of them prosperous and solidly middle class. There was a service entrance in the back of the building, and it was covered by a supplementary car, just in case, but it probably wouldn't be used as a pedestrian exit. Not the local custom, as the sleepers would surely know. Presumably

211

they made conscious efforts to fit in, and not stand out.

'Thank you,' Reacher said. 'Good hunting.'

Griezman asked, 'How long do you expect to need us?'

'Forty-eight hours or less.'

'Any news on the fingerprint?'

Reacher paused a beat.

He said, 'Not yet.'

Griezman said, 'Why does it take so long?'

'We'll get it soon.'

'I know,' Griezman said. 'I trust you.'

TWENTY-ONE

In the Educational Solutions building in McLean, Virginia, it was six hours earlier, still morning, and Waterman and Landry were working together on the background check. They had Wiley's service number, which in the modern way was the same as his Social Security number. Which unlocked a lot of database doors. First up and most obvious were four felony arrests in the 1980s, in Sugar Land, Texas, south and west of Houston. Clearly none of the arrests had led to a conviction. A guy who had gone down the first time wouldn't have been around to collect the next three. But, no smoke without fire. Landry dug into the details. All four arrests had been for selling stolen property. Allegedly. All four cases had failed for lack of evidence. The prosecutors had declined to prosecute. The witnesses had been vague. Possibly for real. There was no proof of threats or tampering. Wiley was a lucky man. Or subtle. After his last arrest there was nothing in his criminal record for five straight years. Then he joined the army.

'We should tell Sinclair,' Landry said. 'We have

confirmation. This guy steals stuff and sells it. That's his MO.'

Waterman said, 'Except that Reacher claims they have nothing there worth a hundred million dollars.'

'They must have.'

'Not stealable by a single guy. Not portable. Not operable by people who live in caves.'

'Intelligence, then.'

'Accessible to a private soldier?'

'So he's in the army because he's a patriot?'

'Maybe a judge advised him to get out of town and serve his country. As an alternative.'

'To what?'

'A fifth go-round with the prosecutors. Maybe Wiley figured he couldn't stay lucky for ever.'

Landry said, 'There's nothing in the arrest record three years ago.'

'There wouldn't be. It would have been a quiet word in the ear. It happened that way all the time.'

'This is the 1990s.'

'Maybe not in Sugar Land.'

'The guy met with the Saudi. Now he's meeting with him again. Has to be a reason.'

Neagley left, and Reacher stayed in his room alone, because that was where Griezman would call first. No doubt about that. Purely as a courtesy. Just simple detectives, hoping for favours, one to the other. Sinclair would be called second. But the phone didn't ring. Reacher's neck itched, like it did after every haircut. He took off his new T-shirt and shook it out. Then he stripped completely and took another shower, with the door open, and one ear or the other out of the water stream. The phone didn't ring. He towelled off and dressed again and looked out the window. Then he sat down in a green velvet chair. The phone didn't ring.

There was a knock at the door.

Sinclair.

Taller than the average, but no wider.

The dress, the pearls, the nylons, the shoes.

The face and the hair.

'I assume this is the best place to wait,' she said. 'I assume Griezman will call you first.'

Not dumb, either.

'I should apologize,' Reacher said. 'I made two errors of judgement. No disrespect was intended.'

She said, 'May I come in?'

'Of course.'

He stepped aside, and she walked in past him. He smelled her perfume. She looked at the phone, and then she sat down in the same chair he had been using.

She said, 'I didn't take offence. We drafted you to get things done. There's no buyer's remorse. Ultimately it's you I'm worried about.'

'Why me?'

'You were right. We ask you to do things, and if they turn out well we all claim the credit, but if they turn out badly you're on your own. That must be stressful. Like the thing you just did in Bosnia. That can't have been pleasant.'

'Actually it was,' Reacher said.

'Technically it was a double homicide.'

'The first guy was the commander of some ragtag ethnic army. The second guy was his second in command. To set an example they arrested a famous soccer player from the other community. The star of the local franchise. They handcuffed him to a radiator and broke both his legs with a sledgehammer. They paid particular attention to his knees and ankles. They left him there for an hour to contemplate his future. Then they had a couple of mattresses hauled into the room. Then they had the guy's wife and daughter hauled into the room. They had the whole battalion line up at the door. They raped them to death, right in front of the guy's eyes. He kept hitting his head on the radiator. He was trying to kill himself. He didn't succeed. His wife lasted nearly twenty-four hours. His daughter was dead in six. She bled out. She was eight years old. I spent two weeks confirming the facts. I saw the mattresses. So all in all I felt pretty good about pulling the trigger. Like a guy taking the trash to the kerb. Maybe not fun in and of itself, but afterwards you have a clean and tidy garage. Which feels good. That's for sure.'

'I'm sorry.'

'For what?'

'That there are such things in the world.'

'Get used to it,' Reacher said. 'Things can only get worse.'

'I got a message from Waterman. Wiley was busted four times for selling stolen goods. Nothing stuck. But you know how that goes.'

'Outstanding,' Reacher said. 'Now he's in the army.'

'Where all kinds of things are streaming back to

storage depots, because the front line suddenly disappeared. Where as a result security isn't what it was. Maybe old habits die hard.'

'But what? What is he stealing and what is he selling?'

Sinclair didn't answer.

The phone didn't ring.

There was a knock at the door.

A bellboy.

Or a bell girl, to be precise. With a trim uniform and a little hat. From the lobby, with a package. A plain white envelope. Large. Unmarked. It looked to have half an inch of paper in it. That kind of size. That kind of stiffness.

The girl said, 'For you, sir.'

Reacher said, 'Who from?'

'The gentleman wouldn't give his name.'

'What did he look like?'

'I didn't see well. A normal American, I think. Quite ordinary.'

One of Orozco's guys, Reacher thought. Not Orozco himself. Too distinctive. His sergeant, maybe. The guy who was driving the car, the first time out.

Deniability.

He took the package and said, 'Thank you.'

The girl headed back down the stairs. Reacher unflapped the envelope and looked inside. Sinclair stood at his elbow. He could smell her perfume. He riffed the top of the papers with his thumb. He saw every first line. They were all familiar. It was a duplicate copy of Wiley's file. The same in every respect, except this time the

217

photocopier had been short on toner. The print was pale.

Horace-none-Wiley, fading away.

Sinclair said, 'Who sent it?'

'Orozco,' Reacher said. 'No one else knows I'm here.'

'Why would he send you a second copy?'

'Did you order yours through the Joint Chiefs?'

'Yes.'

'Maybe somehow Orozco heard about it. Maybe he thought it was a big deal. A high-level panic over a private first class might attract his attention. You had it sent to Hamburg. Maybe he's giving me an early warning. Or a head start. Knowing I'm in Hamburg myself. Not knowing I've already seen the file.'

'The Joint Chiefs wouldn't leak.'

'Then maybe Stuttgart did. Or Personnel Command. Orozco has friends everywhere. He's a very popular guy. He has a sunny disposition.'

He dropped the envelope on the bed. Sinclair was still at his elbow. Very close to him. He could smell her perfume. The dress, the pearls, the shoes. The face and the hair.

The phone didn't ring.

She said, 'Waiting makes me nervous.'

He said nothing.

'I can't relax.'

He said nothing.

'Do you get nervous?'

Yes, he thought. *I'm nervous right now.*

'No,' he said. 'Doesn't help anything.'

'You had your hair cut.'

'Where I got the idea about Wiley. The barber had a picture.'

'The barber did a nice job.'

'I hope so. He charged me five bucks.'

'That's cheap.'

'You think?'

'You should try where I go in D.C.'

He said, 'I think yours is more complicated.'

She said nothing.

Just looked at him.

He said, 'May I?'

She didn't answer. He raised his hand and brushed her forehead with his fingertips, and slid his fingers into her hair, and ran them through, the texture alternately thick and soft as the waves came and went. He swept it all back and left part of it hooked behind her ear, and part of it hanging free.

It looked good.

He took his hand away.

He said, 'That's how you comb it, right?'

She said, 'Now do the other side.'

He used his other hand, the same way, barely touching her forehead, burying his fingers deep, pushing them through. This time he left his hand where it ended up, which was cupped on the back of her neck. Which was slender. And warm. She put her own hand flat on his chest. At first he thought it was a warning. Or a prohibition. A stop sign. Then it became an exploration. She moved it around, side to side, up and down, and then she slid it in behind his own neck, where the cut hair had itched. She pulled down and he pulled up and they kissed, at first tentatively, and then harder. Her tongue was cool and slow. Her eyes were open. He found the zipper tab on the back of her dress. A tiny metal teardrop. He eased it down, between her shoulder blades, past the small of her back, below her waist.

Her lips moved against his and she said, 'Is this a good idea?'

'Feels pretty good to me,' he said. 'So far.'

'Are you sure?'

'My rule of thumb is those kind of questions are best answered afterwards. Experience beats conjecture every time.'

She smiled and shrugged forward and the dress slid off her shoulders and puddled at her feet. She was wearing a black lace bra and black pantyhose. And her shoes. She took the hem of his new T-shirt in her hands and pulled it up over his head, on tiptoe. It fell behind him. She unclipped his belt. He kicked off his shoes. She did the same. She peeled off her pantyhose. Underneath was black lace underwear. Filmy and insubstantial. She pulled his pants down and he stepped out of them. They kissed again, and staggered to the bed like a four-legged creature. She pushed him down, on Orozco's envelope. She climbed on top. He reached behind her and unhooked her bra. She rolled away and lay on her back and peeled her panties off. He did the same, arching one way, curling the other. She climbed back on and rode him like a cowgirl, hips forward, shoulders back, face up, eyes closed. He kept his eyes open. She was a sight to see. She had pale skin, with moles and freckles here and there, and small breasts, and a flat hard waist, and muscles in her bunched and moving thighs. She was still wearing the pearls. They swung and bounced. The hollow of her throat was filmed with sweat. Her arms were behind her, held out and away from her body, her wrists bent, her hands flat and open, her palms close to the bed, hovering, skimming a cushion of air, as if she was balancing. Which she was. She was balancing on a single point, driving all her weight down through it, rocking back and forth, easing side to side, as if chasing the perfect sensation, and finding it, and losing it, and finding it again, and holding on to it, all the way to the breathless end. Which was where he was headed, too. That was for damn sure. No stopping now. He pushed back hard, lifting his hips, floating her up, her feet off the bed, her knees clamping, thrust and counterthrust all in one place.

Afterwards he stayed on his back and she snuggled alongside him. He traced patterns on her hip with his fingertip. She said, 'So now answer the questions.'

He said, 'Yes, I think it was a good idea, and yes, I'm sure.'

'No command and control issues?'

'I thought my control was pretty good.'

'I mean, I shouldn't have. You're my subordinate, technically.'

'Your underling, in fact.'

'I suppose.'

'And thankful for it.'

He traced a pattern on her hip.

With his fingertip.

She said, 'Tell me about Sergeant Neagley.'

He said, 'What about her?'

'Why isn't she an officer? She has more than enough ability.'

'She doesn't want to be an officer.'

'And she's crazy about you, but she won't sleep with you.'

'That's what friends are for.'

'Is she OK?'

'She has haptephobia.'

'Which is what?'

'A fear of being touched. The army made her see a doctor.'

'What happened to her? Was she assaulted?'

'She says not. She says she was born like it.'

'Shame,' Sinclair said, and snuggled closer.

'You bet,' Reacher said.

He traced a pattern on her hip.

With his fingertip.

Then he said, 'Wait a damn minute.'

He scrabbled under her for Orozco's envelope. This time he pulled the copied file all the way out. Taped to the front was a smaller envelope. Griezman's envelope. With the fingerprint in it. From the lever in the dead hooker's car.

Sinclair said, 'I don't believe in coincidence.'

Reacher looked at the envelope and scanned through the file. No notes, no handwriting. Nothing from Orozco. Just the tape. Firmly affixed. A message.

Definitive, but deniable.

'Sometimes we have to believe in coincidence,'

Reacher said. 'Especially a small one. The populations are not large. Guys willing to betray their country for money, guys willing to use a prostitute, guys willing to kill a prostitute. Like a Venn diagram. Not many people where the circles meet. I guess he was celebrating. The deal was halfway done. He had financial prospects. But something got out of hand. Which has a huge silver lining. In a way. For us, right now. Tonight, and tomorrow. It's a regular homicide now. Griezman can come out in the open. He can use federal resources. He can give that drawing to every cop in town.'

Sinclair was quiet for a beat, and then she shook her head and said, 'No, we can never admit we ran that print at his request. And it would only confuse the issue. One thing at a time. We want him for the hundred million dollars. That comes first. That's more important.'

'The hooker might not agree.'

'We can't hang him twice. And we can't have him arrested by the Germans. Because he's ours. But justice will be done. This time it's an order.'

'Yes, ma'am,' Reacher said.

He put the file back in the envelope, and timed it out in his head. Five streets away, in the woman's apartment. Wiley had been there while Reacher was eating dinner with Neagley in McLean, Virginia. *Of all the diners in all the towns.* He lay back down, on his side, and he rolled Sinclair over, on her front, and he put his hand high on the back of her thigh.

She said, 'Already?'

He said, 'I'm younger than you.'

The phone rang.

Griezman, checking in. Reacher put him on the speaker. Griezman asked about the fingerprint. Reacher said there was no news yet. Sinclair looked away. Griezman said there was nothing to report from the surveillance operations. So far there had been no sign of Wiley at the bar. So far at the safe house a mail carrier had brought a package, which had then sat unclaimed on a table in the lobby, and was still there. Apart from that no one else had gone in or come out, except for what was probably a daughter from either the Turkish or the Italian diplomatic families, probably going out for the evening. To a dance club, possibly. She was in her early twenties, with jet black hair and olive skin. Very good-looking, Griezman said, according to contemporaneous reports from his men. The sight had brightened their day. Because absolutely nothing else was going on. But they were nevertheless still committed. They would hold their positions for the time being. They would have to thin out by evening, when street parking would be harder to find, after everyone in the neighbourhood was home from work.

Sinclair said, 'Last time the meeting happened late in the afternoon. Which is right about now.'

'Wait a damn minute,' Reacher said again. 'What about the lamp in the window? Something changed. It is but it isn't. We blew it. It's a messenger but not the same messenger. It's not a man. It's a woman. We fell for it. We're missing the rendezvous. It's happening right now.'

TWENTY-TWO

Reacher told Griezman to get all his units moving immediately, in pursuit of the good-looking girl, but Sinclair told him no, sit tight for the moment. To Reacher she said, 'You're only guessing. She could be Turkish or Italian. Would these people even use a woman?'

'I was in Israel,' Reacher said. 'These people use women all the time.'

'You're gambling.'

'And so far I'm winning. Look at me right now, for instance.'

Sinclair paused a beat.

Then she said to Griezman, 'Keep one car on the safe house. Get all the others moving.'

The new messenger walked south out of the neighbourhood, and then turned west, to loop under the Aussenalster lake, from Saint Georg to Saint Pauli, on her way to her appointment, which was in a club on a street called the Reeperbahn. She had walked the route many times in her imagination, the physical details built up around her by many hours of briefing, the sights and sounds and smells described so many times that reality felt bland and small by comparison. She had been warned that Wiley would choose a rendezvous point he hoped would embarrass a person of the Islamic faith. A male person, to be specific. He wouldn't expect a woman. He had a mean, competitive streak. He would want two out of three from alcohol, girls, and hatred. On this occasion it would be the first and the second, she figured, from what she had been told about the street called the Reeperbahn. Girls and alcohol. But she would handle it. Great struggles required great sacrifices. And she was from the tribal areas. She was sure she had seen worse.

Reacher called Griezman back and asked if the pretty girl had been seen near the bar. The answer was no. Wiley neither. No sign. Reacher said, 'OK, they're meeting somewhere else. Get those cars moving too.'

This time Sinclair just nodded.

Griezman said, 'But those men didn't see the girl.'

'Doesn't matter,' Reacher said. 'They have the drawing of Wiley's face. Where we find one we'll find the other.'

The new messenger turned left into the Reeperbahn and was hit by all the light and all the noise she was expecting. Flashing and blinking and glaring, and thumping and booming and distorting. Not bland and small any more. This time it was more than she had imagined. She took a breath and walked on. She knew the name of the club she was looking for. In a manner of speaking. She knew the shape its letters made. She knew it had a photograph in its window, of a naked woman and a German shepherd. Which was a kind of dog. Inside it would smell of beer. She had been told there would be things she might prefer not to look at.

She heard police sirens, howling and baying in the distance. She slowed down, suddenly uncertain. Many places had the same letters in their names. The same shapes. Mostly at what Westerners would call the end of the word. Like a suffix, repeated over and over. Then suddenly she understood. All such places had steps leading down. To rooms under the ground. Like caves. *Keller*. Part of a word. It meant *underground cave*.

She walked on. She found the place she wanted. It was lit up red. It had a narrow door, with a narrow window alongside it, sandwiched between two other places. A lobby, with a stairhead. The window carried the promised photograph. It was bleached by many daylight hours. It showed a naked woman on her back, with a big dog squatting over her, its hindquarters over her face. She had the dog's penis in her mouth. No big deal. Not to one from the tribal areas. The messenger had seen it done before. Boys on men, mostly, on command, or sometimes goats.

She pushed the door and went inside. There was a sharp chemical smell. Astringent. She had smelled the same thing in the airport bathroom. There was a big man on a stool. Men had to pay him, but women didn't. What they called a cover charge. She had been coached. She smiled at him, shyly, and set off down the stairs. They were narrow. At the bottom was blue light and a roar of noise. Music, talking, the slam of heavy glass pitchers on wooden tables.

She stepped into the basement room. There was a lit stage at the far end. A naked woman was bent double, having sex with a donkey. The donkey was in a kind of hammock, to take its weight off the woman's back. The room was crowded with men, all of them rearing up, and craning their necks. They were shouting and grunting in time with the donkey's bewildered thrusts. She saw Wiley two-thirds of the way back, alone at a table. She had memorized his face. He had a tall glass of golden liquid. It was half gone. Beer, she assumed.

She stood still. Men were looking at her. She had on black pants and her travel shirt, open two buttons. She ignored the looks and threaded her way between the tables. There was a clatter of hooves as the donkey finished and struggled out of its hammock. All around her men clapped and cheered. The naked woman straightened up and waved to them, graciously.

In Reacher's room they heard the phone ringing through the wall, next door in Sinclair's room. Then it stopped and Reacher's own phone rang in turn. It was Bishop, from the consulate. The CIA head of station. He wanted Sinclair. She put him on speaker and he said, 'The Iranian just called it in. About the lamp in the window. The messenger is a woman and as of right now she's out of the house.'

'We're on it already,' Sinclair said.

'But not really,' Reacher said. 'It's a hopeless task. Not going to work. Griezman's guys have got an hour, maximum. Twelve cars in a big city. It's way too random. I suggest we go to plan B immediately.'

'Which is what?' Bishop asked.

'Pull Griezman's guys back to the safe house, and hit the messenger on her way back in. Fast and hard, as soon as they're sure. She might tell us where she went. Wiley might have lingered there. He lingered last time. About thirty minutes, according to Klopp. Maybe he thinks it's a security measure.'

'She won't tell us.'

'We'll ask her nicely.'

'But that way we burn the Iranian.'

'Can you get him out?'

'Tonight?'

'Right now. You must have rehearsed it.'

'I'd have to talk to Mr Ratcliffe at the NSC.'

Sinclair said, 'Damn right you would. All of us would.'

Reacher said, 'We need a decision.'

Sinclair said, 'We won't get one inside thirty minutes. But we still have a car at the house. We'll know when she's back for the night. That gives us hours.'

'That's half a loaf. We don't get Wiley.'

'Not this time. But they must have fixed another meeting. This is a back-and-forth negotiation. She might tell us where and when.'

'Better to hit her now. She thinks her job is done. She's coming down off a high. Her adrenalin is low. She'll be braver in the morning.'

Bishop said, 'I'll call Ratcliffe,' and he hung up, crackly and distant.

The new messenger was touched on the leg by one man and on the bottom by another, but she ignored them both and pushed on through the throng. She wondered if they thought she was an employee of the club. Western behaviours had been explained to her. She could see Wiley up ahead, watching her. A frank and interested stare. Maybe he thought she was an employee too. She walked up to him and leaned close to his ear, so he could hear above the noise, and she said in carefully practised English, 'I bring greetings from your friends in the east. The elevation of Sugar Land Regional Airport is eighty-two feet above sea level.'

Wiley said, 'Well, don't this just beat the band.'

She said, unsure, 'Does it?'

'They sent a girl.'

'Yes, sir, they did.'

'And you speak English.'

'Yes, sir, I do.'

Then suddenly Wiley said, 'Why? Why did they send a girl? Are they saying no?'

'No, sir, that's not the message.'

'Then what is?'

'The message is, we accept your price.'

'Say that again.'

'We accept your price.'

'What, all of it?'

'Sir, what I am permitted to know is, we accept your price.'

Wiley closed his eyes. *Bigger than Rhode Island. Visible from outer space.* His new Swiss friends would be delighted too. It was double what he had told them. He had never expected to get it all. He would have plenty left over. A massive fortune. He would have a portfolio. Guys in suits would call him on the phone.

He opened his eyes.

He said, 'When?'

The messenger said, 'I believe you agreed a delivery date. Your friends in the east expect you to honour it.'

'No problem,' Wiley said. 'As agreed is fine.'

'Then that is the response I will carry back.'

'Tell them it's a pleasure doing business. And tell them thanks for the extra gift. Much appreciated.'

She said, unsure again, 'Sir, I brought nothing with me.'

'You brought yourself,' Wiley said. 'You're the gift. Right? I mean, get with the programme. Why else would they send a girl with the good news? You're the icing on the cake. Like when you get a bottle of Scotch when you buy a car.'

'I don't understand.'

'You like this place?'

On the stage a naked woman was lying on a plastic sheet. Three men were urinating on her face.

The messenger said, 'It seems very popular.'

'We could go to a hotel.'

She had been coached.

She said, 'Sir, this is a business arrangement. It can't proceed any further until I get home safe and sound.'

'OK,' Wiley said. 'I get it. But you got to give me some little thing. We're friends. We're celebrating here. I'm giving you people something you never had before. One more button.'

'What?'

'On your shirt. Right here. Like a token. To seal the deal.'

Great struggles require great sacrifices. And it was a small enough price, she thought. The room was dark. No one was looking. They were all watching the stage. She undid the third button. She parted the seams. Wiley looked and smiled.

He said, 'I knew I could make you do it.'

She walked away, through the crowd, ignoring the grabbing hands, up the stairs, past the doorman on the stool, out to the street, where she walked twenty paces and flagged down a cab. She settled in the back seat and said in carefully practised German, 'The airport, please. International departures.'

TWENTY-THREE

In a different club two miles away two men were having dinner. The club was small, but panelled in oak. The tables were cramped, but the cloths were linen. More wine was served than beer. Lamb chops were on the menu. One of the men was an importer of shoes from Brazil. He was a solid figure, about forty-five years old. His hair was blond, going grey, and his face was red, also going grey. His name was Dremmler. He was in a suit, with a high lapel.

The other man was similar in appearance. Mid-forties, bulky, a little redder, a little less grey. He was also in a suit, a chain store label, but not cheap. His name was Muller. He was a policeman.

Dremmler said, 'One of our members is a man named Helmut Klopp. He saw an Arab talking to an American and reported it. Guess what happened?'

Muller said, 'Nothing, probably.'

'Two secret investigators came here from America. In a big hurry. Your chief of detectives was kissing their ass.'

'Griezman?'

233

'So evidently what Klopp saw was a very important meeting. They questioned him for hours. He says they showed him two hundred photographs, but he recognized none of them. So they made a sketch, from the description he gave them.'

'That's a lot of work.'

'Exactly,' Dremmler said. 'Therefore something is going on. Of great importance to the Americans. One of their own is talking to an Arab. We'd like to know what about. Is one buying and the other selling? We need you to see if Griezman wrote anything down.'

'Why?' Muller said. 'Why help either Griezman or the Americans?'

'We'll be helping ourselves,' Dremmler said. 'Don't you see? We could get in the middle of this. There will be money going one way and something else going the other. Either of which we could use. Or both. And we could use them better than they could. Even part of it could help us make a statement. They've got their cause, and we've got ours. May the best man win.'

'We're planning a hijack?'

'We should at least consider it.'

'OK,' Muller said. 'I'll see what I can find.'

A waiter in a short jacket took their plates away.

Dremmler said, 'One more thing.'

'Yes?' Muller said.

'We have four youth members who were beaten up outside a bar. They were quite badly hurt. They say their attacker was a very big man. An American, holding to a pro-occupation position. He was with a dark-haired woman.'

'And?'

'According to Helmut Klopp, those were the secret investigators from America. The descriptions match exactly.'

'OK.'

'I can't let such a thing go unpunished. Klopp says the man's name is Reacher and the woman's name is Neagley. I would like to find them. I'm sure your chief of detectives knows where they're staying. I need you to see if he wrote it down.'

'OK,' Muller said again. 'I'll see what I can find.'

At ten o'clock in the evening Hamburg time Ratcliffe approved plan B. At eleven o'clock Reacher gave up on it. The messenger had not come home. She was never planning to. That was clear by then. Griezman said she could have taken any one of twenty or more international flights in the last few hours. Or flown domestic to Berlin, where the whole world was a hop and a skip away. Or driven to Amsterdam. Or taken a train to Paris. Or gone to another safe house in the city, which was a separate nightmare all by itself.

Reacher and Sinclair were in Sinclair's room, all showered and dressed long ago. Neagley was back. They had brought her up to speed with the whole sorry mess. The missed cues, the wrong assumptions, the late connections. Which led inevitably to a debate about next steps. Which led inevitably to a debate about the fingerprint. Sinclair said, 'Wiley has Sixth Amendment rights to a speedy trial for the homicide. Which he wouldn't get, because we would tie him up for years about the other thing. And we can't let the Germans have him first, because we might never get him back again.'

Neagley said, 'We could negotiate that ahead of time.'

'We can't be in a position where we have to ask the Germans for permission to run our own national security the way we want to.'

'We'd be giving up all kinds of capabilities.'

Sinclair said, 'Reacher?'

He said, 'I think it's fifty-fifty. A physical search of the city would be a waste of time. Even if they could eyeball a thousand faces a day, it would take nearly five years to cover the whole population. But their records could be useful. Wiley came to town not more than four months ago. We know that for sure. So we have a hard start date. Obviously he rented a place, because he killed the hooker in her apartment, not a hotel room. So he has a lease somewhere. And then a new name, probably German, to go with his new passport, probably also German. He has utility bills. Probably a telephone. We have no access to those databases. That's where Griezman could help us.'

'Yes or no?'

'I'm biased,' Reacher said. 'I owe the guy.'

'He did nothing for you. He didn't find Wiley, and he didn't find the messenger.'

'He tried.'

'What did you think of Mr Bishop, from the consulate?'

'The head of station?'

'The CIA veteran.'

'He's not bad for an old guy.'

'Obviously our older German-speakers were trained under the previous system. For duty in East Germany, not the civilized west. They like to know everything about everybody. For recruitment, back then, and for blackmail, and for a better understanding of the local inside stories. They have extensive files. Not all of them in the official cabinets.'

'And?'

'Chief of Detectives Griezman was the dead hooker's client about a year ago. Four times. We know this for sure. He spent his kids' college fund. Therefore my guess is he wants to close the case so no one goes poking and prying too far back. My guess is his noble quest for justice is not so noble after all.'

Reacher paused a beat.

'OK,' he said.

'So yes or no?'

'Wiley still walks on the homicide.'

'We can't hang him twice.'

Reacher paused again.

Then he said, 'Griezman was stupid.'

'Overcome by lust,' Sinclair said. 'It happens.'

'He was stupid because of what you're going to realize about five seconds from now. Only because you're a nicer person than me.'

Sinclair didn't answer.

Then she said, 'Oh.'

Reacher nodded. 'We can sidestep the fingerprint issue completely. We don't need to trade. We can get everything we want by blackmailing the guy.'

'I hope so,' Sinclair said.

'Except I don't want to do that. So not yet, OK? Wiley is an AWOL soldier in the same city as me. It's money in the bank.'

'How much time would Griezman save you?'

'He's a last resort either way around. I don't want to get bogged down in databases. There are other ways. I was trained under the previous system too. So Griezman's zipper problem doesn't matter yet. There's nothing he can do for us right now.'

'Are you saying that because you owe him?'

'I'm saying it because it's true.'

'What are the other ways?'

'We get to know the guy. We find him from the inside.'

By then Neagley had the transcripts from the original AWOL file, so she and Reacher left Sinclair in her room and headed down to Neagley's, to read them. The physical chronology was straightforward enough. Wiley had failed to return from a routine ninety-six hour pass. Simple as that. He had never been seen again. He had mentioned nothing in advance to his crewmates about where he was going on the pass. Best guess was Frankfurt, where the hookers were plentiful and inventive, because of the convention business. Did Wiley like hookers? No more than the next guy, was the answer.

Then there were background questions, to build up a picture of the guy. Hobbies, interests, enthusiasms, things he talked about. He was from Texas, and sometimes he talked about beef cattle. He was proud of his home town. Sometimes he got all excited and said things he seemed to regret later. Other times he was quiet. One time he said he had joined the army only because an uncle had told him stories about Davy Crockett. He liked beer better than hard liquor, and he didn't smoke. He was unmarried and had never talked about a partner back home. He was extremely happy where he was. He liked his posting and gave the impression he had aimed for it.

'That's weird,' Neagley said. 'Most AWOLs aren't extremely happy where they are. That's kind of the point.'

Reacher said, 'And who would aim for a Chaparral unit on an abandoned front? The guy is still a private. Always will be. He must have known.'

'Was Davy Crockett even in the army?'

'Not this army. It was the Lawrence County militia, in Tennessee. And then he was at the Alamo, of course. Which was a heroic story, for sure, but dying besieged and hopelessly outnumbered is not exactly the image of glory we want recruits to bring in with them.'

'We should find the uncle. Maybe they're close.'

'You think Wiley is sending him postcards?'

'He might have told him something. Apparently he blurts things out and then regrets them later. Maybe that's why he killed the hooker. I've heard of that happening. Guys boast about what they're doing, because they feel good in the moment.'

'OK,' Reacher said. 'Find the uncle. And check with his commanding officers from three years ago. Basic training, and then Mother Sill. Did he really aim for

Germany? As in, aim specifically, like a target? That would change my thinking. That would make this whole thing feel planned, not purely opportunistic.'

'Three years is a very long game.'

'Worth it for a hundred million dollars.'

'We don't have anything worth a hundred million dollars.'

'Make the calls,' Reacher said. 'I'll be back later.'

'Where are you going?'

'For a walk.'

'I noticed Dr Sinclair seemed more relaxed tonight.'

'Did she?'

'She had a definite glow.'

'Maybe she does yoga.'

'Or deep breathing.'

Reacher said nothing.

The man named Muller stopped in at the central police station. It was where he worked. He was second in command in the traffic division. Not ideal for access to Griezman's office, but the place was quiet at night. Griezman's floor had spacious suites with secretarial stations outside. They were all deserted. All the bosses were basically paper-shufflers. They wrote things up and their secretaries did the filing, once at lunchtime, and then again first thing the next morning.

Griezman's secretary's in-box was piled high.

Muller was not a brave man, but he was a loyal comrade-in-arms. He made a deal with himself. He would read through the in-tray, but he wouldn't search Griezman's desk. A sensible compromise. He felt all reasonable people in the movement would agree with him. Information was important, but so was keeping a guy in a job at the highest level. Or close to it.

He clamped the pile of papers between his palms and carried them away, down the hallway, to the fire door, and down the fire stairs, to his own floor, and his own hallway, and his own office.

Neagley called Landry in McLean, Virginia, and asked him about Wiley's family. His uncles, specifically. Possibly one in particular, who maybe lived close by, and had an influence on the kid growing up.

Landry said, 'Wiley has no uncles.'

'You sure?'

'Both parents were only children.'

'Great-uncles?'

'I'll take a look.'

'What was the state of the parents' marriage?'

'The father took off early and was never seen again. The mother raised Wiley as a single parent. No brothers or sisters. Just the two of them.'

'Did the mother get a boyfriend later? He might have been called an uncle in front of the kid.'

'Could have been one after another. Could have been a lot of uncles.'

'Can you check?'

'We'd have to find the mother and get some agents to pay a call. That kind of thing has to be done face to face. It takes time. Old boyfriends aren't in the databases. And some aren't happy memories.'

'It might be worth it. If the great-uncles don't pan out.'

'Could take days. You nearly had the guy.'

'He's still in the city.'

Neagley killed the call and checked the AWOL file for the crewmate who had mentioned the uncle. She dialled the Frankfurt MPs and told them to bring the guy in for further and better particulars. Then she checked Wiley's personnel file for the commanders who had written his initial fitness reports. Fort Benning, and then Fort Sill. She called a friend in Personnel Command. The Benning guy had moved on to Bragg. The Sill guy was still in Oklahoma, three years later. She got the numbers and started dialling.

Muller scanned one scrap of paper after another. Griezman's output was prodigious. Most of it was normal ass-covering bullshit. Trivia from below to be shovelled up above. Standard practice. Everyone did it. No one ever wanted the buck to stop with him. No one ever wanted to be at an official inquiry, saying, 'Yes, it was me who judged it not worth passing on. So it's all my fault.'

There were routine reports from every kind of case. None of them meant anything. Until five stapled pages about Helmut Klopp. An interrogation. Photographs. Issues with the translator. No knowledge of what had been said in the bar. Actual conversation had not been overheard. The American investigators were named as Reacher and Neagley. But that was all. Nothing about where they were staying. Muller thought the consulate, maybe. Or maybe not. They were U.S. Army, not CIA. A hotel? Nothing was mentioned.

He ploughed on. Safe enough, as long as he kept his

light low and his door shut. An unexpected visitor could be counted on to knock. Or at least call out. Not that there would be an unexpected visitor. It was late, and the building was quiet. Eventually he came to an interim report about a surveillance operation. Recent. That evening, in fact. He had dumped the pile upside down. He was reading it in chronological order. The surveillance had been fruitless. The negative result had been communicated to Reacher in his hotel room. Which meant the Hamburg police had run an operation for the American military.

Interesting.

Reacher's hotel was not named, but the switchboard number Griezman had called was recorded. The traffic division had access to a standard reverse phone directory, so Muller started his computer and looked up the number.

And got the hotel's name.

He knew the place very well. A bijou establishment on a side street, in a good but not-quite-best neighbourhood. Sometimes the manager called to complain about people parking right in front. Because that ruined the image. They had a guy with a top hat. Where was he supposed to stand? Muller himself had been out there twice. Nothing he could do. Not without two years of due process to get the kerb changed. Which the city's lawyers would never allow. Suppose all the small hotels wanted the same treatment? Chaos. It was already bad enough with the big brands.

Muller picked up his desk phone and dialled Dremmler at home.

TWENTY-FOUR

Reacher stepped around the guy with the top hat and set out walking. It was midnight local time. The streets were lit by lamps on poles, and by the soft light of storefronts dimmed to a night-time glow, and by the blue flicker of late shows on television sets behind undraped apartment windows. He walked a figure of eight around two random blocks and saw no one behind him. Or ahead of him. Or in the shadows. Just a routine precaution. A habit. He was thirty-five years old and still alive. Had to mean something.

He found the street with the bar in it. Where Klopp had seen Wiley the first time. Where Billy Bob and Jimmy Lee had sold their scrap Berettas. Where German ID was for sale. He stopped forty yards short and eyeballed the place from an angle. The ground floor of the stone building, the centre door, the planked wood façade, varnished and shiny. The small windows, with their lace curtains, and their paper flags. The lights were on inside. By night they looked warm and welcoming.

Reacher crossed the street and went in through the door. Inside it was smoky and loud. It was late, but there were maybe sixty people still in there, mostly men, in tight private groups of three or four. Some were at tables, and some were standing, cramped and back to back with other huddles. There were upholstered benches under the windows. All were full, like seats on a rush-hour subway. Reacher eased through the crowd, gently but firmly, like a police horse at a riot. Most folks got out of his way fast enough. They looked like business people, or clerical workers. Some of them senior, some of them doing well. Reacher didn't see Wiley. He didn't expect to. He was a lucky man, but not that lucky. He sensed people looking at him from behind. Delayed reaction. *Weren't we warned about a man like that?*

He made it to the bar after a roundabout route, and he wedged himself in, and waited to be served. Both bartenders were men. Both had heavy canvas aprons tied around their waists. One glanced his way. Reacher asked for a cup of black coffee. The guy set an espresso machine going, and ducked back for his money. Reacher asked him no questions. Life wasn't like the television shows. Bartenders never spilled the beans. Why would they? Who came first, the sixty people they had to live with every night of their lives, or the lone guy they had never seen before?

Instead he carried his coffee into the crowd and sat down in the spare seat where three guys were at a four-top table. They looked at him like he had committed an embarrassing faux pas, and then they looked away, and a lot of coughing and false starts indicated they were changing the subject. And commenting. Reacher heard the word *Arschloch*, which he knew from many

245

in-country arguments meant *asshole*. But he didn't react. Instead he drained his cup and headed for the pay phone on the opposite wall. He got a coin ready and dialled Orozco.

Orozco said, 'Are we in trouble?'

Reacher said, 'No, we're good. If I get the guy.'

'I thought you almost had him.'

'I screwed up. I didn't expect a woman messenger. Live and learn.'

'So what now?'

'Did Billy Bob and Jimmy Lee tell you who sold them the ID?'

'They won't. They're scared. This is some kind of big mobbed-up thing. But not Italian. Nostalgic Germans instead. They have members and chapters and rules and all kinds of things. Billy Bob and Jimmy Lee are more afraid of them than me.'

'And the bar is where these guys meet?'

'It's their unofficial HQ.'

'And what are they exactly?'

'The biggest far-right faction. So far all talk, but that can't last for ever.'

'OK, tell Billy Bob and Jimmy Lee we don't care who they bought their ID from. Tell them we won't ask again, in exchange for an answer to one simple question. They gave the impression they picked out their new names themselves. One of them said because he liked the sound of it. Ask them if that's true. Could they really get any name they wanted?'

'OK,' Orozco said. 'I'll ask them. Anything else?'

'Not right now.'

'Are we in trouble?'

'Don't worry. We're golden.'

'If you get the guy.'

'How hard can it be?'

Reacher hung up the phone and turned to face the room. By that point lots of people were looking at him. Word had gotten around. There was a huddle at the street door, and another at the back door. Both sets of guys were watching him. Waiting for him. Which meant the fight would be outside. He would leave, and they would follow. If there was a fight. Which was not certain. These were mostly above average people. Above average age, above average weight. Heart attacks just waiting to happen. Discretion would be the better part of valour for most of them. The exceptions were of no real concern. They were younger and a little fitter, but they were desk workers. Nothing to worry about. Reacher was a good street fighter. Mostly because he enjoyed it.

He pushed off the wall and parted the crowd, chest out, as straight and slow as a funeral march. No one blocked him. He made it to the street door. In front of it was a tight knot of six men. In their thirties, probably, and none of them slender. But desk workers. Their suits were shiny on the ass and the elbow. He could read their body language. They were set to let him pass, and then they would about-turn fast and spill out behind him, on the damp and shiny cobblestones.

Reacher said, 'You speak English?'

One guy said, 'Yes.'

'You ever wonder why? Why you speak my language and I don't speak yours?'

'What?'

'Never mind. What are your orders?'

'Orders?'

'If I wanted a parrot I'd go to a pet store. Someone just told you to do something. Tell me what it was.'

'No.'

'Then I'll have to evaluate a large number of theoretical possibilities. One of which is you want a rumble on the sidewalk. Maybe that's not true at all. Maybe I've misjudged you terribly. But I'll have to err on the side of caution. You see that, right? It's my only sensible course of action. So don't follow me out the door. Maybe all you want is a breath of air. But erring on the side of caution means I'll have to interpret it as a hostile act. Current NATO doctrine requires an immediate reaction with overwhelming force. I know you have a welfare state, but a hospital is still a hospital, no matter who pays for it. No fun at all. So my advice is to sit this one out.'

'You're afraid of us.'

'Sadly, no. I'm trying to be fair, is all. No reason for you to get hurt. If one of your bosses has a beef with me, send him out alone. I'll walk him around the block. We'll have an exchange of views. That way everyone's a winner.'

No answer.

Reacher pushed his way between the first guy and the second, and pulled the door. He slid out around its swing and took two fast paces to the kerb and turned around.

No one followed.

He waited in the gutter a whole minute, but no one

came out. He turned his collar up against the night-time mist and set out walking back to the hotel. From the corner he saw the guy with the top hat was gone. The evening shift had ended, and the night shift had started. He slowed down and scanned ahead. Habit.

There was a guy in a doorway on the other side of the street. Barely visible. He was lit from the side, softly, in green, by a pharmacy sign two units farther away. He was wearing a dark parka and a little Bavarian hat. Probably had a feather in the band. He was watching the hotel. No doubt about that. He was face-on to it, wedged in the doorway corner. White, and a little stout. Maybe six feet and two-ten. Hard to say how old.

Reacher walked on. Maybe part of a diplomatic protection team. A courtesy from the German government. Maybe they had found out Sinclair was in town. Or maybe Bishop had sent a guy. From the consulate. A third under-deputy for cultural affairs, with brass knuckles in his pocket. Trained under the previous system.

Reacher walked on, looking at nothing in particular, with the guy in the corner of his eye. But then a car turned in from the four-way up ahead, and bright headlights came straight at him, fast and dazzling, a big vehicle pattering over the cobblestones.

The car stopped alongside him. A Mercedes. A department Mercedes. Griezman. Who buzzed the passenger window down and said, 'Get in. I've been calling you. I thought you must be asleep with the phone turned off. I was coming to wake you up.'

Reacher said, 'Why?'

'We saw Wiley.'

Reacher glanced up.

The man in the doorway was gone.

'Get in,' Griezman said.

Reacher did.

TWENTY-FIVE

Griezman took off fast, his seat back yielding and groaning under the sudden acceleration. He said one of the cops in one of the unmarked cars parked at the bar earlier in the evening had been a night-shift guy, brought in early on overtime rates of pay, and therefore still on duty, still on his regular watch. Still with the sketch of Wiley on the seat beside him. He had been cruising the western edge of St Pauli, and he had seen a guy he swore matched the sketch. Carrying a bottle-shaped carrier bag from an all-night wine store. Walking south towards the water.

Reacher said, 'When?'

'Twenty minutes ago.'

'How sure is he?'

'I believe him. He's a good cop.'

Traffic was light, but the road surface was slick, and most other drivers were heading home from bars, so Griezman wasn't as fast as he might have been. But even so they got where they were going within ten minutes. They stopped between high buildings, twenty yards short of a crossroads. Griezman said the possible Wiley had been seen crossing the street, up ahead, walking right to left from the cop's point of view. Now thirty minutes ago, in total. In that direction lay huge new apartment blocks. A brand new residential development. Immense. On reclaimed land, from when the docks moved downriver, in search of more space. There were thousands and thousands of separate addresses.

Reacher said, 'Rentals, right?'

Griezman said, 'You think he lives there?'

'He was carrying a bottle of wine. Conceivably taking it to a party, but more likely taking it home. Given the late hour.' Reacher looked the other way, to his right. He said, 'I bet I know what he bought. Let's go find the store.'

The store was a clean, well-lit place, with what looked like a fine selection of wines, red, white, rosé, and sparkling, including a shelf of lower-priced items, for folks who didn't live in brand-new residential developments. The clerk was an amiable old guy of sixty-something. Reacher took his copy of Wiley's sketch from his pocket and the old guy confirmed it immediately. The man in the sketch had been in the store about forty minutes previously. He had bought a bottle of chilled champagne.

'He's celebrating,' Reacher said.

'Credit card?' Griezman asked.

'He paid cash,' the clerk said.

Reacher looked at a plastic bubble on the ceiling above the clerk's head. He said, 'Is that a security camera?'

The clerk said it was, and it fed a VHS recorder in the back room. Griezman knew how to work it. It gave a decent black and white picture, looking down from behind the clerk's shoulder. The angle was wide. It was a dual-purpose installation. Customers were clearly visible, but so was the register drawer. In case the clerk was skimming.

Griezman wound the tape back forty minutes and Wiley came in right on cue. No doubt about it. The hair, the brow, the cheekbones. The deep-set eyes. He looked dead-on average height, but scrawny, in a hardscrabble kind of a way. He moved with energy and purpose. And confidence. Almost a swagger. Physically he looked athletic. Not bouncy like a kid, but trained and mature. He was thirty-five years old, like Reacher himself. All grown up.

On the tape Wiley stepped over to a chiller and opened the glass door and took out a dark bottle with a thin neck.

'Dom Perignon,' Griezman said. 'Not so cheap.'

Wiley carried the bottle to the register and took crumpled bills from his pocket. He counted them out and the clerk made change with coins. Then the clerk put the bottle in a bottle-shaped bag and Wiley carried it away. Thirty-seven seconds, beginning to end.

They watched it again.

The same things happened.

'Now show me the neighbourhood,' Reacher said.

They got back in the car and Griezman drove south, pattering slowly over the cobblestones, following what must have been Wiley's earlier route, past where the cop had seen him, between scarred brick warehouses, and eventually to a brand new traffic circle, that led left or right or straight ahead into the new development's feeder roads.

Griezman stopped the car. The engine idled, and the wiper flopped back and forth about once a minute. Reacher looked ahead. He could see a hundred thousand windows. Most were dark, but a few were lit.

He said, 'Are these places expensive?'

Griezman said, 'All of Hamburg is expensive.'

'I'm wondering how Wiley pays the rent.'

'He doesn't. No one named Wiley is registered here. We already checked.'

'We think he's using a German name.'

'That would make a difference.'

'Possibly one he chose himself.'

'Does he offend you?'

'He's betraying his country. Which is also mine.'

'Do you love your country, Mr Reacher?'

'Major Reacher.'

'Perhaps that answers my question.'

'I prefer to think of it as healthy yet sceptical respect.'

'Not very patriotic.'

'Exactly patriotic. My country, right or wrong. Which means nothing, unless you admit your country is wrong sometimes. Loving a country that was right all the time would be common sense, not patriotism.'

Griezman said, 'I'm sorry your country is having these troubles.'

Reacher said, 'Do you love your country?'

'It's too early to say. It was only fifty years ago. We changed more than any other country has ever changed. I think we were doing OK. But the people from the east have set us back. Economically, of course. And politically. We're seeing things we haven't seen before.'

'Like the bar Helmut Klopp called you from.'

'We have to bide our time. We can't arrest them for thought crimes. We need actual crimes.'

Reacher said, 'There was a guy watching my hotel. He left when you showed up.'

'Not one of mine,' Griezman said.

'Federal?'

'No reason. I haven't reported Dr Sinclair's visit. Not yet. No one knows she's here. She's registered under a different name.'

Reacher said nothing.

Griezman said, 'Did you run the fingerprint?'

Reacher said, 'Yes, I did.'

'And?'

'You can call it a cold case now. It will never be solved.'

'What does that mean?'

'It means I know who it was, and I won't tell anyone.'

'But I helped you.'

'I know you did. And I thank you.'

'Do I get nothing in return?'

'She was a very expensive hooker. Her client list was therefore of interest. But I won't tell anyone about that, either.'

Griezman was quiet a beat.

Then he said, 'The CIA? I was of interest?'

Reacher nodded. 'To the part that was trained under the previous system.'

'You're going to blackmail me.'

'Not my style. I already said I won't tell anyone. No strings attached. Whether you choose to keep on helping me is entirely up to you. If you do, I'll take it as two simple detectives getting along, nothing more.'

Griezman paused again.

'I wish to apologize,' he said. 'I'm not the man you thought I was.'

'Doesn't matter to me,' Reacher said.

'I don't know why I did it.'

'I'm not your shrink.'

'But I would like to know why.'

'Was she cute?'

'Incredible.'

'There you go.'

'You think it's that simple?'

'I'm a military cop.'

Griezman said, 'I'll help you if I can.'

'Thank you.'

'What do you need?'

'You could tell your night shift guy to spend the rest of his watch right here. It's a bottleneck. Wiley might come through again. If so, arrest him for walking while foreign. Keep him in the car until I get here.'

'There are many other ways out of the complex. There are cycle paths and footbridges at the back. And a big bridge to the bus stop on the main road.'

'We might get lucky. He might want more champagne.'

'Tell me one thing, about the man whose identity you are concealing. Will he be punished?'

'Yes,' Reacher said. 'He will.'

'That's good.'

'You liked her, right?'

Griezman said, 'I'll drive you back to your hotel.'

Wiley gave the champagne thirty more minutes in the refrigerator, and then he peeled off the foil wrap and eased out the cork, with his thumbs, slowly and gently, until it made a polite little *pock* and fell to the floor.

He poured a glass, which had also gotten thirty minutes in the refrigerator, and he carried it to his table, where his map of Argentina was spread out. The outline of his ranch was rubbed greasy by his fingertips. Truly his ranch now. Or soon, when the money reached Zurich and left again. Or more precisely when some of it left again. Not all of it. He had liked the girl they sent with the message. *Sir, what I am permitted to know is, we accept your price.* She was polite. Kind of deferential. Like when she popped the third button. There would be girls like that in Argentina. Dark, like her. Shy, but with no other choice.

He got up and refilled his glass. He held it high, as if toasting a cheering crowd of thousands. Horace Wiley, from Sugar Land, Texas. King of the world.

Reacher listened at Sinclair's door and heard talking, so he knocked, and she said, 'Come in.' Neagley was there, and Bishop, from the consulate. The head of station. Sinclair was sitting on the bed, and Bishop and Neagley were in the green velvet armchairs. Neagley had hand-written notes in her lap.

Reacher said, 'Progress?'

'You?'

'I think he lives in an apartment complex near the waterfront. One of Griezman's guys got a glimpse of him. He was out buying champagne.'

'Celebrating,' Bishop said.

Reacher nodded. 'We should assume the negotiation is over. We should assume they agreed the price. The wheels are in motion.'

'How big is the apartment complex?'

'Huge.'

'Paper trail?'

'Nothing in the name of Wiley.'

'Is he in there now?'

'Almost certainly.'

'We should lock the place down.'

'There's an unmarked car at the main exit. That's the best Griezman can do. He was already paying overtime earlier in the day.'

Neagley said, 'It appears Wiley has no uncles. The witness who mentioned one has been ordered here for further questioning. Landry is working on possible great-uncles and the mother's possible boyfriends. The latter could take some time.'

'OK,' Reacher said.

'And I spoke to his COs from Benning and Sill. The guy from Benning doesn't remember him at all. The guy from Sill does. He said it was clear Wiley wanted to do his tour in Germany. He was fixated on it. He aimed for

258

it. Every qualification he took narrowed his choices.'

'The guy remembers all that, three years later?'

'Because they had a long conversation at the time. The CO pointed out the consequences of the drawdown. A dead end, a black hole, and so on and so forth. Wiley said he wanted to go anyway. He wanted to serve in Germany.'

'So it was a long game,' Sinclair said, from the bed. 'Now we're trying to figure out what.'

Reacher said, 'There was a guy watching this hotel. An hour ago. He disappeared when Griezman showed up.'

'Not one of mine,' Bishop said.

Muller called Dremmler at home again, and woke him up. It was very late. Or very early, depending on which direction a person was facing. Dremmler composed himself and Muller said, 'Reacher got back to the hotel just before one in the morning. But Griezman came by and picked him up before he went inside. I got out of there real quick, in case Griezman recognized me.'

'What did Griezman want?'

'One of my traffic cars heard it on the radio. The American they're looking for was seen in St Pauli. His name is Wiley. Griezman's men have Klopp's police sketch in their cars.'

'Any other details?'

'One of my guys just checked a car in a no-parking zone near the water. Near some new apartments. It was one of Griezman's detectives, in an unmarked unit, watching for Wiley. My guy asked why, and they talked for a minute. Just blue-to-blue gossip. Griezman's guy didn't know the details, but he said it was obviously some heavy duty thing. His orders came through flagged red.'

'What does that mean?'

'It used to mean organized crime, but now it means terrorism. The guy wasn't clear whether it was supposed to be an old red or a new red. There's some confusion at the moment. But I think it was a new red, because they were also watching an apartment near Reacher's hotel. Earlier in the day. There was supposed to be a Saudi guy coming out. But it didn't happen. I checked the city records and there's an apartment in that building with three Saudis and an Iranian. All young men. I think this is some kind of Middle East thing.'

'Is Wiley in the city records?'

'No trace.'

'Klopp says he saw him in the bar more than once. Maybe someone there knows him.'

'Maybe,' Muller said.

Dremmler said, 'We need you to get us a copy of Klopp's police sketch.'

Neagley left, and then Bishop. Reacher took an armchair. Sinclair stayed on the bed. She said, 'Waterman and White will be here tomorrow morning. And Landry and Vanderbilt. I relocated the whole operation. This is where the action is. We'll work out of the consulate.'

'OK,' Reacher said.

'What are you thinking about?'

'Right now?'

'Yes.'

'Work life or personal life?'

'You can think about both at once?'

'Most of the time.'

'OK, work first.'

'Wiley's hair.'

'What about it?'

'It's a way in. Possibly. He didn't cut it. He let it grow.'

'Maybe he was worried a barber would remember.'

'He could have done it himself. He shaved the sides every day. He could have shaved it all and started over. But he didn't.'

'Why not?'

'I think there's a vanity to him. A kind of flamboyance. He likes Davy Crockett. Maybe he's growing his hair long so he can buy a fringed suede jacket and be the king of the wild frontier. The way he moved on the tape was interesting. He's a small guy, but he swaggers. He's got it going on. And he bought expensive champagne. I think he likes grand gestures. Which combined with the hundred million dollars doesn't make me feel good. It makes me feel like something huge is coming.'

Sinclair was quiet for a moment.

Then she said, 'What about personal life?'

Reacher smiled.

He said, 'You walked right into that one.'

'Which one?'

'Same exact answer,' he said. 'I feel like something huge is coming.'

'I'm counting on it,' she said.

TWENTY-SIX

When they woke up Reacher went back to his own room and showered, and dressed again. He took the stairs down to breakfast, alone. The four guys from McLean were in there already, after their overnight flight. Waterman, White, Landry and Vanderbilt. Neagley was with them. They looked tired. She didn't. Landry said he had traced the great-uncles. But the news was not good. Most were long dead and none had lived near the kid growing up. There was no evidence of contact. Not even circumstantial. They were not necessarily the visiting type. Two had done prison time. Extended influence was thought unlikely.

But Waterman had better news. He said Wiley's mother had been located, and had agreed to an interview about her old boyfriends. She was living in New Orleans, on welfare. The local field office had been alerted. Agents would be dispatched. First results were expected in seven or eight hours. Because of the time zones.

White didn't look happy to be there. The CIA guy. His hair looked longer than ever. He looked thinner. He was twitching and writhing. And wringing his hands, and squinting.

Reacher said, 'What?'

White said, 'They really need to get the Iranian out.'

'None of this comes from the messenger. We missed her completely.'

'Ratcliffe thinks too narrowly. If something bad happens to them in the city of Hamburg, their inquisition will range far and wide. Everybody will be a suspect. They aren't dumb. They'll deduce the facts. How many variables are there? Two different messengers, but only one house. The Iranian will last less than five minutes.'

'You should talk to Bishop.'

'Bishop runs the kid, but he doesn't have the authority to pull him out.'

'He must have.'

'Not for big-picture reasons. Imminent danger only.'

'Which you think is now.'

'It will start the same minute you get your hands on Wiley. The minute their deal falls apart. Which will be when?'

'Soon, I hope.'

'Exactly.'

'You should talk to Bishop,' Reacher said again.

Then Sinclair came in. Black dress, pearls, nylons, shoes. Her hair was damp. Landry and Vanderbilt made a space and she sat down. She said, 'I talked to Mr Ratcliffe. We're assuming the negotiation phase is over and the delivery phase is about to begin. So we need to know what, where, and when.'

'The messenger could be home already,' Neagley said.

'She might have flown direct. Or nearly. Then they'll send a messenger to Switzerland. Because they don't trust the phones. With the account details and the passwords. The transaction might take an hour or two. Could happen tomorrow.'

'Or a year from now,' Vanderbilt said. 'Are they ready to act? Do they have the money?'

'Wiley can't wait another year,' Waterman said. 'He's already been on the run four months. Not easy. A lot of stress, and a lot of risk. He needs to get settled. I think this will happen fast now. Tomorrow, or the next day, or the day after that. I'm sure the money is lined up and ready to go. Probably in the same bank. Different blips in the same computer.'

'OK,' Sinclair said. 'So it's what, where, and soon.'

'The where depends on the what,' Reacher said. 'If it's intelligence or a document, they might do the handover right there in the banker's office. If it's a big thing, right now it must be stored or hidden somewhere in Germany, so they'll have to send a crew over to haul it away.'

'We should watch the bank,' Waterman said.

'Don't know which one. They have hundreds.'

'The airports, then. Here and Zurich.'

Landry said, 'The easiest way would be to figure out what he's selling.'

'No shit,' Neagley said.

'Must be something.'

'But what? He can't go get it now. He would be arrested immediately. Therefore it was stolen or otherwise obtained more than four months ago. Except nothing was reported missing.'

264

White said, 'We need to get the Iranian out.'

'Not yet,' Sinclair said.

'Then when?'

'Talk to Mr Bishop. We're heading for the consulate now. He set up an office for us. Be in the lobby in ten minutes.'

Muller walked up the fire stairs to Griezman's floor. It was still early. Before eight o'clock. No one was in. The secretarial stations were still deserted. Griezman's secretary's in-tray looked like it had before. Muller had replaced the papers carefully. Nothing suspicious. But where was the sketch? Presumably the American investigators had taken as many copies as they wanted. Griezman himself might have taken a couple more, to start a cover-your-ass file of his own. He would have stored the original somewhere safe. In a special drawer, perhaps. He might have dozens of sketches. A whole category. It was a detective bureau, after all.

But where? There was a side-to-side line of drawers behind the secretary's ergonomic typing chair. They formed the base of a wall unit, with shelves above. Muller slipped in behind her desk and bent down to take a look. None of the drawers was labelled. He backed out and glanced through Griezman's door. The inner sanctum. There were identical drawers inside, but with no shelves above. Like a credenza, with framed photographs on it, of a woman and two children. Griezman's wife and kids, no doubt. Plus a statuette trophy for something or other. Probably nothing athletic, given the size of the guy. There was another line of file cabinets on the wall opposite. A total of twenty drawers inside the room, and four outside.

An inconvenient ratio.

Muller made a deal with himself. A one in five chance of success was better than a four in five chance of losing his job. He was useful where he was, in the long term. In the big picture. That fact had to be weighed in the balance. Therefore he would search the secretarial station, but not Griezman's office itself. A sensible compromise. He slid in again behind the secretary's desk. He would go left to right, he figured. A quick look. A sketch should be easy to spot. Probably done on thick paper, from an art store. Possibly a non-standard size. Probably cased in a plastic page protector.

He bent down.

A woman's voice behind him said, 'Hello?'

Surprised, and a little quizzical.

Muller straightened up and turned around.

Griezman's secretary.

He said nothing.

The woman dumped her purse on her desk and shucked off her coat. She hung it on a hook and bustled back. She said, 'Can I help you, Deputy Chief Muller?'

Deputy Chief Muller didn't answer.

The woman said, 'Are you looking for something?'

'A sketch,' Muller said.

'Of what?'

Muller paused a beat.

Thinking.

Then he said, 'There was a traffic accident late last

night. My division is handling it, naturally. A cyclist was knocked down. Hit and run. The driver didn't stop. The cyclist's companion gave us a pretty good description. A distinctive face, and an unusual hairstyle.'

'How can we help you?'

'By a coincidence my officer had just seen one of Chief Griezman's officers, about an hour before. My officer thought it was illegal parking, but it was actually a stakeout. Chief Griezman's officer had a sketch in his car. Of an American named Wiley. Later my officer remembered it and realized it was exactly the same face as was being described to him there and then by the cyclist's companion.'

Griezman's secretary said, 'I see.'

'Therefore I need to show your sketch to our witness. For confirmation.'

'I would be happy to give you a copy.'

Muller said, 'If it's not too much trouble.'

'None at all.'

'Thank you very much.'

The woman ducked into the inner sanctum and Muller heard a drawer roll open. Then she came out again, with a sheet of thick paper in a plastic page protector. She switched on her Xerox machine. Muller heard clicking and ticking and smelled hot toner. He heard the elevator door thump open. He saw two more secretaries step out. Purses, coats, brisk morning motion. Both walked past, smiling and polite, ready to get to work.

Griezman's secretary raised the Xerox machine's lid and placed the sketch face down. She touched a button. The machine whirred. A copy came out.

The elevator door opened again. Not Griezman. Just a man in a suit. Muller knew him vaguely. The man nodded good morning and walked on by.

Griezman's secretary handed the copy to Muller. It was done with coloured pencils. A scrawny man, with a prominent brow, and prominent cheekbones, and deep-set eyes, and long yellow hair.

Muller said, 'Thank you,' and walked away, down the hallway, to the fire door, and down the fire stairs, to his own floor, and his own hallway, and his own office, where he immediately set about creating a phoney log entry about an injured cyclist and a hit-and-run driver. Just in case Griezman checked.

Reacher and Neagley went straight to the lobby. Neagley said, 'We need to get Wiley's movement orders. All of them. That's the key to this thing. He's been in-country a little over two years, and AWOL the last four months. Which gives us a critical period of a little under two years of active service. During which envelope of time he saw something, and planned, and then stole it. So we need to know exactly where he's been. Day to day, from first to last. Because at least one day he was right next to it. Whatever it is. Maybe even touching it. Physically adjacent.'

'Minimum of one day,' Reacher said. 'The day he was stealing it.'

'I think two days minimum,' Neagley said. 'First he saw it, and then he figured it out, and then he came back to steal it.'

'Except he didn't see it. Not exactly. He found it. He

located it. This is a long game. He came to Germany to get it. He knew about it ahead of time.'

'Either way. Maybe more so. There was a physical encounter.'

'I want to know how he's paying his rent,' Reacher said. 'He's a private soldier. He doesn't have a savings plan. See if the movement orders overlap with any kind of cold-case property crimes. He got his seed money somehow.'

And then the clerk at the desk answered a ringing telephone, and pressed the receiver to her bosom, and called out, 'Major Reacher, it's for you.'

It was Orozco, calling from a cellar somewhere, judging by the sound.

Orozco said, 'Are we in trouble?'

'We're good,' Reacher said. 'Currently saving the world.'

'Until we don't.'

'In which case it won't matter anyway.'

'I just got through talking with Billy Bob and Jimmy Lee. They confirm they could pick any name they wanted for the phoney ID. But it had to be German. In case there was a random check inside the division. It was felt foreign names would stand out. But any German name was OK. Whatever they wanted. Whatever sounded good or meant something to them.'

'OK, thanks,' Reacher said. 'Got to go.'

His back was against the counter, and he could see out through the glass part of the front door.

There was a guy in a doorway.

Across the street.

Reacher hung up the phone. He caught Neagley's eye and pointed. She lined herself up with the sliver of view. She said, 'I see him. Hard not to.'

'Let's step out for some air.'

Neagley went first, and then Reacher, and the guy in the doorway startled, and then made an elaborate show of yawning and stretching and sauntering away, on the opposite sidewalk, slowly, as if he had all the time in the world.

Neagley said, 'Shall we see where he's going?'

They kept pace, ten feet behind, two lanes of morning traffic between, as the guy strolled along. He had a wool coat and no hat. He was solidly built. He was bigger than Neagley and smaller than Reacher. He turned right at the four-way. Reacher and Neagley crossed at the light and caught up again, to ten feet behind.

The guy turned right again.

Into an alley, between buildings.

'A trap, obviously,' Neagley said. 'Probably a closed courtyard. No wonder the guy was easy to see. His job was to bring you here.'

'Me?'

'The guy wasn't Griezman's and he wasn't Bishop's. So who was he? Orozco just told you this place is mobbed up. I'm sure Helmut Klopp is a founder member. He knows what we look like and he knows our names. You made four of their foot soldiers cry. When we were here the first time. Now they want a do-over.'

'You think they're still mad about that?'

'Probably.'

'How big do you think the courtyard is?'

'I'm no architect, but maybe thirty by thirty. Like a large room.'

'How many guys do you think they brought?'

'Six, minimum. Seven, with the guy who led you here.'

'Led us here.'

'Until I halted the advance. A sergeant's first duty is to keep her officer safe.'

'Is that what they teach you?'

'Between the lines.'

'Works for me,' Reacher said.

'We should head back.'

'Maybe you're wrong.'

'I don't think I'm wrong.'

'Maybe it's a residential courtyard. Low income housing. Some kind of an inner-city thing. Rooms without a view. The kind of place you live if you're out of work. Which at least leaves you free all morning to stand in a doorway across the street from a hotel.'

'You think he was going home?'

'I think I should go find out.'

'It's a trap, Reacher.'

'I know it is. But we need to make them worried about us. We need to keep the pressure on. We might need to make them give up the passport seller. I'm sure he's one of them. We need Wiley's new name. That might be the only way of getting it. Give me two minutes exactly. If I'm not out already, feel free to come on in and lend a hand.'

TWENTY-SEVEN

Reacher walked on and turned in at the alley. It was about three feet wide. Like a mean hallway in a cheap apartment. Up ahead was a rectangle of light. Morning shade, and sandstone colours. No people. They would be flat against the wall, either side of the alley mouth.

Reacher walked on in the dark, trailing his fingertips against the stone on both sides, to keep himself centred. His footsteps were loud, and a strange quacking echo came first off the walls and then off the roof. Up ahead nothing changed. Morning light, and painted concrete. Fleshy colours. Bright and clean. Bricks underfoot, like some of the sidewalks. No physical obstructions. No well heads or water pumps. All 1950s modernity.

Reacher walked on.

Then three paces from the end of the alley he broke into a run and burst out into the courtyard, moving fast, all the way to the centre, where he jammed to a stop and spun around.

Eight guys.

All still pressed flat against the wall. All evidently expecting a more cautious approach. Four of them were the four from outside the bar, the first time. *Germany is for Germans.* They looked partially recovered. Three of the others looked similar, but as yet undamaged. And possibly older, on average. Possibly selected on merit. One had nothing in his hands. One had a baseball bat. One had a broken bottle. Brown glass, jagged, like a miniature crown. That guy would go down first, Reacher decided. The bat guy could wait. A bat was no use in a melee. The first four would hang back. Once bitten, twice shy. The decoy from the doorway wouldn't fight at all. Not his job. So it would be three on one initially. Not a huge problem. After that, who knew.

The guy with the bat moved first. Which was dumb but predictable. It was the biggest weapon. It set the tone. But it was useless on the run. No one could get a hit while simultaneously sprinting down a track. Not Babe Ruth, not Joe DiMaggio, not Mickey Mantle. Not even Ted Williams at his finest. Wasted effort, but indicative of an attempt at tactics. The idea seemed to be the bat would knock Reacher down, and then the guy with the bottle would follow up, leaning down, jabbing and twisting. Which meant the bottle guy was on the move very early, just two steps behind the bat guy's shoulder, ready for his moment of glory, looking for all the momentum he could get.

But momentum was a two-way street.

Reacher sidestepped the guy with the bat and met the guy with the bottle head on, two opposing masses colliding at high speed, like a wreck on the highway. Reacher was watching nothing but the bottle, which was out in front and coming up in a panic, towards his face, in the guy's right hand. Which made it purely a question of approximate timing. Easier than hitting a baseball. Reacher swept his left forearm up, inside out, like a guy shooing a wasp at a picnic, and it hit the bottle guy's right forearm somewhere along its length, so that the bottle's trajectory was slammed up and out, harmlessly over Reacher's left shoulder, which left time and space for Reacher's right elbow to hook around and smash the guy full in the face, which because of all the kinetic energy was more or less like a stick of dynamite going off in the guy's mouth. He went down faster than gravity and Reacher turned and stomped on the bottle, so no one else could use it, and then he started back towards the guy with the bat, who had spun off uselessly behind him.

He decided he wanted the bat.

The guy planted his feet and started to drop into a crouch, and started to pull the bat back, low, more like a tennis swing than a baseball swing, like setting up for a cautious two-handed backhand return of serve, or a long drive off a golf tee, all his momentum cocking back, and back, and back, ahead of eventually pulling the trigger when Reacher arrived within range. Which made it another question of approximate timing. The only way to defend against the swing of a bat was to get there early, ideally before the swing had even started, or worst case in its first foot or so, where it would still be weak and slow, no more than a soft lateral thump, like walking into a fence rail at night. Getting there early required sudden acceleration, which was not easy for a guy built like Reacher, but which came naturally on that

274

occasion. Because of motivation. Because of the difference between a soft lateral thump and a broken femur or arm or ribs. Reacher exploded at the guy and got there three inches into the bat's forward swing, which gave him time to catch its sweet spot in the meat of his palm, and jerk it away, and add his other hand, and stab the knob of the handle at the guy's head like a rifle butt, and connect, like a ferocious punch through a single knuckle.

The guy went down sideways and Reacher spun around, looking for the next target, which presented itself immediately in the form of the third new guy rushing in, unarmed, his hands up and open as if he was aiming for a wrestling hold. Reacher swung the bat the wrong way around, like a bad switch hitter flailing at a high fastball, a swinging strike for sure, except the third new guy was a lot bigger than a baseball, so a perfect aim was not a crucial requirement. Anywhere between the chest and the head was a bull's-eye. The elbow, the upper arm, the neck, the skull. Or all four at once, which is what happened. The guy brought his arm up to protect his head, and the bat caught his elbow, and his triceps, which impact smashed the heavy bone of his upper arm backward into the point of his jaw, where his neck met his skull. Which dropped him to his knees, but the lights stayed on. So Reacher swung again, this time properly right-handed, probably good enough for nothing more than a fly ball at a July Fourth picnic, but more than adequate against human biology. The guy rocked sideways and then flopped forward on his face.

By that point the clock in Reacher's head told him the

fight had been running a little over four seconds. The decoy from the doorway was still plastered against the wall. Not his business. The four sides of beef from the first bar were lumbering into action. They had broken raggedly from their concealed positions and were haphazardly placed. No rhyme or reason. Just random. Which was a problem. The first two would be easy. The third would not be difficult. But the fourth would be a problem. Reacher could see that. Time and space and movement. Like astronomy. Like planets on collision courses. Orbits and angles and relative speeds. The fourth guy would come pressing in before the third guy was down. No other possibility. It was in the way their centres of gravity were moving. There was no logical sequence beyond one, two, three. No matter where a person started.

All of which made Reacher regret he had told Neagley two minutes exactly. He still had a minute and fifty-five seconds to go. With no logical way of surviving. Against vengeful opposition. He should have left it to her discretion. She would have entered the alley as soon as she was sure his attention was focused ahead, which meant right then she would be already waiting in the shadows of the alley's mouth, watching, doing the same instinctive calculations he was doing, and therefore ready to step in and put a wrench in the fourth guy's works.

A sergeant's first duty is to keep her officer safe.

Maybe she had disobeyed him.

Which of course she had. He launched against the first two, using the bat like a fist, *one*, *two*, forehand,

276

backhand, thinking ahead, lining up for the third guy, executing the pivot with speed and grace and economy, but even so the fourth guy came pressing in way too early, as predicted, just half a step behind, by blind luck timed to arrive just before the bat could start moving again.

But then the fourth guy disappeared. Like he had run full speed into a clothes rope. Like a special effect in a movie. One frame he was there, and the next he was gone. The third guy went down and behind him Reacher saw Neagley, following through from what looked like a roundhouse rabbit punch to the fourth guy's throat.

The decoy from the doorway raised his hands.

Reacher said, 'Thank you, sergeant.'

Neagley said, 'You should have picked up the bottle. Better than the bat.'

Reacher walked over to the decoy and said, 'Tell your boss to stop wasting my time. Tell him to come see me himself. One on one. I'll walk him around the block. We'll have an exchange of views.'

Then they left, back down the alley to the street, first Neagley, then Reacher. They stood in the sun and shrugged and straightened, and then they hustled back to the hotel.

TWENTY-EIGHT

They were late back to the hotel. The others were waiting. Bishop had sent a little bus. Like an airport shuttle. They were all in their seats, all watching out their windows. Waterman, Landry, White, and Vanderbilt. And Sinclair. Reacher and Neagley got in, and the door hissed shut behind them, and the bus took off. Not a long ride, around the Aussenalster lake, to a large and imposing but slightly odd building. It looked like a copy of the White House done purely from memory by a builder who had visited once as a kid. Inside Bishop greeted them and showed them their room. Mostly desks and phones and fax machines and copy machines and telex machines and printers and bulky computer terminals with dirty beige keyboards. Bishop said the phones were set up as a replica of the McLean switchboard. Locally only Griezman had been given the numbers, in his case without being told their location.

It was Griezman who called first.

With a problem.

Reacher picked up and Griezman said, 'Don't put me on speaker.'

'Why not?'

'I screwed up. Or my department did. Which is the same thing.'

'What happened?'

'I think we lost Wiley. Somehow he was in a hit-and-run accident about two hours after you and I left. He was driving a car and he hit a bicycle. He was full of champagne, no doubt. A witness described him perfectly. She was shown Helmut Klopp's sketch and made a positive ID. It's all right there in the traffic division's log.'

'So your guy missed him coming out.'

'At one point he was talking to a traffic cop. It might have happened then.'

'But either way you don't know where Wiley is.'

'Not with an acceptable degree of certainty.'

'Is that something they teach you to say?'

'It sounds sober and mature, and burdened down with technicalities.'

Reacher said, 'Shit happens. Get over it.'

Griezman said, 'I'm sorry we missed him.'

'Don't worry about it.'

'I'll maintain the surveillance as long as I can.'

'Thank you.'

Reacher hung up and told the story and Sinclair asked everyone's first question for them, when she said, 'Was that the delivery? Did we miss it? Was he so stressed he knocked a bicycle over?'

'Too soon, surely,' Vanderbilt said. 'It was the middle of the first night. He can't have been paid yet. So he won't have delivered yet. Not unless he's really dumb.'

'Worst case, he was going to the airport,' Landry said. 'For the early flight to Zurich. Maybe he'd rather wait a day or two there than here. In which case he took the delivery with him. If it's small. To swap in the banker's office, like Reacher said.'

'We should be watching the airports,' Waterman said.

'We are,' Sinclair said. 'Both airports have closed-circuit television. CIA arranged temporary feeds. Unofficial, so they won't last long, but so far Wiley has not passed through.'

'And he didn't come home either,' Reacher said. 'Not unless Griezman's guy missed him twice. So where is he now?'

'Out and about,' Neagley said. 'Somewhere in Germany. The phase before delivery. Like the dealer inspection when you buy a new car. Ahead of the big reveal.'

Wiley was waking up, in his bedroom, the same place he had woken up for the last three months. In his rented apartment on the waterfront. The new development. A village within the city. But not really. It was actually a giant dormitory, full of incurious people who rushed in and out in the dark, and slept the few hours between. He had never seen his neighbours, and as far as he knew they had never seen him. Perfect.

He got up and set his coffee machine going. He rinsed the fumes out of the Dom Perignon bottle and placed it in the recycle bin. He put his glass in the dishwasher.

He picked up his phone and dialled the rental

franchise he had used before. The call was answered immediately, by a man who sounded young and efficient.

Wiley said, 'Do you speak English?'

'Certainly, sir,' the young man said.

'I need to rent a panel van.'

'What size, sir?'

'Long wheelbase, high roof. I need plenty of space inside.'

'We have Mercedes-Benz or Volkswagen. The Mercedes-Benz is longer. Over four metres inside.'

Wiley did the math in his head. Four metres was thirteen feet. He needed twelve. He said, 'How far off the ground is the load floor?'

'Quite normal, I think. I'm not sure exactly.'

'Does it have a roll-up rear door?'

'No, sir. It has hinged rear doors. Is that a problem?'

'I need to back it up to another truck and move stuff across. Can't get close enough with hinged doors.'

'I'm afraid our only option with a roll-up door is in an altogether different class of vehicle. It's a question of gross vehicle weight, technically. In Germany the heavier vehicles require a commercial licence. Do you have one?'

'I'm pretty sure I got the right licence for whatever you want to give me. You can count on that. Like a deck of cards.'

'Very good, sir,' the young man said. 'When do you need the van?'

'Immediately,' Wiley said.

* * *

The phone rang again in the consulate room, and Landry passed it to Reacher. It was Bishop, in his office nearby. Who said, 'There's a U.S. Army soldier at the reception desk claiming he has orders to report to you.'

'OK,' Reacher said. 'Send him up. Or should I go get him?'

'I'll have him escorted,' Bishop said.

The escort turned out to be a woman of maybe twenty-three, maybe a recent graduate, just starting out, but already Foreign Service to the core. The soldier turned out to be an enlisted man with a Mohawk haircut. From Wiley's air defence unit. His crewmate. The witness from the AWOL file, four months earlier. He was an E-4, but only a specialist, not a hard-striper corporal. One step up from private first class, but not yet an NCO. He was in woodland-pattern battledress uniform. He was all squared away. Maybe twenty years old. He looked like a good soldier. His name tape said Coleman.

Neagley put three chairs in a quiet corner, and they all sat down. Reacher said, 'Thanks for stopping by, soldier. We appreciate it. Did they tell you what this is about?'

Coleman said, 'Sir, they told me you would ask questions about Private Wiley.'

His accent was from the South. The Georgia hill country, maybe. He was perched on the edge of his chair like the sitting-down version of standing rigidly to attention.

Reacher said, 'Reports from four months ago suggest

282

Wiley was happy to be in your unit. Were those reports correct?'

Coleman said, 'Yes sir, I believe they were.'

'Happy and fulfilled?'

'Yes sir, I believe he was.'

'Not victimized or oppressed in any way?'

'No sir, not to my knowledge.'

'Which makes him a very unusual AWOL. And which makes it completely impossible for you or your unit to get the blame. This is not your fault. There is no practical way to make this your fault. A hundred bureaucrats could type for a hundred years on a hundred typewriters and still not get close to making this your fault. Understand? We know Wiley took off for external reasons.'

Coleman said, 'Yes sir, that was also our conclusion.'

'So relax, OK? You are not accused of anything. There are no wrong answers. There are no dumb answers, either. We need anything you can tell us. Any little impression. I don't care how stupid it is. So don't hold back. Get it all out. Then you can have the rest of the day in Hamburg. You can check out the clubs.'

Coleman nodded.

'How long have you known Wiley?'

'He was in the unit nearly two years.'

'Old guy, right?'

'Way older than my oldest brother.'

'Did you think that was weird?'

'A little bit.'

'Did you have a theory about why he waited so long?'

'I think he tried some other things first.'

'Did he talk about them?'

'No sir, never,' Coleman said. 'He was all buttoned up. He was a keeper of secrets. We all knew he was hiding things. He was always smiling to himself and saying nothing. But he was old, so we figured it was OK. We figured he was entitled. It didn't stop anyone liking him, either. He was a popular guy.'

'Was he a hard worker?'

Coleman started to answer, and then he stopped.

Reacher said, 'What?'

'Sir, you asked for stupid impressions.'

'I like stupid,' Reacher said. 'Sometimes stupid is all we got.'

'Well, sir, it seemed to me it wasn't just secrets. It seemed to me like a whole secret plan. For his life. Day by day. Yes, he was a hard worker. He did it all and never complained. Even the bullshit parts. And most of it is bullshit now. He would get a look on his face. He was happy, because every day was one day closer.'

'To what?'

'I don't know.'

'Four months ago you mentioned Wiley's uncle.'

'They were asking us if Wiley was a chatty guy. They wanted to know what he talked about. There wasn't much. He told me he was from Sugar Land, Texas. He knew about beef cattle. One time he said he wanted to be a rancher. But that was all. He never talked much. Then one night we were back off an exercise, and we had fired some practice rounds, and we had gotten a pretty good score against the helicopters, so we all laid back and cracked some beers, and we got pretty buzzed. They all got to talking about why they had joined the army. But in a cryptic way. There are some real smart mouths in the unit. You had to put it all in one clever sentence. I'm not so good at that type of thing. When my turn came I said I joined the army to learn a trade. I thought there could be a double meaning. Trade, like automobile mechanic, or trade like killing people. Which would be alternative employment later if automobile mechanic jobs were hard to find.'

'Good answer,' Reacher said.

'They didn't get it.'

'What did Wiley say?'

'He said he joined the army because his uncle told him Davy Crockett stories. Which was short and cryptic, just like it should be. Like a crossword puzzle. Then he smiled his secret smile. It was easy for him to be cryptic. He was always cryptic.'

'What did you think he meant?'

'I remember Davy Crockett on the television show. I saw him every week. He wore a hat made from an old raccoon. Didn't make me want to join the army. So I don't know what he meant. I guess that time it was me who didn't get it.'

'Just uncle, or was there a name?'

'Not then. But later they were ragging on him about talking so much about ranching, when there was nothing in his home town but a big old sugar factory, and he said his uncle Arnold had worked on a ranch before he got drafted.'

'Did that sound like the same uncle? Or a different uncle?'

Coleman went quiet, as if running through his own family members, and listening in his head to what he called them. This uncle, that uncle. Was there a difference?

Eventually he said, 'I don't know. Wiley was the kind of guy who would use a name where he could. A Texas kind of guy. Old-fashioned courtesy. But he couldn't in the cryptic sentence, because it had to be short. So maybe it was Arnold both times, or maybe not.'

'Tell me more about how every day he was one day closer. The secret plan. How was his mood? Did it feel like a step by step plan, slow and steady, or were there ups and downs?'

'I guess neither,' Coleman said. 'Or a mixture of both. He was always cheerful, but he got happier later. Total of two steps only. He was up, and then he was up some more.'

'When did it change?'

'About halfway through. About a year ago.'

'What happened?'

'Nothing I could put in words.'

'Got an impression?'

'It might be stupid.'

'I like stupid.'

'I guess he was like a guy waiting for news, always kind of expecting it would be good news, and then finally getting it, and sure enough, it is good news.'

'Like a guy looking for something he knew was there, and finding it?'

'Exactly like that.'

* * *

In Jalalabad it was much later in the morning. Breakfast was long gone, and lunch was coming. The messenger was called back to the small hot room. Her second visit of the day. She had already delivered Wiley's response, on her arrival at dawn. The fat man had smiled and rocked, and the tall man had clenched his fists and howled like a wolf. Now only the fat man was there. The tall man's cushion was dented but empty. He was elsewhere. Very busy. Very excited. Busier and more excited than he should have been, she thought, about a matter he had claimed was of very little importance.

Silent flies came close, and hovered, and darted away.

The fat man said, 'Sit down.'

The messenger looked at the tall man's cushion.

She said, 'May I stand?'

'As you wish. I am very proud of your performance. It was flawless. As of course it should have been, given the excellence of your training.'

'Thank you,' she said. 'I felt well prepared.'

'Was your German adequate?'

'I spoke very little. Only to a taxi driver.'

'Would it have been adequate if you had to speak more?'

'I believe so. Because of the excellence of my training.'

'Would you like to go back to Hamburg?'

She thought of photographs and fingerprints and computer records.

She said, 'I will go where you in your wisdom choose to send me.'

'The delivery is planned, as you know, but we must have a presence to authorize its collection.'

'It would be an honour.'

The fat man said, 'Are languages your greatest strength?'

She said, 'That's not for me to say.'

'Those who trained you say your memory is excellent and you know your numbers.'

She didn't answer.

She didn't want to talk about numbers.

Not then.

The fat man said, 'Were those who trained you not telling the truth?'

'They were very kind. But too generous. I know hardly any numbers at all.'

'Why do you say this?'

She didn't answer.

'Tell me.'

'Before Hamburg you want me to go to Zurich. Where they also speak German. To a bank. To transfer money to Wiley. With numbers. Account numbers and passcodes. This is how I will be able to authorize the collection.'

'Do you intend to refuse?'

'I would need to know the price.'

'Of course you would. It's one of four important elements. Our account number, our passcode, the amount, and the recipient's account number. A lot to memorize, I know, but it's really a very simple and straightforward transaction.'

'You don't like it when people know the price.'

The fat man said nothing.

The messenger said, 'I will be sacrificed.'

'Not if we get what we want. This time it's different. If this deal succeeds, you will always be part of it. We all will. We will become myths and legends. Stories will pass from generation to generation. The price will be revered as a bargain. It will be celebrated. Little girls will pretend to be you. They'll play games about moving the money. Girls will know they can do this too.'

The messenger said nothing.

The fat man said, 'But if this deal fails, then yes, you will be killed, whether you go to Zurich or not. You are already part of it. You are already a witness. All witnesses will be killed. The humiliation would be too great for us to bear otherwise. A hundred million dollars for nothing? Clearly we would need to erase it from memory. Or we'd be finished as leaders. Our bones would be picked clean.'

The messenger said, 'A hundred million dollars? Is that the price?'

'Go learn the numbers,' the fat man said. 'Be ready to leave tonight. Pray for success.'

In Hamburg Wiley rode down in the elevator, and stepped out of his lobby. He walked away from the traffic circle, past another building, and between two more, to the rear of the complex, where new paving gave way to old granite, and cobblestones, and preserved dockside cranes. There were new footbridges over the dark water, made of teak and steel, looping gracefully over the voids. Wiley took one, and joined another. It was wider, and it led farther, all the way to the main road, and the bus stop. Wiley sat in the shelter and waited. First the wrong bus came, and then the right bus came. It would stop two blocks from the car rental franchise. Wiley got on. He was calm. No longer falling. Now it was a sequence of simple mechanical tasks. Deliver, collect, fly. By which time nine hundred square miles would be waiting for him. Visible from outer space.

He smiled to himself, alone in the crowd on the bus.

Little Horace Wiley.

Hot damn.

A mile from the bus route Muller met Dremmler in a pastry shop. It had four small tables, all of them occupied by pairs of men just like themselves, friends but not really, bound together only by a proposition, be it buying or selling or hedging or insuring, or investing or leasing or renting or flipping.

Or making a stand against crumbling national identity.

Dremmler said, 'Once again, thank you for your help in the matter of Reacher's whereabouts. A plan is now in place.'

Muller said, 'My pleasure.'

'He can't stay in his hotel all day. He's bound to come out. I expect a positive report any moment.'

'Good,' said Muller.

'Did you succeed with the other thing?'

Muller took out the sketch of Wiley and flattened it on the table.

Dremmler said, 'Was it hard to get?'

'It required a tiny paper trail. But it won't lead anywhere.'

'I have never seen this man before. He is not a movement member.'

'But Klopp saw him more than once.'

'Then he goes to the bar to buy or sell. Or both. I'll show this picture to the folks I know. We might get a name and address.'

'We know his name. It's Wiley. And he doesn't have an address. I already checked, remember?'

'I'm sure he purchased a new identity. Or several. That's usually the first thing these fellows do. But don't worry. I know exactly who to ask.'

Neagley told Landry to call his New Orleans field office and script some questions for Wiley's mother, on the subject of any and all old boyfriends named Arnold, and any and all old boyfriends who were ranchers and then subsequently drafted, and any and all old boyfriends who ever talked about Davy Crockett. Then Vanderbilt called her over to a chattering telex, where she tore out an armful of paper. Her request, via Sinclair and the Joint Chiefs, for cold-case property crimes in Germany. Near military installations or areas of activity. During the span of Wiley's active in-country deployment.

There were plenty of crimes.

Reacher said, 'When do we get Wiley's movement orders?'

'Soon,' Neagley said. 'They're working on it.'

The crimes were many and various. All unsolved. There were silent midnight burglaries, and armed invasions and robberies, and stick-ups, and hijacks, all aimed at cash-rich local businesses, like bars and betting parlours and strip clubs. Geographically the locations matched the military map. Because that was where the money was. Hence the cash-rich businesses. Perpetrators in such crimes would come from miles around. From far and wide, like seagulls to a landfill. Very few of them would be soldiers. But some of them would be.

Neagley said, 'Look at the dollar values.'

'They're bullshit,' Reacher said. 'For the insurance. We should cut them in half.'

'Even so. One or two of these would give Wiley all the seed money he needed. Three or four of these would put him in a whole different category. We would need to make new assumptions. He could have multiple locations and major resources.'

'When did he steal the thing he's selling?'

'Somewhere between the day he located it and the end of his final ninety-six hour pass. Somewhere in that ten-month period.'

'Why hasn't it been reported missing?'

'That depends on what it is. Depends on the audit cycle, I suppose. Maybe they're counting something right now. Maybe the news will break tonight.'

'How thorough are the audits?'

'On average not very,' Neagley said. 'Mostly it's a head count. If there are three containers listed on the inventory, they count one, two, three, and they make a check mark.'

'But the containers could be empty or something.'

'Got to be one or the other. Either the count hasn't happened yet, or he fooled them somehow. Those are the only two possibilities.'

'No, I think there's a third,' Reacher said. 'Maybe whatever he stole was never on an inventory. Maybe no one knew it was there, so no one knows it's gone.'

'Like what?'

'Like my pants.'

'What about them?'

'You like them?'

'They're pants.'

'They're U.S. Marine Corps khakis manufactured in 1962 and shipped in 1965. At some point they were delivered by mistake to a U.S. Army warehouse in Maryland. They stayed there thirty years. Never counted, never audited, never on any guy's list.'

'You think someone just bought a hundred million dollars' worth of pants?'

'Not specifically pants.'

'Shirts?'

'Something that got lost in the back of a warehouse. As a third possibility.'

'Like what?' Neagley said again.

'We were going to fight the Red Army here. We had all kinds of stuff. And people screw up. If they can randomly send a bale of jarhead pants to an army base, they can randomly send anything anywhere.'

'OK,' Neagley said. 'It's a third possibility.'

Then the phone rang.

Griezman.

Who said, 'Something weird happened.'

TWENTY-NINE

Reacher put the call on speaker, and all seven people gathered around, and Griezman said, 'A local police station just got a telephone call from the manager of a car rental franchise. Near your hotel, as a matter of fact. A man who spoke in English and sounded American just rented a large panel van. Despite the fact he spoke only in English, his ID was German. The clerk at the desk did the deal. But the manager was in the back office and overheard the conversation. He recognized the customer's voice. The guy had rented there before, not long ago. Afterwards for some reason the manager checked the deal in the computer and saw the guy had used a completely different name than the last time. He had used a whole different set of ID.'

'When was this?' Reacher said.

'Twenty minutes ago.'

'Description?'

'Vague, but it could be Wiley. That's why I'm calling you. I already sent a car with a copy of the sketch. We'll know in a minute or two.'

'Was the name German the last time?'

295

'Yes, but different. Last time it was Ernst, and this time it's Gebhardt.'

'OK, thanks,' Reacher said. 'Get back to us when the rental people have seen the sketch.'

He killed the call.

Sinclair said, 'This is the endgame. Starting now. The van is for the delivery.'

'And then he's getting the hell out,' Waterman said. 'He's burning through his spare ID. He's keeping his Sunday best for the airport.'

'Twenty minutes,' Landry said. 'He could be ten miles out of town by now. Griezman has no more jurisdiction. We need to go federal.'

The phone rang.

Griezman.

Who said, 'Now we have a positive ID on the sketch. It was Wiley who rented the truck. Confidence level is a hundred per cent. I already put out an APB on the plate number. The traffic division will handle it. They can liaise out of town. They do it all the time. We're assuming a fifteen-kilometre radius by now. About ten miles. It's coming up on twenty-five minutes. Almost certainly he's moving south or east. Unless he's going to Denmark or Holland. We have cars on the main roads and the autobahns. Rest assured we'll have a lot of eyeballs on it. It's a large vehicle. And slow.'

'What address did he use?' Reacher asked.

'It was phoney. Nothing but a hole in the ground. For another new apartment building on the other side of town.'

'Anything else?' Reacher said.

'Just that the clerk at the rental franchise said Wiley was concerned about the height of the load floor, and that he needed a roll-up rear door, not hinged, because he said he intended to back the truck up to another truck and transfer a load across.'

'Thanks,' Reacher said.

He killed the call.

Sinclair said, 'At least now we know what kind of thing it is. It's not a document. It's not intelligence. It needs a large panel van with a roll-up door.'

'To back up to a similar vehicle,' Neagley said. 'Why? If the load is already in a truck, why get another truck?'

'Maybe the first truck was stolen,' Reacher said. 'Maybe he's worried about getting pulled over.'

Neagley turned and leafed through the telex concertina. Cold-case property crimes in Germany, near military installations, during Wiley's deployment. She traced her finger down the faint grey list.

Her finger stopped.

She said, 'Seven months ago a delivery truck with a roll-up door was stolen from a mom-and-pop furniture store on the outskirts of Frankfurt. Local and then national police were given the number, but the vehicle was never found.'

Her finger started again. She licked her thumb and turned the pages.

She said, 'Nothing else. Plenty of cars, but no more roll-up doors.'

Reacher said, 'That was three months before he went AWOL.'

'It was a long game.'

'Did he steal the thing the same night he stole the truck?'

'Almost certainly. Which begins to define a location. If he's the kind of guy who worries about getting pulled over, he would steal the truck close by, drive it the minimum, steal the thing, drive the minimum again, and hide the truck as soon as possible. In a barn, or something. With the thing still inside. A triangular route, fast and focused. Minimum mileage. Minimum risk. We could be looking at a fairly small area, some-where near Frankfurt.'

'But then he returned to his unit. For three months. Why?'

'He was lying low. Waiting for a reaction. Hiding in plain sight. Which was a smart move. We'd have been looking at AWOLs and outside bad guys. Not grunts on the post. But the thing was never missed. The alarm was never raised. There was no reaction. So as soon as he felt sure of that, he left, at the next opportunity. He holed up in Hamburg. It took him four months to sell the thing. Now he's headed back to pick it up.'

'Those are big conclusions,' Sinclair said. 'Aren't they? Anyone could have stolen that furniture truck.'

Reacher said, 'We need to know where Wiley was seven months ago. We need his movement orders.'

'They're coming,' Neagley said.

And right then the telex machine burst into chatter-ing life.

Wiley had driven the big new van back towards the

centre of town, slowly, carefully, inching through the city traffic, waiting at lights, checking his mirrors. He looped around the Aussenalster lake, and crawled through St Georg, curving west, heading towards where he lived, but long before he got there he turned left and rumbled over a boxy metal bridge, into the old docks, where the piers were too small for modern freighters, which meant the warehouses were also too small, which made them cheap to rent.

He parked in front of a dull green double door, and slid down from the high seat. The double door had padlocked bolts top and bottom, and a padlocked hasp in the middle. He had all three keys. He opened the right-hand door, and propped it, and then he walked back and opened the left-hand door, and propped it.

The space inside was about thirty feet by forty, by more than fifteen feet tall. Like a double garage in a nice suburban house in Sugar Land, but swollen up some. The right-hand slot was empty. The left-hand slot had the old furniture truck. He had driven it from Frankfurt seven months before, the same night he stole it. The same night he loaded its precious cargo. The crazy sprint was not strictly necessary, because he had changed the plates, to be on the safe side. He could have taken his time. But he had wanted to get where he was going. He wanted to hunker down. He only just made it. It was an old truck. A piece of shit, basically. The oil light was on the whole way. The engine was making noises. It was close to dying when he parked it, nose in, thankful to have gotten it there. Thankful to have avoided a tow truck. Some things would have been hard to explain. He shut it down and it never started again. Seized solid. Hence the rental. He parked it next to its predecessor, and he closed the dull green doors, and padlocked the bolts again, and the hasp, and he put the keys in his pocket. He crossed an old iron footbridge to a different pier, and then the new footbridges took over, soaring teak and steel, carrying him from one pier to the next, to the rear of his development, where he walked between two buildings and past another, to his lobby, and his elevator, and his apartment door.

Muller closed his office door and called Dremmler on his desk phone. He said, 'The man in the sketch has left town in a truck. We just got a request for assistance from Griezman's division. We're putting an APB on the plate number. Starting fifteen kilometres out, going national if we need to.'

'He's delivering,' Dremmler said. 'We missed it.'

'No, the truck is clearly empty. He just picked it up from a rental franchise.'

'Then he's collecting something from somewhere else. Which is much more interesting. Keep me informed. Make sure I'm the first to know.'

'I will.'

'I'm afraid the other thing didn't work out.'

'Reacher?'

'He predicted it. He brought people with him. He ambushed the ambush. A squad of twelve, my guys said. All armed with military weapons. Plus him. My guys didn't stand a chance.'

* * *

300

Wiley was on a ninety-six hour pass the night the truck was stolen. Whereabouts unknown. That was the first thing his movement orders revealed. His immediately previous location had been his regular billet, on a post some miles north and east of the mom-and-pop furniture store. But not many miles, Reacher thought. Dozens, not hundreds. He knew the area. He had been there many times. It was all reasonably local. Like Sugar Land to downtown Houston. A bus ride.

Beginning to end the orders showed Wiley arriving in the country, and then bouncing back and forth between what used to be a forward position in the battle area, to a rearward position in a maintenance depot. Which was the post north and east of Frankfurt. There were also regular voluntary detachments to a storage lager thirty miles west. What was once a supply depot was by then a dump for stuff no one needed any more. Members of Wiley's unit could volunteer to go cannibalize parts from retired machines. The XO called it hands-on training in on-the-field maintenance. Which Reacher agreed sounded better than the guy admitting he had to scavenge retreads to keep his unit limping along. But despite the hard sell it was not popular duty. There had been four opportunities. No one had volunteered more than once.

Except Wiley.

Wiley had volunteered three times.

The first three.

But not the fourth.

Neagley said, 'That's where he saw it, obviously. Whatever it is. In the storage lager. Has to be. Maybe the first time, he searched for it. The second time, he found it. The third time, he planned it. Then he stole it, seven months ago. Which meant he didn't have to go back the fourth time. The thing was gone by then. He already had it.'

'Hidden nearby, according to you. We need to confirm it. We need eyes on the road. Four guys with binoculars, like a visual trap. Maybe on the autobahn south of Hanover. He can't have gotten that far yet.'

He dialled Griezman, who said he would take care of it.

Sinclair said, 'He's very helpful.'

Reacher said, 'So far.'

'Are you blackmailing him?'

'I said I wouldn't, but I'm not sure he believes me. So I guess I am, in a way. The end result is the same.'

'Long may it continue.'

'It won't,' Reacher said. 'Griezman will dump us as soon as he gets a bigger problem.'

'Is there a bigger problem than this?'

'He doesn't know how bad it is.'

'Should we tell him?' Sinclair said. 'Should we make an official request for assistance?'

White said, 'That would be a political disaster. It would project weakness. Russia is practically next door. We can't wash our dirty linen in public.'

Waterman said, 'And it's too late anyway. The Germans would take half a day even to respond. It would take a whole day to brief them in properly. Maybe more, because they're starting from cold. Which means Wiley would get at least a thirty-six hour start.

302

By then he could be anywhere. This is a big country now.'

Dremmler's office was on the fourth floor of a building wholly owned by him. He rode down in the elevator, which was the original 1950s item. Reliable, but slow. It took twenty seconds to reach the lobby. During which time Dremmler imported and sold thirty-three pairs of Brazilian shoes. Which was a comforting statistic. A million pairs a week. More than fifty million pairs a year.

He left his building and walked through the weak midday sun, a block, two, three, to the bar with the varnished wood front. Once upon a time it would have been considered early for a lunch break, but the place was already crowded. Because new staggered office hours meant lunch breaks happened throughout the day, in a ceaseless ongoing relay.

Dremmler pushed through the crowd, nodding and greeting, until he saw Wolfgang Schlupp on a stool at the bar. Not an impressive specimen. Dark hair, dark eyes, lean dark face, built like a shivering dog. But useful. About to be more useful. Dremmler elbowed in next to him, shoulder first, his back to the room. He said, 'How's business, Herr Schlupp?'

Schlupp said, 'What do you need?'

'Information,' Dremmler said. 'For the cause. The new Germany depends on it.'

A barman in a heavy canvas apron came over and Dremmler ordered a litre of beer.

Schlupp said, 'What kind of information?'

'You made a driver's licence and maybe a passport for an American gentleman.'

'Hold it right there. I didn't make nothing.'

'OK, you passed a customer's order to your partners in Berlin. They made it. All you did was keep half the money.'

'So what?'

Dremmler squeezed himself some extra space and took out the drawing. He smoothed it on the bar.

He said, 'This guy.'

The hair, the brow, the cheekbones. The deep-set eyes.

Schlupp said, 'I don't remember him.'

'I think you do.'

'What of it?'

'It's important to the cause.'

'What is?'

'What new name did this man take?'

'Why do you need to know?'

'We want to find him.'

Schlupp said, 'You know I can't tell you. What kind of business would I have? No one would trust me.'

'This is one time only. No one will ever know. This guy is in trouble already. But we want him first. Right now he's heading somewhere in an empty panel van. To pick something up. Presumably a heavy load. Given the size of the van. Could be weapons. Could be Nazi gold from a salt mine.'

'And you want it.'

'For all of us. For the cause. It would make a huge difference.'

Schlupp didn't answer.

Dremmler said, 'There would be a finder's fee, of course. Or a consultation agreement. Or a straight commission, if you like.'

Schlupp said, 'I would be taking a risk. It's like being a priest. It's understood I won't talk.'

'The size of the fee would of course reflect the size of the risk.'

Schlupp looked at the sketch.

He said, 'I think I remember him. I've done a lot of Americans. I think this guy chose three separate names. The first two were identity cards and driver's licences only. But I think the third had a passport.'

'What were the names?'

'It was months ago. I would have to look it up.'

'You don't remember?'

'I hear hundreds of names.'

'When can you do it?'

'When I get home.'

'Call me at once, will you? It's very important. To the cause.'

'OK,' Schlupp said.

Dremmler nodded in satisfaction and left the way he had come, leading with the other shoulder, pushing through the crowd, nodding and greeting, back to the weak midday sun beyond the open door.

The barman who had served his litre of beer picked up the phone.

The phone rang in the consulate room. Vanderbilt picked it up and gave it to Reacher. It was Orozco. He said, 'Are we in trouble?'

'Not yet,' Reacher said. 'We think Wiley's heading for Frankfurt. We think he stole something from the storage lager near his home base, about seven months ago. Then we think he hid it. Now we think he's heading down there to pick it up.'

'We have plenty of people in Frankfurt.'

'I know,' Reacher said. 'I'll call them if I need them.'

'I just finished up with Billy Bob and Jimmy Lee. They saved the best for last. Turns out they sold an M9 to Wiley. So bear that in mind. He's armed.'

Wiley's phone rang, and he took the call in his kitchen. He knew immediately from the background noise who it was. The friendly barman, made friendlier still by liberal applications of folding money, in amounts somewhere between tips and bribes. Plus an extra wad for just-in-case emergencies. Or warnings. Or whatever else in the opinion of the guy who was taking the cash would be appreciated by the guy who was giving the cash. The same the world over. All unsaid and unspoken but well understood.

The guy said, 'Wolfgang Schlupp is going to sell you out to Dremmler.'

Wiley said, 'For how much?'

'A percentage. Dremmler says you're on your way to find Nazi gold.'

'I was on my way to the bathroom.'

'You've got until Schlupp gets home.'

The phone rang again in the consulate room, and Landry picked it up, and gave it to Neagley, who gave it to Reacher. It was Griezman. He said, 'It turns out our traffic division needs extreme detail for a remote operation like Hanover. We'll all save time if you give them the specifications direct. Better accuracy, too. I've alerted their deputy chief. He's expecting your call. I'll give you his number. His name is Muller.'

'OK,' Reacher said. 'Anything else?'

'Nothing. Good luck.'

'Thank you.'

Reacher hung up and redialled.

The phone rang on Muller's desk. He closed the door and sat down and picked up. An American voice said, 'Is that Deputy Chief Muller?'

Muller said, 'Yes.'

'My name is Reacher. I believe Chief of Detectives Griezman told you I would call.'

Muller moved a file and found a pad of message forms. He picked up a pencil. He noted the date, the time, and the caller. He said, 'Apparently you wish autobahn traffic to be monitored south of Hanover.'

'You have the plate number. I need to know if it's heading from here to the Frankfurt area.'

'What exactly do you envisage from us?'

'Cars on the shoulders. Or on the bridges. Four pairs of eyes. Like a regular speed trap, but with binoculars, not radar guns.'

'We have no experience of such things, Mr Reacher. There are no speed limits on the autobahns.'

'But you get the gist.'

'I have seen American television.' Muller wrote *gist* on the message pad.

Reacher said, 'Communication needs to be instant. I need time to arrange things at the other end.'

Muller said, 'Do you know where he's going?'

'Not exactly. Not yet.'

'Tell me when you work it out. I could allocate resources.'

'Thank you, I will.'

Muller hung up. He tore the top sheet off the message pad. He tore it in half, and in quarters, and eighths, and sixteenths, like confetti, which he dropped in his trash can. Reacher could claim the conversation had taken place, but Muller could claim it had ended with a last-gasp never-mind withdrawal, and hence cancellation of all just-agreed points. Couldn't be proven either way. A classic he-said-she-said, which the cops always won.

He dialled Dremmler.

He said, 'Believe it or not, I just had Reacher on the phone. A problem Griezman dumped in my lap. Reacher thinks Wiley is heading to Frankfurt. He promised to tell me the exact destination, just as soon as he has it.'

'Excellent.'

'Did you get his new name?'

'It's on its way very soon.'

Wolfgang Schlupp left the bar as soon as he was good and ready, and he took two alleys and a bus, which let him out one alley and two left turns from home, which was a top-floor apartment in a pre-war townhouse. No elevator, given the age of the place. But plenty of equity.

There had long been a rumour the whole townhouse row had been incorrectly repaired after the wartime bombing. But then an engineer's report had proved exactly the opposite. Prices had doubled overnight. Schlupp had gotten in early. He had overheard a conversation in the bar, back to back with two city officials, swapping gossip.

He walked up the stairs, through the second-floor lobby, through the third, and onward.

Wiley heard him coming. He was leaning on the wall, in the shadow between a fire cabinet and a hot-water riser. He had a gun in his hand. His Beretta M9, army kind-of surplus, bought from two chuckleheads stealing from a supply company, in the very same bar where the talkative Mr Schlupp plied his not-so-secret-after-all trade.

Schlupp stepped up from the top stair, and hunched left, and unlocked his door. Wiley came out of the shadow and shoved him through it, the gun in his back, kicking the door shut with his heel, pushing him on down the hallway, to a spacious living room, all urban and grey and bare brick, where Schlupp tripped and fell on a black leather sofa, and lay there helpless.

Wiley stood above him and aimed the gun at his face.

He said, 'I heard you're going to sell me out, Wolfgang.'

'Not true,' Schlupp said. 'I would never do that. What kind of business would I have?'

'You told Dremmler you would.'

'I was going to make up a name and send him on a wild goose chase.'

'You got records here?'

'All in code.'

'Why not make up a name in the bar? Why wait to get back to the records?'

'Was it Dremmler who told you?'

'Doesn't matter who. You were going to sell me out. You were going to look me up in the records. Dremmler told you to call him at once, because it was very important to the cause.'

'No way, man. That's bullshit. How could I? Who would trust me again?'

'Why didn't you make up a name in the bar?'

Schlupp didn't answer.

Wiley said, 'Show me the records.'

Schlupp struggled to his feet and they went down the hallway the same way they came up, but slower, the gun in Schlupp's back all the way, to a small bedroom in use as an office.

Schlupp pointed to a high shelf.

He said, 'The red file folder.'

Which was like a three-ring binder, except it had four. Pre-punched pages had lines of handwritten code, nonsense non-words in separate columns, maybe old name, new name, passport, licence, national ID.

Wiley said, 'Which one am I?'

'I wasn't going to sell you out.'

'Why didn't you make up a name in the bar?'

'Dremmler's full of it, man. Right now he thinks you're deep in the country in a panel van, looking for

310

Nazi gold. But evidently you're not. So he's wrong about that, which means he could be wrong about everything. That's logical, right? Why even listen to him?'

'I didn't,' Wiley said. 'I listened to the barman. Dremmler asked and you answered. You were going to sell me out. If you didn't want to, you would have given up a phoney name right there and then. Or OK, maybe you froze, but a minute later you would have figured it out and said, yes now I remember, he calls himself Schmidt. Or some such. But you didn't.'

'He scares me, man. He can make trouble. OK, I was going to to tell him. But I changed my mind.'

'When you saw me?'

'No, before.'

'I don't believe you.'

'What kind of business would I have?'

'Dremmler told you he'd cover the risk.'

'I swear, man. You're wrong. I changed my mind. I would never do it.'

In for a penny, in for a pound.

All or nothing.

Wiley said, 'Better safe than sorry, pal.'

He swapped hands on the gun, fast and smooth and fluid, and he cracked Schlupp hard on the temple, backhand, with the heel of the butt. He didn't want to shoot him. Not there. Too noisy. He hit him again, forehand, on the other temple, and the guy's head bounced around like a rag doll. When it came to rest Wiley hit him again, a vicious downward chop, right on the top of his skull, like an axe or a hammer. Schlupp fell to his knees. Wiley hit him again. Schlupp pitched forward and fell on his face. Wiley leaned down and hit him again, and again, and again, and again, and again.

Bone cracked and blood oozed and spattered.

Wiley stopped and took a breath.

He checked Schlupp's neck for a pulse.

Nothing.

He gave it a whole minute, just to be sure. Still nothing. So he wiped his gun on Schlupp's shirt, and he picked up the red file folder, and he left.

THIRTY

Reacher sat quiet in the corner of the consulate room, waiting for the phone to ring, wondering who would call first, either New Orleans or Deputy Chief Muller in the traffic division. It was like waiting for the winner of a slow-motion race. He pictured dawn breaking over the delta, languorously, and local FBI agents waking up and eating breakfast, slowly, and then heading out. At which point the process might get a little faster. Presumably their appointment with Wiley's mother would be their first of the day. Given the pressure from Waterman and Landry. Possibly as early as eight o'clock in the morning, given that a welfare recipient would want to stay cool with the government. Against that semi-leisurely Louisiana timeline ran Wiley's panel van, five thousand miles away in Germany, cruising at maybe sixty miles an hour, closing in on Hanover, and bypassing it, and leaving it behind, and rolling on south towards the unmarked cars. Who would get there first?

The phone rang.

Neither New Orleans nor Deputy Chief Muller.

It was Griezman.

Who said, 'I have a serious problem.'

Reacher said, 'What kind?'

'We have a homicide in the old part of town. A small man with his head bashed in. It's a very fresh scene. A neighbour heard a noise. I feel obliged to send all my men there, at least for today. I really have no alternative. So I'm very sorry, my friend, but I am forced to suspend our temporary assistance.'

'And you're wondering how I'm going to feel about that.'

Griezman paused a beat.

'No,' he said. 'I took you at your word.'

Reacher said, 'Good luck with the homicide.'

'Thank you.'

Reacher killed the call. Sinclair looked a question, and Reacher said, 'We're on our own now.'

'Because you're such a gentleman.'

'We have time.'

'The messenger could be in Zurich by now.'

'Doesn't matter. It's this part that matters. Something physical in a panel van. Which can't move like money. Not secretly in the blink of an eye. It's slow and ponderous and noisy and visible, because it's real.'

'Except Muller hasn't seen it.'

'Yet.'

'How long will you give it?'

'Two hours, maybe.'

'Then what?'

'I'll conclude Wiley wasn't headed for Frankfurt.'

The phone rang again.

This time it was the New Orleans FBI, patched

through direct from their car outside the one-room shack where Wiley's mother lived. Two agents, a man and a woman. Immediate reports, as requested. They had led off their interview with the scripted questions, about the name Arnold, and the drafted rancher, and the Davy Crockett fan. Turned out they were all the same guy. His full name was Arnold Peter Mason. Born and grew up in Amarillo, Texas. As a kid he worked on a ranch, then he did twenty years in the U.S. Army, and then he lived with Wiley's mother in Sugar Land, Texas, for a six-year spell, from when young Horace Wiley was about ten years old until he was about sixteen. And yes, young Horace had called Arnold his uncle. He was an older man than Wiley's mother had been accustomed to, and he was a still, silent man with secrets, but at first he had been a good provider. More details would follow.

Landry, Vanderbilt and Neagley all plugged the name into their respective systems. Arnold Peter Mason. Landry got nothing of immediate top-line interest. Neither did Vanderbilt. Neagley got a twenty-year NCO in the airborne infantry. No gold stars, no red flags. Plenty of time in Germany, way back when anything could happen.

Still alive, according to the Social Security mainframe. Sixty-five years old. Still working, according to the Internal Revenue Service. A modest income, declining year on year. Maybe odd jobs or labouring, slowing up ahead of retirement.

The owner of a passport, according to the State Department.

No address within the United States.

The IRS said his tax returns had been filed from overseas.

CIA flagged him as living in Germany.

The Berlin embassy showed him registered as a retired military U.S. citizen resident in a small village near Bremen. An hour away from Hamburg.

Reacher said, 'Is this a co-production? Is this the two of them together?'

Neagley said, 'Maybe that's where the first truck is hidden. At Uncle Arnold's place, not Frankfurt.'

'Then why bring a second truck now?'

'Maybe Uncle Arnold let the tyres go flat.'

'Or maybe they're going to split the load. If it's a co-production. Maybe the hundred million is for Wiley's half only.'

'Wait,' White said. 'Look at this. Uncle Arnold has been in Germany nearly twenty years. Since Wiley was sixteen. That's a hell of a long game.'

'And look at this,' Vanderbilt said.

Also listed along with Mason on the embassy's register were two non-citizen dependants.

Landry said, 'A buck gets ten that's a wife and a kid.'

Then the phone rang again. The New Orleans FBI, direct from their car, with an important bullet-point update. After six years of relative happiness Mrs Wiley had kicked Arnold Mason out of her house because she accidentally discovered he had a wife in Germany. And a son. The boy was handicapped. Mrs Wiley didn't have much, but she had her standards.

Wiley was a practical man, so he cleaned his gun in the

dishwasher. Why not? The M9 was built to military specifications. It was designed to withstand continuous salt water immersion. He used the full pots-and-pans cycle, with the full drying phase. Then he would oil the parts and put the gun back together again, pristine and good as new.

He had balled up his spattered clothes with the red file folder and put them in the kitchen trash. A considered decision. First instinct was to take them out and dump them in a can on the street. Not too close, but not too far, either. No one liked to walk a long distance with a suspicious object in his hand. And then hypothetically there might be a full-court press, and hypothetically the trash cans on the street might get searched, so why let them draw a circle on the map and figure out where you live? Better to leave it right there. The landlord would find it in a month. By which point it wouldn't matter.

Wiley picked up the phone and dialled his travel agent. The same girl who had booked his trip to Zurich. She spoke good English. She knew he liked a window seat. She had all the details from his shiny new passport.

Muller didn't call. No one was surprised. The working hypothesis had changed from Frankfurt to Bremen. To Uncle Arnold's place. Bishop brought a CIA map and spread it on a table. The embassy showed the top line of the address as Gelb Bauernhof. A name, not a street number. Therefore possibly rural. Possibly a farm. Reacher pictured barns and garages and outbuildings, and piles of worn-out tyres.

317

Hiding places.

He said, 'We need a car.'

Bishop said, 'You need a plan.'

The telex machine started up.

'Uncle Arnold's service record,' Neagley said.

Reacher said, 'The plan is Sergeant Neagley and I will conduct surveillance and gather intelligence.'

'Negative,' Bishop said. 'CIA and the NSC must be represented. Dr Sinclair and I will come with you. And the rules of engagement are no engagement at all. Strictly observation only. That's a dealbreaker. Legally, this is a complex situation.'

'Bring a weapon,' Reacher said. 'Wiley has one. And if it's a farm, they'll have a shotgun.'

'I said observation only.'

'Bring one anyway.'

White said, 'You have to get the Iranian out. You're saying one hour from now there could be a shooting war. At that exact moment their deal is dead and the Iranian won't survive it. If you leave him there, you'll kill him.'

Bishop said nothing.

The phone rang.

Griezman.

Who said, 'Do you believe in coincidence?'

Reacher said, 'Sometimes.'

'Our homicide victim was a regular patron of Helmut Klopp's bar. He did his business there. Everyone's lying, of course, but I think he was the one who sold the ID.'

'Why?'

'Whispers, from other people with other things to hide.'

'Do you have a suspect?'

'Someone preventing or avenging betrayal.'

'Was someone just betrayed?'

'No.'

'Preventing, then.'

'There are no written records in the victim's apartment. There is however a space in an otherwise neat shelf of file folders.'

'Mission accomplished,' Reacher said.

Then he said, 'Which could be ironic.'

Griezman said, 'How?'

'It's a question of timing. You buy ID and decide to kill the supplier and remove his records to prevent future betrayal. But when do you do it? That's the question. Would a new client take that risk immediately after delivery? Or an old client at a time of maximum pressure, with his plan finally in motion, and maybe already going a little ragged at the edges?'

'I don't know.'

'Neither do I. I guess it's about fifty-fifty.'

'You think it's Wiley.'

'No, I don't. There could be any number of old clients under stress. And I think Wiley was driving a van at the time. But you're a responsible copper. You'll put him on your list. You'll have to. Which means your temporary assistance just started up again.'

'I thought you gave up on that.'

'On what?'

'Driving the van. Muller told me you cancelled your request.'

'When?'

'I spoke to him an hour ago.'

'No, when did I cancel?'

'He said you discussed specifics for a while and then suddenly changed your mind.'

'Last thing I said was I didn't know exactly where Wiley was going. He said to tell him when I did. Maybe I misunderstood. Maybe he was waiting for me to call. Maybe he never even started.'

'He said you cancelled.'

'Then he misunderstood, not me.'

'I agree, his English is not excellent.'

Bishop called across the room, 'The car is here.'

THIRTY-ONE

Bishop's CIA car was exactly the same as Orozco's MP car, a big blue Opel sedan identical in every respect, except it had no bulletproof divider. Bishop drove, and Sinclair sat next to him in the front. Reacher and Neagley sat in the back. Neagley was comfortable and Reacher was not. Traffic was moving. The sky was grey.

Neagley read out loud the telex summary of Arnold Mason's service career. He had been drafted at the age of twenty, in 1951, but sent to Germany, not Korea, where he stayed for twenty years, apart from stateside trips for training and manoeuvres. He was airborne infantry throughout, trained for the Soviet conflict, and deployed with good but not elite units. He was honourably discharged at the age of forty, in 1971, terminal at staff sergeant.

Sinclair said, 'Prior to which he married a German girl and had a kid. Who he returned to twenty years ago after just six years away. Yet Wiley feels connected. This is a weird relationship.'

By then the view out the window was agricultural, in a flat, perfect, close-to-the-city kind of a way. The fields were as neat as vegetable gardens, and not much larger. Every road and every street had a name, neatly lettered in Gothic script, black on cream. The passing villages were very small. Not much more than crowded and crooked crossroads. There were barns and outbuildings here and there, but smaller and fewer than Reacher expected. It wasn't what he had pictured. It was less private and more orderly. It was clean and tidy. Not densely but uniformly populated. Everything was pretty close to everything else.

Bishop said, 'Next but one dot on the map and we're there.'

The next but one dot was a little larger than previous versions. A little denser. They picked up the name of Arnold Mason's road at a free-for-all five-way in the centre of town. It hooked back west of north, away from Bremen in the distance. It was lined left and right with tiny pocket-handkerchief farms, no more than small and perfectly neat houses with a few immaculate acres. There were sheds, but no barns.

Each farm had a name. All appropriately modest. All no doubt picked out by the owners, with a measure of pride. Reacher watched for Gelb Bauernhof, and suddenly understood what it meant. It was German for Yellow Farm. Yellow in Spanish was Amarillo. Where Arnold Mason was born. Amarillo, Texas. The guy had named his farm for where he grew up.

They found it fifth on the right. They were going slow, to read the names. So they got a good look. Not much to see. Maybe four acres planted in perfect lines, growing something dark green, possibly cabbages, and a small

322

neat house, and a small neat stand-alone garage, and a small neat stand-alone shed, set back a little ways. And that was it. The garage would take a Mercedes station wagon. The shed would take a small tractor or a ride-on machine. Neither one would take a stolen furniture truck.

Bishop stopped the car a mile down the road.

Reacher said, 'I should go back and knock on the door.'

Sinclair said, 'That's a risk.'

'Wiley isn't there. No new van. No old van, either.'

'That doesn't prove Uncle Arnold isn't involved somehow.'

'He won't shoot me straight off the bat. He'll play dumb. He'll try to talk his way out of it. I'll let him, if necessary. I agree, if the vans were here it would be different.'

'Wiley might arrive while you're in there.'

'It's a possibility. But unlikely. If it happens, I'm sure Sergeant Neagley will think of something.'

'We should all go.'

'Works for me,' Reacher said.

Bishop said nothing.

'Arnold Mason is an American citizen,' Sinclair said. 'You're from the consulate. You're entitled to make contact.'

Bishop said, 'We can't afford to screw this up.'

'We'll shut it down at the first sign of trouble.'

'Don't stand close together,' Reacher said. 'Not at first, anyway. Not until we're sure.'

Bishop turned the car around on the narrow road.

Gelb Bauernhof was a property about a hundred yards wide by two hundred deep. Like a high-end suburban lot in America. But a farm nonetheless. Albeit in miniature. There was nothing yellow about it. The sky was grey, and the dirt was brown, and the cabbages were army green. Bishop turned in at the driveway. Which was dirt, hand scraped to a consistent camber. The big blue Opel hissed over it. The garage was dead ahead. The house was to the left. About eighty yards from the street.

Bishop rolled on. There was no reaction. He stopped where a footpath left the driveway and led to the house. Now twenty yards away. Still no reaction.

Then a man came out of the house.

He left the front door open, and took two steps, and stood on the path and watched. He was about Reacher's own age. Maybe thirty-five. He stood tall and straight. Fair hair, a shapeless grey sweater, and shapeless grey pants.

Nothing on his feet.

Reacher said, 'I'll go first.'

He got out of the car slowly, and took a step. The guy on the path just watched. Another step. All good. So Reacher kept on going, a step at a time, until he was face to face with the guy. Like a salesman calling. Or a neighbour in need of advice.

Reacher said, 'I need to speak with Arnold Peter Mason.'

The guy didn't answer. Didn't react at all. Like he hadn't heard. He was looking past Reacher's shoulder into the middle distance. Nothing there but cabbages.

Reacher said, 'Herr Mason?'

The guy looked at him. Blue eyes. Empty. Nothing going on back there. The lights were on, but no one was home. The handicapped son. Same age as Wiley. Same generation as the so-called nephew. Thirty-five years old, but still a dependant.

Reacher pointed to the house with one hand and made an arm-around-the-shoulder shape with the other, and said, 'Let's both of us go inside.'

The guy did nothing for a moment, and then he turned and walked briskly back to the house, his bare feet slapping, and he leaned in the open door and pounded on the wall, and shouted out, 'Mutti!'

Then he stood back and waited.

A woman came out. She was small and trim. She had fading blonde hair cut short. She was maybe sixty-five years old. A kind face. Worn, but still handsome. She smiled benignly at Reacher, as if to say she was sure he understood, and then she turned away and thanked her son for a job well done, squeezing his hands, patting his shoulder, cupping his cheek, sending him back inside.

Then she stepped up to where Reacher was waiting. She looked at him for a second, and then she said, 'Are you from the army?'

She spoke in English, with an accent but no hesitation.

Reacher said, 'How did you know?'

'Arnold said you would come.'

'Did he?'

'Although he thought sooner. But still.'

325

'I'm Major Reacher.'

'I'm Frau Mason.'

'Is Arnold home?'

'Of course.'

The others got out of the car and followed Reacher and the woman through the door. The house was small inside, but light and cheerful, with white paint and sprigged wallpapers. The woman led Reacher to a back parlour. She went in. He followed. She crossed the room and bent down and hugged a man in a wheelchair. She kissed him awake. She said, 'Darling, this is Major Reacher from the army.'

Arnold Mason. Once a teenage ranch hand, then an infantry soldier, then a family man with two different families. Now collapsed in a wheelchair, slack on one side, one eye looking, the other eye shut.

Reacher said, 'Good afternoon, Mr Mason.'

The guy didn't answer. He was sixty-five years old, but he looked ninety-five. He had no strength. No focus. Reacher looked at the woman and said, 'Frau Mason, can we talk?'

They went back to the hallway. Bishop and Sinclair introduced themselves as government workers. Reacher asked, 'What happened to him?'

The woman said, 'Don't you know?'

'No, we don't.'

'He has a growth in his head.'

'Like a tumour?'

'It's a long word I don't understand. It's crushing his brain. One part after another. Day by day.'

'I'm sorry.'

'He knew you would be.'

Reacher said, 'When did it start?'

'A year and a half ago.'

'Can he talk?'

'A little. He lost movement on one side, so he sounds funny. But he's not upset about it. He was never much of a talker. And now he can't remember anything anyway.'

'That could be a problem. We're here to ask him questions.'

'I thought you were here to help him.'

'Why?'

'He said if he got sick someone from the army was sure to come.'

'Has he been treated by the army before?'

'No, never.'

'How bad is his memory?'

'Patchy, but mostly very bad.'

'How tired does he get?'

'He'll lose track after the first few questions.'

Reacher said, 'Would you wait outside?'

'Has he done something wrong?'

'The questions are about the period immediately after he mustered out. The six years he wasn't here. He might not want you to hear his answers. I'm obliged to consider his privacy.'

The woman said, 'I know all about Mrs Wiley, in Sugar Land, Texas. Is that all this is about?'

'Her son,' Reacher said.

They went back in the parlour. Mason was still awake, and a little brighter. He acknowledged introductions with a vague one-eyed glance and a movement of his hand. His wife crouched behind his chair and hugged his shoulders, as if to reassure him, and Reacher squatted in front of him, to get in his line of sight.

Reacher said, 'Mr Mason, do you remember Horace Wiley?'

Mason closed his working eye, and held it shut a moment, and then opened it again. His gaze was far-away and watery. The working half of his face moved with exaggerated diction and he said, 'Call me Arnold.'

His voice was low and breathy, and half his mouth was frozen, but the words came out clear enough.

Reacher said, 'Arnold, tell me about Horace Wiley.'

Mason's eye closed again, longer, as if he was consulting an internal source of information, and then his eye opened, and with half a hint of half a smile he said, 'I used to call him Horse. Sounded about the same in Texas anyway.'

'What was the last time you heard from him?'

A pause.

Mason said, 'I guess I never heard from him. Not since I left.'

'Did you tell him Davy Crockett stories?'

A longer pause.

Longer.

Mason said, 'I don't remember any of that.'

'He said he joined the army because you told him Davy Crockett stories.'

'Horse joined the army? Hot damn.'

'What about the stories?'

'I don't remember.'

'You sure?'

'Maybe it was a television show the kid was watching.'

'Nothing more?'

'I don't think I would have told stories. Not back then. People said I didn't talk much.'

Then his eye closed again, and his chin fell to his chest. His wife propped his head comfortably and hauled herself up. She said, 'He'll sleep now. That was more talking than he's used to.'

They filed out to the hallway with the sprig wallpaper. The woman said, 'Can you help him?'

Bishop said, 'We'll check with the Veterans' Administration.'

Reacher said, 'Did he ever tell you the Davy Crockett stories?'

The woman said, 'No, never.'

Sinclair said, 'How is your son?'

'He's well, thank you. A little slow. By now like a seven-year-old. But placid, not boisterous. We have much to look forward to. Except that Arnold blames himself. Which is why he went back to Texas after his discharge. All those years ago. He ran away. He couldn't face it all day every day. Because he thought it was his fault.'

'Why?'

'It's genetic. It's him or me. He says it's him. Truth is it could be both of us. But he insists. But he came back in the end. It all calmed down. He did very well. But he still blames himself. And now he worries what will become of us.'

* * *

They got back in the car, and they turned around, and they drove away. Reacher said, 'Did you believe him?'

'Believe what?' Sinclair said. 'He couldn't remember anything.'

'Did you believe he couldn't remember anything?'

'Didn't you?'

'I wasn't sure. On the one hand, OK, he's dying from a brain tumour. On the other hand, I didn't like the call-me-Arnold bullshit. He was buying time. He was an infantryman twenty years, so he can smell MPs a mile away. He wanted to think about his answers.'

'Which were, in the end?'

'No, Wiley hadn't contacted him, and no, he didn't remember telling Davy Crockett stories.'

'You think he was lying?'

'A person in that condition is hard to read. I think the first part was probably true. He was sad, not defensive. But he paused an awful long time after the Davy Crockett question. Maybe it was the brain tumour. Or maybe he was putting two and two together. The passage of time, plus Horace Wiley's inborn nature, which he observed at close quarters, plus whatever was in the Davy Crockett stories, plus then many years later the sudden appearance of an O-4 investigator, equals some kind of an eventual bad outcome. And therefore a need for denial. Which our natural sympathy excuses as memory loss. Which it might actually be. But we'll never know for sure. Because we can't find out. We can't smack the guy around. So to speak.'

330

Bishop said, 'He can't be actively involved. He's been sick a year and a half.'

'Agreed,' Reacher said.

'So it's all about the Davy Crockett stories. Which at face value sound like nothing. Just stupid fairy tales for kids. But they were top of Wiley's cryptic list. So clearly they have personal meaning for him.'

Sinclair said, 'Personal meaning how?'

Neagley said, 'He didn't tell his wife. So they were work-based stories, not home-based. They were army stories. Of which there are millions. All kinds of unit legends. Maybe Mason told Wiley his unit's legend, man to man, trying to bond with the kid. Like in the movies. The mother's new boyfriend always does that. Maybe Wiley always remembered the stories. Maybe they were powerful enough to make him come check them out, all these years later.'

'What kind of legends are there?'

'We could try a Hail Mary,' Neagley said. She was reading Arnold Mason's service record like a sheet of music, moving her finger from measure to measure, head cocked, listening to the tune. She said, 'It's a long shot, but if you start way back, a first lieutenant with these guys might have rotated back in as a captain. Maybe again as a major or a light colonel. Back then airborne infantry could build careers. If such a guy did well, he could still be with us. Very senior now, but he'll remember. Everybody remembers their first unit.'

'It's forty years ago.'

'If he graduated the Point at twenty-two, he's still short of retirement.'

'He'd be a general by now.'

'Probably.'

'How would you find him?'

'I would call a friend in Personnel Command. Someone would figure it out.'

'Do it,' Sinclair said. 'As soon as we get back.'

They drove on. Outside the sky grew darker. Either rain coming, or late afternoon. Or both.

In Jalalabad dusk was already falling. The messenger was leaving the white mud house. She climbed into a Toyota pick-up truck. Same system as before. Drive all night, and take the first flight out. She was ready. Still a clean skin, more or less. Not that the Swiss cared. All money was the same to them. She had been coached.

She knew the address in Zurich. She knew Zurich would look different from Hamburg. She knew all the numbers. Their account number, their passcode, one hundred million dollars, zero cents, Wiley's account number. She had Swiss francs in her pocket, for taxis.

Pray for success, the fat man had said. But not hers. Her job was easy. He should have said pray for Wiley's success. She didn't like Wiley. Not because of the assault on her modesty. Because he was weak and furtive and easily distracted. Which worried her. His job wasn't easy. Her success depended on his. *If this deal fails, then yes, you will be killed.*

It wouldn't fail because of her.

The Toyota bucked and bounced over washboard roads, heading away from the last of the sunset.

* * *

Neagley got on the phone in the consulate room and called her friend in Personnel Command. She explained the Hail Mary. Her friend said the theory sounded simple enough. Look for junior commanders in about 1955, in the airborne divisions in Germany, who were still in the army forty years later. Neagley bet five dollars on low single digits. Her friend put ten on the zero. Because of natural attrition, he said, plus three major upheavals, first Vietnam, and then the Soviet collapse, and then the modern-day volunteer high-tech military machine, all lean and mean, with body armour and women and night-vision goggles. No guy could survive all that.

Then another phone rang, and it was picked up by Vanderbilt and handed to Reacher. It was Griezman. Who said, 'I need to speak with you in private.'

Reacher said, 'Go ahead.'

'No, face to face. And alone. Where are you?'

'I'm not supposed to tell you that.'

'I can't help you if you won't let me.'

'I'm at the U.S. Consulate.'

'Be outside one minute from now.'

THIRTY-TWO

Reacher waited at the kerb, with his back to the not-exactly White House, and he saw Griezman's Mercedes in traffic a hundred yards to his left. He got in when it reached him, and Griezman pulled a U-turn and headed back the way he had come. He was as big as ever. And quiet. He had something on his mind.

Reacher said, 'Where are we going?'

Griezman said, 'The railroad station.'

'Why?'

'Because I'm a responsible copper. I added Wiley as a potential suspect. Which meant the uniformed division got his picture. The feet on the street. They showed it around. A money changer at the railroad station recognized it. From a couple of days ago. Which makes him your business, not mine.'

'Thank you.'

'However,' Griezman said.

'That doesn't sound good.'

'You have seen our facilities. Unbelievable results are obtained. We think our victim was hit seven times on the top of the head. Almost a frenzy. All in the same place, so the wound is mush. Except two of the seven blows erred slightly, one to the left, one to the right, and by combining opposite halves of those two crisp impressions, we can see the overall shape of the implement used as the bludgeon.'

'Good work.'

'We have an extensive database of such things, for reference and comparison.'

'I'm sure you do.'

'It was the butt of a Beretta M9 pistol.'

Reacher said, 'I see.'

'Which is the U.S. Army's standard-issue sidearm.'

'Wasn't me.'

'Was it Wiley?'

'I don't know.'

'There's one more thing,' Griezman said.

But it had to wait, because a light turned green and the Mercedes rolled into the square in front of the station. The grey sky made it dark early. The street lights were on. People streamed in and out, fast and purposeful, flowing around others standing dazed and mute. There was a lit-up booth halfway back. Foreign currency. One guy.

Griezman parked and they walked the rest of the way. The guy in the booth was small and dark. He spoke fast, even in English. Reacher showed him the sketch and he said, 'Yeah, two days ago, in the evening, Deutschmarks and dollars into Argentinian pesos.'

'How much?'

'About four hundred bucks.'

'Was he nervous or excited?'

'He was gazing all around. Like he was thinking.'

'About what?'

'I have no idea, man.'

Reacher stepped back, and gazed all around. It was getting darker by the minute. He saw streams of people, and behind them the railroad station, all lit up, as big and fancy as a museum or a cathedral. He saw city lights and the grind of traffic.

Griezman said, 'Now get back in the car.'

They drove two more blocks in the traffic and then they turned off and parked in a quiet street. They sat side by side in the front of the car, staring ahead through the windshield. Griezman seemed to prefer it that way. Alone, but not exactly face to face. He said, 'I told you there was a space in an otherwise neat shelf of file folders.'

'You found the missing item?'

'No, we found something else. The file folders were made of stiff board covered in vinyl. All different colours. With four rings inside. They line up like books. Are you familiar with this product?'

'Ours have three rings inside.'

'Suppose there were ten such items neatly lined up on a high shelf. Numbered from one to ten. Suppose I asked you to take down number six. How would you do it?'

'I'm tempted to say it ain't rocket science. Except it probably is. I've seen your facilities.'

'They ran an experiment. They simulated the scene and randomly selected thirty-four subjects. Basically anyone who passed their office door. Every single one pulled the file exactly the same way. A hundred per cent.'

'How?'

'You reach up and touch the pad of your index finger to the spine of your chosen file, in our case number six, as if you've traced it and now you're claiming it, very discreetly. It's yours. The ownership issue is psychologically settled. But it's lined up perfectly. There's nothing to grip. But you can't move your index finger. Subconsciously you can't give up your claim. So you put the edge of your thumb on number five, and the pad of your middle finger on number seven, and you ease them back, very respectfully, because it's a neat shelf, and then you jump your thumb and your middle finger inward, to pincer the sliver of spine you've just exposed, and you pull the file out, with your index finger exactly where it always was, on the spine, ready to balance the load as it comes down towards you.'

'Good work,' Reacher said again.

'Reverse the numbers for left-handed people, of course.'

'But I'm guessing he wasn't left-handed.'

'We have a perfect print. From the spine of the adjacent file. The pad of his right-hand middle finger. Pressed gently against the vinyl.'

'Is it in your system?'

'An exact match.'

'That's good.'

'With the print we took from the dead girl's sports car. From the chrome lever. The unknown suspect. It's the same guy, Reacher. The prints are identical.

Same finger, same angle, same cautious pressure. It's uncanny.'

Reacher said nothing.

'First a woman and then a man were savagely murdered,' Griezman said. 'You know who did it.'

'Help me find Wiley and I'll tell you.'

'Would I also be helping myself?'

'Let's ask him when we find him.'

'But you could tell me now.'

'Tell who now? The simple detective, or the obedient bureaucrat who will pass it all on to his intelligence service in Berlin about ten minutes from now? Whereupon I would go to jail about ten minutes after that.'

'Do you not tell your superiors what they should know?'

'I tell them as little as possible. Short words, no math, and no diagrams.'

'You'll go to jail anyway. In Germany it is illegal to withhold this kind of information.'

'You going to arrest me?'

'I could make you a material witness. You would be obliged to answer. Refusal would be deemed contempt of the judicial system.'

'I'm sure there's a joke in there somewhere.'

'This is a serious business.'

'There's a case to be made ours is more serious. I'm sure my president would be happy to explain it to your chancellor. But we don't need to go that route. Help me find Wiley, and then we'll figure out this other thing together.'

'Did he do it?'

'Forget the print. A lawyer wouldn't like it anyway. It could have been left months ago. You need to come at it another way. The Beretta was a good catch. They're for sale in your victim's favourite bar. Did you know that? Who could have bought one there?'

'Wiley,' Griezman said. 'He bought his ID there.'

'Good theory. Promising. Doesn't prove anything yet, but clearly the next step would be find him and talk to him.'

'Where is he?'

'I don't know.'

At that moment Wiley was a hundred yards away, crossing the street at a walk light two blocks east of the train station. He was dressed in black pants and a black hooded sweatshirt. He was carrying a small black duffel. It was heavy. Its load shifted and clanked as he walked. At first he followed a familiar route, from the bus stop towards the bar with the varnished wood front. But halfway there he turned off and stepped into a vehicle entrance and walked past two head-high trash receptacles. He opened a stairwell door marked Exit Only, and he walked up a flight, to the hotel parking garage. Where he had met the hooker. He remembered the way she turned around and beckoned him to her car, like she couldn't wait.

He remembered every detail.

No cameras.

He walked to the far corner of the floor, smelling cold gasoline, cold diesel, cold rubber, and cold cement dust.

He picked out a silver BMW. Six cylinder, gasoline. An older model. It had the look of a car parked a long time. The windshield was dull. The paint was filmed with neglect. He squatted in front of its radiator grille. He took a cross-head screwdriver from his duffel. He unfastened the front licence plate and stored it in his bag. He moved around and squatted behind the trunk. He unscrewed the rear plate and put it in his bag.

He took out a single-burner camp stove. Bought new for the occasion. It was about eight inches square, made of pressed steel, with a rubber tube and a knurled brass valve. He took out a head-sized canister of propane. Bright blue, cheap, easy, and convenient. He attached the valve. He turned the knob and heard a hiss of gas. He shut it off.

He lay down on the cold concrete and slid the burner two feet under the rear of the car. He took six wooden blocks from his bag. Children's toys. From Sweden, he thought. Each one was about six inches long and an inch square. Each one was lacquered a different bright colour. He built them into a tower on top of the burner. Where a coffee pot or a tea kettle would go. He put two one way, then two the other, and finally the third layer the same way as the first. Like a little camp fire. He took out a silver foil dish, the size and shape of a roast chicken. He balanced it on the tower of wooden blocks.

He took out a box of nine-millimetre Parabellum ammunition. A hundred rounds. One of two bought with the M9 from the chuckleheads in the bar. He threaded his hand through the space under the BMW's suspension and laid the box gently in the silver foil dish.

Finished. Good to go. The propane, the tube, the burner, the short stack of wood, the roasting dish, the handgun rounds.

The BMW's gas tank, directly above.

He checked his position and rehearsed the backward scoot. Then he took out a Zippo lighter. He checked the knurled brass knob. He turned on the burner. He heard the hiss of gas. He flicked the lighter and brought the flame to the burner's rose. The gas caught with a thump. He dialled it back to a lower setting. A click below medium. Like a fast simmer.

Then he slid out backwards and stood up and grabbed his bag and hustled.

A mile away Dremmler came out of his fourth-floor office, and spent twenty seconds in the elevator, which was thirty-three pairs of Brazilian shoes, and then Muller fell in step with him on the sidewalk, and said, 'You've heard, I expect.'

'About Wolfgang Schlupp?' Dremmler said. 'I've heard about nothing else. The police have been all over that bar. My members there are very upset. My phone has been ringing off the hook.'

'Was it Wiley?'

'I thought he was out of town.'

'So did everybody. They were all focused outward. No one even looked the other way. So I did, just to be sure. Two cameras on traffic lights. For flow, supposedly, but recorded all the same. And there he is. Driving the other way. Towards St Georg. He never left town. He's in town right now.'

'Where?'

'It's a large white vehicle. Every traffic cop on the force is looking for it.'

Dremmler walked a couple of steps in silence.

Then he said, 'Herr Muller, in your professional opinion, concerning Wolfgang Schlupp, how serious will the investigation be?'

'Extremely. His head was bashed in.'

'They'll make a list of people he spoke to today. I'll be on it.'

'Naturally. Chief of Detectives Griezman likes lists. He likes paperwork in general.'

'I can't afford to be implicated. It would be politically inconvenient.'

'Just make up a story. You're a businessman, he's a businessman. You were talking about the stock market. It's not like he can contradict you.'

'Will that be enough?'

'It was just a weird coincidence. Maybe you saw him at a business dinner. He was a nodding acquaintance. You were merely saying hello. A professional courtesy. You hardly knew the fellow.'

Griezman drove Reacher back to the consulate, and let him out on the same kerb he had got in from before. Then Griezman drove away and Reacher went inside, where he discovered Neagley had won her five-dollar bet. She had a sheet of telex paper to prove it. Low single digits, she had predicted, and she had scored with the lowest digit of all.

In 1955 the United States Army was considerably

north of a million strong. Part of that strength was a young first lieutenant by the name of Wilson T. Helmsworth. He was a recent graduate of West Point and several specialist schools. He was hunting one airborne command after another. He was technically Arnold Mason's superior officer several different times. It was even theoretically possible the two had met. In some kind of a formal setting. Maybe a parade. Not cracking beers. Then later Helmsworth moved onward and upward, and along the way he qualified in anything and everything related to a parachute. At one time or another he held all the records. Free fall included. He wrote book after book about paratrooper tactics.

Then he survived a long jungle war where the canopy was thick and the air was misty and the infantry didn't give a damn about paratrooper tactics. And he came out of it promoted. He got on board early with special forces theory, and about twenty-odd generations later he was still there in the thick of it, now in overall command of training at Fort Benning, Georgia. Where the tough stuff was invented. Major General Wilson T. Helmsworth. The only Cold War airborne junior commander still wearing the green suit. From the brown-boot army to the black-boot army to the New Balance army. Tenacious. A million to one, literally.

Neagley said, 'As of this moment he's located at Benning.'

Sinclair said, 'He needs thirty minutes to set up a call. He's a busy man.'

'We can't do this by phone,' Reacher said. 'It has to be done face to face. He's been in the army forty years. He knows how to bullshit. We need to be in the same room. We need to see his body language.'

'We? We can't all fly back. Not now. None of us should fly back.'

'None of us is going to. Helmsworth is going to come to us. If he's at Benning, he can get to Atlanta. For the night flight. He could be here in the morning. I think the Joint Chiefs should order him to report to the Hamburg consulate immediately.'

'Because of someone else's cryptic half-remembered childhood legend?'

'Ratcliffe said we get what we need.'

'He's a two-star general.'

'Which means he'll run away from anything soft or speculative, at a hundred miles an hour. And anything even remotely controversial at two hundred miles an hour. Won't work on the phone. He needs to see the face of the NSC. And we need to see his.'

'It's a big deal for a Hail Mary.'

'It's a foreign country. Possibly there's a foreign enemy here. They'll give him another medal. Theoretically he could get a Silver Star.'

'For flying in?'

'He's a two-star general. They get medals like frequent flier miles.'

'Are you sure we need him?'

'No stone unturned.'

Sinclair made the call.

Then outside the window there was a faint, distant sound. A dull and hollow *pop pop* and a blunted hiss of air. And then more. *Pop, pop pop*. The back part of

Reacher's brain said *handgun, probably nine-millimetre rounds, urban setting, probably half a mile distant.* He stepped to the window and heaved it open. He heard sirens in the distance. Then more gunfire, four rounds, then five, very faint but louder because of the open window, and then more sirens, two different tones, probably ambulances and cop cars, and then a furious volley of gunfire, impossibly fast, like a continuous explosion, like a hundred machine guns firing all at once, like the best firework show the town park ever had, and then there was the muted concussive thump of a fuel explosion, and two more handgun rounds, and then nothing but sirens, the scream of cop cars, the yelp of ambulances, the deafening bass bark of fire trucks, all blending in a howl that sounded more like sorrow than help.

Reacher looked out at the street and saw cops racing past, all in the same direction, most in cars, some on motorcycles, one on foot, half running. He saw two ambulances and a fire truck. The whole place was flashing red and blue.

Sinclair said, 'What was it?'

Neagley said, 'It sounded like a house fire, where someone left a box of ammunition on the kitchen counter. Then the propane tank went up. Except we should have heard the sirens earlier. But maybe it was a stone building. Maybe the fire was concealed from exterior view. Therefore the alarm was sounded late.'

'Deliberate?'

'Maybe, maybe not. Either way sounds the same.'

'Related?'

'Can't say,' White said. 'This is a big city. There's a lot going on.'

There was a second fuel explosion. Faint and far away, but unmistakable. A thump, a silent vacuum, the suck of air, and the sensation of blooming heat, however impossible. Reacher watched the street. Every cop in town was heading in the same direction.

THIRTY-THREE

Wiley took the padlock off the hasp, in the centre of the door, and then off the top bolt, and the bottom, and he dragged the door open, and he ducked inside. He was calm. He had simple mechanical tasks ahead of him. First up were the plates. He took off the rental's fresh new issue, and he put on the old BMW's number in their place. Then he took out his cans of spray paint, bought at the hardware store, lurid greens and yellows and orange and red and silver. He sprayed fat initials on the side of the van, his own, just for the hell of it, but reversed, WH, all swelled up like balloons, like you saw on the subway cars. He shaded the letters with silver, and sprayed random swirls in the background, and added a fat S and a fat L, like a tag for a second artist, except it wasn't. It was Sugar Land, right there on the truck, because why the hell not? It was where he was from, and it was where he was going.

Then he sprayed a mist of grey over everything else, to calm it down, to give it age. He stood back. He was light-headed from the aerosol fumes. But he was satisfied. It was no longer a new white truck. It was a piece of urban junk. It was no longer worthy of a passing glance. Not that anyone would be passing. Everyone was at the hotel. There would be crowds of law enforcement and all kinds of perimeters. Firefighters and SWAT teams in the centre, because of the handgun rounds and the gasoline fires. Then all kinds of security and rubberneckers and glory hunters. *I was there, man. The bullets were zipping right over my head.*

He opened the double doors all the way, and then he climbed in and started up the rental. He reversed it out, and manoeuvred it around, sawing it back and forth until it was lined up perfectly. He watched his mirrors and backed it up slowly, slowly, until its rear bumper kissed the old truck's rear bumper. He put on the parking brake and shut down the motor. He climbed through from the cab to the load space. He rolled up the rear door from the inside. The old truck's rear door was right there, an inch away. He unlocked it and rolled it up from the outside.

A wooden crate.

It was six feet high and six feet wide and twelve feet long. It was solidly made from tight-grained softwood, straight and true, once pale, now aged to a tobacco amber. It was a prototype of a standardized container system the Pentagon experimented with in the 1950s. A survivor. A piece of history. It was stencilled here and there with faded whitewash numbers.

It weighed more than six hundred pounds. No way to move it without a forklift truck. One of which he no longer had. He took out a regular slot screwdriver from his bag. Old-fashioned. Like the crate. It had screws the size of buttons. They were set on six-inch centres all around the perimeter of the end panel. Forty-four in total. Probably the result of a study by a research and development corporation. Some guy in a suit got a fat cheque for saying more was better. Which made everyone happy. The Pentagon's ass was covered. The screw supplier was making out like a bandit. Probably charged a dollar each. Military spec.

Wiley got to work.

The phone rang in the consulate room. Griezman. Who said, 'Something is happening in the hotel parking garage. Where the hooker vanished. There were gunshots and then a car blew up. Then two more. The fire is contained because there are sprinklers and foam on the ceiling. But we can't get close. Not until we're sure about the gun.'

Reacher said, 'You think the guy is still in there?'

'Don't you?'

'We didn't like the sound. It could have been ammo cooking off. Some kind of a delayed mechanism. You need to consider someone set it up on a timer. In which case he's long gone. He's where you're not.'

'Who?'

'Horace Wiley, maybe. He's keeping to a busy schedule right now. He might be in need of a decoy. You should put half your men back on the street.'

'You think he's back in town?'

'I'm beginning to think he never left. He could be moving his truck right now. You should put guys on the street.'

'Impossible. This is a government protocol. There were gunshots and explosions in the centre of town. It's not my decision. They planned for a year. The mayor's office is in charge and we're doing it by the book.'

'How long do they plan to wait before they go in?'

'A unit with body armour is on its way. Thirty minutes, possibly.'

'OK,' Reacher said. 'Good luck.'

He clicked off the call. No one spoke.

Reacher said, 'I'm going out for a walk.'

Forty-four screws cost him just shy of twenty minutes, plus a lot of burn in his forearms. But then the panel came free and he laid it down to bridge the gap between the load floors. A flat surface, from one truck to the other. As planned ahead of time. He had thought of everything.

The air in the crate smelled still and stale. Old wood, old canvas, old dust. The old world. The contents were exactly what Uncle Arnold had told him about, all those years before. Ten identical items. All the same. Each one weighed fifty pounds. Each one was ready-packed in a transport container. What Uncle Arnold had called an H-912. Wiley still remembered all the details. The containers had straps all over them. Easy to grab. Easy enough to haul and slide and drag and push. One at a time. From the old truck to the new truck. All the way in. Butted up tight, starting in the far back corner.

Then a pause, and a breath, and back for the next one.

* * *

350

Reacher walked south to the Aussenalster lake. The city was quiet. A learned response. Europe was full of explosions. Factions and groups and people's armies. A big deal for a day or two, until the next thing happened. He turned east at the water, looping around. He was two miles from where Wiley lived. Which had no inconspicuous place to park a panel van. But it made sense to keep it close by. Which was a relative term. A circle on a map would be drawn cautiously large. Some of it would be water. But most would be land. Of which Reacher could cover nothing more than a random and insignificant sliver. But doing something felt better than doing nothing. Walking felt better than sitting around. So he walked.

Fifty pounds was a hell of a weight, especially when you had to do it over and over. Wiley took a break after seven units, breathing hard, half bent over. Partly nerves. A simple mechanical task, but the whole ballgame right there, nonetheless. The moment of maximum exposure. But much longer than a moment. Close to half an hour already, with vapour lights all over the old docks, and the two trucks jammed together rear end to rear end like some kind of vehicular sodomy, complete with rocking and thumping and grunting inside, while all the time half in and half out of a tumbledown shed no one had used in the last thirty years.

Vulnerable.

Not good.

He took a breath and rolled his aching shoulders and got back to work. He dragged number eight the length of the crate, and up over the lip, and across the last yard of the old truck's floor, and over the flat wooden panel, slowly, slowly, until it seesawed in the middle and clapped back down, and then onward into the new truck, where he left it standing upright against number seven.

He went back to the crate, to the far back wall, and he got number nine. He dragged it out, and over, and in. All the way. He took a breath and went back for number ten. The last. He pulled it away from the wall. The book was right there. Right where Uncle Arnold said it would be. A khaki file folder striped in red, set in a neat receptacle made of thin plywood, with a half-moon shape scooped out for fingers. Maybe an apprentice's work, all those years ago. In the crate factory. The folder held mimeographed copies of typewritten pages, all held together with brass fasteners gone dull with age.

He carried the folder in one hand and dragged number ten with the other. He stood ten upright next to nine and wedged the book between them. He dragged the bridge back into the old truck and rolled down the new truck's door from the outside. He squeezed around the empty crate and climbed out of the old truck through its cab. He hustled around and got in the new truck and started it up. He moved it forward and backed and filled until he had gotten it turned around again, and then he drove it in nose first on the right hand side, and he shut it down and locked it up. He re-packed his duffel and closed the double doors, and bolted the bolts, and closed the hasp, and clicked the padlocks shut.

Nearly forty minutes. A long time. He walked to the

corner and risked a look up the cobblestone street. All the way to the metal bridge. Beyond it on the main road the traffic was moving. Left to right, and right to left. Normal speed. No sirens. No squealing tyres. No flashing lights.

Logical.

He carried his bag and used the footbridges, from pier to pier, all the way home.

Reacher walked halfway into the St Georg neighbourhood, curving west with the road around the lake. He saw nothing of interest. Cars, but none of them contained Wiley. Pedestrians, alone and in groups, but none of them Wiley. Eventually he stopped at a crosswalk. The main road ran straight ahead to St Pauli. There was a narrow left turn that led to a boxy metal bridge. He saw cobblestones and moonlight on black water. All quiet. No movement.

He gave it up and turned around and headed back. Folks in their homes were watching television. Hundreds of rooms were glowing blue. Live news, no doubt. The handgun rounds had been a pretty smart move. Explosions could be spun as accidental. Gunshots, not so much. Way to get attention. Textbook, literally. They had planned for a year.

He got back to the consulate, where the evening guard let him in, and where Neagley told him the Joint Chiefs had issued the order to General Helmsworth. He was booked on Delta, on the night flight, nonstop out of Atlanta. A consulate car would pick him up in the morning.

'A Silver Star for sure,' Neagley said. 'We had explosions and gunfire. He'll call it a war zone.'

Then the phone rang. Griezman again. Who said, 'There was no one in the parking garage. Just three burned-out cars, still smouldering. And bullet holes everywhere. It's crazy.'

'It was a set-up,' Reacher said.

'But by who?'

'It would be a big coincidence if it was someone else.'

'The mayor's office is in charge. They don't know the history.'

'Can you give me some unmarked cars?'

'Impossible, I'm afraid. I'm standing by to be briefed. Which at this rate might be tomorrow. Someone already said that corner of the garage is near the hotel kitchen, so we should look at animal activists worried about foie gras and crate-raised veal.'

'I don't think it was them.'

'Neither do I. But you see my point. This is going to be a long night. The mayor's office doesn't know any better.'

Twelve hours until the Swiss banks opened.

Reacher said nothing.

Griezman killed the call without saying goodbye.

Later Bishop's airport bus took them back to the hotel. They all went to their rooms. Reacher heard Neagley's door click shut. Then Sinclair's. Then a minute later she called him on the house phone. She said, 'When should we ask for help?'

He said, 'Not before tomorrow.'

'You say that every day.'

'I live in hope.'

She said, 'Will it happen tomorrow?'

'It might.'

'Will you come over and talk to me?'

She was waiting for him, standing in the middle of her room, in her black dress, with her pearls, and her nylons, and her shoes, and her uncombed hair.

She said, 'What are you thinking about?'

He kissed her, long and slow, and then he moved behind her. She leaned back and rested against him.

He said, 'Personally or professionally?'

She said, 'Professionally first.'

He bent her forward an inch and found the tag on her zipper, at the back of her neck. The metal teardrop. Tiny, but perfectly cast. A quality item. He eased it down, past the clasp of her bra, to the small of her back.

He said, 'Where do they plan to use what they're buying?'

She said, 'I don't know.'

'In Germany?'

'That would make no sense politically.'

He tipped the dress off her shoulders, and it fell, and caught, and fell again, and puddled on the floor around her feet.

She leaned back.

She was warm.

She said, 'More likely D.C. or New York or conceivably London.'

'Then they'll ship it by sea. We wasted a day. Wrong

assumption. Wiley was never headed out of town. It's a big heavy thing that needs a large-size panel van. Driving is not the best way to get it out of Germany. They can't drive it all the way to D.C. or New York or London anyhow. It has to go by sea eventually.'

He bent her forward again, just an inch, and unhooked her bra. He smoothed his hands over her shoulders, snagging the straps, pushing them off.

The bra joined the dress.

He cupped her breasts.

She leaned back, and turned her head, and kissed his chest.

He said, 'Wiley drove the furniture truck straight here, seven months ago. Even though he never served here. He chose Hamburg because it's a port. The second largest in Europe. They call it the gateway to the world.'

He hooked his thumbs in the top of her pantyhose.

She said, 'He's going to put it on a ship.'

'That's my guess.'

'When?'

He eased her pantyhose down.

Panties too.

Clumsy thumbs.

He said, 'When he gets paid.'

'Which could be tomorrow.'

He said nothing.

She stepped out of her shoes, and turned to face him. Naked, apart from the pearls. A sight to see.

She said, 'When should we ask for help?'

He said, 'Not this exact minute.'

He took off his T-shirt.

She said, 'Now your pants.'

'Yes ma'am,' he said.

She rode cowgirl again, but this time reversed, with her back to him. Which visually speaking had a complex balance of pluses and minuses. Overall it was no kind of a hardship. He felt like an observer of a private pleasure. She was going for the big one. That was clear. OK with him. Whatever worked. Whatever got you through the night.

THIRTY-FOUR

Bishop sent the bus early, because of General Helmsworth coming in. The driver said Delta's wheels-down in Hamburg had already happened, just as dawn was coming up. The general was being met at the airport and would be driven straight to the consulate, where he would freshen up in the guest quarters ahead of moving to a meeting room provided by Bishop. Apparently Helmsworth's interpretation of his orders was narrow. He would speak only to Sinclair, Reacher and Neagley, who were in his chain of command, broadly understood. The others were not. Which in practical terms was no problem at all. They had already decided among themselves to keep it lean. It was felt someone else's cryptic half-remembered childhood legends would not survive a formal one-against-seven across-the-table grilling. It was felt a casual atmosphere would be more productive. A smaller gathering. Sinclair and Reacher and Neagley had already been chosen ahead of time.

So the others went to the regular office, and Bishop led the way to the room he had chosen. It looked a lot like the room in Fort Belvoir where Reacher had gotten his medal. Same kind of gilt chairs, same kind of red velvet, same kind of flags. Maybe the ceiling was higher. It was an older building. Neagley found four chairs with arms, and she set them in a square, like a casual group. All equal. Just folks passing the time of day.

Then Bishop left, and a minute later Helmsworth came in. He was a compact man close to his middle sixties. He had a silver buzz cut and bright grey eyes. He was wearing battledress uniform, starched and pressed, with two black stars in the collar. He had flown all night, but he looked in reasonable shape. Introductions were made. Hands were shaken, except for Neagley, who nodded politely. Then they all sat down, where Neagley had placed the chairs.

Reacher said, 'General, how annoyed are you right now, on a scale of one to ten?'

Helmsworth said, 'All things considered, son, about an eight or a nine.'

He sounded like a guy reading out a death sentence.

Reacher said, 'It can only get worse.'

'I have no doubt about that, soldier.'

'But we don't have time for bullshit. So cheer the hell up, general. We're here to talk about the good old days.'

'Yours or mine, major?'

'A sergeant named Arnold P. Mason. He served in an 82nd Airborne unit. Your path and his crossed in 1955, and a couple of times later. But only technically. You were moving up by then. You won't remember him.'

'I don't. It was forty years ago.'

'But we need to know what you remember about his unit.'

'What is this, a folklore project? Oral history month?'

'We're looking at a guy named Wiley. As a kid growing up, for a six-year period, from the age of ten to the age of sixteen, his mother's boyfriend was a twenty-year veteran of the 82nd Airborne in Europe. We think the boyfriend told the kid stories. We think the kid remembered the stories, and then many years later joined the army himself, because of them.'

'That's how it's supposed to happen. I'm glad to hear it.'

'It wasn't like that with Wiley. It was like the stories were a treasure map, and he joined the army only because he wanted to dig up the treasure.'

Helmsworth said, 'That's absurd.'

'Now he's got it and he's AWOL.'

'Got what?'

'We don't know. But it's worth a lot of money.'

'AWOL from where?'

'Air defence with the armoured divisions near Fulda.'

'Major, why am I here? Please tell me you had a good reason for bringing me to Europe.'

'We want to hear the buried treasure stories. From that old 82nd Airborne unit. We're sure you remember them. Every officer remembers his first command.'

'There were no buried treasure stories.'

'Our boy Wiley got in a unit competition over smart-mouth one-liners about why they joined the army. When his turn came he said because his uncle told him Davy Crockett stories.'

Helmsworth didn't answer.

Reacher noticed.

He said, 'The uncle was really the mother's boyfriend. The twenty-year veteran. Uncle Arnold. A polite honorific. Possibly appropriate when the kid was ten. Maybe a little weird by the time he was sixteen.'

Helmsworth said, casually, 'What were the Davy Crockett stories?'

'We don't know,' Reacher said. 'That's why we're asking.'

'What years did the mother's boyfriend serve?'

'From 1951 through 1971.'

Helmsworth was quiet a long moment.

Reacher said, 'General?'

'I can't help you,' Helmsworth said. 'I'm very sorry.'

Reacher said, 'How mad are you now?'

Helmsworth almost answered, but then he stopped short.

'Exactly,' Reacher said. 'A one or a two out of ten. You're no longer angry. Because now you've got bigger things to worry about.'

Helmsworth said nothing.

Reacher said, 'General?'

Helmsworth said, 'I can't discuss it.'

'You'll have to, I'm afraid.'

'I mean I'm not permitted to discuss it.'

Sinclair said, 'General, with respect, you're talking to the National Security Council. There is no higher level of clearance.'

'Is this room secure?'

'It's in a United States consulate and it was selected by the CIA head of station.'

'I need to speak with the Joint Chiefs' office.'

'On this issue they'll say what we tell them to say. Why not cut out the middleman and tell us direct?'

'It was classified a long time ago.'

'What was?'

'It's a closed file.'

Reacher said, 'Tell the story, general. Our boy Wiley is AWOL with stolen material. We need to know what it is. We're going to sit here until you tell us. I'd like to say we've got all day, but I'm not sure about that. Maybe we haven't.'

Helmsworth paused again.

Then he nodded. He hitched his chair in and sat forward. He said, 'I'll tell you what happened to me, and then I'll tell you what else was going on. This was Europe in the early 1950s. We knew the battle plan. The Red Army would advance through the Fulda Gap in strength and depth. Our first job was to stop their spearhead and then prevent reinforcement. Which we planned to do by targeting roads and bridges behind their lines. To halt their incoming armour. Maybe also power plants and other large items of infrastructure. To degrade their capability. Except the air force was unreliable. Back then there were no smart bombs. A bridge is a very small target. We needed certainty. We raised a couple of engineer companies. They were regular combat paratroops trained in demolition. The idea was they would jump with an explosive charge, and hike or if necessary fight from the landing zone to the target, and affix the charge with great precision, to the bridge support or the power plant wall, or whatever it may be.

That was the plan. Back then a paratrooper with an explosive charge on his back was the smartest bomb we had.'

'Good work,' Reacher said.

'Not really. What's the maximum they could carry on their backs?'

'From an LZ to a target? A hundred pounds, maybe.'

'Which was the problem. A hundred pounds of TNT doesn't put a scratch on a bridge support. It's a fire-cracker. And a power plant is even bigger. So we put the human smart bomb technique on the back burner for the time being. Pending improvements to portable ordnance. Which were generally slow back then. The glamour was all at the other end of the scale. Which was the stuff I didn't know at the time. Los Alamos was busier than ever. They were working on the hydrogen bomb. They tested it just before I graduated West Point. On Bikini Atoll, in March of 1954. It was a fifteen-megaton explosion. By far the most powerful in all of recorded history. It was five times more powerful than all the bombs dropped on Germany and Japan in World War Two put together, including the atom bombs we dropped on Hiroshima and Nagasaki. Probably more powerful than all the ordnance ever exploded in the whole world before. All in one split second. It was a big-ass explosion, people. So big no one ever seriously thought about going bigger. They thought the atmos-phere would catch on fire. Not that I knew any of that stuff at the time.'

Reacher said, 'When did you find out?'

'Later in the 1950s. Things were going crazy by then.

We found out other things, too. For example, we found out we had two secret nuclear labs, not just one. Not just Los Alamos. There was another place. They had a theory at the time. It was behind everything the Department of Defense ever did back then. In their words they believed rivalry fosters excellence and is imperative for supremacy. It was written in stone. So they gave Los Alamos a rival. It was called Livermore. Near Berkeley, in California. There were smart people working there right from the start. They saw there was no point in designing a bigger bomb. So they went the other way. They designed smaller bombs. They got better and better at it. Eventually they built a whole new nuclear weapons system around a very neat new warhead called the W-54.'

'Good to know,' Reacher said.

'Now go back to my original problem. A guy carrying a hundred pounds on his back was no good to me. But I was a commander with a tactical problem to solve. My target list included major civil engineering projects. Roads, bridges, viaducts, power plants, infrastructure. Could a guy carry two hundred pounds on his back?'

'Maybe,' Reacher said. 'But not very far.'

'Still not good enough. Still just a firecracker. What about four hundred pounds?'

'No.'

'What about a ton? Could a guy carry a ton of TNT on his back?'

'Obviously not.'

'What about ten tons? Or a hundred tons? Or a

thousand tons? Or fifteen thousand tons? Could a guy carry *fifteen thousand tons* of TNT on his back?'

Reacher said nothing.

Helmsworth said, 'In the end that was what they offered us.'

'Who did?'

'Livermore. The new lab in California. Truth is, their new weapons system was a failure. They got small, but not small enough. They packed the power of the Hiroshima bomb into a cylinder eleven inches wide and sixteen inches tall. It weighed just fifty pounds. The same fifteen-kiloton yield as Little Boy. Equivalent to fifteen thousand tons of TNT. But Little Boy was ten feet long and weighed five tons. So Livermore's cylinder was a triumph of miniaturization. But unfortunately it wasn't quite enough of a triumph. It was still too big to use as an artillery shell or a mortar round. There was no reliable man-portable launcher. It was a curiosity, nothing more. It was a solution in search of a problem. But waste not, want not. They found a relevant problem. They gave the cylinder a new name, SADM, for special atomic demolition munition, and they gave it to the 82nd Airborne. Now my guys could jump with just fifty pounds on their backs and take out any road or bridge or viaduct they wanted.'

'With nuclear bombs?'

'As big as Hiroshima.'

No one spoke.

Reacher said, 'What was the SADM's old name?'

'Take a guess.'

'Davy Crockett.'

Helmsworth nodded. 'That was the name they gave to the W-54 warhead. I don't know why. But it took over. No one ever said SADM. They called the things Davy Crocketts instead. They came with padded canvas transport containers built like backpacks. You strapped it on, and you were good to go. But it was unpopular duty. The cylinders leaked radiation. Or so people said. Some folks got sick. They worried about cancer. But mostly they worried about the newsreel film they had seen from Hiroshima. That immense explosion. They were carrying the exact same bomb. Their orders were to strap it to a bridge support, set the timer, and run like hell. Very different than dropping it out of an airplane eight miles up.'

Neagley said, 'How long was the timer?'

'A maximum of fifteen minutes. Plus or minus. It wasn't very accurate.'

'That's insane. The Hiroshima lethal blast radius was one mile. The fireball radius was two miles. That's twelve minutes for most guys on a running track. Across mixed terrain it would likely be impossible. Especially if they had to fight their way in. They'd have to fight their way out again. While waiting to be incinerated. It was a suicide mission.'

Helmsworth nodded again. 'It was a different calculus back then. We would have given up two companies to stop a million men and ten thousand vehicles getting out. We would have thought of it as a bargain.'

Reacher said, 'Two companies?'

'We had a hundred Davy Crocketts.'

'Each with its own target?'

'Carefully planned.'

'Widely distributed?'

'Like measles on a map.'

'Except there aren't a hundred bridges. Or power plants. Or roads or viaducts. It's a narrow funnel. That's why they call it a gap.'

'There was redundancy built in. About half were to proceed to standby positions.'

'In the spaces. Linking everything up.'

'Like a chain.'

'You were making a radiation barrier. Like a minefield. With a hundred bombs it could have been ten miles wide by ten miles deep. Any shape you wanted. You wanted to force the Soviets to go left or right. Where you were waiting.'

'The file is closed.'

'Because as time passed all kinds of treaties were signed. You couldn't do it any more. You couldn't even admit planning it.'

'Yes,' Helmsworth said. 'The SADMs were retired, but not strictly for military reasons. They were all brought home. They were not replaced. Eventually nuclear weapons below a certain size were banned altogether.'

Sinclair said, 'Arnold Mason is sick. His wife claims he told her the army would be interested. He told her someone would come.'

'Sick how?'

'Brain tumour.'

'It was a very long time ago. Most cases were much earlier.'

'There were others?'

'A sprinkling,' Helmsworth said.

Reacher said, 'Such stories wouldn't make me want to join the army.'

Helmsworth said nothing.

Reacher said, 'General?'

'Different recruits have different reasons.'

'Horace Wiley was a thirty-two-year-old thief. I don't think training for a suicide mission and getting sick and then seeing the weapons go home anyway would have done the trick for him.'

Helmsworth said nothing.

Reacher said, 'General?'

'This is classified at the presidential level.'

Sinclair said, 'For these purposes, so is everyone in this room.'

Helmsworth said, 'It's possible there was an inventory error.'

THIRTY-FIVE

Helmsworth said, 'Initial cargo manifests show ten crates leaving Livermore. Each crate held ten Davy Crocketts. Ten times ten is a hundred, which was the number of bombs we trained with. Later cargo manifests show the same ten crates going home again, each one with the same ten bombs inside. Ten times ten is a hundred. All accounted for. All properly delivered and safely stored inside the United States. All subsequently checked and physically examined and counted in front of witnesses. There are exactly one hundred in our possession.'

Reacher said, 'So what was the error?'

'Those were the cargo manifests. A hundred out, and a hundred in. They matched all known army paperwork. But years later at the Livermore lab someone found an unsent invoice for an eleventh crate. Ten more Davy Crocketts. There was no coherent delivery paperwork. The production figures were ambiguous. It was possible an eleventh order was filled.'

'But not paid for. Which is unlikely. Which means the invoice was probably the error. Possibly why it was never sent.'

'That was the initial conclusion,' Helmsworth said. 'Unfortunately the crate manufacturer had contradictory evidence, from an unlikely source. An apprentice's log showed eleven crates had in fact been built. The foreman of the shop had signed off on them all. The eleventh crate wasn't in the crate factory. It wasn't at Livermore. And if ten more bombs had been built, they weren't at Livermore either. So where the hell were they? Did they even exist? Half the argument was philosophical. The other half was better safe than sorry. So they started searching. Didn't find anything. Not at home, and not overseas. Maybe the apprentice was wrong. But then the foreman had to be wrong, too. They went back and forth.'

'Until?' Reacher said.

'It was a split committee. The majority said the ambiguous production figures should be read the other way around, and that therefore the eleventh order had not been manufactured in the first place, and that the invoice was incorrectly raised. Or fraudulently raised, perhaps.'

'That sounds like a threat, to make the problem go away.'

'Perhaps it was.'

'What did the minority think?'

'That Livermore wouldn't have ordered the extra crate unless it had bombs to put in it. The crates were prototypes of a standardized system. They were modified inside to carry the load. But on the outside they all looked the same. The error could have been in the delivery paperwork. The crate could have left Berkeley and gone to the wrong destination. Or the right destination with the wrong product description. The inventory codes were very complicated. A single-digit mistake could have been fatal.'

'That's a lot of could-haves,' Reacher said. 'That's a cascade of three separate errors. Wrong delivery paperwork, wrong inventory code, and the invoice was never sent.'

'Every year we were spending billions of 1950s dollars on millions of tons of equipment. The sample size was enormous. It was a frenzy. There was scope for every kind of error. How long have you served, major?'

'Twelve years.'

'You ever known anything go wrong?'

Reacher glanced down at his pants. Marine Corps khakis, sewn in 1962, shipped in 1965, to the wrong branch of the service entirely, undiscovered for thirty years.

He said, 'We're talking about nuclear weapons here.'

Helmsworth said, 'In our history we've had a total of thirty-two accidentally launched, fired, detonated, stolen or lost. We closed the files on twenty-six of them. The other six were never traced or recovered. They're still missing. We know those numbers for sure. They're solid. Another ten isn't outside the bounds of possibility. Especially given their nature. Davy Crocketts were small and mass-produced. They were not glamour weapons. They were treated like regular everyday ordnance.'

'How good was the search?'

'We looked everywhere. Literally everywhere in the

371

world. We didn't find them. So the majority view prevailed. They never existed in the first place. The invoice was an intended fraud, but someone got cold feet and never submitted it.'

'What was your personal opinion?'

'We were preparing for a land war against the Red Army in Europe. We had hundreds of supply depots all over Germany. The largest was bigger than some of their cities. The smallest was bigger than a football stadium. I thought the majority was sticking its fingers in its ears and singing la-la-la.'

'Would Arnold Mason have been involved in the search?'

'Almost certainly. This was years later, don't forget. Those were the guys who actually knew what they were looking for.'

'So those were the stories young Horace Wiley heard. The missing crate. Ten lost bombs as big as Hiroshima. Buried treasure.'

Sinclair said, 'Why would he expect to find them when no one else could?'

'Different people have different talents,' Reacher said. 'Maybe Uncle Arnold gave him half a clue. Maybe he hit on something no one else did. Maybe he was the right kind of smart.'

'This sounds completely impossible.'

'I agree.'

Helmsworth said, 'Ma'am, nothing was impossible. It was the Cold War. It was a kind of madness. One time they sewed a microphone and a transmitter in a cat's neck, with a thin antenna threaded through inside its spine and up its tail. They were going to train it to wander into the Russian Embassy compound and pick up loose talk. Its first day on the job it was run over by a car. Nothing was impossible and everything went wrong sooner or later.'

Neagley said, 'Does it even matter? Because who knows the arming codes? Were they ever issued? Even if they were, they'd be split between two personnel. That was a basic nuclear safeguard. For ten bombs, that's twenty veterans. Who exactly?'

Helmsworth said nothing.

Reacher said, 'General?'

Helmsworth said, 'It gets worse.'

'Is that possible?'

'You've seen the movies about D-Day. Anti-aircraft fire, map reading errors, wind and weather, swamps and rivers, immediate ground combat. The chances of landing two personnel in the same place at the same time were precisely zero. Which would have left us with a hundred useless hunks of metal. But it was essential we were effective. Therefore the split-code safeguard was considered a tactical impediment.'

'Considered by who?'

'Tactical commanders.'

'Like you?'

'I told my quartermaster to tell our armourer to write the whole code on the bomb itself with yellow chalk. That way the guy carrying it could get killed and someone else could still complete the mission. It was the Cold War. Looking back we know it didn't happen. It felt like it could at the time.'

'But the eleventh crate never made it to the field.'

'In which case it has its codes in a top-secret file placed in a custom receptacle on the inside back wall. That was the part the apprentice made. Eleven times over.'

No one spoke for a very long time.

Then Sinclair said, 'OK, one minute from now I have to call the president and tell him we may have ten loose atom bombs, complete with full arming codes, each one as powerful as the Hiroshima bomb, which means up to ten world cities could soon be completely destroyed. Can anyone give me a reason why I should not make that call?'

No one spoke.

Chief of Detectives Griezman took the elevator to Herr Dremmler's office. It was very slow. An original installation, no doubt, part of the rebuilding. But it got there in the end. A minute later Griezman was sitting uncomfortably in a too-small visitor chair across the desk from Dremmler, who first ordered coffee from a secretary Griezman took to be South American, and then asked how he could help.

Griezman said, 'It's about Wolfgang Schlupp.'

Dremmler said, 'You know, I talked to him earlier in the day. Purely by chance.'

'That's why I'm here.'

'He said nothing of interest. Certainly nothing that would shed light on what happened to him afterwards.'

'What did you talk about?'

'It was all pleasantries. I saw him once at a business dinner. He was a nodding acquaintance, nothing more.

I was merely saying hello. A professional courtesy. I hardly knew the fellow.'

'Were you trying to sell him shoes?'

'No, no, not at all. It's a politeness. It oils the wheels.'

'Do you go to that bar often?'

'Not very.'

'Why that day?'

'To see and be seen. I have many different places. On rotation. It's what we do.'

'We?'

'Entrepreneurs, civic leaders, business people, wheelers and dealers.'

Griezman said, 'Did you notice who your back was to?'

Dremmler paused a beat. Remembered elbowing in next to Schlupp, shoulder first, his back to the room. Who was behind him? He couldn't recall.

Griezman said, 'It was a fellow about to run into trouble with the taxman. He overheard the whole conversation. He was very specific about the details.'

Dremmler paused again. He had a good memory. Solid judgement. He was also nimble and creative. A man in his position needed such qualities. He rewound the tape in his head and played the day-old conversation from the beginning, from when he had asked how was business, and Schlupp had asked what he needed. He skimmed it fast and picked out the important parts, which were the words information, and cause, and new Germany, and driver's and licence, and the question about the American's new name, and the bribe, and the word important, and for the fourth time, the word cause.

Busted.

He said, 'I have people in places that might surprise you. It would be hard for this city to run without them. And none of them has broken any law. Myself included.'

'Yet.'

'Which is to say, none of them has broken any law.'

'We'll be ready when you do.'

'Persecuting us will only increase our numbers.'

'Prosecuting is not persecuting.'

'Think for yourself, Herr Griezman. You're facing a powerful force. Soon to get even more powerful. It might be time to abandon obedience to your masters. You should side with us. Our interests are perfectly aligned. You have nothing to fear. Your job will be safe. Even in the new Germany there will be petty criminals.'

Griezman said, 'Did Schlupp call you back before he died, with the American's new name?'

Dremmler said, 'No.'

And Griezman believed him. He expected nothing less.

Sinclair made the call to the White House from the regular office. Helmsworth had left. Bishop had arrived. Waterman repeated his gloomy predictions, that it was too late anyway, that the Germans would take half a day even to respond, and a whole day to brief in. Maybe more, because they were starting from cold. Then they heard that a NATO clause had been invoked, which only added to the complexity. Sinclair predicted a significant delay. Reacher called Griezman, and was told he was out in his car. His secretary said she would make sure he called back just as soon as he could. She sounded like a very pleasant woman.

He hung up.

Sinclair said, 'Wiley is an AWOL soldier in the same city as you.'

Reacher said, 'I need his new name.'

'Good luck with that.'

'We could attempt a prediction.'

'Based on what?'

'We know customers were free to choose what names they wanted. We know Wiley used Ernst and Gebhardt at the rental franchise. Why choose those two? And if they were number three and number two on a list, what was number one?'

'That would be highly speculative.'

'What the MP business would call a wild-ass guess.'

'Is that better than a Hail Mary, or worse?'

'It leaves a Hail Mary so far behind you can barely see it. It's a gut call. Like closing your eyes and swinging the bat.'

'So what's his new name?'

'I'm not sure yet. It's in the back of my mind. Can't get it all the way out. I might need to check a book or make a call.'

'Call who?'

'Someone who grew up in southeast Texas.'

The phone rang.

Griezman.

Who said, 'How may I help you?'

Reacher said, 'I'm not sure you can yet.'

'Then why did you call me?'

'I hoped to be ready.'

Sinclair said, 'Gamble, Reacher.'

He remembered raising his hand and brushing her forehead with his fingertips, and sliding his fingers into her hair, and running them through. He remembered the texture, alternately thick and soft as the waves came and went. He remembered sweeping it back and hooking part of it behind her ear, and leaving part of it hanging free.

It had looked good.

He had gambled then.

He said to Griezman, 'I need you to check city records for the development where Wiley lives.'

Griezman said, 'For what name?'

'Kempner.'

'That's fairly common.'

'Single males, middle thirties, living alone, not much else going on in their lives in terms of a paper trail.'

'That's hours of work. Are you in a hurry?'

'We're stepping a little faster than we'd like to be.'

'Then you better be sure. This could be your only wish. No time to rub the lamp again.'

'Try it.'

'Kempner?'

'Get back to me as soon as you can,' Reacher said.

He killed the call.

Sinclair said, 'Why Kempner?'

'Why Ernst and why Gebhardt? Wiley grew up in Sugar Land, Texas, and then one day years later he was

378

asked for three German names. What came to the surface? There's a lot of German tradition in Texas. An ancient community. A lot of success, and a lot of stories. Legend has it the first German to arrive was a guy named Ernst. He founded the colony. I'm sure Wiley heard all about him. Then years later another guy brewed a hot sauce. Now you can get it in plastic bottles from the PX or the supermarket. It's all over Texas. I'm sure Wiley has put it on his food all his life. The brand is Gebhardt.'

'Coincidence,' Sinclair said. 'Both of them.'

'But what if? If Ernst and Gebhardt came from a subliminal association with growing up in southeast Texas, what would come next?'

'I don't know. I have no idea.'

'Wiley was proud of his home town. That was in the original AWOL file. And Specialist Coleman confirmed it. Wiley's crewmate from the Chaparral truck. Wiley's home town was all about Imperial Sugar. Founded in 1906. Sugar Land was a company town, side to side and top to bottom.'

'How do you know this stuff?'

'There was a movie. And I read about it once, on a bus, in the *Houston Chronicle*. Imperial Sugar was founded by Isaac H. Kempner. He was the father of the town, essentially. He built it. I'm sure he's very famous there. Maybe they named a street for him.'

'Hell of a gamble.'

'You made me do it.'

White said, 'They should close the port.'

'I'm sure they will,' Sinclair said. 'I'm sure those

discussions are already under way. The White House will call us back and let us know.'

She checked the clock on the wall.

The banks in Zurich were open for business.

The phone didn't ring.

THIRTY-SIX

The phone didn't ring during the first hour. Or the second. Reacher said, 'I want to bring Orozco on board.'

Bishop said, 'Why?'

'We need an extra pair of hands. We're running short of time.'

'What could he do for us?'

'He's a good interrogator. If we find Wiley before we find the crate he's going to have to tell us where it is. Orozco would be good for that. People respond to him.'

'How much does he know already?'

'Some of it.'

Sinclair said, 'Call him.'

So Reacher did, there and then. He told Orozco as of ten hundred Zulu and eleven hundred Lima he was TDY to the NSC and for further detail an immediate 10-16 was required at the front desk number.

Then he killed the call.

Neagley looked at him.

He said, 'I'll be back in a moment.'

He left the office and walked down the stairs. To the front lobby. He waited at the desk. The phone rang. The guard picked up. He looked confused for a second, and then he handed the phone to Reacher. It was Orozco. A 10-16 was MP radio code for a report by land line. An immediate 10-16 meant call back right away. At the different number, Orozco would understand, for reasons of privacy.

Orozco said, 'Are we in trouble?'

Reacher said, 'Not yet.'

'That sounds like the guy who just jumped off a building. How does it feel? Pretty good so far. Like flying.'

'All we need to do is get the guy.'

'Are we going to?'

'How hard can it be?'

'What do you need from me?'

'I told them you're coming in as an interrogator. But you're not. You're coming in to get the Iranian out of the safe house. They've forgotten all about him. Or else they're set on taking a stupid risk. We can't let either thing happen. They'll kill him. So get him out as soon as we make a move.'

'Are you going to make a move?'

'I remain optimistic.'

'How will I know which are the Saudis and which is the Iranian?'

'I'm sure a man with your level of cultural sensitivity will have no trouble at all.'

'What do I do with the Saudis?'

'They can be collateral damage, if you like.'

'That's hardcore,' Orozco said.

'There are ten missing bombs.'

'Is that what this is about?'

'We just figured it out.'

'What kind of bombs?'

'Nuclear bombs,' Reacher said. 'Atom bombs as big as Hiroshima.'

'Are you serious?'

'As lung cancer.'

'Ten of them?'

'In a crate.'

Orozco was quiet for a long, long moment.

Then he said, 'I would want to bring my sergeant.'

Reacher said, 'I would expect nothing less.'

'I'm on my way,' Orozco said.

Reacher hung up and took the stairs back to the regular office. The phone rang as soon as he got there. Sinclair put it on speaker. Not the White House. Not new orders from NATO. It was Griezman. Who said, 'There are five Herr Kempners in Wiley's development. Four look unlikely based on age. The fifth is a strong possibility. His lease expires in less than a month. He has no employment records. The source of his funds is unclear. He is registered as Isaac Herbert Kempner.'

'That's him,' Reacher said. 'That's the guy who founded Imperial Sugar. The exact same name. We found Wiley.'

'I'll pick you up in five minutes,' Griezman said. 'But please, just you, Sergeant Neagley, and Dr Sinclair. No CIA. I haven't told Berlin yet. I'm out on a limb with this.'

Sinclair killed the call.

She looked at Reacher, and said, 'Congratulations, major. Another medal.'

Reacher said, 'Not yet.'

Muller closed his office door and called Dremmler from his desk phone. He said, 'Griezman is checking city records for a guy named Kempner. In the new development where they think Wiley lives. Where they had the unmarked car.'

Dremmler said, 'It's a common name.'

'I looked for myself and found five in that neighbourhood. Three are old men. One is a student. The fifth is thirty-five years old. He has a driver's licence. Which gives me access to his record. Which is completely empty. There's nothing there. No speeding tickets, no parking tickets, no warnings or cautions, no insurance claims, no witness statements, no nothing. No contact whatsoever with the bureaucratic world. That's not normal for a thirty-five-year-old. I don't think he's real. I think Kempner is Wiley's new name.'

'You have the address?'

'We should think ahead. Griezman will go to the apartment. It will be inaccessible to us. But think like a traffic cop. He has a long-wheelbase panel van. Where does he park it? Not on the street, because my guys have been looking for it, and they haven't found it. And not in a garage, either, because it's the high-roof model, as well as too long. So it's in a large shed, or possibly a small warehouse. Near enough to where he lives to be convenient. It's there right now. Just waiting for us. It's what we want. Not Wiley himself.'

'Where exactly?'

'You need to ask the people you know. Did anyone rent out an old shed or a warehouse? Possibly for cash, certainly to someone they never saw before, who had some type of vague bullshit story for why he needed it. It's the kind of thing you people talk about, right? A guy who knows a guy who knows a guy?'

Dremmler said, 'I'll make you chief of police.'

Bishop led the way to his office, which had an old-fashioned combination safe in the corner, as big as a basement washing machine. He spun the dials and turned the handle and opened the door. Inside was a mess of stuff, including four handguns stored butts-up in a long cardboard box. He took out three and passed them around. One for Sinclair, one for Reacher, and one for Neagley. They were Colt Government Model .380s. Seven-shooters, blued steel, plastic grips. Short barrel, but accurate. They were loaded.

'Try not to use them,' Bishop said. 'And if you do, for God's sake don't shoot anyone but Wiley. The legalities would be a nightmare.'

Reacher said, 'Tell Orozco where we are and what we're doing, as soon as he gets here. Tell him to stand by.'

Bishop said, 'Sure.'

Sinclair put her gun in her bag. Reacher and Neagley put theirs in their pockets.

Good to go.

* * *

Griezman stopped on the same kerb as the day before, and Sinclair climbed in the front of the car. Reacher and Neagley climbed in the back. Then Griezman took off and threaded through the centre of town, on a road Reacher remembered. Eventually they came to the crossroads. High brick buildings on every side. The champagne store was a right turn, and the new urban village was a left.

They turned left.

They drove around the brand new traffic circle and took the middle exit, straight ahead into the apartment complex. The buildings looked high-rise in their surroundings, but none was more than fifteen storeys tall. Exterior panels that in America would have been glass or mirror were sometimes metal painted bright simple colours. As if the dwellings had inspired or been inspired by a child's construction toy. Or maybe children were supposed to feel at home there. Reacher couldn't see how. He had been a serious kid. He felt the relentless cheerfulness would have driven him mad.

Griezman slowed the car.

He said, 'It's the next building on the left.'

Which was an identical structure, like a giant shoebox laid on its side, piebald with coloured panels, peppered with windows, which were smaller than they might have been, and which had thick, efficient frames. The lobby was a bite out of the lower two floors, like a grand arcade, presumably with entrances right and left. Two elevator banks.

Griezman said, 'Should we park and walk, or drive right up?'

'Drive,' Reacher said. 'Let's get this done.'

So Griezman accelerated again and then coasted to a stop outside Wiley's lobby. There were young trees planted in the shoulders. There was another building dead ahead, and then two more in the distance, with a wide footpath running between them, to the preserved part of the cityscape, and then to a footbridge made of teak and steel. It looped over the water, and away.

They opened all four doors at once and got out of the car. According to his unit number Wiley's lobby was the left-hand option. There were two elevators serving that half of the building. Both cars were waiting on the lobby level. The morning rush to work was over. Wiley's unit was on the ninth floor. SOP for an apartment raid was to send people up in every elevator simultaneously, plus more on the stairs. A full-court press, to prevent a lucky escape. Reacher had known it happen. He had seen security video of a guy strolling out his door and getting in an elevator literally half a second before the cops burst out of another elevator. Unfortunate timing. A teaching moment. Reacher figured Griezman would get a heart attack if he had to climb nine floors, so he suggested he ride in one car, with Sinclair in the other. Neagley took the stairs. Reacher went with Sinclair. Her gun was still in her bag. Not good practice. Getting it out would be slow, and the Government Model's only real weakness was a prominent magazine release near the trigger. A fumble in a bag could unload it. Not ideal.

The elevator doors closed on them. The car moved up. Sinclair said, 'How do you feel?'

Reacher said, 'Personally or professionally?'

'About Wiley.'

'I saw him on the liquor store video. He looked as quick as an outhouse rat. And he has a gun. And he's about to do the deal of the century. But that's OK. I like a challenge.'

'We'll arrest him as soon as he opens the door. He won't have time to do anything.'

'Suppose he doesn't open the door? Suppose he looks out the peephole and waits in the bedroom?'

Sinclair didn't answer.

The elevator stopped.

The doors opened.

Griezman was already out. Apart from him the corridor was empty. There were doors every thirty feet. Unit numbers were marked on narrow vertical panels next to the doors. The panels had an integrated wall sconce above, and the number below. They were all different bright colours. The numbers were written like a book from elementary school. Wiley's was 9b. His panel was green, and his door was yellow. Like a playhouse. My first apartment.

There was no peephole in the yellow door. Instead there was a head-height plastic eye on the green panel, the size of an egg, bulging out, smoky grey. A camera. Presumably with a screen on the wall inside. A big fisheye picture. Below the camera at elbow height was a doorbell button. A visitor who got close enough to ding the bell would have his face right in front of the camera. Which made sense.

Neagley tapped her chest. *I'll go first.* She kept close

to the wall, approaching the fish's eye at a ninety-degree angle, and when she was an arm's length away she clamped her left palm over the lens, and took out her Colt, and used the muzzle to press the bell.

THIRTY-SEVEN

There was no response. Neagley pressed the bell again. Reacher heard a soft chime inside the apartment. Gentle, melodious, not urgent.

No response.

Nothing.

Silence.

Neagley stood back.

Griezman said, 'We need a warrant.'

Reacher said, 'Are you sure?'

'In Germany it is essential.'

'But he's American. And we're American. Let's do this the American way.'

'You need a warrant also. I have seen it in the movies. You have an Amendment.'

'And credit cards.'

'What for? To buy something? To pay someone off?'

'For ingenuity and self-reliance. That's the American way.'

Neagley asked Sinclair for a credit card, and got a government Amex in return. She took it to Wiley's door, and stood sideways, her back to the hinge, her inside hand on the handle, her outside hand holding the card, fingertips only. She pressed on the door with her shoulder, and hauled straight back on the handle, against whatever extra compression the hinges could give her, and she slid the government Amex into the frame and touched it to the tongue of the lock. She dabbed it and tapped it, and moved the door a fraction one way by pushing with her shoulder, and a fraction another way by hauling on the handle a degree more or less, trying random combinations, until finally the lock snicked back and the door came open. At which point she ducked low, because she knew Reacher would be aiming centre mass at anyone standing behind it.

There was no one there.

There was no one anywhere.

They cleared the place room by room, first with hasty left-right glances over iron sights, and then again patiently, and slower.

Still no one there.

They gathered in the kitchen. There was a map folded open on the counter. Large scale, plenty of detail. The centre section of a country. Ocean to the left, ocean to the right. A perfect square rubbed greasy by a finger. The city of Buenos Aires in the top right corner.

'Argentina,' Reacher said. 'He's buying a ranch. Has to be a thousand square miles. He changed his money for pesos at the railroad station. He's going to South America.'

Neagley opened cupboards, and checked the dishwasher, and pulled drawers. She reached into the recycle bin and came out with a dark bottle with a thin neck. Rinsed and empty. A dull gold label. Dom Perignon. Then she checked the trash. Crusts and rinds and coffee grounds. And a bloody shirt, and spattered pants, and a red file folder. Made of stiff board covered in vinyl, with four rings inside, and pre-punched pages with lines of handwritten code, in five separate columns.

'That's Schlupp's,' Griezman said. 'That's all the evidence I need.'

Sinclair came back from the bedroom.

'He packed a bag,' she said. 'But it's still in the closet. He's still in town.'

At that moment Wiley was nine floors below them, in the lobby. But not yet approaching the elevator bank. He was standing in the middle of the floor, half turned, looking back at the car parked on the kerb. He knew about cars. He had been a broker. Other people stole them, he sold them. To Mexico, mostly. Sometimes the Caribbean. He was a good judge of value. It was a price-sensitive market, the same as anything else. The car on the kerb was a Mercedes, about three or four years old. It looked well maintained and very clean. But under the polish it was worn and scuffed. It had done a lot of city miles. It had an antenna on the trunk lid. Like a taxi or a town car. But it was not a taxi or a town car. No light, no meter. As a town car it was too old to be from an upmarket service. If it had been sold on second-hand to a downmarket service, it would be covered in stickers and phone numbers.

And it wasn't a town car because the driver's seat was

crushed way back into the rear passenger space. No date night couple would tolerate that.

It was a cop car. Not a plain vanilla detective's ride, but a sheriff's, or a captain's. Why? Not for him, surely. He was invisible. He was confident of that. So who? There were nearly two hundred apartments in the block. There had to be a bad guy in one of them. Statistically certain, in the new Germany.

He needed his bag, obviously, and he wanted his map. He planned to have it framed. He planned to hang it on a fieldstone fireplace, in a great room with a soaring cathedral ceiling. Where it belonged. It was of great sentimental value to him. It had gotten him through many a long night. It was his inspiration. He couldn't just leave it. He could re-buy the stuff in the bag if he needed to. That would be a trivial task. Although he would have to change pesos back to marks, which would be a nuisance. But he couldn't abandon the map. Apart from anything else it was a clue. A pencilled square, rubbed away with his fingertip. He had killed the hooker for less. So he had to get it.

But later, he thought. Not now. Just in case. The cops could be on his floor. There was a one-in-fifteen chance. He didn't want to get involved with witness statements. What could he say? He didn't know his neighbours. Which would be taken as weird. So he turned back and walked out of the lobby, to the footpath towards the water, past the next building, between the last two, to a bench set at the feet of a preserved dockside crane. He sat down and slid along until he had a clear line of sight back the way he had come. About three hundred yards.

The car was a speck. Therefore so was he, from the other direction. He waited.

Dremmler made his calls from his fourth-floor office, and the people he called made calls of their own, like a cascade through a certain section of society, where the deals were done, where everyone knew a guy who could get it cheaper, where everyone knew who was up and who was down. Then calls came back, like distant sonar pings, and a consensus grew around a guy who would never admit it. Because it stemmed from failure. The guy had bought some dockland south of St Georg. He was going to sell it for apartments. But the city fathers developed St Pauli instead. The guy was left with nothing but a bunch of tumbledown warehouses. Having paid a premium price. He was embarrassed.

But Dremmler was a leader, and like all leaders a man of charisma, so he called the guy and asked for the story. And sure enough he got it, after five minutes of obfuscation and delay, all because it was a cash deal. The warehouse guy was hiding it. His creditors were all over his bank accounts. But he needed walking-around money. So no questions asked. Wiley had shown up seven months ago. They met face to face. Wiley had a red ball cap and his chin tucked low. And wads of cash. He was impatient, as if the clock was ticking on an urgent plan. He paid well above the market rate. He didn't think twice.

The guy told Dremmler where the warehouse was located. Dremmler knew the spot. He knew the boxy bridge. He thought: *You honestly believed they would put apartments there? No wonder you're bankrupt.*

He said, 'Thank you so much for your help. When the time comes, your service will not be forgotten.'

They debated waiting in the apartment for Wiley to come home, but Sinclair said since Helmsworth's testimony the game had changed, and the long-wheel-base high-roof panel van was now the new number one priority. Not Wiley himself. He was now the number two priority. So Griezman made a call on Wiley's phone, and kidnapped a surveillance unit from the mayor's office, where the panic was dying down a little. The guy said he could be on station outside Wiley's building in about five minutes. So as close as they could they left the apartment the way they had found it, and they went back down to the street the same way they came up, for the same reasons. Both elevators and the stairs, all at once.

They stepped out to the sidewalk. To the left was a footpath towards the water. In the distance Reacher could see an old dockyard crane, repainted black and gold, stooped like an ancient carnivore. There was a park bench at its feet, and maybe a guy sitting on it. Too far to see. Just a speck. Beyond the crane was a foot-bridge, to the next pier, which had two more, like a branching tree.

He said, 'What happens over there?'

'At first it's like an urban park,' Griezman said. 'Then farther out it's undeveloped.'

Reacher glanced around and lined himself up, north, south, east and west. He looked straight ahead, beyond the crane, into what would be a fan-shaped spread, first of neat urban parkland, and then of derelict lots. Which had to be the same fan shape he had seen from the side, the night before. If his mental map was correct. Beyond the boxy metal bridge. Where he turned back. He remembered moonlight on black water.

Derelict lots.

Old buildings.

Places to hide a long-wheelbase panel van.

He said, 'We should go take a look.'

They walked four abreast, at Griezman's pace, which was slow. They passed the next building and kept on going. In the distance the speck on the bench got up and wandered away. Break over. Back to work. They walked on, between the last two buildings, towards the old dockyard crane. Beyond it the footbridge skipped ahead to the next pier, and then there was a choice of two bridges, half left or half right, to two more piers, each one different in the way it had been restored, with different sculptures, like different rooms in the same museum. From those piers the number of footbridges doubled again, two choices on the left, and two on the right, fanning out like fingers. The piers were massive granite constructions, worn and black and slimy, and the bridges were new and light and airy, spidering their way from one to two to four and onward. Whimsical. Like a maze, but not exactly. The city had spent some money.

But not enough. Beyond the last sculptures in the far distance were weeds and broken brick and clusters of sway-backed old buildings. Back there the footbridges were old iron affairs. A dismal panorama, covering acres.

A lot to search.

But logical.

Reacher said, 'He wouldn't want to park on the other side of town. He'd want to keep it local. These footbridges help him out. He's got a hundred derelict warehouses within walking distance. Maybe a thousand. I bet half of them have no owners. He could move right in. Change the locks, and the place is his.'

Sinclair said, 'Is that where we'll find it?'

'It would make a lot of sense. It's close at hand. It's a short drive to the port, when the time comes.'

They walked back to the car. The surveillance vehicle had arrived. It was a good one. It blended in well. They got in the Mercedes and drove out of the complex, around the new traffic circle, and back to the crossroads, with the high brick buildings. They turned right, on the road Reacher knew, past a body of water, some kind of a deep-water dock or a basin, and then they turned right again, on the narrow cobblestone track that led to the boxy metal bridge Reacher had seen in the moonlight.

Beyond the bridge were the ruins of a lost civilization. Longshoring, nineteenth-century style. There were cobbled streets wide enough for flatbed trailers with iron rims and teams of horses. There were sheds and warehouses of every old-time style and size, some of which had fallen down, and some of which were about to. Walls bulged, and small trees grew in the rainwater gutters. There were side streets everywhere. It was like a city within a city. A lot to search.

Griezman said, 'I could check the rental records, for the name Kempner.'

'He probably paid cash,' Reacher said. 'Off the books. Or he's squatting.'

'I'll check anyway. There might be reports of unusual activity. We can't do this at random. It's too big.'

Griezman turned around in the gap between a rope maker and a sail loft, and drove away again, over the boxy metal bridge.

'We need a car at the bridge,' Reacher said. 'It's a basic requirement. This bridge is the only way in or out. He can't drive his van to the port any other way.'

Griezman said, 'The mayor's office hasn't released my men.'

'You got one out.'

'I can't get two.'

Reacher said nothing.

Griezman said, 'I suppose I could ask the traffic division. They're not involved at the hotel garage. I'm sure Deputy Chief Muller would be willing to do us a favour.'

'Tell him in German,' Reacher said. 'His English is lousy.'

By that point Wiley was more than two miles away. A fast walk in the opposite direction, and then a short ride in a bus. He had gotten a very strange feeling. Not exactly a fright, but a powerful sense of something. He had seen the four tiny specks come out of the building and stand by their car. But then they had started walking towards him. Slowly and ominously. Past the next-door building and onward. He started to make out detail. Two men, two women. Somehow staring at him.

As if they knew. Either the women were tiny or the men were huge. One was wearing grey and the other was wearing khaki. Far away, nothing more than a grainy thumbnail smear of colour, but the shape looked boxy. Like a Levi's jean jacket. Like his own. One of which he had seen, not long ago, in a park, from the bus. With the chuckleheads from the bar.

Impossible.

He was invisible.

Wasn't he?

He got up and walked away. Slowly, not a care in the world. Until he was out of sight. Then he hustled.

Now he crossed the street to a mid-grade Turkish coffee shop and went to the phone on the wall. He had plenty of coins. A waste, almost certainly, because it was too early, but he was suddenly nervous. The guy in the jean jacket had upset him. Staring, like he knew.

He dialled Zurich, and he gave his passcode number.

He asked, 'Has there been a deposit to my account today?'

A keyboard pattered.

There was a pause.

'Not yet, sir,' was the answer.

THIRTY-EIGHT

Muller called Dremmler from his office. He said, 'Griezman's division has asked mine for a favour. Their people are all tied up at the hotel. They want one of my officers to watch the bridge, right where the warehouse is. They already know about it.'

'They don't,' Dremmler said. 'Only that the van is in there somewhere. If they knew exactly where, they'd have it already. All they can do is watch the bottleneck.'

'How long do you need until you're ready?'

'I don't know. I suppose half an hour would be good.'

'I can't delay half an hour. That's a lifetime. Griezman might check. I already didn't do the thing south of Hanover.'

'How much time can you give me?'

'None at all,' Muller said. 'I'm supposed to do it right away.'

'Then do you have a reliable officer?' Dremmler said.

'Reliable in what sense?'

'I mean one of us. Someone who might be persuaded

to be selective about what he reports. For the good of the cause.'

Muller said, 'That's possible, I suppose.'

'Tell him I'll make him deputy chief,' Dremmler said.

Reacher met Griezman's secretary outside his office. She was indeed a pleasant woman. Griezman spoke to her in rapid-fire German, and she bustled off and came back at intervals with men in suits from the city planning department, each one bearing sheaves of maps and plans and historic surveys. Griezman laid out the best and most relevant on his conference table. One map was of the new footbridge arrangement. Another was a brittle sheet from the archives showing the area in the olden days. Another showed how beautification was planned to march on outward, in a shape like a slice of pizza. No doubt one day it would be finished. But not soon. So far the pointed end was pretty well covered, and a couple inches more, but the bulk of the pie hadn't been touched in fifty years, since hungry postwar women in tattered clothing had hauled bricks and made repairs.

There were eight new footbridges at the outer extremity of the urban park, and clearly the idea was to use one, sniff the air, then turn around and come right back. But there were also circuitous onward routes, if desired, using old iron bridges, and catwalks, and dog-legs, and detours. Not part of the park. But a person could get to the ghost town.

Eight final footbridges. Eight onward options, plus a

couple of left-right choices, and then more. An additive effect. In the end there were close to twenty possible itineraries. Close to twenty possible end-points. Each one of which was a five-minute walk to block after block of sheds and garages and storehouses. The cumulative total was the size of a town.

Wiley took the same bus, in the opposite direction, and got off where he had gotten on. He walked over the footbridge, but used a different footpath, that led him behind a neighbouring building, to its corner, where he could see his own stretch of kerb from cover.

The suspicious Mercedes was gone.

But now closer to him was another Mercedes. Brand new. The top model. A limousine. It was deep black, polished to an infinite shine. There was a driver with gloves and a peaked cap in the seat. An upmarket service for sure. Wiley knew about cars. A bank, maybe. Giving a junior executive a taste of the high life. To keep him hungry. To keep him in line. Or a couple with an anniversary. Going to Paris. Cars at both ends. Maybe the guy had done something wrong. Maybe he was making an effort.

Wiley came out around the neighbouring building and walked down to his lobby. Both elevators were on the ground floor. The middle of the day. Nothing going on. He rode up to nine and took out his key.

Out on the kerb the limousine driver keyed his radio and said, 'Wiley has come home. I repeat, Wiley is home.'

402

His dispatcher said, 'Stay on the air. I'm supposed to call Griezman.'

There was dead air, and then the dispatcher came back, and said, 'Griezman says sit tight, and he'll be there as soon as he can. With the Americans. Four in total. In Griezman's car.'

'Understood,' the limo driver said. He hung up his microphone and re-adopted his pose, cap low, nose high, hands on the wheel at the ten and the two, even though the engine was off and the car wasn't moving.

Wiley unlocked his yellow door and stepped inside. He went straight to the bedroom and grabbed his bag. Then straight to the kitchen. He folded his map on its original creases, and smoothed it out, and zipped it in the pocket of his bag. With the paper wallet from the travel agent. With the airplane ticket. He picked up the phone and dialled Zurich. He gave his passcode number.

He asked, 'Has there been a deposit to my account today?'

A keyboard pattered.

There was a pause.

'Not yet, sir,' was the answer.

Wiley put the phone down.

Then he stood a second. Looked around. He had a weird feeling. The air was disturbed. Something had happened.

What?

Who cared? He was never coming back. He closed the door behind him and walked to the elevator. It opened right away. It had waited there. To save

403

energy, he supposed. The Germans were all over that.

He pressed the button and the doors closed and he rode down to the lobby. He walked out to the path and turned towards the water. Toward the old dockside crane, and the footbridges beyond.

The limo driver hit his radio hard and said, 'Wiley is out again. Repeat, Wiley has left home again. He was in there less than five minutes. Now he's walking away from me carrying a bag.'

His dispatcher said, 'Griezman and the Americans are currently en route. Can you follow?'

'No. Wiley is on a footpath and I'm in a car two metres wide.'

'Can you follow on foot?'

'I'm restricted to vehicular duty only. It's a disability posting. I hurt my back.'

'Can you at least see where he's going?'

'He's walking towards an old dockside crane.'

'How far away is he now?'

'About two hundred metres.'

'No sign of Griezman?'

'Not yet.'

Griezman was stuck in traffic. A fender bender, at the crossroads with the high brick buildings all around. He bumped up on the sidewalk and squeezed through whatever gaps he could find. Sinclair was next to him in the front. Reacher and Neagley were in the back. At that point they were impatient, rather than anxious. Until finally they made the turn, and drove around the new traffic circle, and pulled up behind the surveillance unit, and got the news from the driver.

Griezman said, 'How long ago?'

'Ten minutes.'

'He's gone.'

'With his bag,' Sinclair said. 'Which means he ain't coming back.'

Reacher stared ahead, at the old crane, and beyond. Twenty itineraries. Twenty end-points. Block after block of sheds and garages and storehouses. A cumulative total the size of a town.

'No one's fault,' he said. 'I'm sure we all imagined he had come home for lunch. We were entitled to expect thirty minutes at least.'

'You're very cheerful,' Sinclair said.

'He's on a man-made island with one road out. The situation is contained. Now all we need to do is hunt him down. Most likely we'll find him with his vehicle. Two birds with one stone, right there. Our winning streak continues.'

'This is winning?'

'That really depends on what happens next.'

'It's a very large area. There are twenty ways in.'

'Twenty ways out,' Reacher said. 'Only one way in. Because it's a very large area. He must have scouted it by car. I'm sure he got a four-day pass every time he did volunteer duty at the storage lager, which would have given him plenty of time for reconnaissance, but even so, he was coming all the way from the Frankfurt area. He would need a car. Rented, or borrowed. Or stolen, I guess. So think about it from his point of view. One day he'll need to hide a truck. He drives in over the metal bridge. What does he look for?'

'I don't know.'

'Not the first thing he sees. This is a very big deal. At this point he's thinking hard, but he's also listening to his subconscious. He wants secrecy and isolation. He wants a dark furtive corner. Above all he doesn't want to stand out. He doesn't want to be the nearest or the farthest or the biggest or the smallest.'

'He wants to be in the middle.'

'Now it's not such a large area. We just narrowed it down.'

Neagley said, 'He would want solid construction. And a live phone number for the rental. He wouldn't squat. Too insecure for a very big deal. Anything could happen. He'd want to do it face to face. With a big wad of cash. He'd let himself get taken for a little extra. Like a rube. Because then he's the golden goose. They'll leave him alone in the hopes of coming back for more at the end of his term. So we're looking for a solid door, with an inquiries number thumbtacked to it.'

Reacher said, 'Now we narrowed it down some more.'

Sinclair said, 'Still no decision from the White House.'

'Why not?'

'Perhaps the complexities surpass human understanding. Or perhaps they haven't admitted to the world what happened yet. Too embarrassing. In the hopes that in the meantime the problem will go away, because of us.'

'Which is it?'

'I feel like I'm supposed to know. But I don't.'

'I think it's the latter. My guess is they want us to continue.'

'Are you advocating immediate action?'

'Let's go park the car at the bridge,' Reacher said. 'Let's at least do that. Then we'll see what happens next.'

THIRTY-NINE

The old dockside quarter still had telephone booths, and being German they still worked. Wiley dialled Zurich, and paid the toll, another long stream of foreign coins, and he gave his passcode number, and he asked if a deposit had been made to his account that day.

A keyboard pattered.

There was a pause.

'Yes, sir,' was the answer. 'A deposit was made.'

Wiley said nothing.

'Would you like to know the amount?'

Wiley said yes.

'One hundred million U.S. dollars and no cents.'

Wiley said, 'There's a plan in place.'

'I see that, sir. The project in Argentina. Shall we execute immediately?'

'Yes,' Wiley said.

He closed his eyes.

His place.

Visible from outer space.

Little Horace Wiley.

He opened his eyes, and he hung up the phone, and then he walked back the way he had come.

In Zurich the messenger came out of the bank, through a glossy but anonymous door, to the street, where she walked to the corner and flagged down a cab. She settled in the back seat and said in carefully practised German, 'The airport, please. International departures. Lufthansa to Hamburg.'

The driver started his meter and pulled out into traffic.

Dremmler had gotten the rental van's plate number from Muller, which enabled a friend at a Mercedes-Benz dealership to trace its security code through its vehicle identification number, which enabled another friend at an auto parts store to make a duplicate ignition key. Which Dremmler gave to a third friend, one of a team of two assembled for the occasion. They were both big men, both competent, both resourceful. They had been in the army. Now one was a motorcycle mechanic. The other worked security for visiting Russians.

'The traffic cop at the bridge is mine,' Dremmler said. 'As far as he's concerned you're invisible. He's like a blind man. But even so, don't push your luck. Get in and out real fast. You know where to find it, and you know where to take it afterwards. Any questions?'

The guy with the key said, 'What's in it?'

'Something that will bring us great power,' Dremmler said, which he figured was vague, but probably true.

* * *

They found a traffic division black-and-white parked ahead of the boxy metal bridge. The guy inside rolled down his window and told them nothing had passed, either coming or going. No trucks, no vans, no cars, no bikes, and no one on foot. No traffic at all. Reacher asked Griezman to tell the guy to block the road with his car if he saw a panel van coming. Probably white, and probably with the plate number it was born with, but neither thing was definite. It could have been repainted or otherwise disguised. Better safe than sorry. Any kind of a panel van, the guy should block the travel lanes and ask questions later.

Griezman asked why.

Reacher said to get the job done before NATO got its finger in the pie. Which he figured Griezman would interpret as a chance for individual glory and recognition. Maybe the guy wanted to run for mayor one day.

Griezman told the traffic cop what to do.

Reacher said, 'Let's go take a look around.'

Griezman drove down the street, with the cobble-stones pattering under his tyres, then across the boxy metal bridge, its deck humming and ringing, then more cobbles, and then a choice of two main ways to explore the place from nearest to farthest. One was the wharf itself, and the other was an arterial route set back from the water.

'Which way?' Griezman said.

'The back street,' Reacher said.

There were signs of life here and there. A guy was welding a sports car in a garage with its doors propped open. Another guy had an electronics store. But overall

410

the tide was out. That was clear. From nearest to farthest was two miles exactly, and the number of bustling enterprises could be counted on the fingers of two hands.

Griezman said, 'Should we go back now and look at the middle third?'

Reacher nodded.

He said, 'I think that's what Wiley did.'

Griezman threaded through a loading bay, and drove back on the wharf. Technically the middle third would be more than a thousand yards long. Two-thirds of a mile. About the same amount deep. Like the business district of a decent-sized city.

Wiley was in there somewhere.

Griezman said, 'Where do you wish to start?'

'Think about it from his point of view. He's got a van to hide. What does he see? Where does he go?'

Griezman slowed, and then turned between two warehouses, on a narrow street that broadened out into a yard, flanked left and right by storehouses with narrow wooden doors.

'Not here,' Reacher said. 'For whatever reason he rented a second van. Which tells us he had somewhere to put it. By accident or design he rented a place with room for two. So it's not a solid door with an inquiries number tacked to it. It's a pair of solid doors with an inquiries number tacked to one of them.'

Of which there were many. Some notices were old and faded. They inspired no confidence. Some were crisp and new. But other than head back to the office and try them all out there was no way of knowing which numbers were live, and which were not. Reacher looked around as they drove, and pictured the map he had seen, on Griezman's office table, on the brittle archive paper, dense with ink, crowded with detail.

He said, 'Wiley grew up in Texas. How does he feel about driving in Europe?'

'Not great,' Sinclair said. 'It's narrow and awkward and the turns are too tight.'

'We should add that feeling to the list. He had to manoeuvre a commercial vehicle. He didn't want to feel trapped or boxed in. I think he rented on one of the wider streets.'

Of which there were a significant number. They repeated, like an architectural plan. Some side streets were wide too. For heavier wagons and larger loads. Griezman stopped in one of them. He said, 'This could take for ever.'

Reacher said, 'We have for ever. As long as your traffic cop stays awake.'

'He will.'

'We could add one last factor. I think he changed the locks. Or added new. This was a very big deal.'

So Griezman set off again, slowly, quartering the neighbourhood, and all four on board craned their necks, looking for solid double doors, with a plausible phone number attached, and manoeuvring room out front, and new locks.

The messenger was once again in the immigration line at the Hamburg airport. The same four booths were operational, still two for the European Union, and two for outside. She was using the same Pakistani passport.

412

But this time she was dressed in black and her hair was down. She could see her reflection in the glass. She had been told not to worry if she got the same guy. He wouldn't remember. He saw a million people every day.

She moved up, from third in line to second.

From the back of the car Reacher saw a phone booth on a corner. He said, 'I need to make a call.'

Griezman pulled over and Reacher got out. He dialled the consulate room. Vanderbilt answered. Reacher asked him if Orozco had gotten there yet. Vanderbilt said yes, and put him on the line. Orozco said, 'I'm standing by, boss.'

Reacher said, 'You should do it now. We have an active roadblock here. Either way the deal is not going to happen. Sooner or later they'll know it.'

'Have you found him yet?'

'We're close.'

'Pretty good so far. Like flying.'

'You bet,' Reacher said.

He hung up the phone and stood in the silence. He could hear Griezman's Mercedes behind him, idling at the kerb. He could hear a faint penumbra of noise from the city, a mile away, and a ship's horn far down the river. Closer by he could hear a compressor running somewhere. Maybe someone was spraying paint. There were occasional engine noises, in the middle distance, as if things were being hauled back and forth.

Not totally dead.

Wiley was in there somewhere.

Reacher stepped back to the car and said, 'Sergeant Neagley and I will walk from here.'

The messenger walked through baggage claim and out to the meet-and-greet concourse. She sidestepped hugs and balloons and made it to the street. Which was somewhat underground. The departures level was above it. She had been told she would find the two she was looking for at the left-hand end of the covered section. Near a corral full of small three-wheeled carts.

She saw them as she approached, exactly as described. Small men, wiry, bearded, dark-haired and dark-skinned. They had overalls unbuttoned to the waist, with undershirts beneath, and ear defenders around their necks, and elbow protectors around their elbows, and knee protectors around their knees, and see-through ID panels around their biceps, all items firmly held in place with thick elastic straps. The IDs were from the airport. The bearers worked for a freight forwarding company known to have excellent relationships with the cargo divisions of many Middle Eastern sovereign airlines.

The messenger said, 'The Mercedes-Benz was named for a customer's daughter.'

The guy on the left said, 'You're a woman.'

'This is a serious business. What better disguise?'

'Do you know what you're doing?'

'Do you?'

'You're supposed to tell us.'

'Then you'd better trust me. We're going to take a cab to the old docks. A man is going to give us a long-wheelbase panel van. You're going to drive the van back to the airport and load it on the plane. Do you understand?'

The two guys nodded. Pretty much what they expected. They were airplane loaders with badges that could get them through any airport gate. Horses for courses. They didn't expect to get called out to the hospital to do brain surgery.

Reacher and Neagley took opposite sidewalks, and checked doors, and peered around corners. They tried to see what they saw like a slow-motion version of Wiley himself, scouting from his car, pausing at the end of every block, feeling, choosing, left or right or straight ahead, whichever felt best, and safest, and secret, and secluded.

By that point they were deep in the heart of the middle third. And by a happy circumstance the best-feeling places all had the same phone number. Crisp, laminated notices. Fairly recent. Wiley would have liked them. They would have given him confidence. They spoke of a small real estate enterprise. Reliable. Professional. And he would be one tenant among many. He wouldn't stand out.

'I've seen that same number for thirty square blocks,' Neagley said. 'This guy bought a big chunk of land.'

'Maybe he wants to put up an apartment building.'

They moved on, pausing at the end of every block, feeling, choosing, left or right or straight ahead. Reacher stopped on a corner. He glanced left. He saw a pair of double doors. Solid. Dark green. Weathered, but not rotted. A phone number. The left-hand door had sagged ajar a foot or so. Open padlocks hung askew on bolts and a hasp. The right-hand door was propped all the way wide. A small warehouse. Dark inside, against the bright daylight.

Reacher walked closer.

There was a sound inside. Fast wheezing breaths, bubbling and gurgling, each one ending in a tiny gasp or yelp. The sound of a guy breathing hard with broken ribs and blood in his throat. Reacher took his Colt out of his pocket. He clicked the safety. He put his finger on the trigger. He kept close to the wall, and tried to see in through the crack of the hinge. A big dark mass.

He followed the angle of the left-hand door, and flattened his back against the last part of it. Neagley waited a yard away. She would replace him when he moved.

He listened to the breathing.

Wheezing, bubbling, yelping.

He moved off the door and peered around its edge.

He saw a two-truck space. One half was full, and one half was empty. The full half had an old delivery truck, dusty and settled on softening tyres. The word *Möbel* was painted on its side. Which was German for furniture. Its rear door was up. Inside was an empty wooden crate. Maybe twelve feet by six by six, made of old timber as hard and bronzed as metal.

The empty half of the space had a guy on the floor.

He was lying in a spreading lake of blood.

The hair, the brow, the cheekbones, the deep-set eyes.

It was Horace Wiley.

FORTY

Wiley's blade of a nose was busted, and one of his arms, Reacher thought, from the way he was holding it. His other hand was pressed hard against his stomach. Bright red blood was pulsing out between his fingers. He was staring blankly at the far horizon, with wide-open tragedy in his eyes. More shock and misery than Reacher had ever seen before. More abject crushing disappointment, more pain, more betrayal, more open-mouthed incredulity at the unlikely ways the world can crush a person.

Reacher stepped closer.

He said, 'What happened?'

Wiley gasped and bubbled and his voice came out low and halting.

He said, 'They stole my van. Stabbed me. Bust my arm.'

'Who did?'

'Germans.'

'How?'

'I was waiting here. Two guys came. Stabbed me and stole my van.'

'Waiting for what?'

'Guys who were coming for the van. Part of the deal.'

'When?'

'I need a doctor, man. I'm going to die.'

'That's for damn sure,' Reacher said. 'Treason gets the death penalty.'

'It hurts bad.'

'Good,' Reacher said.

Then he heard a car. He looked around the open door. It was Griezman and Sinclair, in the department Mercedes.

Sinclair knelt down next to Wiley, talking, listening, promising a doctor in exchange for cooperation, already debriefing a mile a minute. Neagley looked at the empty crate in the furniture truck. She caught Reacher's eye and pointed to the receptacle for the secret file. Thin plywood, with a half-moon shape scooped out for fingers. The part the apprentice had made, eleven times over. Then Reacher went with Griezman, all the way back to the iron bridge, to see what the traffic cop had snared. One panel van, presumably. But no. When they got there the traffic cop swore nothing had passed by. No vans, no cars, no people, no nothing.

Reacher and Griezman drove back to the warehouse. They got out of the car and heard nothing at all. Sinclair and Neagley were standing in the gloom, still and silent. The lake of blood on the floor was bigger. But it was no longer increasing.

Wiley had bled out.

He was dead.

Griezman said, 'Nothing crossed the bridge.'

Silence.

Then Reacher heard another car.

He stepped out a pace. A taxi. Three passengers. A woman, her head ducked down, shovelling money out of her purse. Paying the fare. And two men, climbing out, small and wiry, dark and bearded, wearing work clothes and protective equipment, looking around, seeing Reacher, looking him right in the eye, and nodding a cautious greeting. As if they expected to see him there. Which they did, he guessed. Generically. They knew a man was going to give them a panel van. They had come to drive it away. Part of the deal.

Reacher put his hand on his gun in his pocket and stepped all the way out to the sunlight. The woman was stuffing her purse back in her bag. The taxi was driving away. The woman looked up. She saw Reacher and looked momentarily confused. Reacher was not the guy she was expecting to see. She was in her early twenties, with jet black hair and olive skin. She was very good-looking. She could have been Turkish or Italian.

She was the messenger.

The two guys with her were waiting patiently, stoic and unexcited, like labourers ahead of routine tasks. They were airport workers, Reacher thought. He remembered telling Sinclair that Wiley had chosen Hamburg because it was a port. The second largest in Europe. The gateway to the world. Maybe once. But the plan had changed. Now he guessed they planned to drive the truck into the belly of a cargo plane. Maybe fly it to Aden, which was a port of a different kind. On the coast of Yemen. Where ten tramp steamers would be waiting to complete the deliveries, after weeks at sea. Straight to New York or D.C. or London or LA or San Francisco. All the world's great cities had ports nearby. He remembered Neagley saying the radius of the lethal blast was a mile, and the radius of the fireball was two. Ten times over. Ten million dead, and then complete collapse. The next hundred years in the dark ages.

The messenger said, 'Hello?'

Not Turkish or Italian. Pashtun, probably, from the Northwest Frontier. A tribe as old as time. Dutiful map-makers drew lines and wrote India or Pakistan or Afghanistan, and the Pashtun smiled politely and went about their eternal business.

The messenger said, 'Who are you?'

Reacher nodded beyond the half-open door and said, 'Mr Wiley is in here.'

The men hung back and let the messenger lead the way. Reacher watched their faces. He saw the truth dawning. An empty space. A dead man on the floor. A lake of drying blood. Three unexplained figures standing back from its edge.

Not right.

Reacher pulled his gun.

The two men and the woman turned to look.

Reacher said, 'You're under arrest.'

Their reactions differed by gender. Reacher saw a cascade of ancient, hopeless conclusions in the two men's eyes. They were guest workers in a foreign nation. They had no status, no power, no leverage, no rights, no expectations. They were bottom of the pile. They were cannon fodder.

They had nothing to lose.

They went for their pockets. They scrabbled at puckered fabric, hitching and bending, ramming their hands in, hauling them out. Reacher yelled *no* in English and *nein* in German, but they didn't stop. They had weird little sawed-off revolvers. Pale steel, pale pinewood grips. Barrels about an inch long, like stubs. Reacher thought Washington D.C. and New York and London would be top of the list. Then maybe Tel Aviv, and Amsterdam, and Madrid. Then Los Angeles and San Francisco. Maybe the Golden Gate Bridge itself. Like Helmsworth had said. *Their orders were to strap it to a bridge support, set the timer, and run like hell.*

He shot them centre mass, a fast double tap, left to right, and when they were down he shot them again, in the head from the same range, to be completely sure and certain. The shattering noise died away to an ear-damaged hiss. On the side of the empty broken-down furniture truck the word *Möbel* was spattered with blood.

Reacher aimed at the messenger's face.

The messenger raised her hands.

She said, 'I surrender.'

No one answered.

She said, 'I have good information. I know their bank accounts. I can give you their money.'

Sinclair took charge. She was the ranking officer, after all, in a NATO kind of way. From a municipal perspective Griezman took it meekly enough, possibly because of realpolitik, which was a German word for knowing when you're beat. She told him if he thought the van hadn't yet crossed the bridge he should pull all his men free from the mayor's office and set up a solid perimeter. She sent Neagley to the phone booth, to get Bishop on the scene, and White, and Vanderbilt. Waterman and Landry could stay home and mind the store.

Within minutes Griezman had two cars on the bridge. The traffic cop was thanked and sent home. Then two more cars arrived. They funnelled through the road-block and set up ahead of the nearest buildings. Simply a question of numbers. A panel van was a substantial item. A long line of men walking shoulder to shoulder could hardly miss it.

Reacher looked at Wiley, and then at Sinclair. He asked her, 'Did he tell you how he found the crate?'

She said, 'Something his Uncle Arnold told him.'

'What kind of something?'

'All about the atom bombs. Even Uncle Arnold thought it was crazy. Even though he was a paratrooper, and basically everything he was trained for was a suicide mission. He was going to be part of the first wave in the greatest land battle in history. But even so there was something weird about the atom bombs. Too much power for a single person. Then he told him the story about the missing crate. They all believed it was true. There was panic behind the scenes. Too much for a cover-your-ass. Uncle Arnold figured the natural ebb and flow would bring it to one particular storage depot.

He was sure of it. But it wasn't there. Apparently he took it as a lesson in humility.'

'What did Wiley take it as?'

'A lesson in something was labelled wrong.'

'How did he figure it out?'

'Something else Arnold told him. A different subject entirely. Arnold was there very early. Germany was still in ruins. People were starving. The army employed local civilians. Mostly women, because that's about all there were. Like a kind of welfare, and it saved drafting GIs to do shorthand and typing. He put it together with something else Arnold said. The local women would do anything for money. Anything for a candy bar or a pack of Luckies. Arnold made hay while the sun shone. One time a girl gave him her sister's address. She was game too. But he couldn't find the right house. The girl had written 11, and he thought it was 77. Because of her handwriting. Europeans put a long tick on the front of their ones. Like the opposite of a tail. A one looks like a seven. They put a little crossbar on the seven, to make it look different. Eventually Wiley wondered what would have happened if a German clerk made a handwritten note, and then an American clerk typed it up. Or the other way around. He figured mistakes could be made.'

'Was it that simple?'

'He figured surely the army would think of that. He figured they would make charts and tables and change ones for sevens and sevens for ones. But apparently Uncle Arnold's stories were crazy. There was extreme bureaucracy going on. Eventually Wiley wondered what would happen if a number went through three steps, not two. As in, suppose a German clerk made a handwritten note, and then an American clerk typed it up, and then another German clerk made a handwritten note off the typed-up page? Or the other way around. Starting with either ones or sevens. He made charts and tables of his own. He figured it was a step the army wouldn't take for itself. He figured the army would be blind to the faults of its own system. And he was right. The crate had been there all along. He found it on his third try.'

Reacher said nothing. Just nodded and walked away. The messenger caught his eye. She said, 'I can help.'

He said, 'I don't want your money.'

She said, 'Something else. The fat man is wrong. A van did cross the bridge. It was driving out as we drove in.'

FORTY-ONE

Neagley carried Wiley's bag to the trunk of Griezman's car, and she set it down on the lid, and she unzipped it. Reacher called Griezman over, and asked him to search it. Griezman said, 'Why me?'

Reacher said, 'I would appreciate your opinion.'

Griezman did the kind of job Reacher expected. Like a veteran taking a test. Practised, but suddenly cautious. As if he knew something must be wrong. A trap. Was he on trial about how fast he could find it? What was at stake? He didn't know.

In the end only three items were worthy of comment. First was Wiley's new passport, in the name of Isaac Herbert Kempner, because it was a thing of beauty. It was completely, utterly, entirely genuine. Second was the map they had seen in his kitchen, now neatly folded, because it was of limited cartographical utility, and therefore possibly sentimental, which might bring a clue as to his state of mind.

Third item was a Mercedes-Benz key.

Probably not for a sedan. A little too large. Too much plastic. Too everyday. It was the kind of key that one day would be grimy. The kind of key that came in a panel van.

Griezman agreed.

Reacher said, 'Can a brand new Mercedes-Benz start without a key?'

Griezman said, 'No.'

'Therefore the van was stolen with a duplicate.'

Griezman said, 'Yes.'

'Hard to get.'

'Yes.'

'Your department has been very impressive. Since the first moment. Your performance has been excellent. Would you agree?'

'Modesty forbids.'

'I mean it sincerely.'

'Again, I can't comment.'

'There was only one weak spot. The surveillance south of Hanover never happened.'

'That was the traffic division.'

'They put the car on the bridge for us.'

'What are you saying?'

'I'm saying a sequence of events can be explained in a large variety of different ways.'

'Give me one way, for example.'

'Everything is a really strange coincidence.'

'Give me another way.'

'The police department leaks through the traffic division.'

'Leaks to who?'

'Some kind of a mobbed-up community. But not Italian. Nostalgic Germans instead. With members and chapters and rules and all kinds of things. And goals and ambitions. That's what we heard.'

Griezman said nothing.

'I'm sorry,' Reacher said. 'We're withholding secrets and prying into yours.'

'Do you have an overall theory?'

'Only two possibilities. First is they stole the truck from one garage and hid it in another garage about three blocks away. Why? For what possible reason? Are they planning to sneak back at night and get it? Is it a double bluff? Is it a triple bluff? It all gets way too weird and complicated. I prefer the second possibility.'

'Which is?'

'The cop at the bridge was lying.'

'That's a big thing to say out loud.'

'They stole the truck and drove it away. The guy at the bridge turned a blind eye. These things happen. Get over it. It's what mobbed up means. It's a port. You need to make mental adjustments.'

Griezman didn't answer.

Reacher said, 'It would make sense of what the messenger just told me.'

'Hardly a reliable witness.'

'I agree.'

Griezman said, 'What is in the truck?'

'What would you most hate it to be?'

'One of a number of things.'

'It's worse than any of them. Believe me. Therefore we need to question everything. So we can figure out where to look.'

Griezman said, 'I suppose a corrupt traffic policeman is a theoretical possibility.'

'You know these people. You told me you were biding your time. You told me you can't arrest them for thought crimes. You told me you need actual crimes.'

Griezman was quiet a beat.

Then he said, 'I talked to their leader this morning. As a matter of fact he was the last man to see the forger alive. He wanted Wiley's new name. He had a copy of the sketch. His name is Dremmler. He imports shoes from Brazil. I had to go to his office. I couldn't ask him to come to mine. He said he has people in places that would surprise me. He said I was facing a powerful force, soon to get more powerful.'

'We need to go pay Herr Dremmler a visit.'

Griezman drove, to a mixed-use street about four blocks from the bar with the varnished wood front. Apparently neon was permitted in that part of town. Dremmler's place was a narrow four-storey building, part of the 1950s reconstruction, with a lit-up sign running side to side in the space between the top-floor windows and the rainwater gutter. It was written in red, in a complicated copperplate script, as if it was a famous brand. Like an old-style Coca-Cola sign in America. It said *Schuhe Dremmler*, which Reacher figured meant Dremmler's Shoes.

The elevator was slow. And the guy wasn't there. His secretary said he had taken a call and gone out. She had no idea where. She had no idea when he would return.

* * *

They drove back to the consulate. Griezman was invited in. The others were there before them. Wiley's corpse was en route to the morgue in the American military hospital at Landstuhl, in a meat wagon organized by Orozco. The messenger was locked in a basement room, waiting for a U.S. Marshal, and a handcuff, and an airplane to Dulles. The Iranian was sitting in a chair by the window. Orozco and his sergeant had brought him in. Smooth and easy. No collateral damage. Happily the Iranian himself had answered the door. After that it had been a straightforward abduction. The guy looked unsure. His old life was over. His new life was about to begin, in a place he had never seen. Orozco said no one was upset about it. He said Bishop claimed he was about to give the order anyway. The after-action report would be written up accordingly. But he said Bishop had thanked him afterwards, for saving time, at least White was happy. He cared about agents in the field. Vanderbilt was gloomier. He said now the CIA in Hamburg was blind.

Then Sinclair took the floor. She had spoken to Ratcliffe and the president. All kinds of back channels were open. NATO and the European Union were standing by. For a task as yet unspecified. Next step was to fill in the blanks. The U.S. would take a deep breath and admit it had lost track of a crate of nuclear weapons forty years ago. Germany would take a deep breath and admit it had neo-Nazi gangs strong enough to steal such a crate. Which was a step neither the U.S. nor Germany really wanted to take. Neither admission was felt likely to inspire widespread admiration. A final decision was to be taken soon.

'They want us to fix it for them,' Sinclair said. 'Before soon becomes now.'

'Did they say that in words?' Reacher asked.

'The hints were pretty heavy.'

'I would like to know for sure.'

'I guess some questions are better answered afterwards.'

'How long have we got?'

'They can't wait for ever.'

Outside the window it was going dark. Northern latitude, late afternoon.

Reacher asked, 'How big of a deal is Dremmler's Shoes?'

Griezman said, 'He boasts of a million pairs a week. Fifty million pairs a year. Probably bullshit, but even so, I'm sure it's a large number.'

'So the office we saw must be clerical only. Orders and invoices and that kind of thing. The heavy lifting must get done elsewhere.'

'At the docks,' Griezman said. 'He owns part of a wharf.'

'And he has people in places that would surprise you.'

Sinclair said, 'Is this a Hail Mary?'

'No, ma'am,' Reacher said. 'It's a wild-ass guess.'

'About the shoe guy?'

'At first as a theoretical example. Let's say he's the grand wizard of something or other. He's got members everywhere. Including the police department. As a result he's been with us every step of the way. He heard about the deal back at the beginning. Then he decided to hijack it. For the greater glory of whatever it is he's the grand wizard of. He piggybacked on our investigation. And it worked for him. He got the van. But it was a crazy scramble. He was always short of time. Always playing catch up. He couldn't plan ahead. No further than getting it out. Now he doesn't know what to do with it. He doesn't even know what's in it. That information never leaked. I think he stashed it somewhere close. Temporarily. He needs to take a deep breath. He needs to figure it out.'

'Plausible,' Sinclair said. 'But so are a hundred other possibilities.'

'Not a hundred,' Reacher said. 'Ten, maybe. But this one fits what we know. Dremmler asked the forger about Wiley's new name. That can't be a coincidence. And he owns a wharf. A million pairs of shoes a week. That's a lot of trucks. An extra one wouldn't be noticed.'

'We get only one shot at this.'

He remembered moving his other hand, the same way, barely touching her forehead, burying his fingers deep in her hair, pushing them through. That time he had left his hand where it ended up, which was cupped on the back of her neck. Which he remembered felt slender, and warm.

He had gambled then.

He said, 'Your call.'

'You don't have an opinion?'

'I'm going anyway. Just in case. Because if this is the guy, this is also the guy who got his ego in a wad when his junior varsity got beat. Ever since then he's been setting people on me. I left word he should come out and meet me himself. I told him we could walk around the block and have a discussion. Maybe it's time to make that happen.'

FORTY-TWO

They waited for full darkness to fall, and for rush-hour traffic to die away. And for all kinds of diplomatic discussions to be over. Bishop said he had to be there. He would drive White and Vanderbilt in his car. Sinclair said she would join them. Griezman felt he should observe, on behalf of the city. He was happy to invite Waterman and Landry to ride with him. They were FBI, after all. It would be an honour.

Reacher and Neagley would go with Orozco, in Orozco's car, driven by his sergeant, who was a guy named Hooper. He was taller than Neagley, but not a huge guy. He and Orozco had army Berettas. Reacher had a new mag in his Colt. He had been four rounds down.

Griezman led the convoy. He had local knowledge. He took the scenic route. The city got serious as the docks approached. It got fast and efficient and hard at work, lit up bright, and crawling with movement. There were acres of stacked containers, and miles of cranes, and queuing semis. There were huge metal sheds, one after another, some with names Reacher knew, and some he didn't. They moved on, and mile by mile they saw the same kind of things again and again.

Then they saw a huge metal shed, fat and bulbous in a modern way, with a blazing red old-style neon sign on its roof, on an old-style iron frame, way up high, written in a copperplate script, like an old-time Coca-Cola sign. It said *Schuhe Dremmler*, which meant Dremmler's Shoes.

Griezman dropped his speed and they drove past going slow. The place was lit up like a stadium. On the other side of the shed was the wharf. Presumably shoes came off the ships, into the shed from the far side, into some kind of a routing or packing or inventory system, and then out of the shed again on the road-side, where the trucks were loaded for onward delivery. A million pairs a week. Which clearly required an evening shift. But maybe not a full contingent. The place looked to be working about half capacity. Maybe a little more.

Orozco said, 'You sure it's in there?'

Reacher said, 'What part of wild-ass guess didn't you get?'

'Are we going to wait for later?'

'They might work all night.'

'There could be fifty people there.'

'With jobs to do. We could be a hundred yards away. They won't pay attention. The truck might have a guard detail. But there are four of us. It's a done deal.'

'If it's there.'

They stopped the cars two units further on, and got out in the damp night-time air.

Sinclair said, 'Are the missing items recognizable for what they are?'

'I never saw one,' Reacher said. 'But from what Helmsworth told us, they're fifty-pound metal cylinders in canvas backpacks. They could be anything.'

'Do they have writing on them?'

'I'm sure they have codes for serial number and date of manufacture. But not like the back of a car. It won't say what it is.'

'Which is why they're not panicking yet.'

'Unless they found the code book. That might give them a clue.'

'It's in code.'

'Like the man said. Think about D-Day. I'm sure it's easy to follow along.'

'It's a warehouse full of shoes. I think you guessed wrong. It's surreal.'

'So is strapping an atom bomb to a bridge support and running like hell.'

'That was then.'

'They don't know what they've got. They were hoping for machine guns. Maybe grenades. They're scratching their heads in there.'

'It's one possibility. But we only get one chance at this.'

'Then let's hope it's the right possibility.'

'But is it?'

'Let's ask Griezman's opinion,' Reacher said.

Griezman shrugged. In his opinion Dremmler was a bold and ambitious shit-stirrer and rabble-rouser. The man was a lover of history, and of movements and causes, and of the power accrued by great men who strike when the time is right. Griezman thought one day he might be very dangerous. But so far he was all talk and no action. Thus inexperienced. Thus likely to be overwhelmed by his first major project. No one ever plans for afterwards. Thus it was plausible he would pause for breath. In a place of safety. Therefore it was plausible he would choose his own premises. In fact more than plausible. A virtual certainty. He would be in control there. Human nature.

'If it's him,' Sinclair said.

Reacher said, 'There's only one way to know for sure.'

There was no point in attempted concealment. The dock road was brightly lit. The truck loading areas were brightly lit. The metal sheds were brightly lit. Beyond them the wharf was brightly lit. The only darkness was the water. They turned around in the road and drove back to Dremmler's Shoes. First Griezman and then Bishop slowed and stopped at the kerb. Orozco's guy Hooper leapfrogged them and drove straight ahead. Level with the red neon sign. To the main gate.

He turned in.

Up close the shed was enormous. Some kind of glittery galvanized metal. No slits or windows or portholes. The roof was bigger than the walls. Swelled up and bulbous, like a loaf of country bread. Like a bouffant hairstyle. It was ribbed and stressed and physically complex. Below it the walls looked short. The wall facing the road had about fifty vehicle entrances. Roll-up doors, like suburban garages, but bigger, in primary colours, with plastic porthole windows. Light blazed out. Maybe thirty doors were open, in an orderly line from the left, reaching beyond halfway. The first twenty or so were busy. Trucks were driving in and out. Then ten doors were open but apparently idle. On the right the last twenty were closed up tight. The evening shift. Maybe rush orders only.

They drove closer.

Inside the shed was as big as a football stadium. There were rushing conveyors, and piles of boxes rising to immense heights, and bustling forklift trucks. And noise, apparently. The guys inside were wearing big yellow ear defenders.

Which might help.

Reacher said, 'They were paratrooper weapons. Immediate ground combat was anticipated. Therefore stray rounds passing through the backpacks must have been predicted. So they probably don't explode from that. Almost certainly not. But if possible I would prefer not to test that theory.'

'If it's in there,' Orozco said.

'Let's go find out.'

Hooper drove in through the last of the open but idle doors, and turned right, away from the busy end of the warehouse, towards the quiet end, in a vehicle channel marked out with tape. He drove behind the line of closed doors, and braked, and stopped, and Neagley got out. He drove on, and braked again, and Orozco got out. He drove on, and braked for a third time, and Reacher got out.

Reacher stood and watched Hooper drive away. First thing that hit him was the noise. The conveyors were howling and squealing and rattling. The forklifts were chugging and beeping. The second thing was the smell. A million pairs of new shoes. Like a childhood memory. Like a shoe store on Main Street, but a thousand times stronger.

Behind him none of the trucks was a panel van. Ahead of him nothing was moving. Nothing was parked. No vehicles were visible. He could see all the way out to the wharf. A long distance, but a clear view. The lights were bright. Nothing there.

But there were mountains of boxes. Many different places. The smallest was taller than Kansas. The biggest was immense. Jagged, like the Rockies from a distance. A left to right panorama. Near the end wall. But not on the end wall. There was space behind it. Not much, visually, against the hugeness all around. But up close and human it might be a useful slice. Maybe as wide as a vehicle.

Reacher looked back. There were maybe fifty guys working. They were suited up like football players, in high-visibility overalls, and hard hats and ear defenders, with plastic cups over their knees and elbows, like the airport workers. Most were putting their time in. A couple were standing and staring. Unsure. Reacher waved. They waved back, and turned away. An old lesson. *Act like you belong there.* Like you just bought half the company. Meet the new boss.

Reacher turned back. Fifty yards ahead Hooper had pulled over. He was waiting. Orozco arrived at Reacher's elbow. Then Neagley. They had to talk loud, because of the noise. Orozco said, 'Either it's hidden behind the boxes or it ain't here at all.'

'No shit, Sherlock.'

'Argument against would be that's a lot of boxes to stack on a moment's notice.'

'I think they're permanent,' Neagley said. 'I think the office must be back there. I don't see it anyplace else. They walled themselves off. Peace, quiet, and parking spaces.'

They walked closer. The smell was intense. Like walking through a department store. The mountain range of boxes was set end-on to the last but one roll-up door, blocking it completely. Which meant the very last roll-up door was the office staff's private driveway. Just like the army.

They detoured to door number forty-seven, to see how it worked. The good news was it had manual override. An up button and a down button. Both plastic, both brightly coloured, both the size of a saucer. Like someone's first magic mushrooms. The bad news was they were on a panel on the left of the door. The far side of the lane. The rear corner of the commandeered space.

Orozco said, 'It could be parked facing out. Like a fire engine. It could be out of here in a second. If it moves, shoot the tyres.'

Reacher said, 'If it moves, shoot the driver. The Davy Crocketts are about two feet tall. Head shots should be safe enough.'

'If it's there.'

Reacher remembered Sinclair's hand on his chest. A stop sign. But no. An assessment, and then a conclusion. Not remotely trust, or even confidence, or much interest, but a solid gamble. He was worth taking a chance on.

'Yes,' he said. 'If it's there.'

FORTY-THREE

It was there. Reacher peered around the last corner of the mountain range, one eye only, and he saw the panel van, no longer white, now daubed with imitation graffiti, with balloon-like letters, W and H, and S and L. It was facing out. Its rear door was up. Inside were stout canvas packs, covered with straps, padded and round, in camouflage colours that were still dark and strong. They had never seen the light of day.

To the left of the truck was a wall of windows, into a large but empty office room. To the right was the back face of the mountain range. Maybe three feet of space either side of the truck. Not cramped at all. Up close the area felt generous.

There were no people in sight. No guards.

Reacher pulled back and checked the other way. Another two workers were standing and staring. He stepped back to where Orozco and Neagley were waiting. Hooper was there. He told them the news. They took a look for themselves, one at a time, one eye only. Orozco stepped back and said, 'The office suite must be two rooms deep. They must be in the rear section.'

Reacher said, 'Or they went out to get pizza and a pitcher of beer. Why stand guard over a bunch of tin cans? They don't know what they've got.'

'First priority is the panel van. Not the personnel.'

'Agreed,' Reacher said.

'So let's go steal it back. Right now. We have a key. Like boosting it off the kerb while the owner is inside watching the ball game.'

Reacher nodded. One time he had rotated through an army fight school, where the toughest instructor liked to say the best fights are the fights you don't have. No risk of defeat, no risk of injury. However slight or unlikely. Plus in this case a political dimension. If the van just disappeared, who could say it ever existed? Deniability was always useful. It would fit the narrative. What crate?

Clearly the noisiest element would be raising the warehouse door. It was driven by an electric motor, through chains. Long and slow. It would need to open all the way. It was a high-roof van. Thirty seconds, probably. Grinding, rattling, shuffling upward. A very characteristic sound. Like putting a notice in the newspaper. They would come running at once.

Better to back it out. The other way. Reverse it carefully, deep towards the centre of the shed, as far as possible, and then swing it around and escape through the body of the warehouse. Through the nearest of the open doors. The same way Hooper drove in.

Now seventy yards away four workers were standing and staring.

Reacher said, 'OK, let's do it. Who wants to drive?'

Neagley said, 'I will.'

'If they hear the engine they'll approach on your side. So you'll need cover. But not from the passenger seat. You could get shot in the face. I'll walk on the blind side. When you stop reversing I'll jump in and you can take off forward. Then Hooper and Orozco can tuck in behind.'

'I plan on reversing faster than you can walk. They're paratrooper weapons. They can stand a little slamming around. Sit in the passenger seat. Just don't do the part where you shoot me in the face. It's not complicated.'

Reacher glanced the other way. Still four workers watching.

'Brisk,' he said. 'Not crazy. Make it look like regular business. It drove in, and now it's driving out again.'

He peered around the corner, one last time. Both eyes. The windows, blank. The truck, waiting. Nothing else. No people.

Now there were six workers watching. They had moved up a step, into a loose arrowhead. The nearest guy was sixty yards away. Isolated by distance and noise, but staring.

Reacher gave Neagley the key.

He said, 'Go for it.'

Orozco and Hooper drifted back towards their blue Opel. They got in and moved it to where they could see into the hidden bay, obliquely, for mission support, but where they wouldn't impede Neagley's rearward progress. They left space for her to back up alongside them. Then she would pull forward on full lock, and turn tight in front of them, and drive away. They would fall in close behind, on the same curve.

Neagley checked the view, and took a breath, and stepped into the hidden bay. Reacher followed. She walked down the blind side of the van to the passenger door. He paused near the tailgate. He watched the office windows. She tried the passenger door. It was unlocked. She opened it wide and climbed across to the driver's seat. He stretched up tall and caught the strap and inched the rear door down. *They're paratrooper weapons. They can stand a little slamming around.* Maybe so. But he didn't want them spilling out during a violent manoeuvre. He didn't want them rolling and bouncing across a Hamburg street corner.

He tugged on the strap and the door came down quiet and slow and easy, whirring and spooling on nylon bearings. A foot. A foot and a half. Two feet.

He stopped.

Shit.

He caught Neagley's eye in the mirror and chopped his hand across his throat.

Abort.

Now.

She climbed out over the passenger seat. Out the passenger door. Along the painted flank. She followed him back to safety.

Orozco and Hooper came back from their car.

In the other direction a dozen workers were watching. A whole regular crowd. Still a shambling arrowhead. Fifty yards away. Shuffling closer.

Neagley said, 'What happened?'

444

'Should be ten bombs in the truck,' Reacher said. 'But I only counted nine.'

Hooper and Reacher had never met before, so Reacher was sure Hooper wouldn't say it. Or Orozco. Too much old-world courtesy. It would be Neagley who said it. She would assemble a dozen alternative theories, starting with ships sailing back to Brazil, or with trucks rolling on to Berlin. And then ending, either with successful resolutions, or with blast zones and fireballs and a million dead. All depending on one critical question.

Which she would ask.

She said, 'Are you sure you counted right?'

He smiled.

'Let's use the two-personnel rule,' he said. 'Basic nuclear safeguard. Hooper should go. He hardly knows me. He's still an unbiased observer.'

So Hooper went. He checked from the corner, one eye, very carefully, and then he stepped into the hidden bay. Reacher replaced him at the corner, one eye, and saw him at the tailgate. He was too short. The height of the load floor plus a couple of feet to the top of the backpacks meant he was looking up at the front rank only.

Then Reacher saw a man in the corner of the office room. On the right. In the far back. On an exact diagonal from where Reacher was. Which meant the guy couldn't see Hooper. Not yet. The angle was wrong. The corner of the truck was in the way.

The guy in the room moved. He was looking for something. He was going from desk to desk, opening drawers, stirring a thick finger through, moving on. He was a big guy. He looked competent.

Hooper stepped back and went up on tiptoe.

The guy moved on, the length of a desk.

Now the angle was right.

The noise was loud. Howling, squealing, rattling. Chugging and beeping.

Reacher called, 'Hooper, get in the van.'

Loud enough to be heard, he hoped, by one and not the other. Hooper froze for a split second, and then he vaulted up on open palms and scrambled over the backpacks into the shadows.

The guy in the office looked out the window.

He took a step closer.

He checked the van. He checked the space behind the van.

He watched for a moment.

Then he turned and walked away, to the far back corner again, and through a door, to the hidden part of the suite.

Reacher waited.

The guy didn't come back. Not in one minute. Not in two. Which he would, if he had heard. Human nature. He would have grabbed his guns and his buddies and come back right away.

He hadn't heard.

Reacher called, 'All clear, Hooper.'

No response.

Howling, squealing, rattling.

Reacher called again, louder this time, 'Hooper, all clear.'

Hooper stuck his head out the back of the truck. Then he jumped down, and bounced up, and walked back to safety.

'Nine bombs,' he said. 'The code book is missing too.'

FORTY-FOUR

In the other direction the crowd had grown to about twenty strong, and they were forty yards away. Still tiny, in the industrial vastness. Not threatening. Reacher felt the opposite was true. They were standing up in puzzled solidarity against what they saw as a threat against their bosses in the office. They were ready to close ranks against the intruders. They were loyal employees. Or more. Maybe some of them were low-level members of the cause. Maybe that's how a guy got a foreman's position, at *Schuhe Dremmler*.

Reacher said to Hooper, 'How good is your German?'

'Pretty good,' Hooper said. 'That's why I work here.'

'Go tell them to calm down and get back to work.'

'Any particular form of words you want me to use?'

'Tell them we're American military police here on behalf of the Brazilian military police, conducting a routine audit connected to shoes, and if we're forced to report a hostile reception they'll get extra scrutiny.'

'Will they believe me?'

'Depends how convincing you are.'

They watched him, forty yards away, face to face with

448

the guy at the tip of the arrowhead. He was talking in long composed sentences. The crowd wasn't buying what he was selling.

Orozco said, 'Stand by to rescue him.'

Reacher said, 'Don't kick them in the knees.'

'Why not?'

'They're wearing knee pads.'

Hooper kept on talking. And talking. Forward motion ebbed away. The crowd went still. But not convinced. Hooper took the long walk back. He said, 'I did my best.'

'Are they going to call the cops?' Reacher said.

'Not their place. They're confused, is all. And concerned. It's a family business.'

'Then we better be quick.'

'Where do we start?'

'With data. Which means the office. And the guy in it.'

'Rules of engagement?'

'We'll figure them out afterwards.'

They did no more one-eye checking. Too much scrutiny. Didn't look right. Instead they walked around the pile of boxes, brisk and routine, into the hidden bay, as if all they needed was a signature on their paperwork, or an answer to a supplementary question, or a copy of a document. They pulled their guns as soon as they were out of sight. The entrance to the office suite was a door in the far back corner of the space, beyond the van, near the manual panel for the roll-up exit. The door led to the first room, which had a matching door in the far back corner, which led onward, to wherever the guy had gone. To the rear part of the suite, presumably. Unknown territory.

Opening the door let in a pulse of factory noise, so they got through fast, and fanned out, ready. Hooper walked backwards. He was tasked to be eyes-on-rearward at all times. Essential for confidence. Nothing worse than not knowing what was behind. The crowd could get restless again. Reinforcements could show up. The night shift, reporting early. Or expert opinion. German army veterans, maybe, called in especially, and asked a simple question: What the hell are these?

They didn't know what they'd got.

They moved on, towards the next door. It was narrow. A bottleneck. What stun grenades were invented for. But they had none. The door was open a crack. Reacher peered through. Saw nothing. A slice of empty room. He put his ear to the opening. He heard talking in German. Male voices. Questions and answers. Frustrated, but not angry. Puzzled, but patient. They were trying to figure something out. Three guys talking, Reacher thought. Were there others saying nothing? The sound was off to the left, and it had a boxed-in, glassy tone. As if they were in a walled-off executive office in the left-hand corner. Which he couldn't see.

He backed off a step. Glanced out the window. No one was coming after them. Not yet. He made hand signals, minimum three people, located far left, in the corner. They paced it out, back to back on their side of the dividing wall. It was an awkward distance. Two steps too long for total surprise. Hooper would guard the door, facing out, and first Neagley and then Reacher and Orozco would go deep, fanning out, splitting the target, giving three different lines of sight. Any monkey business, waste all but one.

They took up station in operational order, first Neagley, then Reacher, then Orozco, then Hooper facing backward. Neagley burst through the door and headed for third. Reacher took second. Orozco stopped at first. Where home plate should have been was a glassed-in cubicle. Set up like an office within an office. Flanking the desk were two guys. One was the man Reacher had seen before. A big guy, and competent. The other was similar.

Propped in a chair in front of the desk was the tenth Davy Crockett. Like a human visitor. Like a suspect in a police station. Its canvas pack was unlaced and pulled down. The cylinder was dull green. It had white stencil writing. It had a screwed-on panel up top, with six small chicken-head knobs, and three small toggle switches.

Behind the desk in a chair was a guy Reacher took to be Dremmler. He looked like the boss of something. He looked like a leader. He was about forty-five years old. An imposing individual. His hair was blond, going grey, and his face was red, going grey. He was wearing a suit, with a high lapel. An old German style. His elbows were on the desk. His fingers were steepled. He was studying the secret file. Or he had been. Now he was staring at Reacher. Or his Colt Government Model. Which was aimed at his face.

Reacher said, '*Hände hoch.*'

Like an old black-and-white movie.

Hands up.

Dremmler did nothing. The men either side went for the biding-his-time tough guy version, their hands coming up halfway, fingers straight, tense and speculative. A cease fire, but not a surrender.

Reacher stepped closer.

He said, 'Do you speak English?'

Dremmler said, 'Yes.'

'You're under arrest.'

'On what authority?'

'The U.S. Army.'

Dremmler glanced down, at the crumpled camouflage canvas.

Reacher said, 'Did you mess with that thing?'

'Not yet,' Dremmler said. 'We don't know what it is.'

'It's nothing of interest.'

'We clicked the knobs a little. To see what they were, really.'

'And the switches?'

'On and off, a couple of times.'

'And now you're studying the file. Trying to puzzle it out.'

'What is it exactly?'

Reacher said, 'Step out of the room one by one.'

The first guy came out. The man Reacher had seen. He walked on his toes, tense and ready, biding his time. Then the second guy came out, just the same.

Reacher said to Dremmler, 'You stay there.'

Dremmler stayed at his desk, his fingers still steepled.

Reacher said to the two guys, 'You are in the custody

of the United States Army. I am obliged by law to tell you if you mess with us we will hurt you very badly.'

The two men didn't move.

Reacher said to Orozco, 'You and Hooper take these guys out to Griezman. Send Neagley out to guard the truck. New departure time is fifteen minutes from now.'

'Why?'

'He messed with the switches.'

'It has to need more than that.'

'I sure hope so. But I would like to check. Herr Dremmler can help me. He has the file, after all.'

FORTY-FIVE

Dremmler stayed at his desk and Reacher sat in an empty chair next to the Davy Crockett. Like a host and two guests. A three-way conversation. Three points of view. But nothing was said. Not for the first many minutes. Reacher took the file off the desk and tried to make sense of it. A six-digit code was entered by turning the chicken-head knobs. Officially one guy did three digits, and clicked his arming switch, and then the second guy did three more, and clicked his arming switch. The centre switch stayed off. What was it for? The file didn't say.

Ten six-digit codes were listed. They were indexed against ten serial numbers. Ready for an armourer's stick of chalk.

Dremmler said, 'What is that thing?'

Reacher said, 'What were you hoping for?'

'I don't know what you mean.'

'To help your cause make a statement.'

'You should leave now,' Dremmler said. 'This discussion is over.'

Reacher said, 'Is it?'

'You have no authority here. This is a simple mis-understanding. I don't even know what that thing is.'

'It's a bomb. You stole it. After asking about Horace Wiley's new name.'

'Griezman would find it very difficult to make legal progress against me.'

'Because you have people in places that might surprise him?'

'Hundreds and hundreds of people.'

'Are you their leader?'

'I have that honour.'

'Where are you leading them?'

'They want their country back. I will make sure they get it. And more. I'll make sure they get the country they deserve. Strong again. With purity of purpose. All pulling together in the same direction. No more dead wood. No more outside interference. Nothing of that kind will be tolerated. Germany will be for Germans.'

Reacher was quiet a long moment.

Then he said, 'How much do you know about the history of your country?'

'The truth or the lies?'

'The terror and the misery and the eighty million dead. We learned that stuff in class. Then at night we'd be shooting the shit, and someone would talk about a time machine, which meant you could go back and take the guy out. Before he even got started. Would you do it?'

'What was your opinion?'

'I was all for it. But it was a dumb question. There are no time machines. And hindsight is always twenty-twenty vision. I figured the real challenge was to ask the question backward. Starting in the here and now. Looking ahead. With foresight. Which is the opposite of a time machine. Is there a guy you could take out today, so no one would need to dream about time machines tomorrow? If so, would you do it? Suppose you were wrong. But suppose you were right. Eighty million lives for one.'

The clock in his head told him fifteen minutes had passed. The bomb was fine. Random twisting and click-ing meant nothing. Which made sense. A bad parachute landing could have been worse.

He said, 'It was a hardcore moral question. Some said no, because the guy has broken no laws. Not yet. But that was true of all of them once. If you would come back in a time machine to do it, why wouldn't you do it now? Some worried about degrees of certainty. What if you're only ninety per cent sure? Some said better safe than sorry. Which logically meant anything better than fifty per cent. But not really. Anything over one per cent might be worth it. A one-in-a-hundred chance of saving eighty million people from terror and misery? Do you have a view, Herr Dremmler?'

Dremmler said nothing.

Reacher said, 'We were undergraduates. West Point is a college. It's the kind of thing we talked about then. Were we serious? Didn't matter. There was no way to prove we would do what we said. Or not. But life's a bitch. Now I get to answer the question for real. Was I bullshitting all those years ago?'

He shot Dremmler in the heart, and when he settled he shot him again, in the head, from the same range, to be sure and certain. Then he put his gun in his pocket, and stuffed the file in the camouflaged backpack, and hoisted the Davy Crockett up on his shoulder, and walked out to the van. He stepped one way and hit the green magic mushroom, to open the door, and then the other, to dump the backpack down with its nine other siblings. He pulled the door on them and locked the lever tight.

He got in the passenger seat.

Neagley said, 'You OK?'

'Never better.'

'You sure?'

'What are you, my mother?'

The door came all the way up.

Reacher said, 'Drive.'

The NSC ran an emergency protocol whereby the participants were immediately dispersed, to reduce the risk of visual identification, and consequently the risk of subpoenas. Within sixteen hours Reacher was in Japan. He heard a nuclear recovery company had been sent out to unload the van. They had an old-style vehicle, from back in the days when nuclear-tipped missiles would fall off planes and land in fields. Later he heard White and Vanderbilt had flown direct to Zurich with the messenger. They had drained one account and filled another. The CIA was up six hundred million. The Iranian was given a condo in Century City. Within a week he had a job in the movies. The Saudis were called home to Yemen. After that, there was no further trace of them. Wiley was buried in a potter's field, on the

457

shoulder of a German highway, with no stone or marker.

Reacher saw Sinclair one last time, about two months later, when he was called to Washington. To get a medal. She sent a note and asked him to dinner. The night before the ceremony. At her place. A suburban house in Alexandria. He wore his Marine Corps pants, and his black T-shirt from Hamburg, both washed and folded by a Japanese laundry. No jacket, because it was warm. His hair was cut and he had showered and shaved. She was in a black dress. With diamonds, not pearls. They ate at a table as long as a boat. Candles flickered. The diamonds sparkled. She told him some of the news was good. The bad guys were hurting. Their financial setback was significant. Six hundred million was a good chunk of change. Hamburg was off the table for air transportation. Because the two guys had been key. The messenger had been helpful. She had mapped out some structure. They had filled in some blanks. Some of the news was not so good. Wiley had made no will, and so far he still owned the ranch in Argentina. They couldn't unwind it. There was still a lot they didn't know. They were still running around with their hair on fire.

After dinner they made a half-hearted attempt to clear the dishes, but they ended up stalled close together in the kitchen doorway. He could smell her perfume. He was nervous again.

She said, 'Do it like you did before.'

He raised his hand and brushed her forehead, with his fingertips, and he slid his fingers into her hair. He swept it back and left part behind her ear, and part hanging free.

It looked good.

He took his hand away.

She said, 'Now do the other side.'

He used his other hand, the same way, barely touching her forehead, burying his fingers deep. He left his hand where it ended up, on the back of her neck. Which was slender. And warm. She put her own hand flat on his chest. She slid it up behind his neck. She pulled down and he pulled up. They kissed, suddenly at home again. He found the tiny metal teardrop on the back of her dress. He eased it down, between her shoulder blades, past the small of her back.

She said, 'Let's go upstairs.'

They went to her bedroom, where she climbed on top. She rode him like a cowgirl, but facing him again, hips forward, shoulders back, head up, eyes closed. The diamonds swung and bounced. Her arms were behind her, like the first time, held out away from her body, her wrists bent, her hands open, her palms close to the bed, hovering, skimming an invisible cushion of air, as if she was balancing. Which she was. Like before. She was balancing on a single point, driving all her weight down through it, rocking back and forth, easing side to side, chasing sensation, and finding it, and losing it, and finding it again, all the way to the breathless end.

The next morning he got to Belvoir early. The same inside room. The same gilt furniture and the same bunch of flags. The Chief of Staff presiding. Which was nice.

There were five awards to be made. The first four were Army Commendation Medals, for Hooper, and Neagley, and Orozco, and Reacher. Not as handsome as the Legion of Merit. But not the worst thing he had ever seen. It was a bronze hexagon, with a sculpted eagle. The ribbon was fresh myrtle green with white pinstripes and white edges. A Bronze Star equivalent, except not in a war.

Take the bauble and keep your mouth shut.

The fifth award was a Silver Star to Major General Wilson T. Helmsworth.

Afterwards there was milling around, and small talk, and shaking of hands. Reacher moved towards the door. No one stopped him. He stepped out to the corridor. No sergeant met him. The rest of the day was his.

**Exclusive extract
from the new
Jack Reacher thriller**

THE
MIDNIGHT
LINE

Coming in November 2017

ONE

Jack Reacher and Michelle Chang spent three days in Milwaukee. On the fourth morning she was gone. Reacher came back to the room with coffee and found a note on his pillow. He had seen such notes before. They all said the same thing. Either directly or indirectly. Chang's note was indirect. And more elegant than most. Not in terms of presentation. It was a ballpoint scrawl on motel notepaper gone wavy with damp. But elegant in terms of expression. She had used a simile, to explain and flatter and apologize all at once. She had written, *You're like New York City. I love to visit, but I could never live there.*

He did what he always did. He let her go. He understood. No apology required. He couldn't live anywhere. His whole life was a visit. Who could put up with that? He drank his coffee, and then hers, and took his toothbrush from the bathroom glass, and walked away, through a knot of streets, left and right, towards the bus depot. She would be in a taxi, he guessed. To the airport. She had a gold card and a cell phone.

At the depot he did what he always did. He bought a ticket for the first bus out, no matter where it was going. Which turned out to be an end-of-the-line place way north and west, on the shore of Lake Superior. Fundamentally the wrong direction. Colder, not warmer. But rules were

462

rules, so he climbed aboard. He sat and watched out the window. Wisconsin flashed by, its hayfields baled and stubbly, its pastures worn, its trees dark and heavy. It was the end of summer.

It was the end of several things. She had asked the usual questions. Which were really statements in disguise. She could understand a year. Absolutely. A kid who grew up on bases overseas, and was then deployed to bases overseas, with nothing in between except four years at West Point, which wasn't exactly known as a leisure-heavy institution, then obviously such a guy was going to take a year to travel and see the sights before he settled down. Maybe two years. But not more. And not permanently. Face it. The pathology meter was twitching.

All said with concern, and no judgement. No big deal. Just a two-minute conversation. But the message was clear. As clear as such messages could be. Something about denial. He asked, denial of what? He didn't secretly think his life was a problem.

That proves it, she said.

So he got on the bus to the end-of-the-line place, and he would have ridden it all the way, because rules were rules, except he took a stroll at the second comfort stop, and he saw a ring in a pawn shop window.

The second comfort stop came late in the day, and it was on the sad side of a small town. Possibly a seat of county government. Or some minor part of it. Maybe the county police department was headquartered there. There was a jail in town. That was clear. Reacher could see bail bond offices, and a pawn shop. Full service, right there, side by side on a run-down street beyond the restroom block.

He was stiff from sitting. He scanned the street beyond the restroom block. He started walking towards it. No real reason. Just strolling. Just loosening up. As he got closer he counted the guitars in the pawn shop window. Seven. Sad stories, all of them. Like the songs on country radio. Dreams, unfulfilled. Lower down in the window were glass shelves loaded with smaller stuff. All kinds of jewellery. Including rings. Including class rings. All kinds of high schools. Except one of them wasn't. One of them was West Point 2005.

It was a handsome ring. It was a conventional shape, and a conventional style, with intricate gold filigree, and a black stone, maybe semi-precious, maybe glass, surrounded by an oval hoop that had *West Point* around the top, and *2005* around the bottom. Old-style letters. A classic approach. Either respect for bygone days, or a lack of imagination. West Pointers designed their own rings. Whatever they wanted. An old tradition. Or an old entitlement, because West Point class rings were the first class rings of all.

It was a very small ring.

Reacher wouldn't have gotten it on any of his fingers. Not even his left-hand pinky, not even past the nail. Certainly not past the first knuckle. It was tiny. It was a woman's ring. Possibly a replica for a girlfriend or a fiancée. That happened. Like a tribute or a souvenir.

But possibly not.

Reacher opened the pawn shop door. He stepped inside. A guy at the register glanced up. He was a big bear of a man, scruffy and unkempt. Maybe in his middle thirties, dark, with plenty of fat over a big frame anyway. With some kind of cunning in his eyes. Enough to calibrate a response to his sudden six-five two-fifty visitor. Driven purely by instinct. He wasn't afraid. He had a loaded gun under the counter. Unless he was an idiot. Which he didn't look. All the same, the guy didn't want to risk sounding aggressive. But he didn't want to sound obsequious, either. A matter of pride.

So he said, 'How's it going?'

Not well, Reacher thought. *To be honest*. Chang would be back in Seattle by then. Back in her life.

But he said, 'Can't complain.'

'Can I help you?'

'Show me your class rings.'

The guy threaded the tray backward off the shelf. He put it on the counter. The West Point ring had rolled over, like a tiny golf ball. Reacher picked it up. It was engraved inside. Which meant it wasn't a replica. Not for a fiancée or a girlfriend. Replicas were never engraved. An old tradition. No one knew why.

Not a tribute, not a souvenir. It was the real deal. A cadet's own ring, earned over four hard years. Worn with pride. Obviously. If you weren't proud of the place, you didn't buy a ring. It wasn't compulsory.

The engraving said *S.R.S. 2005*.

The bus blew its horn three times. It was ready to go, but it was a passenger short. Reacher put the ring down and said, 'Thank you,' and walked out of the store. He hustled back past the restroom block and leaned in the door of the bus and said to the driver, 'I'm staying here.'

'No refunds.'

'Not looking for one.'

'You got a bag in the hold?'

'No bag.'

'Have a nice day.'

The guy pulled a lever and the door sucked shut in Reacher's face. The engine roared and the bus moved off without him. He turned away from the diesel smoke and walked back towards the pawn shop.

TWO

The guy in the pawn shop was a little disgruntled to have to get the ring tray out again so soon after he had put it away. But he did, and he placed it in the same spot on the counter. The West Point ring had rolled over again. Reacher picked it up.

He said, 'Do you remember the woman who pawned this?'

'How would I?' the guy said. 'I got a million things in here.'

'You got records?'

'You a cop?'

'No,' Reacher said.

'Everything in here is legal.'

'I don't care. All I want is the name of the woman who brought you this ring.'

'Why?'

'We went to the same school.'

'Where is that? Upstate?'

'East of here,' Reacher said.

'You can't be a classmate. Not from 2005. No offence.'

'None taken. I was from an earlier generation. But the place doesn't change much. Which means I know how hard she worked for this ring. So now I'm wondering what kind of unlucky circumstance made her give it up.'

The guy said, 'What kind of a school was it?'

'They teach you practical things.'

'Like a trade school?'

'More or less.'

'Maybe she died in an accident.'

'Maybe she did,' Reacher said. Or not in an accident, he thought. There had been Iraq, and there had been Afghanistan. 2005 had been a tough year to graduate. He said, 'But I would like to know for sure.'

'Why?' the guy said again.

'I can't tell you exactly.'

'Is it an honour thing?'

'I guess it could be.'

'Trade schools have that?'

'Some of them.'

'There was no woman. I bought that ring. With a lot of other stuff.'

'When?'

'About a month ago.'

'From who?'

'I'm not going to tell you my business. Why should I? It's all legal. It's all perfectly legitimate. The state says so. I have a licence and I pass all kinds of inspections.'

'Then why be shy about it?'

'It's private information.'

Reacher said, 'Suppose I buy the ring?'

'It's fifty bucks.'

'Thirty.'

'Forty.'

'Deal,' Reacher said. 'So now I'm entitled to know its provenance.'

'This ain't Sotheby's auction house.'

'Even so.'

The guy paused a beat.

467

Then he said, 'It was from a guy who helps out with a charity. People donate things and take the deduction. Mostly old cars and boats. But other things too. The guy gives them an inflated receipt for their tax returns, and then he sells the things he gets wherever he can, for whatever he can, and then he cuts a cheque to the charity. I buy the small stuff from him. I get what I get, and I hope to turn a profit.'

'So you think someone donated this ring to a charity and took a deduction on their income tax?'

'Makes sense, if the original person died. From 2005. Part of the estate.'

'I don't think so,' Reacher said. 'I think a relative would have kept it.'

'Depends if the relative was eating well.'

'You got tough times here?'

'I'm OK. But I own the pawn shop.'

'Yet people still donate to good causes.'

'In exchange for phony receipts. In the end the government eats the tax relief. Welfare by another name.'

Reacher said, 'Who is the charity guy?'

'I won't tell you that.'

'Why not?'

'It's none of your business. I mean, who the hell are you?'

'Just a guy already having a pretty bad day. Not your fault, of course, but if asked to offer advice I would have to say it might prove a dumb idea to make my day worse. You might be the straw that breaks the camel's back.'

'You threatening me now?'

'More like the weather report. A public service. Like a tornado warning. Prepare to take cover.'

'Get out of my store.'

'Fortunately I no longer have a headache. I got hit in the

head, but that's all better now. A doctor said so. A friend made me go. Two times. She was worried about me.'

The pawn shop guy paused another beat.

Then he said, 'Exactly what kind of a school was that ring from?'

Reacher said, 'It was a military academy.'

'Those are for, excuse me, problem kids. Or disturbed. No offence.'

'Don't blame the kids,' Reacher said. 'Look at the families. Tell the truth, at our school there were a lot of parents who had killed people.'

'Really?'

'More than the average.'

'So you stick together for ever?'

'We don't leave anyone behind.'

'The guy won't talk to a stranger.'

'Does he have a licence and does he pass inspections by the state?'

'What I'm doing here is legal. My lawyer says so. As long as I honestly believe it. And I do. It's from a charity. I've seen the paperwork. All kinds of people do it. They even have commercials on TV. Cars, mostly. Sometimes boats.'

'But this particular guy won't talk to me?'

'I would be surprised.'

'Does he have no manners?'

'I wouldn't ask him over to a picnic.'

'What's his name?'

'Jimmy Rat.'

'For real?'

'That's what he goes by.'

'Where would I find Mr Rat?'

'Look for a minimum six Harley-Davidsons. Jimmy will be in whatever bar they're outside of.'

THREE

The town was relatively small. Beyond the sad side was a side maybe five years from going sad. Maybe more. Maybe ten. There was hope. There were some boarded-up enterprises, but not many. Most stores were still doing business, at a leisurely rural pace. Big pick-up trucks rolled through, slowly. There was a billiard hall. Not many street lights. It was getting dark. Something about the architecture made it clear it was dairy country. The shape of the stores looked like old-fashioned milking barns. The same DNA was in there somewhere.

There was a bar in a stand-alone wooden building, with a patch of weedy gravel for parking, and on the gravel were seven Harley-Davidsons, all in a neat line. Possibly not actual Hell's Angels as such. Possibly one of many other parallel denominations. Bikers were as split as Baptists. All the same, but all different. Apparently these particular guys liked black leather tassels and chromium plating. They liked to lay back and ride with their legs spread wide and their feet sticking out in front of them. Possibly a cooling effect. Perhaps necessary. Generally they wore heavy leather vests. And pants, and boots. All black. Hot, in late summer.

The bikes were all painted dark shiny colours, four with orange flames, three with rune-like symbols outlined in silver. The bar was dull with age, and some shingles had slipped. There was an air conditioner in one of the windows, straining to keep up, dripping water in a puddle below. A cop car rolled past, slowly, its tyres hissing on the blacktop. County Police. Probably spent the first half of its watch ginning up municipal revenue with a radar gun out on the highway, now prowling the back streets of the towns in its jurisdiction. Showing the flag. Paying attention to the trouble spots. The cop inside turned his head and gazed at Reacher. The guy was nothing like the pawnbroker. He was all squared away. His face was lean, and his eyes were wise. He was sitting behind the wheel with a ramrod posture, and his haircut was fresh. A whitewall buzz cut. Maybe just a day old. Not more than two.

Reacher stood still and watched him roll away. He heard a motorcycle exhaust in the distance, coming closer, getting louder, heavy as a hammer. An eighth Harley came around the corner, as slow as gravity would allow, a heavy machine, blatting and popping, the rider lying back with his feet on pegs way out in front. He leaned into a turn and slowed on the gravel. He was wearing a black leather vest over a black T-shirt. He parked last in line. His bike idled like a blacksmith hitting an anvil. Then he shut it down and hauled it up on its stand. Silence came back.

Reacher said, 'I'm looking for Jimmy Rat.'

The guy glanced at one of the other bikes. Couldn't help himself. But he said, 'Don't know him,' and walked away, stiff and bow-legged, to the door of the bar. He was pear-shaped, and maybe forty years old. Maybe five-ten, and bulky. He had a sallow tan, like his skin was rubbed with motor oil. He pulled the door and stepped inside.

Reacher stayed where he was. The bike the new guy had glanced at was one of the three with silver runes. It was as huge as all the others, but the footrests and the handlebars

471

were set a little closer to the seat than most. About two inches closer than the new guy's, for example. Which made Jimmy Rat about five-eight, possibly. Maybe skinny, to go with his name. Maybe armed, with a knife or a gun. Maybe vicious.

Reacher walked to the door of the bar. He pulled it open and stepped inside. The air was dark and hot and smelled of spilled beer. The room was rectangular, with a full-length copper bar on the left, and tables on the right. There was an arch in the rear wall, with a narrow corridor beyond. Restrooms and a payphone and a fire door. Four windows. A total of six potential exits. The first thing an ex-MP counted.

The eight bikers were packed in around two four-tops shoved together by a window. They had beers on the go, in heavy glasses wet with humidity. The new guy was shoe-horned in, pear-shaped on a chair, with the fullest glass. Six of the others were in a similar category, in terms of size and shape and general visual appeal. One was worse. About five-eight, stringy, with a narrow face and restless eyes.

Reacher stopped at the bar and asked for coffee.

'Don't have any,' the barman said. 'Sorry.'

'Is that Jimmy Rat over there? The small guy?'

'You got a beef with him, you take it outside, OK?'

The barman moved away. Reacher waited. One of the bikers drained his glass and stood up and headed for the restroom corridor. Reacher crossed the room and sat down in his vacant chair. The wood felt hot. The eighth guy made the connection. He stared at Reacher, and then glanced at Jimmy Rat.

Who said, 'This is a private party, bud. You ain't invited.'

Reacher said, 'I need some information.'

'About what?'

472

'Charitable donations.'

Jimmy Rat looked blank. Then he remembered. He glanced at the door, somewhere beyond which lay the pawn shop, where he had made assurances. He said, 'Get lost, bud.'

Reacher put his left fist on the table. The size of a supermarket chicken. Long thick fingers with knuckles like walnuts. Old nicks and scars healed white against his summer tan. He said, 'I don't care what scam you're running. Or who you're stealing from. Or who you're fencing for. I got no interest in any of that. All I want to know is where you got this ring.'

He opened his fist. The ring lay in his palm. *West Point 2005*. The gold filigree, the black stone. The tiny size. Jimmy Rat said nothing, but something in his eyes made Reacher believe he recognized the item.

Reacher said, 'Another name for West Point is the United States Military Academy. There's a clue right there, in the first two words. This is a federal case.'

'You a cop?'

'No, but I got a quarter for the phone.'

The missing guy got back from the restroom. He stood behind Reacher's chair, arms spread in exaggerated perplexity. As if to say, what the hell is going on here? Who is this guy? Reacher kept one eye on Jimmy Rat, and one on the window alongside him, where he could see a faint ghostly reflection of what was happening behind his shoulder.

Jimmy Rat said, 'That's someone's chair.'

'Yeah, mine,' Reacher said.

'You've got five seconds.'

'I've got as long as it takes for you to answer my question.'

'You feeling lucky tonight?'

473

'I won't need to be.'

Reacher put his right hand on the table. It was a little larger than his left. Normal for right-handed people. It had a few more nicks and scars, including a white V-shaped blemish that looked like a snakebite, but had been made by a nail.

Jimmy Rat shrugged, like the whole conversation was really no big deal.

He said, 'I'm part of a supply chain. I get stuff from other people who get it from other people. That ring was donated or sold or pawned and not redeemed. I don't know anything more than that.'

'What other people did you get it from?'

Jimmy Rat said nothing. Reacher watched the window with his left eye. With his right he saw Jimmy Rat nod. The reflection in the glass showed the guy behind winding up a big roundhouse right. Clearly the plan was to smack Reacher on the ear. Maybe topple him off the chair. At least soften him up a little.

Didn't work.

Reacher chose the path of least resistance. He ducked his head, and let the punch scythe through the empty air above it. Then he bounced back up, and launched from his feet, and twisted, and used his falling-backward momentum to jerk his elbow into the guy's kidney, which was rotating around into position just in time. It was a good solid hit. The guy went down hard. Reacher fell back in his chair and sat there like absolutely nothing had happened.

Jimmy Rat stared.

The barman called, 'Take it outside, pal. Like I told you.'

He sounded like he meant it.

Jimmy Rat said, 'Now you've got trouble.'

He sounded like he meant it too.

Right then Chang would be shopping for dinner, probably. Maybe a small grocery close to her home. Wholesome ingredients. But simple. She was probably tired.

A bad day.

Reacher said, 'I've got six fat guys and a runt. That's a walk in the park.'

He stood up. He turned and stepped on the guy on the floor and walked over him. Onwards to the door. Out to the gravel, and the line of shiny bikes. He turned and saw the others come out after him. The not-very magnificent seven. Generally stiff and bow-legged, and variously contorted due to beer guts and bad posture. But still, a lot of weight. In the aggregate. Plus fourteen fists, and fourteen boots.

Possibly steel capped.

Maybe a very bad day.

But who cared, really?

The seven guys fanned out into a semicircle, three on Jimmy Rat's left, and three on his right. Reacher kept moving, rotating them the way he wanted, his back to the street. He didn't want to get trapped up against someone's rear fence. He didn't want to get jammed in a corner. He didn't plan on running, but an option was always a fine thing to have.

The seven guys tightened their semicircle, but not enough. They stayed about ten feet away, with better than a yard between each of them. Which made the first two plays obvious. They would come shuffling in, slowly, maybe grunting and glaring, whereupon Reacher would move fast and punch his way through the line, after which everyone would turn around, Reacher now facing a new inverted semicircle, now only six in number. Then rinse and repeat, which would reduce them to five. They wouldn't fall for it a third time, so at that point they would swarm, all except

Jimmy Rat, who Reacher figured wouldn't fight at all. Too smart. Which in the end would make it a close-quarters four-on-one brawl.

A bad day.

For someone.

'Last chance,' Reacher said. 'Tell the little guy to answer my question, and you can all go back to your suds.'

No one spoke. They tightened some more and hunched down into crouches and started shuffling forward, hands apart and ready. Reacher picked out his first target and waited. He wanted him five feet away. One pace, not two. Better to save the extra energy for later.

Then he heard tyres on the road again, behind him, and in front of him the seven guys straightened up and looked around, with exaggerated wide-eyed innocence all over their faces. Reacher turned and saw the cop car again. The same guy. County police. The car coasted to a stop and the guy took a good long look. He buzzed his passenger window down, and leaned across inside, and caught Reacher's eye, and said, 'Sir, please approach the vehicle.'

Which Reacher did, but not on the passenger side. He didn't want to turn his back. Instead he tracked around the trunk to the driver's window. Which buzzed down, while the passenger side buzzed up. The cop had his gun in his hand. Relaxed, held low in his lap.

The cop said, 'Want to tell me what's going on here?'

Reacher said, 'Were you army or Marine Corps?'

'Why would I be either?'

'Most of you are, in a place like this. Especially the ones who hike all the way to the nearest PX to get their hair cut.'

'I was army.'

'Me too. There's nothing going on here.'

'I need to hear the whole story. Lots of guys were in the army. I don't know you.'

'Jack Reacher, 110th MP. Terminal at major. Pleased to meet you.'

The cop said, 'I heard of the 110th MP.'

'In a good way, I hope.'

'Your HQ was in the Pentagon, right?'

'No, our HQ was in Rock Creek, Virginia. Some ways north and west of the Pentagon. I had the best office there for a couple of years. Was that your security question?'

'You passed the test. Rock Creek it was. Now tell me what's going on. You looked like you were fixing to fight these guys.'

'So far we're just talking,' Reacher said. 'I asked them something. They told me they would prefer to answer me outside in the open air. I don't know why. Maybe they were worried about eavesdroppers.'

'What did you ask them?'

'Where they got this ring.'

Reacher rested his wrist on the door and opened his hand.

'West Point,' the cop said.

'Sold to the pawn shop by these guys. I want to know where they got it.'

'Why?'

'I don't know exactly. I guess I want to know the story.'

'These guys won't tell you.'

'You know them?'

'Nothing we can prove.'

'But?'

'They bring stuff in from South Dakota through Minnesota. Two states away. But never enough to get the Feds interested. And never enough to put a South Dakota detective on an airplane. So it's pretty much a risk-free system.'

'Where in South Dakota?'

'We don't know.'

Reacher said nothing.

The cop said, 'You should get in the car. There are seven of them.'

'I'll be OK,' Reacher said.

'I'll arrest you, if you like. To make it look good. But you need to be gone. Because I need to be gone. I can't stay here all day.'

'Don't worry about me.'

'Maybe I should arrest you anyway.'

'For what? Something that hasn't happened yet?'

'For your own safety.'

'I could take offence,' Reacher said. 'You don't seem very worried about their safety. You talk like it's a fore-gone conclusion.'

'Get in the car. Call it a tactical retreat. You can find out about the ring some other way.'

'What other way?'

'Then forget all about it. A buck gets ten there's no story at all. Probably the guy came back all sad and bitter and sold the damn ring as fast as he could. To pay the rent on his trailer.'

'Is that how it is around here?'

'Often enough.'

'You're doing OK.'

'It's a spectrum.'

'It wasn't a guy. The ring is too small. It was a woman.'

'Women live in trailers too.'

Reacher nodded. He said, 'I agree, a buck gets ten it's nothing. But I want to know for sure. Just in case.'

Silence for a moment. Just the engine's whispered idle, and a breeze in the telephone wires.

'Last chance,' the cop said. 'Play it smart. Get in the car.'

'I'll be OK,' Reacher said again. He stepped back and straightened up. The cop shook his head in exasperation, and waited a beat, and then gave up and drove away, slowly, tyres hissing on the blacktop, exhaust fumes trailing. Reacher watched him all the way to the corner, and then he stepped back up on the sidewalk, where the black-clad semicircle reformed around him.

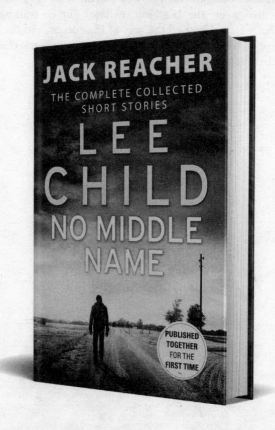